THE SPECTERS OF FEAR

"Go back," a voice whispered softly. "It is not yet time. Go back."

He looked to the shadows and another form drifted from the swirling darkness. "Who are you?" Michael whispered.

It started to turn. "Michael," the spirit said, "where were you to protect them?"

The shadows started to draw away, into the darkness of night.

"Wait!" he cried.

The apparitions stopped, turned. Their faces were no longer human—dark, skull-like eyes peered out at him. He felt his sanity drifting away. Suddenly he recognized the images, and he screamed...

Also by William R. Forstchen
Published by Ballantine Books:

ICE PROPHET

THE FLAME UPON THE ICE

WILLIAM R. FORSTCHEN

A Del Rey Book

BALLANTINE BOOKS • NEW YORK

A Del Rey Book
Published by Ballantine Books

Library of Congress Catalog Card Number: 83-91240

ISBN 0-345-31137-X

Manufactured in the United States of America

First Edition: April 1984
Cover art by Darrell K. Sweet

For Ida Singer, Betty Keller, and, of course, for Thomas Seay, who had said I could.

When there was the need for a teacher, I always found one.

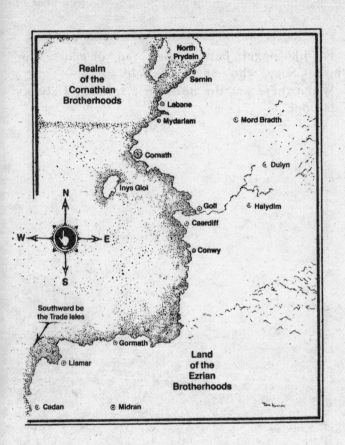

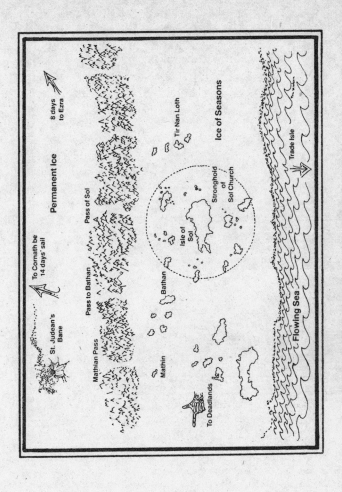

Permanent Ice

Ice of Seasons

8 days
to Ezra

To Cornath be
14 days' sail

St. Judean's
Bane

Pass of Sol

Pass to Bathan

Matthian Pass

Mathin

To Deadlands

Bathan

Isle of
Sol

Stronghold
of
Sol Church

Tir Nan Loth

Trade Isle

Flowing Sea

PROLOGUE

It was a war unlike any witnessed on the Frozen Sea, as the fleets of Michael Ormson carried his word across the Southward Sea. The old orders crumbled against the onslaught of the new. The islands of the south, the harbors of piracy, and the religious colonies of old knew that the days of northern dominance were finished at last. The power of the Prophet grew with a fierceness and vitality undreamed of. In the north, there was war as well. Not of fleets but of maneuver, innuendo, and the poisoned dagger.

All were linked, all intertwined, and all knew that a final confrontation must come.

Five years had passed since the miracle before the Mathinian Pass. To some it was the twenty-ninth year of the Prophet; to others, it was the year 1029, the five hundredth anniversary of St. Elbreck the III, first of the Holy Sees to die from assassination. He was not the last.

BOOK III

Ice Cruiser

CHAPTER 1

"DECK HO! DEAD AHEAD, NOT FOUR LEAGUES OFF."

The captain came up behind the hooded form of the archbishop and shouted against the shrieking wind. "My lord Zimri, the lookout's spotted them dead ahead. Shall I send up the recognition flares?"

Without turning to face the sailing master, Zimri of Mor gave a curt nod and continued to look forward across the glaring, frost-white sea.

Behind him, the roar of the rockets slashed across the deck, then flamed upward to burst downwind in the colors of recognition. Moments later, four rockets exploded on the horizon several leagues ahead. He breathed an involuntary sigh of relief.

The riggings of the *Golau du Mor* shrieked as the light frigate ran across the wind at nearly a hundred miles an hour. The thundering gale forced Zimri to huddle against the scant protection of the wind barrier, but the icy wind cut through him, numbing his hands and feet. In another minute, the approaching frigates were hull up over the horizon, riding on their downwind outriggers as they kept full canvas to the howling gale. The deck lurched beneath Zimri's feet as the *Golau* turned to the northwest and slid into the eye of the wind.

"Ease off all sheets; fasten down all sails," Gimrath shouted. His commands were taken up by the mast captains, who drove their men aloft.

Zimri leaned back and watched as the crew scurried up the riggings, struggling against the wind, which could pluck a man off the ropes and hurl him to the ice below. The frigate reached the eye of the wind, and the loosened sails cracked and thundered as the wind struck them evenly on either side. Zimri turned his attention away from the ice sailors aloft and watched as two frigates closed in on the port side, their runners kicking up a wake of showering crystals that the wind whipped away to the southeast—toward Cornath, two score miles below the horizon.

"All gunners stand by your guns," Gimrath shouted through the hatchway. Zimri could feel the deck vibrating beneath his feet as the guns were run out.

The two frigates were closing up fast and now stood only half a mile off, approaching in line abreast as the *Golau du Mor* slowed to a walking pace. Zimri walked over to Gimrath and said softly, "Remember, only on my command do you fire."

The two frigates turned to the northwest and swept in on the *Golau*. It was a tense moment, and Zimri watched them closely. The two ships dropped into a line astern formation, and the first one drew abreast of the Morian ship. Zimri recognized it as belonging to Mord Rinn, the Brotherhood of the Inquisition. He held his breath as it skated across the ice with guns run out. Zimri noticed the tense silence as his monks watched the ship sail by.

"Blessings of the Saints," Zimri whispered as the ship passed them without a shot. Good, they were holding to their bargain. It wasn't a trap.

The second ship, belonging to the monks of the First Choice, crossed astern of the *Golau* on the starboard side, sailed past them, and parked several hundred yards downwind, so that the three stationary vessels formed a rough triangle on the frozen, windswept sea.

A red rocket rose from the deck of the Mord Rinn ship, and with a smile, Zimri turned to Gimrath. "Gimrath, send up the blue in response; only Madoc knew that signal, and only I know the final blue." Zimri could barely conceal his relief.

"Have your men stand down but ready for battle stations at a moment's notice. I think we're safe, but if this meeting doesn't work, we might have to fight our way out of here."

Gimrath nodded slowly, keeping a wary eye on the flagships of the two rival orders.

Zimri turned away and walked over to the rope ladder that two priests had lowered over the side. Zimri waited for his four escorts and eyed them approvingly as they came to stand by his side. They walked with catlike ease, their goggles removed to improve their vision. Their eyes never rested on a spot but were always shifting, always moving, always searching. They were the best the brotherhood could buy. He had lost three so far, but each had died protecting him from assassination.

Gimrath turned his attention from the two ships and shouted a command through the open hatchway, his orders echoing across the decks below. Zimri felt a vibration underfoot, and looking over the railing, he saw the stern hatch of the *Golau* swing outward. Several dozen monks swarmed from its interior, carrying bundles of lumber, which they dragged across the ice to the center of the triangle formed by the three ships. With practiced skill, they fitted the pieces of wood together, forming a wind barrier twelve feet on a side and eight feet in height. Another half-dozen monks from the *Golau* carried a large brazier filled to the brim with shimmering coals that burned fiercely in the howling gale. Three high-back chairs were carried out as well and set inside the temporary shelter, the bearers returning quickly in order to escape the cold.

"Hoist the banner," Zimri shouted. And the guard next to him raised the standard of Mor, the silhouette of an iceboat on a blue field, the Arch overhead. From the other two ships, the banners rose heavenward in response, the scarlet field of Mord Rinn and the black banner of the Brotherhood of Ceauth Cerath.

With a bow to the sacristy and the sacred relics held aloft by the priests, Zimri made the Sign of Blessing as clouds of incense wafted across the windswept deck. Turning away, he lowered himself over the side and started toward the temporary shelter, his four guards in an arc behind him. From the other two ships, similiar processions emerged, from the one, the burgundy robes of Mord Rinn, and from the other, the jet black robes of the Protectors of the First Choice. A wave of excitement passed through Zimri—after five years he was returning.

After the disaster at Mathin, there was only one recourse open to Zimri—to avoid abdication, he and his followers went into self-imposed exile on the windswept barrens of North Prydain. A forced abdication was barely avoided when the survivors of the battle before Mathin claimed that he had betrayed them. As planned, Peter took most of the blame and spent several years in ecclesiastical prison before going into exile as ambassador to one of the minor Ezrian brotherhoods. Zimri thought of Peter for a moment and then forced him out of his mind. There were more important things to deal with now.

With a subtle hand gesture, Zimri ordered his guards to stop a hundred yards out, and he proceeded alone, walking slowly toward the leaders of the other two groups. They approached each other across the frozen sea until they were ten yards apart.

"My lord Madoc of Mord Rinn?"

"Yes, it is I, my lord Zimri of Mor," responded a cold, chilling voice from beneath the folds of the swirling burgundy robes.

"And my lord Balor of the First Choice?" Zimri looked closely at the masked and hooded form before him. They had met on the night of Zimri's ascension to Archbishop of Mor; it was Balor who revealed the final truth of the First Choice. Only Balor, his fifty assistants, and the ruling hierarchy knew that the Arch was merely the rubble of a destroyed moon, and that the legends of the Garden and its loss were nothing more than fables. That was the final insight that weighed upon the ruling elite—the true and hidden purpose of the Churches was to save man from his own knowledge and the destruction such knowledge created.

Without another word, the three archbishops walked into the relative warmth of the enclosure and gathered around the glowing brazier. Removing his goggles and face mask, Zimri turned and faced the archbishops, waiting for them to open the parley. Madoc ignored Zimri for several minutes, and then, with a gesture of disdain, he pulled aside his mask to reveal sharp, cunning eyes and full red lips, which were compressed in a sardonic smile. Balor stood next to him, masked and silent.

"It's been five years now, has it not?" Madoc said coldly. "I was surprised to receive your request for this rather unorthodox meeting. So tell me, Zimri, how does your self-imposed exile fare these days?"

"Difficult, my dear Madoc. Difficult and painful when I see what we have sunk to. And that is why I have decided to return."

Madoc nodded slowly; his face an impenetrable mask. "I must assume, Zimri, that you do not drag me fifty miles out here to inform me of your desire to reenter the Council of Archbishops. I think it interesting that your timing coincides with the assassination of our good Holy See, Alnar the III. I take it that you look for something else in this unusual meeting that you've requested."

"Of course, Madoc, there is a reason," Zimri said, suppressing a retort to Madoc's barb. "You see, I wish to do several things. The Holy See—our third in five years—is dead, and Michael Ormson rules the Southward Ice. We are losing, Madoc; I warned the archbishops five years ago about this, and they would not listen. The Prophet and the dark ones behind him have sprung forth, and the dogmas of our past no longer apply. Look at us, Madoc. Look how we meet here—alone and afraid, in secret, half a hundred miles from land. You know who is behind this, don't you?"

"Inys Gloi." Madoc spit out the distasteful words.

Zimri hesitated for a moment, nervous at having to say the name aloud to his rival archbishops.

"Yes, Madoc, Inys Gloi." Zimri looked to the two hooded forms before him. Placing his hands over the brazier, he rubbed them vigorously, attempting to drive out the numbness.

"It's Inys Gloi and their damned Prophet," Balor said at last, breaking his silence.

Madoc turned away from Zimri and casually examined the carvings on the wooden barrier that protected them from the wind and from being overheard. "What are your thoughts on this, Zimri?" he asked, his back still turned to the other two.

"First of all, Madoc, can I trust you?" Zimri asked coldly. "I know you want the seat of the Holy See. I could be an obstacle, could I not?"

Madoc turned and examined Zimri dispassionately. "Why do you speak the obvious, Zimri?"

"Because it is time to go beyond the obvious and look to

what is hidden within. Each of us wants the Holy See; only one can succeed next spring. But damn it, that is the least important issue confronting us. Madoc, we have to bury our rivalry for the moment if we wish to survive."

"Ah, my lord Zimri," Balor whispered, "you say that it's time for trust, but can we trust you? After all, the disaster at Mathin is the working of your hand."

"I know that, Balor," Zimri said heatedly. "But you had your hand in Mathin. If my reports are correct, you and Rifton sent a messenger to Ormson as well. Of course, that never came out in the Council meetings, did it?"

Balor nodded his head. "I told my friend in the beginning to kill that boy, but he would not listen. I should have done it myself, but now it is too late."

Balor turned away from Zimri and looked at Madoc. "We have to listen to him, Madoc. The rivalry within the Church must end if we are to survive."

Madoc looked at Balor with disdain, "So, you'll forgive him, will you?" And he pointed an accusing finger at Zimri. "Damn it, you had them all in the palm of your hand. I still can't believe that you let that Seth Facinn of Inys Gloi escape from you. Damn you, Zimri, I can't forget, nor will I trust you. I need you as an ally against Inys Gloi, but I will be damned if I trust you. The Prophet would be dead now except for your inept bunglings."

Zimri looked into the eyes of Madoc, and their gazes locked. Balor could sense the battle of wills as each one tried to force the other down. After several moments of uncomfortable silence, Madoc's gaze broke away, and he shifted his feet uneasily while poking the glowing coals with the butt of his staff.

"I will only say it once, Madoc," Zimri said. "I was wrong. I lost the Holy See as a result, and I've taken my punishment. But my time of exile is over, and I shall return to vote next summer. Mark my words, Madoc. My vote will be crucial."

"We were talking of Inys Gloi," Balor said softly, shifting the topic to grounds of mutual agreement. "Or did you summon us to argue about the past?"

Overhead, the wind increased in its fury, and Zimri looked heavenward. The faint shadow of the Arch was etched across the afternoon sky. So far away, he thought whimsically, and then forced his thoughts to return.

"My brothers," he said softly, his voice barely audible against the shrieking of the icy wind. "We've lost three Holy Sees in five years, one definitely from poison, and possibly another. Five archbishops have died as well. All this at the same time that the Prophet appears. With Ezra, the confusion is the same."

"You think that Inys Gloi is behind all of the deaths, then?" Madoc asked cautiously.

"Obviously," Balor exclaimed. "Damn it, let's stop wasting time. You know the truth, Madoc, and so does Zimri. Their agents are in all our brotherhoods. This Seth managed to get all the way to the Prophet in spite of Rifton's precautions. What we say here better not get beyond the three of us. I don't even trust some of our fellow archbishops. If Inys Gloi's agents heard of this meeting, their blades would find us within the month."

"We're already marked," Zimri said. "We'd be fools to think otherwise."

"So why are we meeting, then?" Madoc said sarcastically. "To share our fears, then scurry back to our holes and wait?"

"Ah, my dear Madoc," Zimri responded, "at last you bring us to the arena where we can find agreement. We have to act against both Inys Gloi and this Prophet at once; otherwise, we are doomed."

"How?" Madoc said in response, looking into the fire. "Their fortress is impregnable and could withstand a siege of years. From what little information we have, it can be assumed that Inys Gloi has at least five hundred monks in disguise across the Ice and on the Flowing Sea. Each of them gathering information, sowing discord. Each trained as an assassin. If we openly attack Inys Gloi, we would all be dead within a year. For the time being, such action is closed to us."

"We can never take them directly; at least not yet," Zimri responded. "But there is another way. Madoc, tell me, how many of your men are secretly enlisted in my ranks?"

Madoc looked up at Zimri and smiled. "Ah, if you only knew!"

"Of course," Zimri said with a grin and a mock bow. "I wager not as many agents as I have in your brotherhood, to be sure."

"Get to the point," Balor said impatiently.

"I'm at the point," Zimri replied. "We've dismissed Inys

Gloi for too long, never bothering to take them seriously. A generation ago, they were viewed with a mixture of tolerance and superstition. We are paying for that mistake. We must now treat them the way we've treated each other for generations. Our only hope is to get some of our own into their ranks."

The two archbishops looked at him. His idea had been theirs, but they had never dared venture it alone.

"We must move now, my brothers," Balor responded eagerly, "and bury our differences for the moment. A storm approaches. We have only felt the first light breeze, but soon it shall be a thundering gale that will sweep all in front of it. Inys Gloi has begun the overthrowing of our Cornathian Brotherhood. The final blow might not come for another generation, but with the power of this Prophet, it will come unless we lay the groundwork for our resistance here and now. The recent deaths within our orders have paralyzed us."

"Through the Prophet, they plan to destroy Cornath," Zimri whispered.

Madoc nodded in agreement. "But how do we get our people into Inys Gloi? Are they to go to the doors of the citadel and beg admission? No one knows how a person becomes one of Inys Gloi. Some say women are hidden within the citadel and the brothers breed their own. They have no churches, no sanctuaries, no seminaries or monasteries, only that damned rock in the middle of the sea."

"Then it's time we learned," Zimri said forcefully.

"Ah," Madoc whispered, "*there* is something my brotherhood has had experience with. We can be most persuasive."

"Your bloody rack won't help with this. Their agents are too well trained for that."

"The hell with you, Zimri. We can wring confessions from anyone. More than one of your men has spilled your plans on the rack, and I dare say, we can get the same from Inys Gloi."

Zimri leaned over the brazier and stared at Madoc, who grinned malevolently.

"Brothers, let's not start again," Balor said quickly. "Zimri, tell us your plan."

Zimri nodded to Balor. "From each of our orders, we should quietly select the most skilled and cunning of our men. Set them into the cities and onto the Ice. Let them assume the guise of the common people, leaving all traces of the brotherhoods aside. Send most of them south, into the lands of the Prophet. Let them look and learn, and most of all, let them be available. If we dispatch many, and if they wait long enough, perhaps some of them will be approached and recruited by Inys Gloi. Then we shall have our answers. All we need is one man to gain the Inner Council. We can't do it alone, but among the three of us, one should succeed, and by sharing information, we can identify the traitors in our ranks."

"What you say, Zimri, is what I hoped I would hear when you summoned us," Balor said quickly, attempting to sway Madoc to the plan. "If we do this now, hope remains for our Church and for the sacred goal of the First Choice as laid down by our forefathers. Otherwise, the original intent of the Church and the power we hold as a result will be lost forever."

"Let us all understand one thing, though," Zimri interjected, fixing the other two archbishops with his gaze. "This action is to be done by us alone; none of the other brotherhoods must hear of it. We three are alike in spite of our rivalries, and for that we can trust one another. But of the other brotherhoods, we can never be sure."

"But what of this Ormson?" Madoc asked cautiously. "By the time our plan for Inys Gloi is completed, that heretic will have strengthened his hold on the Southward Isles. His heresy is spreading to our land and to that of the Ezrians, as well. My prisons are choked with his followers, arrests are made without letup, the Inquisition meets day and night, yet his heresy spreads."

"Something even deeper is here," Balor replied. "He knows the First Choice of our forefathers. I fear that he will use his knowledge. Once that demon is released to the people, it will never be contained. Can we hope to defeat him in open battle?"

At last, Zimri thought, the waiting, the fortune in bribes, have paid off. For with Balor's words, Zimri knew that the other brotherhoods were ready to accept a return of Mor in order to save their own hides.

"My brothers," Zimri said coldly, staring at Balor, "in order to force the barrier lines and to defeat Michael upon the Southward Ice, we would have to violate the First Choice. That would be necessary to give us the weapons required. He has had five years to build and to prepare. It would be a war unlike any that has passed before—in all the wars of the past, it was agreed never to force the issue to the death as stated in the First Choice. With the Prophet, this no longer applies. We do not now have the power to defeat Michael upon the Southward Sea."

"We can't violate the First Choice," Balor replied. "That would require a unanimous vote of the Council and of the fifty brothers under my control. And I will not vote for it; I cannot throw over the mandate of a thousand years. If you try it without my permission, Zimri, I'll see you dead."

"You can't even order a fleet action," Madoc interjected. "We'd have to go before a full Council to get that. I doubt if we can trust all our archbishops even on that question."

"What if Michael attacks us?" Zimri said softly, extending his hands to warm them over the flickering fire.

The two archbishops facing Zimri were silent for a moment. They both knew that to attack Michael would be nearly impossible, but a defense against him would, of course, be accepted by the Council without question.

"How?" Madoc asked. "He's too strong in the South, and surely he would see the folly of coming into our own territory. Ormson's too logical to attack us now, when all he needs to do is wait."

"We have to make him illogical," Zimri replied.

"How?" Balor inquired.

"Revenge. A desire for revenge that will drive him and his followers to the edge of madness. We need to make the Prophet human. We must make him hate us with a blinding hatred that will transcend all other dreams, all other goals."

Madoc looked at Zimri and smiled. From Balor there was no sign of emotion, his face still masked by hood and goggles.

Zimri reached over to the bucket of coal sitting next to the brazier and threw a handful onto the fire, which flickered greedily at the fuel. He knew that the time was right to say what he had planned for the last three years.

"We must murder his wife and only son."

Balor did not respond at first, but Madoc let the idea flow through him, and he nodded slowly at the wisdom of the plan. "I see," Madoc said cautiously. "If we murder the Prophet, then we create the martyr both for Inys Gloi and for his own followers. But if we let him live, we can destroy him completely by unmaking all that he dreams."

"And we can save the First Choice," Balor interjected. "Remember always that this is the prime directive, the prime goal to bring about the Return of the Garden."

"Are your own men to do this, then, Zimri?" Balor asked in an offhand manner.

Madoc looked at Zimri closely, waiting for his response. If Zimri would shoulder the responsibility, then of course he could shoulder the blame. No matter what the result, Madoc realized, he could then profit from it. Zimri could provoke the war but also bear the blame for it. It would go poorly for him at the next Council meeting. Madoc savored the thought and its infinite possibilities. It would eliminate any hope Zimri might have for the Holy See and would, of course, provoke a deadly response from Inys Gloi and the vengeance of the Prophet.

Zimri, shaking his head, looked at his two rivals and smiled. Do they take me for a fool? he thought angrily.

"But that would be impossible, my dear Balor, for any number of reasons which I think should be obvious to all of us."

"Oh? And what would those be?" Balor asked casually.

"First, my men are not trained for such a mission. There is only one group that is capable of reaching Mathin and successfully completing the task—the Hidden Order of the Knife. You, Balor, and you, Madoc, have the power to release them with the chair of the Holy See vacant."

Madoc cursed under his breath; he knew that his dream was too much to hope for. "What is your other reason, Zimri? If I might be so bold to ask."

"But of course, Madoc. I would be glad to answer," Zimri said with a disarming smile. "If I undertake the mission alone, you, Madoc, would be sure to pin the onus of war upon me at the next Council meeting; that would ensure the Holy See for you and assassination for me as a self-seeking renegade who's forced the Church into war."

Balor threw his head back and laughed. "Ah, Madoc, we can't cheat him, that's for sure."

Madoc threw Balor an evil, threatening glance.

"So, Zimri, you wish to force us into this move?"

"Damn it, Madoc, it's the only way we can hope to win. We have to transcend our own politics for the moment; otherwise, someone else will end our plans, anyhow."

Madoc turned to Balor. "The Black Brothers answer directly to you. I can only select a proven heretic as their target, nothing more."

Balor gazed at Madoc in the darkening shadows. "Do you request that I release the Brothers of the Knife to seek out the Prophet's family? By your own words, Madoc, you have the power to choose assassination for any heretic."

Madoc shook his head and looked toward Zimri, who stood silent, gazing into the fire. "It was Zimri, as the leader of the Warrior Brotherhood, who first suggested this."

"Damn you, Madoc," Zimri shouted. "If we continue this way, we'll still be arguing while the Prophet's fleet knocks at our city's gate. Let it simply be the decision of all three of us—I as the planner of war, you as the defender of the faith, and Balor as Protector of the First Choice. We have the power— let us use it."

Balor looked from one to the other. Madoc would agree there and then plead ignorance to the wider implications when the war started. Madoc would maneuver well the following spring, when the fury of Ormson descended upon them. He could sense Zimri's plans, as well. The war would come at last, and the power of Mor would rise again. Yes, he could sense their hidden plans, and he smiled, for they fit his, as well.

"It shall be done," Balor said forcefully. "The three of us shall declare that together we reached this decision. I shall meet with the Master of the Knife upon my return to Dulyn and command him to fulfill this mission."

Zimri breathed a sigh of relief. He looked to Madoc, and the archbishop of the Inquisition gave him a curt nod of agreement.

"Then we are agreed; in our name, the knife shall seek the family of the Prophet, and together we shall send out our agents to seek the hidden way of Inys Gloi. Before you sail, Balor, one of my men shall bring a sealed locker to your ship. It is to be delivered unopened to the Master of the Knife. Within will be the necessary maps and information. I shall be in Cornath for the Supplication Night, and there I will answer any questions he might have."

Zimri looked from one to the other, then he smiled at Madoc while pulling up his hood, concealing his face beneath its billowing shadows. Yes, my dear Madoc, he thought, you think you will pin this on me, but the game has only started. Zimri bowed with full ceremony to the two archbishops.

"So let it be done by the blessing of all the Saints and for the Return of the Garden."

Reaching over with his staff, Zimri tipped the brazier over, sending the flaming coals across the frozen sea.

CHAPTER 2

THEY WALKED ALONE THROUGH THE SACRED GROVE. THE meeting of the morning completed, the hundreds of followers had finally drifted away into the forest, returning to the walled confines of Mathin. They were not really alone, to be sure; just out of sight were the Companions, the ever-present guards dedicated to one thing only—the protection of the Prophet.

The sheltered grove echoed to the shouts of the boy who scampered up the path to the Place of Watching, waving his small sword and calling on his "men" to follow him. For a moment, he was lost from view.

Michael looked at Janis and smiled softly, and her eyes were drawn away from their son and met his.

"You seemed so distant this morning," she said softly, "as if some darkness was pressing in upon you."

He shook his head, turning away so she could not see his expression. "No, it's nothing, nothing at all."

How could he explain the dream that had swept over him in the night? For five years, the darkness had hovered on a distant horizon, its presence felt but not really acknowledged. But with the dream the night before, a cold sense of dread had come to him, as if someone or something were seeking him

18

out, closing in on the fragile peace he had managed to preserve.

"You're lying. You fool, don't you think that I, of any, can see when our Prophet attempts to deceive?" she said with a gentle look of concern.

They walked on through the forest, beneath the shadows of the towering pines, breathing in the sharp, crisp air of early winter. Reaching the high stone pedestal of the Place of Watching, they settled down together into the oversized chair carved out of the frost-covered rock. He placed his arm around her and drew her close. The shouts of the boy echoed in the distance.

He looked out over Mathin, its log walls and great warehouses crowding halfway up the slopes to the Sacred Grove. In the last five years, it had tripled in size as the power of the Southward Isles came into his grasp. Here and there, a church tower rose heavenward as symbols of his decree that all thought, be it religious or secular, was to be welcomed as long as it accepted the principle that each man, not the churches, would decide what he was to believe. Off to the south, almost concealed by the trees, Michael could see the Aithe du Eolas, the Place of Knowledge—the dream of Zardok come to pass. Hundreds had come from as far as North Prydain and even from beyond the Flowing Sea to debate questions, to learn reading, and to spread the growing truth of knowledge against the fallacies and superstitions of the church.

The harbor was aswarm with ships—dozens of merchant craft ready to venture northward, bearing food and lumber, which would be exchanged for fur, oil, black rock, and iron. And beyond them, parked in orderly rows, was his striking arm—the fleets of rams and armored ships, ready to sail if war threatened. There had been skirmishes aplenty in the last five years, especially when rebellions against the holdings of the three churches were supported, but a mass sailing of the entire fleet had not been seen since the Battle of the Mathinian Pass.

Near the great wharf of the house of Ishmael rested half a dozen light schooners, each one bearing a pennant of command from the mainmast—the great bear of Daniel Bjornson, the upraised hand with a golden eye in the middle for Seth Facinn, and the flags of Finson, Cowan, and Eldric. They had arrived the day before and the previous night to join in council, and he knew that even now they were awaiting his return. However, for the moment at least, that could wait.

"Dada, Mama, look at me!"

He was drawn from his thoughts as Andrew came running toward them, waving his play sword. With a resounding shout, he charged up to the chair and crawled into Janis's lap.

"Andrew, your feet are wet. We better take you home."

"No, let's stay here and play."

Michael looked at his family—the only true joy in his world. He smiled at Janis, and she leaned over and kissed him lightly on the brow.

"Don't worry, my love," Michael said gently. "It won't hurt him."

"Let's play," Andrew demanded in a loud voice.

Michael stood up and swept Andrew off his feet, raising him up high to sit on his shoulder as the boy squealed with delight.

Janis put her arm around Michael's waist.

"Can't we stay here awhile longer?" she asked softly.

He looked down at her and smiled sadly. "No, love, they're waiting for me again. So much must be seen to this year," he said with a distant, almost wistful voice, "so much to plan, and with the freezing of the ice, we must begin again."

She hugged him closer. This was as she always knew it would be. The meetings would start again, and ships would again sail, and soon he would be gone for the winter—traveling from one port to another, talking, planning, and building a future he seemed to be creating from the energy of his mind and dreams. But his uneasiness had been such a stranger of late. Since the Battle Before the Pass, he had gone forth radiant with confidence, sure of his every move, as if it was preordained that the renaissance of thought would be brought about in just one lifetime. Now she could sense his anxiety, and as they started down the hill, she talked to him softly about the most trivial of things to distract his troubled mind. Between their conversation, Andrew chattered away happily, drawing Michael into soft laughter that masked his doubts.

"So, what say you, Seth? Has your voyage northward been profitable for the master?"

Seth turned away from the fire and stared at Cowan du Renarthson. He could see the resemblance that all of Zardok's family line carried—the meaty build that in later years would drift into true rotundity, the fair skin, light eyes, and red hair that all of Zardok's many nephews and nieces seemed to share.

After Zardok's death, Cowan had taken control of the family fortune through his hard-driving determination and even-handed method of dealing with all sides of the family. In the last two years, he had drifted ever closer to Michael, sharing his interests in exploration and the establishment of a secular school of learning, which he had underwritten with part of the wealth that his family had amassed. Cowan was almost as much a part of Michael's Council as Seth himself was, and for that Seth felt a sense of envy.

Seth broke away from Cowan and walked to the far corner of the audience room. They were all there—the five commanders of the various fleets, the envoys to the three churches, the representatives of the free islands confederated under Michael, and, of course, the Inner Circle, the friends who had been with him at the start. All were waiting, and all were quietly talking about the hundred various plans that had been instituted in the past five years.

A single horn sounded in the distance, and a shout went up from the great square, visible through the open doors of the room. There was a flash of white and burnished steel at the end of the plaza. Cowan could see Michael, his guards flanking him and holding the crowd back. Cowan smiled. Michael's progress was so like a religious procession, even though Michael would deny it passionately—the sound of the horn, the shouts of the faithful, who reached out for his blessing, all of them believing that he was the Prophet, the Deliverer Preordained. The call rose in a steady rolling chant.

"Michael, Michael, Michael!"

By Michael's side, Janis walked, dressed in a robe and cape of rich burgundy. Between them, dressed in a child-size uniform of the Companions, was Andrew, his arms outstretched, holding his parents' hands. Cowan turned away for a moment and looked across at Seth, whose gaze seemed aflame with some inner fervent light.

Seth smiled as he felt the presence, the power, that rippled through the square. Yes, the dream was true—it was real. He was the Prophet. The multitudes in their ignorance had turned from the Church and had made Michael and his Chosen Ones the objects of their veneration. Not one in a hundred truly understand what Michael is really saying, Seth thought quietly. Few of them grasp the Truth that he is trying to teach—that religion is not the answer, that it is the mind of man that should be the guide. No, they look to him—in fact, many in their fervor pray to him. He is the new idol—the living icon ready for worship. It had come to pass as Seth always knew it would ever since that day, a decade earlier, when he had first seen Michael and had prepared the mushroom for his first meal.

The chanting swelled louder and louder. "Michael, Michael, Michael!"

All in the room fell silent and turned to face Michael as he strode into the hallway, laughing at some little joke shared with his son.

Stopping at the entrance to the room, he leaned over and hugged the boy, who grabbed hold of him, refusing to let go. They talked for a moment, and all in the room watched the private moment of their leader; many looked to each other and smiled shyly. Finally, the boy let go and ran to his bodyguard, Elijah. The two walked off together hand in hand, and Michael drew Janis to his side, both of them watching as the boy disappeared from view. Together they entered the room as the doors to the square closed behind them, shutting out the calls of the followers and pilgrims.

He beckoned for his followers to be seated.

Seth always found that moment to be amusing—Michael so hated the ritual his followers pressed upon him. In his simple flowing robe of brown, he looked more like a wandering friar than a great leader who could command fifty thousand men and half a thousand ships. Seth could still detect Michael's slight flush of embarrassment at the attention of the crowds and the deferential treatment he received from his closest friends and advisors.

"So, my friends," Michael began softly, "again the ice has hardened. And again we meet to plan for the season to come. Eldric, did you have clear ice on your sail?"

Eldric, captain general of the freebooters' island of Bathan, stood to face Michael. Dressed in a gaudy tunic taken from the body of an Ezrian archbishop, he towered over them. His coal black eyes shone from an oiled curly beard that wreathed his face in darkness.

"Aye, Michael, the ice is formed well indeed! No snow to ruin the surface. It was a fast run here, with the wind less than a day, and nary a ripple to bother us."

The men mumbled their agreement. Two years earlier a heavy snow at the start of the season had ruined the ice for all but the slowest passage for a fair part of the winter. Now that the sea was formed, there would be little chance for a heavy blow for six months to come.

"The passes, then?"

"A bad double buckling scars the Bathian and Uzbarth channels. I have nearly a thousand men on the task now, and before the week is out, the passages will be cleared to the north. All other channels have held open through the season, and reports indicate that once beyond them, it's smooth ice and a fair run to Ezra—or Cornath, for that matter."

"Yes, to Cornath," Seth said quietly.

Michael looked at him for a moment. "In due time, Seth, in due time."

"Cowan, what is the latest to be said on Sol?"

Cowan looked to his leader with the soft, disarming grin, which concealed beneath it the mind of a master merchant and diplomat. "His Holiness, the prelate Valmarka, has conveyed to me privately that he is willing to make a discreet agreement."

"But not a public statement; is that it?"

"No, of course not, Seth," Cowan replied. "If it was known to the other two churches that Sol was ready to form a pact of mutual consideration, then it would break the sacred agreement of all three churches to support each other against any heretic who threatened to unbalance the status quo that they have held."

"But it must be an open statement," Seth insisted, "for in so doing, it will finish our drive to take hold upon the Southward Ice, leaving only the agreed-upon trading outposts of Cornath and Ezra to contend with."

"What you say has weight, Seth, my friend, but let us hear Cowan's reasoning first." Michael nodded for Cowan to continue.

"It is simply this, Michael. If you will forgive my saying so, you are still an outlander—one not born to the Southern Ice, and above all else, a declared enemy and renegade of the

Cornathian Church, and as such, a supposed enemy to all three churches."

"So are most of us here, Cowan," Daniel growled softly. "If I remember correctly, your uncle, venerated be his name, was considered by most to be a bloodthirsty pirate in his younger days."

"And so what is wrong with that?" Eldric shouted out with a laugh. "By Hell's mouth, half of us on the Southward Ice are renegades according to the pus-faced priests of the north."

"So much more the reason for having a public declaration of acceptance by Sol and thereby gaining even more power in the Ezrian court," Seth replied evenly.

"But it is not the reality of the situation," Janis interrupted gently. "At least they will accept us in private, and so their prelate states; that is a first step."

"Thank you, Janis," Cowan stated quickly. "If we have their agreement privately, at least that means they will no longer harass the spreading of our word. It implies, as well, that Sol realizes Cornath and Ezra can no longer stop us, and in the end, realizing that, the others will acknowledge us as part of the Ice. In time, Michael, we can bring Sol into the open and have them sign the Concordia of Religious Acceptance. Once we have that, we will have broken one-third of the powers."

"Then I must ask the Council, will we accept at this time the private agreement of the prelate?" Michael continued forcefully. "In so doing, we must agree that any and all ships of Sol are free to pass and to moor in our harbors, exempt from taxes, search, or attack." As he finished his statement, he looked to Eldric, who controlled most of the freebooters.

"Ah, Michael," Eldric replied playfully, "but that will take away some of the fun of my men. Chasing down the occasional priest of Sol has been such fine entertainment for us in years past."

"You pox-eaten pirate," Janis replied, "you'd attack your own mother's ship if there were a profit in it."

Eldric threw back his head and laughed. "If I knew who she was, my dear. If I knew who she was."

Michael and the others looked at Janis and laughed, as well. Then, turning to Eldric, he said calmly, "I and those who follow me will agree. Can I count on you to do likewise?"

Eldric was quiet for a moment. "If the shadows of my

forefathers could only see this, I, master of Bathan, pledged in alliance to a brown-robed Prophet. But damn me, I pledged myself to this Confederation of yours, and I shall agree to your words, Ormson."

Michael looked to the others.

They nodded in agreement, all except Seth, who looked at Michael with a quiet, determined gaze.

"Good, then. Cowan, reply to the prelate in my name that the arrangement shall be made. We shall pledge safety to all ships, both by mine own men, which, of course, has always been our policy, and by our allies as well. In return, he shall allow our people freely to spread the word, to teach, to recruit, and to inform of knowledge and doctrine outside the teaching of the Holy Brotherhood of Sol."

Changing the subject, he looked to Daniel. "How stand the Companions?"

Daniel leaned back in his chair, the wood creaking in protest at the strain put on it. The giant was dressed in the white tunic, leggings, and helmet covering of the Companions—the elite guard and military strength of the Prophet.

"Ah, by me own eyes, 'tis good. Morale could never be higher. There be a thousand here in Mathin, two thousand aboard our ships, and another two thousand scattered across the Southward Sea. At a moment's notice, five thousand more could be brought into the ranks, if need be."

"But there is no need at present," Michael replied quietly.

Daniel looked at him and voiced no protest.

"And, Finson, our fleet?"

"In the shipyards of Mathin, Bathan, and Wallen, there be four hundred battle rams ready to sail with a week's notice. There are also twenty frigates, three old ice cruisers, and a hundred other ships of war, including the corsairs and privateers of Eldric."

"The best on the Ice," Eldric replied proudly.

"Not as good as Mathin's," Finson retorted.

"My *Golden Star* can do five the wind, running full abeam, you yapping dog."

"Pox, you say," Finson replied heatedly, "not four the wind and no match for *Red Flame* of Mathin. And she carries a third again the cannon of your twisted-keel hulk."

The argument had run for years, and Eldric still bore a knife

scar on his shoulder from a time when the hot words had flowed
with too much ale.

"Stop it, damn you all," Janis shouted above the rising
voices. "Finson, you can take him running close hauled, and
all know it, but on a beam reach, nothing can run against the
Golden Star, which I must remind you, Eldric, was laid down
by my father in the shipyards below this window."

The two looked to her and, bowing low, mumbled the usual
words of courtesy reserved for the woman of the Prophet.

"All right," Michael continued, "what of harbor defenses
and cannons?"

"We have nearly seven hundred cannons of all weights—
five hundred and ten shipboard, the rest in harbor defense. We
are still woefully short. The blockade of Mor and the Horthian
Brotherhoods has been difficult. Since the Cornathian destruction of Sol's one foundry, we still have no source south of the
Tracks."

"Can not our own men cast them yet?"

"Remember, Michael, when Cornath destroyed the foundry
four years ago, they slaughtered every man who might know
all the secrets," Seth responded quietly. "We are working on
the problem. We have cast weapons to be sure, but as yet our
manufactures are brittle, burst easily, and cannot throw an
accurate shot. Several years will pass before we perfect the
technique."

"And by the nature of this conversation, we must turn to
Cornath," Seth interjected forcefully.

"Yes," Michael replied wearily, "to Cornath, then."

"Michael, I must state something that has changed all of
our plans. We have received fairly reliable reports that His
Holiness Alnar the III is dead, most likely from poison."

Michael cast him a sharp look of reproach—Seth had arrived
late the night before, with important information that he should
have told Michael before the Council meeting. Believing that
Seth had withheld the information so that in the meeting he
might be forced by his followers to take a more aggressive
stance, Michael felt a wave of resentment.

"How reliable?" Michael replied coldly.

"Good enough, Michael. I have my sources. The Council
of Archbishops is trying to keep it quiet as long as possible
while they formulate what must be done. Remember that until

the next Church Council meeting in the spring, issues of war will now be under the control of Balor, Madoc, and Zimri."

"And what sources might those be?" Cowan asked in a cold, icy voice.

The room fell silent. Most of them knew that somehow Inys Gloi was behind them, but its involvement was a topic never openly discussed. Michael looked around the room and decided that now was not the time to begin.

"They wouldn't dare to launch a full war without Council support," Michael said quickly, trying to divert the conversation.

"One never knows."

"But for all practical purposes, Zimri is powerless. He's in self-imposed exile and deeply mistrusted by the other archbishops," Janis stated, as if trying to reassure herself.

"Ah, but that can change," Padraig Toverson responded from the far end of the table, where the ram fleet commanders and island chieftains sat. "Remember, I served aboard a Morian vessel for thirteen seasons and know them well. No matter how much the other brotherhoods fear Zimri, they still need Mor to insure their survival."

"But perhaps we read too much into this," Janis replied. "We all knew that Almar was a compromise See, elected in the turmoil after our victory. The peace element still holds a majority, and surely they cannot forget how Zimri tried to maneuver them five years ago."

"Memories are short," Daniel mumbled more to himself than to the others.

"Still," Seth replied, "I must counsel action now! We have the fleets. We have followers who are willing to die for our cause—to spread the word across the Ice until all the plague-rotted churches are dead and the way of the master rules over all."

Seth rose as he spoke, a fanatical expression on his face. Michael swept the room with his gaze. To his dismay, he could see that old familiar look mirrored on the faces of his followers. Most were nodding with wolfish grins of delight at the call to arms. Daniel was half out of his chair—his fists clenched, his dark eyes alight with the thought of battle. Only Cowan and Janis sat back, shaking their heads sadly.

"Speak, Cowan. I see you agree not with our brother Seth."

"Now is not the time," Cowan responded. "First of all, there is no provocation to attack. Granted, our brothers are harassed and hunted in the north, but Eldric does the same upon the Southward Ice. And we must consider the cost—it would be horrifying, my friends, so horrifying it would make all the other wars pale to insignificance. And for what good, when we can gain all we desire by adroit maneuver and diplomacy? The churches are dying of their own corruption. All we need do is wait until they topple over from within, and then we shall fill their place."

"No, that is nonsense," Seth responded, turning to look Michael in the eyes. "We should strike now, Michael. Strike before a day comes when you might regret it!"

Michael looked at Seth calmly. "My friend, I have always taken your advice to heart. I, too, have worried about Cornath, somehow sensing that they will not let the final issue rest without a fight. But if we are the ones to attack, then it changes all."

He looked around the room. "Remember what I have said, what we have started, and what we believe for the future. Religion as the cause of war, the forcing of our belief upon another, will not happen as long as I live and think. We are trying to end that cycle, not continue it. If we attack Cornath, then the onus will be upon us, and in fighting to deliver Truth, we will be repressing it. No, I cannot agree, Seth, my friend. I am sorry."

He looked around the table. He was still amazed how his men would follow him. His mere wish carried such power with them that they would agree to anything he asked. He never ceased to be amazed at the reverent looks hardened men of combat gave to him. He did not understand, but over the years he had come to accept and, when necessary, to use it. He looked confidently at them and waited.

The room was silent as the men looked one to the other.

"Your wish has always been my command, master," Daniel said quietly, gazing at Michael with a confused look of frustration and heartfelt admiration.

The other picked up Daniel's words and murmured their agreement. Then Seth faced Michael and nodded to him with a slight bow. "Of course, Michael Ormson, if you wish it, so shall it be."

Michael leaned across the table and clasped Seth's hand. "My first and closest friend, though we might not agree, your counsel and love I shall always hold next to my heart."

Seth looked at him and spoke quietly. "I pray, Michael, that your decision here shall not one day haunt you."

Michael looked at him and tried to dismiss a vague unease. He knew of Seth's connection to Inys Gloi and from the beginning had accepted it as one of the links to his own power. After all, it was the cult of Prophecy, established by Inys Gloi, that had guaranteed his rise. But the words of Peter of Mor drifted back to him, the warning that in the end Inys Gloi would destroy Michael when he was no longer needed. What was their plan? Michael pushed the thoughts away, then looked to Janis and smiled.

"There is so much more to be discussed," he said with forced cheerfulness. "Let us take our meal together and talk of the future. I wish to share with you some of the things that are being debated in the school. A most remarkable young man there, a former priest of Sol, claims that he can prove that the Arch is the remnant of what was once another world."

Murmurs arose around the room. Some of the men exclaimed over the nonsense of such thoughts, while several of the island chieftains made subtle gestures to ward off evil.

"And, of course, we must share the plans for the great voyage around the world, which shall leave at the end of the season." Michael stood up from the table. "Let us go to the next room where the table is already set."

Taking Janis by the hand, he walked from the room. The others rose to follow, many engaged in heated conversation as they debated Michael's decision concerning Cornath.

As Michael walked from the room; the doubts flooded back to him. His dream of the night before still hung at the edge of his consciousness—a room, somehow familiar, covered in blood and he, alone in the middle of it. At the far end of the room stood a specter, a specter that he knew, concealed in the hooded robes of the Church, and at the specter's feet lay something too dreadful to gaze upon. And even as he started to look down on it, his fear had driven him from the dream into consciousness. The dream was a warning—he knew that—but of what?

CHAPTER 3

THEIR CHANT ECHOED IN THE DISTANCE, THE WORDS REVER-
berating with soft, whisperlike tones through the darkened
chambers. Upward they came, a single torch lighting the way
in the long, narrow corridor that shimmered with crystalline
frost. The chanting stopped for a moment, and as the words
echoed away, the silence was broken by the soft rustling of
robes and the measured step of the procession. They turned
the final corner. The single light flickered in the distance,
weaving and bobbing as the high priest held it aloft, guiding
the way for the white-robed forms that appeared silhouetted by
reflected light in the darkness of night.

The chanting started again, the steady single note weaving
the Hymn of the Holy Light—the liturgy of Inys Gloi.

The climb upward had started nearly half an hour before.
Alone, he had watched them as they gathered in the courtyard,
five hundred feet below. For the last week, Riadent, Grand
Master of Inys Gloi, had watched with grim satisfaction as half
a thousand men had gathered in the courtyard and harbor,
enclosed within the island fastness of the Holy Island. They
had arrived by the hundreds, usually at night, carrying single
skatesails or standing on the decks of aging corsairs and cutters.
They had arrived wearing the garb and carrying the pennants
of half a hundred cities. Many were dressed in the heavy non-

descript robes of the ice runner, here and there were the fine furs and wrappings of a guild master or merchant prince, and scattered throughout were the robes of the three churches. Several had come from Mathin, wearing the pure white battle garb of the Companions. The tunics and shields of the Mathinians shimmered in the reflected light of the Arch, and all eyes were upon them as they strode alone into the mountain fortress of Inys Gloi.

All had come together, answering to the voice of his command, and now, at last, they were weaving their way up the mountain to the meeting that would reveal the next act of their drama, planned a thousand years earlier. The secret brotherhood was meeting for the first time in nearly thirty years, for the first time since the birth of the Prophet.

Thirty years had passed, and now he was the master, the Guide of the Path Hidden. When last this happened, he was but the Ail Meistr, the second to the master, knower of the secret, Gwybod o Cyfrinc. But at last the final power was his to control, and he took quiet joy in that thought. He who had started as a young deacon, working his way into the inner circle of St. Awstin, a trusted companion to a future archbishop of St. Awstin, who had unwittingly controlled the future. He thought of Rifton for a moment and smiled sadly at the memories of that simple priest who had so well served their cause.

The procession was entering the chapel, and the monks' chanting swelled with a deep, passionate fervor as the words of praise to the ancient Church, the Founder of All, echoed through the chambers and drifted out from atop the pinnacle of Inys Gloi to the frozen night beyond.

He turned and, with his robes billowing out, strode across the chamber. With quick, easy steps he walked to the front of the altar, the darkness no hindrance, so often had he taken that path. There were twenty-one steps to climb, and then, reaching out into the darkness, he parted a heavy gauze curtain that concealed the Holy of Holies and the throne reserved for the master. Behind the curtain, his form appeared to be a ghostly shadow, while the torchlight in the chapel revealed those who entered into his presence.

The procession crossed the threshold into the chapel and fell into silence as the brothers stopped before the altar and, genuflecting to the Holy of Holies, filed to the sides of the room. It took several minutes for the brothers to gain the doorway to the Ard Capel du Inys Gloi, the High Chapel, the room revealed only to the Elect. As the last brother entered the room, the doors closed silently behind him.

These were his instruments—sharpened and ready. If one of them should die, a novice waited below to take the place of the fallen and to enter a world where he would lead two lives—the one on the surface, the other within—for the advancement of the Sacred Cause, the return of Inys Gloi to power. Each of them was merely a cell in a living organism that he controlled. Riadent smiled at the thought. They were his—a sacred trust that had been passed down by the eighty-seven masters who had preceded him across two thousand years of time, and in turn two thousand years before that. All was coming to form at last. Soon the screen would be removed forever. Riadent knew with a grim certainty that he would be the last Grand Master of the Hidden Age. He knew, as well, that he would be the first master of the new.

The single bell in the towering steeple peeled its solitary call, and with the first note, all fell to their knees and assumed the position for meditation. It would last until the first light of dawn, when the watcher above could distinguish the white thread from the black. Riadent went slowly to his knees, as well, and silently crossed his hands in the ritual posture of ninth-degree meditation—the bringing together of all thought into one collective whole. So he would remain till dawn. Then the final decisions concerning the Prophet would be made.

The night passed in silence as Riadent's thoughts and the thoughts of those with him turned across the frozen sea. And they could sense the stirring—the awareness that greeted them.

"Michael, are you all right?" Janis whispered sleepily.

He was silent.

"Michael, is something wrong?"

She could feel the tension in his body. It had brought her out of sleep, and in the darkness, she could sense that he was staring at something unseen.

"I don't know, love. I felt something in the night."

"What, Michael?"

"Nothing, love. Nothing. Go to sleep," he said quietly. "It was nothing."

She held him close but knew that he would not sleep.

Riadent smiled. He turned away, and then his thoughts crossed to the other side—to a monastery hidden deep beneath the Sacred Cathedral, a place known only to the Inner Circle of Cornath and to those who walked undetected in that Circle of Knowledge. They were preparing, as well. It was going as planned, and all smiled in their dreamlike trance.

The night passed quietly. The only sound was the soft, measured breathing of five hundred brothers, all drawing breath and exhaling together, as if their bodies had been joined in one flesh, one thought, one dream.

The Arch cut across the sky, its light matched only by the flaring of the aurora that shimmered in shifting patterns of polychromatic light. Curtains of fire washed the heavens, blanketing the night with icy flames that reflected across the eternal frozen sea.

He sensed at last that the dawn was approaching and that the watcher above was holding the two threads aloft, judging the moment when the bell would be sounded.

The master waited in silence, his thoughts standing with the watcher, and in his mind he could see the guard turn away from the threads and approach the cord to the single bronze bell suspended atop the highest tower. Before the striker log cut its arc, the master opened his eyes and clapped his hands three times, the bell above sounding even before the last clap echoed away into silence.

An involuntary sigh rippled through the chapel. From behind the curtain, the master could make out the shadows of the brothers as they stood up and formed into ranks of ten. A whispered command sounded from the rear of the room, and all the brothers save three turned away from the altar. Without chant or ritual, the brothers of Inys Gloi filed out of the chapel while overhead the deep booming of the bell rolled through the citadel and carried far out across the icy silence of the Frozen Sea.

Involuntarily, he checked the ceremonial face mask to make sure that it was in place. Arising, Riadent walked in front of the altar and tore the curtain aside. He looked at the three and smiled. They were the Chosen Ones, the Inner Circle. All had taken the vows with him nearly forty years earlier. With a curt wave of his hand, Riadent beckoned for them to follow.

From the corner of his eye, he saw another form standing in the far corner of the chapel. He acknowledged her presence with a brief nod and then led his men into the chambers of the master, concealed behind the altar.

The Yawinder passed around the table, and Riadent laid aside his ceremonial robes, stretching his arms and groaning with delight after twelve hours of immobility. Finally, he turned and looked across at the three men who sat casually around the table, sipping the wine and awaiting his decisions.

Riadent looked at them with pleasure—how the others would love to know who they really were, he thought. How little the outside truly knew of Inys Gloi. Riadent sat down with a casual air, picked up the Yawinder, and poured himself a drink.

"So, my friends, it is time at last."

The others nodded, looking one to the other.

"All that we have planned has come to pass," a lean, dark-visaged man whispered. The robes of Mor were revealed, for the habit of Inys Gloi was draped over the high-back chair behind him.

"The same for Ezra," said the second.

The third was silent.

Riadent and the others looked to him.

"And of him, what can you say?" the Morian asked coldly. There was no response.

"Go on, my friend; speak freely," Riadent said gently.

"You already know what I have said," the man dressed as a Companion said darkly.

Riadent looked at the Companion, fixing the man with his gaze, trying to somehow reach into the inner thoughts. But his friend was silent, returning his gaze without fear or emotion.

"You realize, of course, what is to come?" Riadent asked quietly. "Again, we could see it in the meditation of five hundred joined together as one."

"Yes, we realize it."

The Cornathian turned and faced the one from the south.

"By all the Saints, man, we've discussed this a hundred times. It all depends on your people."

"I know that," the Mathinian replied, "but you know our observations, as well, and they are most disquieting."

Riadent slammed the table with his fist, jarring the bottle of Yawinder.

"Damn it all, that's been settled already. We created the Prophet, we shall guide him, and we shall use him. So it has been from the beginning and for every step that he has taken, and damn it, so it shall be in the future. We have waited a thousand years for this moment, and your misgivings will not sway us from this course." Riadent leaned over the table and stared menacingly at his old friend. "Now, do you understand, my friend, for if not, we can make the proper arrangements."

The threat was clear, and the others waited cautiously for the response.

"But, Riadent," the Mathinian said softly, "what if the Prophet knows more than we think? I should know. I've been there, I've watched him nearly every step of the way, and I think I can judge on that matter far better than anyone else here, either alone or by our collective meditation. And what of the other churches, as well? Surely they must be onto the game by now, or are they complete fools?"

"Of course they are becoming aware," Riadent replied with barely concealed impatience. "As the game comes to the end, we become more visible. We know that the Cornathian and Ezrian archbishops whom we do not control are increasingly aware of us of late, but that is to be expected. But by the time they gain full recognition of our plans, it will be too late; our people will be in control."

"However," the Mathinian replied quietly, "we must accept the maxim laid down by our forefathers. 'The greater the risk, the greater the probability of the improbable.'"

"That we accept," Riadent replied coldly. "We would be fools not to acknowledge the risk. Since the consolidation of our order and the gathering of the records, we have known the risk. Since the acceptance of the goal from the Before Time we have always known the risk." As he uttered the last words, he hit the table sharply.

"The Prime Choice of the Churches was inevitable," Riadent

continued softly, "but we knew that in the end it would corrupt them. We knew that all too well when the other brotherhoods cheated our order out of its birthright as rulers of the Ice. Of course, there is risk, but look at our cards. We have three archbishops of Cornath, five of Ezra, and, of course, it is obvious the control we exercise in Mathin."

He stopped for a moment and smiled, and two of them acknowledged his pleasure.

"But," the Mathinian argued, "we have always moved on the predictable. This action is the unpredictable."

Riadent looked across the table.

"It has already been decided. Through this action, the Prophet will serve our cause. If he dies by his action now, that we can accept, for we can make a martyr of him. But we must force him to action, and we must do it now! If we wait any longer, his power will grow beyond our ability to control.

"His rallying of the freebooters and this secret pact with Sol have come faster than we were able to perceive either through agents or meditation. We must seize a tighter control, and now! He has already destabilized Sol beyond any hope of recovery. That is as we wished, but again, it is too soon. If we have peace for even five more years, he would simply overwhelm Cornath and then Ezra. We want a vacuum, not another power!"

Riadent paused for a moment and refilled his glass with the burgundy richness of Yawinder; draining his cup, he fixed the Mathinian with his gaze.

"When he dies, we must be the heirs, not the rivals. Our action shall guarantee that before his death he shall come to our door asking for admittance, and behind him shall come the people and his multitude of followers. Then we shall be the priests of the New Movement. The Choice shall be loosened, but not beyond recall, and at last we shall be the inheritors, ready to lead our race into the Peace of God, as was our right from the very beginning of time."

"If it works," the southlander said defiantly.

"It will work," Riadent said forcefully, cutting any further argument with a cold-blooded stare. "Our order planned for all the probabilities long before any of us walked upon the Ice. This drama has been planned, and we are merely the actors created in the dreams of our forefathers, two thousand years before the seas ever froze.

"As the Grand Master of our sacred brotherhood, I have spoken. Last night's meditation again reaffirmed the correctness of our action. And as that has been confirmed, then so it shall be done. We are pledged to our order unto death, and as by our pledge, so we must act."

Riadent stood up, signaling that the meeting had come to an end.

"I will meet with each of you in private. Bring your intelligence reports and a full evaluation of all your agents. There are some indications that our good friend Zimri is planning something—that private meeting of his is still a mystery in regards to his actions concerning us."

With a curt nod, Riadent dismissed the two from the northern churches. He waited until the door had closed, and then he turned to face the Mathinian.

"Damn you," he said angrily, "can't we ever agree?"

The Mathinian stood up and faced him stoically.

"You're not there, Riadent. I am. That is why I am so afraid."

"Of what?"

"Of all that we have discussed. I still feel it at times."

Riadent looked at him appraisingly.

"Riadent," the Mathinian said in a whisper, "there are times that he looks at me and I can't help but feel that he knows all—everything. At moments like that, I am afraid. For forty years, I have believed in nothing but Inys Gloi and the plan. But I have grown fearful. I ask myself, Have we created the legend, or is that legend real and beyond our own understanding and merely using us for its own ends?"

Riadent looked away for a moment. Yes, the fear, he thought, the damnable fear, but he was the master, and he of all could not show it.

"That is nothing but nonsense. The question is settled; our meditations have proven that our actions are right and we are the controllers. So stop this damnable worrying; there are other things to attend to now." He picked up the half-empty bottle of Yawinder, started to pour another drink, and then, deciding against it, replaced the bottle on the table. "I think it is time that we went to talk to her," he said quietly.

"Yes," the Mathinian replied sadly, "I guess it is."

"Let us go, then."

"Funny, of late I recall a poem from the Before," the Mathinian said softly.

Riadent looked at him.

"You see, there is a phrase: 'Are we nothing but the dream within the dream.'" The Mathinian chuckled softly.

Riadent was silent. Turning away, he looked out the window—to the early light of dawn.

The dream within the dream, he thought quietly. Strange, how often of late those precise words had come to him, as well.

He appeared to float out of the darkness. His heavy, square-shouldered form was silhouette by the single candle that flickered on the jet-black altar. Behind him, in the niche above the Sacred Stone, rested the bloodstained icon of St. Mawr, protector of the Briath du Cyllel, the Brotherhood of the Knife. Bowing low, he made the final prayers of ritual in preparation for what was to come.

"Guide me in the darkness so that it is light. For life is nothing, hope is nothing, dreams are but dreams, and all is dedicated to the One—the preservation of Holy Church. Amen."

In the distance a deep, sonorous chanting could be heard; the initiates were coming to him at last. He could hear the soft swish of robes and the pad of bare feet on the icy rock, which heralded the approach of his order.

Ulric du Cyllel, forty-third Master of the Order, stepped up to the altar and extinguished the only source of light; then, bowing to the icon, he turned away from the shrine with graceful, catlike ease. He was ready. The procession entered the chapel in silence, the chant ending as the first monks entered the room. There was no sound from the monks, no calling of age-old prayers, just a quiet filling of the darkened room by dark forms that drifted through the shadows and merged into the surrounding darkness. He could sense, rather than see, their presence. He waited for several minutes, until the last of the two hundred entered the chamber.

They awaited his command.

"Is all in readiness?" Ulric demanded in a full, booming voice.

"It is as it must be," a voice called from the darkness.

"Then I call upon my brothers to bear witness, for the time

of initiation is at hand. Let the three come forward."

From the darkness, three phantoms emerged, dressed in the gray robes of initiates. He stepped down from the altar and stood before them.

"Do all of you, of your own free will, take part in this act?"

"We do, by the blessing of St. Mawr," they said, as if with a single voice.

"Do all of you understand that which you must face in order to gain admittance into our Sacred Brotherhood?"

"We do, by the blessing of St. Mawr."

"You have been asked twice this evening, and I ask you again. From this final answer, there is no retreat. Do you swear yourselves unto me to live by my command and to die by my word?"

"We do, by the blessing of St. Mawr."

Ulric turned and walked to the altar. He unbuttoned his hooded cassock and let it fall to the ground, revealing a loose-fitting tunic and trousers of deepest black. His head was wrapped in a turban of black cloth that covered all but his eyes. His massive shoulders and barrel chest rippled as he stretched his arms to the altar.

"May St. Mawr approve of these, his initiates."

"And guide them in the trial to come," the hooded monks whispered in reply.

"Let it begin."

The members of the brotherhood arose as one and filed out of the chapel. With his back turned, he waited until the doors closed behind them and then extinguished the single flickering candle. His breathing was quiet and controlled. He was ready.

Ulric could hear the three initiates at the far end of the chapel as they removed their gray cassocks to stand naked in the cold chamber. He waited for several minutes, attuning himself to their presence, listening for the whisper that would betray movement. Good, very good; nothing so far.

Ulric slipped away from the altar, his muscles rippling fluidly. Slowly, he made his way into the middle of the chapel. Crouching low in the darkness, he closed his eyes. They were a useless distraction; all attention must be given to the senses that could pierce the darkness.

Yes, something at last! A faint rustle sounded to his left. Still crouched low, Ulric backed away several paces. He turned

his head from side to side—listening, waiting. There it was
again. His prey stopped, sensing that Death was near.

With flared nostrils, Ulric took long, deep breaths, catching
the faint smell of sweat and fear. Walking lightly, he back-
tracked with a crablike motion, shifting to the left until his
outstretched hand brushed against the damp, chilled wall. Yes,
he was closer. Ulric reached up and silently removed the black
steel garrote from his headband. The presence moved again;
Ulric could sense the panic as his victim tried a desperate sprint
past his right.

Ulric cut across the room to stop in the middle of the chapel.
The presence came closer. He poised himself, his muscles
coiled and tense.

Now! He leaped into the darkness, his aim perfect, as his
garrote wrapped around the neck of a struggling form. Ulric
slammed his forearm against the victim's head, pushing it over
while the garrote tightened. The vertebrae separated, and the
spinal column snapped with an audible crack. A bad kill; the
snap was too loud. The body kicked spasmodically as Ulric
lowered it to the ground.

From behind! Ulric sprinted to the front of the altar and
leaped into the darkness. He caught hold of a foot that kicked
out viciously. Ulric rolled, twisting the leg out, pulling the
victim down. Even as they fell, Ulric kicked out with his right
leg, catching the initiate on the knee, shattering the bone. A
body crashed down next to him, and an open hand caught him
a glancing blow to the shoulder, just missing his face. Ulric
delivered a blow into the darkness. His hand drove into the
sternum, cracking the rib cage. He cut upward with a forceful
punch, driving his thumb into the throat, collapsing the initiate's windpipe. A muffled cry filled the chamber as his victim
began to choke on cartilage and blood. Ulric leaped aside, not
bothering to finish off the prey. The noise would be a good
distraction. He waited. Yes, the other one was still in front of
him, not a dozen feet away. Crouching, he waited for several
minutes, trying to panic the initiate into moving. He plays the
game well, Ulric thought, but he'll have to move eventually.
There was a soft rustle to his left. Ulric turned to face it. A
stunning blow slammed into him on the right, knocking him
off his feet. Ulric rolled over backward, alighting and kicking
out again to his left. He brushed something. Ulric leaped into

the darkness, connecting again, striking his victim in the small of the back. But he received another blow, as well, across the side of the head, that sent him reeling. He rolled quickly to absorb the impact and came up on the run. Weaving and dodging, Ulric ran down his foe. Directly ahead now! He leaped for the kill, and caught the initiate across the small of the back, knocking him to the chapel floor.

"Sanctuary!" the victim shouted before Ulric could raise his hand for a killing blow.

Ulric relaxed. The initiation was over, the one survivor had reached the altar.

Ulric drew himself up in the darkness. "You have done well," he whispered.

Turning away from the altar, Ulric clapped his hands three times. The door at the end of the chapel, where the brotherhood waited expectantly for his command, opened.

At the head of the column, four monks held flaming torches that flooded the chapel with a warm, fiery glow. In the flickering light, Ulric saw the two who had failed the final test. The one in the middle of the room was still. His neck twisted obscenely to one side. A puddle of blood spread from beneath him. By the steps of the altar was the other, still kicking spasmodically. A river of pink foam gushed from between his quivering lips—his face was contorted in agony. In the distance came a soft, even chant in praise to St. Mawr. Ulric walked over to the dying boy, his face wreathed by a strange, distant look.

Kneeling, Ulric made the Sign of Blessing. The boy looked at him, trying to mask his fear, but terror was obvious on his face. With unexpected gentleness, Ulric bent over and covered the initiate's eyes with his left hand while he raised his right hand into the air. A deacon stepped forward from the column and placed a razor-sharp stiletto in Ulric's hand. With a quick downward sweep, Ulric slipped the knife into the base of the skull behind the boy's ear. The boy kicked once, sighed, and was still.

Ulric withdrew the knife, laid it on the boy's chest, and returned to the altar, his hands stained with blood that gave off a warm, metallic smell. Two deacons stepped from the orderly ranks with a steaming bowl of scented water. Ulric washed his hands and, turning, faced the initiate who stood before him.

"You have survived the final test."

"And now shall be as us," the assembly behind responded.

"By my word, you shall live, and by my command, you will die."

"For the Return of the Garden, for the protection of Good and Holy Church, it shall be done," the two hundred monks replied.

"The initiation is complete."

Half a dozen monks stepped forward and picked up the bodies on the chapel floor. The column chanted the praise of St. Mawr as they carried the corpses to the altar. With a quiet reverence, they placed them on the altar so that the blood of the fallen would mingle with the blood of those who had died before. Though they had failed in life, still their blood offering would bring blessings in death. The sacred icon was removed from its niche, while four monks waved censers that gave off a cloud of sweet smoke. The bottom of the icon was dipped in the wounds of the fallen, while all in the chapel and the corridor beyond bowed low, chanting their praise. Ulric waited until the icon had been replaced in its sacred spot, then rose and stepped down from the altar. Their chants echoing down the corridors carved in stone, the monks parted before him, and he disappeared into the darkness.

Six ceremonial guards led the way, but in the labyrinth hidden beneath the cathedral of St. Eglais, he knew no fear. The guards were ceremony, for none would ever dare to strike. He was the master, the strike arm of Holy Church, and though the others might loathe him in their hearts, he knew that his was truly the power of the Church.

Where the corridor grew wider, a hooded form with a flickering torch met him. The figure came up to him and whispered, "Balor and Madoc are here."

He concealed his surprise. His agents had already told him that the two had sailed to some secret rendezvous two weeks before, and he had half suspected that there would be a calling as a result. But their presence was a breaking with tradition— usually *he* was summoned when the killing of a heretic was to be performed.

Ulric gave a hand gesture, indicating that he was to be left alone, his guards to remain out of sight. He walked down the dark, cold hallway and entered the audience chamber.

Madoc looked up as the shadow loomed in the doorway. Every time he met Ulric, he felt ill at ease. He knew that the man had personally executed more than fifty assassinations, a master who was considered one of the best in the long history of the Church. Madoc noted the heavy scent of blood as the hooded form drew closer, bowed reverently, and then pulled back his hood. A thin white scar marked Ulric's forehead and craggy brow. Ulric's jet black eyes stared at him with a cold, frightening gleam—their color matched by the dark mane that was cut square at the shoulders. Alone of all the brotherhoods, the assassins did not shave their heads; their missions so often required them to mingle with those outside the Church.

There must have been an initiation that night, Madoc thought distastefully, perhaps replacements for the assassins lost against the guild master who had divined the Hidden Secret of Reading. Many a time he had summoned Ulric, and once, long before, there had been a private commission—the one his own were not good enough for. Perhaps that might be necessary again.

"My lords, I bid you welcome." Ulric bowed low to each of them. "I trust that your visit is of some importance."

Madoc nodded slowly. Ulric never bothered with political niceties. "There has been a meeting, and an important decision has been reached. Your services are needed."

"Yes?"

"Michael Ormson," Balor said.

"Ah, so you've finally come to your senses over him. I was wondering how long my lord archbishops would take. His following is growing at an alarming rate. In fact, if it continues, I fear that it will soon be beyond the control of Cornath. He can rally a hundred thousand men to his cause and a thousand ships, most of them battle rams, but quite a few of them the remnants of the Sol fleet and corsairs of the freebooters. In battle, his ram fleets are invincible, as demonstrated, of course, by our good lord Zimri."

"Can he be defeated on the open ice?" Balor interjected.

"With a fleet, no. There's no reason for him to come northward, and we can't force the barrier lines he's erected across the Broken Tracks. We'd have to attack his barriers while our fleet was vulnerable on the open ice. He would have the protection of the channels from which to launch his ram attacks. Fortunate for us all that he still allows the trade ships to go through—after paying taxes, of course. But with the pressure from elsewhere, that could change at any time."

"From elsewhere?" Madoc asked curiously.

"Inys Gloi awaits." Ulric smiled.

"Can he be killed?" Balor inquired.

Ulric was silent for a moment. Three of his best had already been sent—one by Balor and Rifton and two others the following year. All had failed, as if Ormson held a special charm conferred by the Saints. The Holy Father had halted further attempts. But that Holy Father had been dead for a month. Ulric thought of that for a moment and then pushed it away—it was not for him ever to question the decision of a Holy Father, master of them all. Yes, it was a question of pride; the execution of a heretic, if properly commissioned, must be completed.

"It can be done, but the cost will be high. Ormson's guardians are the best on the Ice. They come from that brotherhood that even I cannot enter."

He looked at them with lowered eyes, waiting for their next move. This was a risky business—ordering a death when the Holy Throne was empty.

"It is possible?" Madoc asked.

"I take it that we are talking of a private commission. Who would order this to be done? Since I have not the power to order it myself."

"Zimri," Madoc replied coldly.

Ah. Zimri has returned at last, he thought. But such a foolish move. It will merely create a martyr for the mobs to follow. Prophets are always more believable when they are dead. If Zimri orders this, then the war that follows can be blamed on him. Ulric visualized the net that was already half woven—as soon as the new Holy Father was selected with the return of the sun month, there would be another commission—to eliminate the archbishop of Mor.

"Does Zimri want the prophet dead?"

"No," Balor replied carefully, "and I must agree with this. You can see our problem and have stated it clearly. The prophet controls the trade lanes, and we have not the strength to force them. We could perhaps take him, but only after a long effort. We would have to triple the size of our fleet and forge a firm alliance with Ezra, but Ormson has masterfully played off Ezra by granting it preference in trade, thereby keeping us at odds with each other. No, Zimri wants to force Michael to attack us. We need him alive for that. The 'Ilad o Focred' that he commissions is the one act that will bring Ormson out in open attack. You are to execute his wife and only son."

That was something that Ulric had not expected. And perhaps somewhat easier to perform.

"But there is one element to the plan that we must insist upon," Balor stated in a cold, even voice. "The assassination must be performed in such a way as to bring Ormson and all of his followers out unto the northward shelf, and the action must be accomplished before this season of ice is over."

"In other words, before another Holy Father can be selected, like the last, who blocked your moves."

The two archbishops looked at him, but neither would comment. He ignored their stares. The wish of the Church was the command he must follow. He would have to strike openly and with a violence that would bring Ormson out. Yes, he could see the wisdom in the idea. But in order to guarantee success, he would have to use sufficient force to gain the citadel of the Prophet—a fortress protected by the Companions, the elite guard of the Prophet. To kill the woman and child by poison or an attack in an alleyway would not have the necessary impact. Stealth would play a part, but brutality would be necessary, as well. This would indeed be a difficult task—one that could be led only by a Master.

"This is an action that requires the approval of you two, as well," Ulric stated formally, "since I am required by custom to demand that. You alone, Balor, can release me for this mission, since it does involve a violator of the First Choice."

Balor nodded in response. "I shall release you to serve Zimri's wish, since he has requested it as archbishop of our warrior brotherhood. I do this only in the absence of a Holy Father."

"This needs your agreement, as well, Madoc, since you stand as Protector of the Faithful in your capacity as Secretary of the Church, while awaiting the election of the next Holy See."

"I agree to the request," Madoc responded, "as stated by Zimri."

Ulric looked from one to the other.

Madoc eyed the master assassin coldly. Ulric's appearance did not fit the image he thought the master should project. He had always felt that the master should be a thin, shadowy form who drifted in darkened corners. Instead, Ulric was broad, almost bearlike, with thick, powerful arms and a massive chest. Yet one look at Ulric's swarthy complexion and icy eyes told anyone that there was a man who can kill effectively—and without emotion.

Balor reached into the folds of his robe and produced a thick bundle of documents. "I have here the necessary information from Zimri's agent. You'll find detailed maps of Ormson's fortress, the island of Mathin, and the various approaches to his city. If you accept this task, I am to inform Zimri's agent at once. You are to sail on Supplication Night and to rendezvous with Zimri at the Place of Souls, thirty leagues to the northwest. There he will give you your final orders."

Taking the bundle of parchment, Ulric bowed low to the two archbishops. "By the order of my fathers and by the guidance of all the Saints above, I shall fulfill your command for the Return of the Garden."

"May the Saints above guide you for the preservation of our Good and Holy Church, and may you and all your brothers feast at the Blessed Table of the Saints through the long darkness of night, till the Return of our Father," the two archbishops responded.

Balor and Madoc looked at each other and nodded. Ulric had accepted, as they had known he would. And if the mission failed, Zimri would suffer the blame. Turning, they walked through the low archway where they were met by Ulric's guardians, who guided them through the darkened corridors back to the sanctuary of the cathedral above.

Ulric watched them disappear into the shadows. He looked down at his hands and saw traces of the blood of the novice whom he had killed only an hour before. It was the blood of his nephew, and he stared at the darkening stains. As he had feared, the boy had failed, but nothing could be done for that. Ulric looked to the small icon of St. Mawr, which was half hidden in the shadows. Without remorse or pity, he mumbled the prayer for the recently dead. Opening up the bundle of papers, he was soon lost in thought, pondering the path to action.

CHAPTER 4

HE STOOD ALONE ON THE DECK, THE CROSS-LACING OF RIG-
gings and masts silhouetted overhead by the fiery light of the
Arch and the flame of a blood-red aurora. Ulric looked heavenward and smiled—it was a good omen, he thought with a
grim sort of humor. Rubbing his tunic, he felt the gritty dust
of the black rock, which seemed to have seeped into every
pore of his body. The ship reeked with the smell of sulfur. The
stench was similar to that of black powder; it reminded him of
battle, and beneath his mask he grinned at the thought of the
mission to come.

Barneth came from the shadows and touched him lightly on
the shoulder. "All's ready, master."

"The men secured below?"

"As planned, Ulric."

"Good, make sail on my command."

He turned and walked across the deck of the collier—the
first obstacle overcome. The use of the collier was a simple
ruse, but like all simple things, it took deep insight to discover
the way. Barneth had approached him with the idea when Ulric
had finally confided that he needed to transport a hundred men
south of the fortress line that Ormson had created at the passes.

"Have you thought of a black-rock ship?" Barneth had ventured.

"How's that?"

"Me father told me of it from when he was a privateer fifty years ago. They built false bulkheads belowdecks, filled the outer ones with coal in case they were boarded, and concealed in a hidden deck, they placed nearly two hundred men. They gained the harbor of Sol, sprung a trap door on the bottom of the ship, and before the defenses could be raised, had taken half a dozen prizes and cut their way out of the harbor. A rare fine trick, it was."

The problem was solved. Ulric had placed his request with Madoc, and within the week an old collier out of North Prydain had disappeared—lost in a storm, it was later reported. A hundred miles off the coast, Barneth, with a dozen skilled carpenters from the brotherhood, constructed the false rooms, while Ulric completed his plans ashore and picked the men who would sail with him. The Chosen boarded the ship in secret after it entered the harbor and were secured below.

All was ready except for one final act—an act that Ulric knew was a break with law and tradition, but for the good of the Church, it would have to be done. "Barneth," he called softly.

"Yes, master."

"The sails ready?"

"At your command, Ulric."

"Good, will you follow me?"

Ulric went to the ship's ladder and lowered himself to the ice, and Barneth alighted next to him.

"Go to shore."

"Master?"

"You heard me. To hear is to obey; now go to shore."

The years of training faltered. Barneth started to turn, then hesitated, looking into the darkness, seeking an answer. "Why this, Ulric? Are you displeased with my work?"

"It is because I wish it, Barneth. I need not explain."

"Then you will have to kill me, for I refuse to obey."

Ulric was silent.

"I know where we are going, and it is my duty to go with you, Ulric."

"If you know where we are going, then you know why I am ordering you to stay."

"No, I don't, damn it."

"Because there's no return from this."

Barneth was silent for a moment. "Damn it, Ulric," he whispered. "Don't you think I know that?"

Ulric clapped him on the shoulder. "I've left instructions with Balor that you are to be the master, and he has agreed."

He could feel Barneth tense; his third in command had not expected that. All had assumed that Williams would be the heir, but Ulric needed Williams. Besides, Williams didn't have the political mind of Barneth. And the order would need a politician in the days ahead.

"In a month, you will know I am dead. Make your peace with Madoc, but when the time comes, and you will know when that is, go with Zimri."

"I know."

"Good, Zimri is the only one who can face this madman and defeat him in the war to come. And Zimri, I dare say, will be the only hope of our Church against Inys Gloi."

The Order would be entrusted to him, then, after all. Torn between loyalty to Ulric and the realization of what was being offered to him, he hesitated for a moment, then bowed low. "The Saints bless you, Ulric."

"And you, too, Barneth, until the Return of the Garden." He made the Sign of Blessing, lowered his hands, and turned away. Ascending the ladder, he called out his commands. "Make sail! Make sail!"

From overhead, the black sails snapped into place as straining crews worked at the windlasses to tighten the sheets down until they were cleated into place.

The craft broke free of the ice and quickly started away, far quicker than a collier should. Ulric noted the flaw. He didn't bother to look astern, for he knew that Barneth would watch until they disappeared into the shadows of night.

The collier cleared the harbor of Cornath, and soon the lights of the city were mere flickers—illumination dimmed to insignificance by the splendor of the Arch and the soaring aurora that crackled and whipped overhead. Sailing at night, especially for such a cumbersome craft, was somewhat dangerous. But it did cloak their actions—and a rendezvous was to be made at dawn.

It was nearly first light when the call came to his cabin, announced by a light knocking, coded to reveal who was beyond the doorway.

"You may enter, Fredrenson."

"Master Ulric."

Putting aside the documents that concerned the attack, Ulric looked up at Fredrenson, the sailing master in command of the night watch. His billowing ice-runner robes were far too big for the slender body of a practiced killer who had survived ten missions thus far.

"Report from the mizzentop watch. Appears to be a single ship trailing us; they can see it against the eastern horizon."

"Fine, it's what we want."

"Do you have any orders?"

"Come into the wind, we'll wait for her."

Ulric could sense the questioning in Fredrenson's mind.

"It's all right. It's according to plan."

"Yes, master." And the aide left the room.

For a moment, Ulric was tempted to put on his ceremonial robes, then decided not to; there was always the chance that it was not the ship he expected. Pulling on the tattered cloak of a black-rock sailor, he went topside.

The frigid air stunned him as he stepped onto the windswept deck. Walking astern, he could already see the ship in question silhouetted by the flaring scarlet of sunrise. Turning to Williams, the second commander, he ordered that all men were to remain concealed belowdecks and the morning prayers to be postponed.

The ship heeled beneath his feet as Fredrenson piloted the craft off a beam reach to turn her directly into the wind.

"Leave the sails luff," Ulric shouted. "This shan't take long."

The approaching schooner appeared to hover motionless on the ice, its speed undetectable, though it approached across the vast frozen waste. It wasn't until the ship was several hundred yards away that the motion became apparent; the ship trailed twin tails of spray, kicked heavenward by the blades to catch the early-morning light.

Her master let the schooner drop off from the wind, cutting

down astern of the collier, not a hundred yards off. As she drew abeam, the craft turned smartly into the eye of the wind. From beneath her deck, several braking blades appeared, tearing into the ice with a high-pitched whine, while from astern, the shower of ice redoubled. The craft cut across the bow of the black ship and came to rest upwind of the collier. Without a comment to his men, Ulric lowered himself over the side and trotted across the ice to the waiting schooner. On deck, his men waited tensely, knowing that when their master returned, their fates would be decided.

Zimri stood alone—his form concealed beneath the robes of a wandering friar of the Braith de Narn, the silent brotherhood. His guards stood in the distance, discreet but visible, and ready if need be.

Ulric surveyed the defensive arrangement on the deck and the watchful crossbowmen in the riggings. Good, very good, he thought. I gave that bastard some of my best; at least he knows how to use them.

Ulric reached the ship's ladder and without ceremony quickly scurried up it to land on the deck. He looked around at the dozen sailors and the cluster of Morian priests that stood on the deck, eying him cautiously. He searched for the subtle signs—the slight deference of positioning and the defensive patterns of the guards. All were silent. Yes, it must be him, the friar, the way several of the men kept darting quick glances to the most humbly dressed one on deck.

Without hesitation, Ulric strode forward and bent his knee before the man dressed in the plain, undyed robe.

"I seek your blessing, holy one."

There was a quiet murmur; he could sense fear from several of the Morians.

A mild chuckle arose from the friar who stood before him. "I told my brothers that you would be able to pick me out even though we have never met, brother Ulric. I give you my blessing in the name of all the Saints and in the hope of the Return of the Garden." Zimri made the Sign of the Arch over his head and, touching Ulric's shoulder, beckoned for the assassin to follow him below.

The cabin was lightly furnished, the only illumination coming from the light of dawn, revealed through one small window. Without ceremony, Zimri threw back his hood and removed the mask and goggles.

Ulric knew of the injury, but the ugly scar that ran from brow to jaw was something that held him, compelling him to look. He could sense the discomfort his scrutiny caused Zimri, but he didn't care, feeling that the injury was part of the mold that had shaped the leader of Mor.

"I thought a man such as yourself was accustomed to the sight of injuries," Zimri said sarcastically.

"On fighting men, yes; on archbishops and future Sees, no."

Zimri decided to let the challenge pass. Antagonizing this most important of men at such a crucial moment could serve no use. "I take it that all is in order," Zimri ventured, wishing to direct the conversation to the business at hand.

"Yes, my lord."

"Is there anything that you require of me?"

"No, my lord. The plans that Madoc gave me were quite detailed. My compliments to your people who prepared the information."

"Good, and I shall convey your thanks."

"Zimri, why did you call for this meeting? It is dangerous if all you intend to do is see us off with a blessing and some encouraging words."

Zimri pondered Ulric's directness. If this man were an archbishop, he would be dangerous beyond all measure. If Rifton had allied with him, Zimri thought, I would be a dead man now. The thought was unnerving, and he pushed it away.

"A fair statement, and one simply answered," Zimri responded. "There are three things I wish to convey to you, and I wanted to do it face to face—no envoys, no go-betweens, and no leaks."

"Go on, then, Zimri, but there's a fair wind, and I wish to take advantage of it."

Zimri couldn't help but smile. Any other man would have been in fear of him, but this one knew that Zimri could do nothing to him. If he ordered his death, the mission would fail; if he removed him, he could talk, and besides, he was going to die, anyhow, and knew it.

"Right, then, my dear Ulric. I shall not waste your time.

First of all, under no circumstances must the Prophet be hurt. If he is harmed in any way whatsoever, then the mission has failed, and you and all your brotherhood will be held accountable, both in this world and in the next."

Ulric was silent.

"Do you clearly understand what I have said?"

"Yes, my lord."

"Remember, if the Prophet is hurt, your mission will be a failure and your soul damned to the darkness forever."

"My lord Zimri," Ulric replied in a cold, even voice, "you need not threaten my immortal soul. I have agreed to undertake this mission. If I agreed to do it, then you can be assured that I have also agreed to all the particulars. If I thought it could not be done, then I would not have taken the responsibility that Holy Church asked me to assume. Your threats are unnecessary—twenty years ago, I swore to be the knife of Holy Church, and my life has always been dedicated to the moment of my final mission. I can assure you, I know the price of failure." He almost shouted the last words, knowing that his honor and ability had been questioned.

Zimri watched him closely. If need be, he was ready to kill Ulric and to order the frigates in from over the horizon to destroy the collier if any double-dealing was suspect on the part of Ulric. He watched closely and believed. So rare, he thought sadly, so rare indeed that a man states what he truly believes and cares for, that nebulous thing called honor. Honor, such a strange thing, Zimri though as he reached out to touch Ulric's shoulder in a gesture of reassurance. "I had to be sure, my dear Ulric. I hope you understand. And, of course, I am confident that you will follow the mandate of Holy Church."

"The other points, then, my lord," Ulric responded, shrugging off Zimri's touch.

"Yes, the others."

Zimri turned away from Ulric and looked out the window; he could see the light of dawn approaching through the frosted pane. There was no warmth; never was there any warmth to that baleful light—even there, inside the cabin, his breath froze, the chill cutting into his every bone, stabbing him with fingers of pain. It's so damned cold, always so damned cold, he thought sadly.

"Yes, the others," Zimri said again absently. "I personally charge you to be the one to finish the task. If you reach your objective, you and you alone must deal the fatal blow. If the Prophet is there, he is to be rendered harmless, but he must see their deaths. If he is not there, then someone must live who can carry the message back to him."

"And what is that message?"

"Yes, that is the final point," Zimri said quietly, turning around to face Ulric. "You see, my dear Ulric, I want you to tell Michael Ormson that I alone sent you."

"My lord, you realize what that means for your dealings with Madoc and the rest of the Council? If such a statement is revealed afterward."

Zimri thought it strange the way Ulric phrased the last comment. This man was talking about his own death without a trace of emotion. "Go on."

"Madoc will wash his hands of the affair and turn the Council against you when time comes to select the next Holy See."

"Yes, I realize that."

"Why, then?"

"I don't fear Madoc, nor do I fear you, my dear Ulric. In fact, I don't even fear this Prophet—for I know that I shall beat him. What I need more than anything else is for this self-proclaimed Messiah to act according to my plan, and your action is essential to that plan for the good of Holy Church."

Ulric was silent for a moment. It was not his to question, so he left the words unsaid.

"By the way," Zimri suddenly asked in an offhand manner, "who did you designate as your heir?"

Ulric smiled and looked through Zimri as if he weren't there.

"Ah, Zimri, so you wish to know if your man is the one. I regret to say that Williams was not left behind as you wished; in fact, he is aboard my ship even now. I don't want my order to be your pawn. We serve you now, and in the days to come we shall serve you again, but if there ever comes a day when for the good of Church and the First Choice, it is decided that you must go, then I don't want one of your agents to be the master. No, Williams will die in the first wave of the attack. You'll have to deal with Barneth, who will answer to no one but the ultimate good of Holy Church. By the way, I've already lectured him about you in some detail."

Zimri nodded begrudgingly. "All right, then, it was worth the try at least, wasn't it?"

Ulric smiled. "Of course, my lord, of course. If there is nothing else to be said, I would like to leave."

"Yes, you know the way out."

Ulric bowed. "Your blessings, my lord."

"Yes, of course. May the Saints watch over you and guide you, may the Ice give up your soul, and may you feast at the Long Table of Our Fathers until the Return of the Garden. Amen."

Ulric stood up and started for the door.

"Ulric."

"Yes, your lordship?"

"Anything I can do for you?" Zimri asked hesitantly. "Anyone I can help out, take care of, that sort of thing?"

Ulric looked at him sadly. There was no one, nothing at all, ever since the great plague. He stopped for a moment and looked away, shaking his head. "Only the Church," he said sadly, "only the Church."

The door closed behind him with a gentle creak of the old leather hinges.

Helping hands reached out and pulled Ulric up over the icy railing.

He could see the questions in their eyes, but he would follow his original plan. Orders would not be given until the barrier line had been forced and the target was in sight—a prisoner, deserter, or solitary spy could defeat everything. Inys Gloi was only fifty miles away, he thought with a shudder, far too close for comfort.

"Back her off," Ulric called to the sailing master. "Set a course two points off abeam the wind."

"Yes, master."

The booms creaked overhead as the men strained to bring the sails over against the wind. After several minutes, the blades shuddered and broke free, gently pushing the ship backward, her rudder blades forcing the craft abeam the wind. When the sailing master judged the moment right, the booms were released and clinched down. The backward momentum stopped, and ever so gently the ship started to glide forward. Velocity increased, and the apparent wind started to shift forward until,

56 *William R. Forstchen*

after several minutes, it felt like a gale was running nearly straight down the deck as the ship accelerated to twice wind speed.

Ulric looked astern. Already the schooner was cutting back in the opposite direction. Before her a blood-red sun broke the horizon, bathing the sea in cold, crystalline light.

"Michael, I think it's time."

He pulled away from her, ever so gently. In the faint half light of early dawn, he could see the vague outline of her face, wreathed by her dark flowing hair. "Not quite yet, my love. We still have a little time yet."

"No, Michael, I can hear the guards below. It wouldn't be proper for us to keep them waiting."

He drew her close, his body merging into hers. How could he explain it to her? Ten days earlier—the night after the Council meeting broke up—it had come again. Seth had left early, claiming business to the north, and there had been something vague about that. And the sense of something's being wrong had pressed harder and harder upon him. How could he explain the dream of the previous week—the fire of light in the east, and coming from it a danger, real and palpable, drawing ever closer?

He had tried again the night before, after she had slipped into sleep, exhausted from their passion. He had calmed his breathing, drawing inward, trying vainly for the release that would send his thoughts abroad to seek and to find. But each time he thought he was on the edge of release, an indefinable presence had restrained him, as if forcing him down with a giant, unseen hand.

"Michael?" She brushed her hand lightly down his side, pressing her body against his.

"I thought you said it was time?" His thoughts returned to the warm presence by his side.

"I changed my mind. They can wait for a few more minutes."

The noise from below finally broke the lingering spell as he kissed her one last time and rose from the bed. Together they dressed, he in the simple robes of an ice runner and she in the long, flowing dress of blue that reminded him of the

light blue robes of St. Awstin. She started to tie her hair with
a ribbon that matched the dress, and then, stopping for a moment, she looked away, out the window, which was flooded
with the light of early dawn.

"What is it, love?" he asked gently, his dark thoughts dis-
pelled for the moment by the fire of their lovemaking and the
anticipation of the voyage ahead.

"Oh, nothing," she said absently, and turning to him, she
forced a smile.

"Remember this ribbon?" she said quietly.

"No, should I?"

"I suppose not. Silly of me, but when you returned from
the Battle of St. Judean's Bane, you still wore your robe of
St. Awstin. I burned the thing—it was so filthy. But first I
cut this one ribbon from it as a keepsake." She drew closer to
him. "Keep it with you for the next voyage, my love." She
pressed it into his pocket, then looked up at him and smiled.

Kissing her lightly on the forehead, he put the ribbon in his
pocket.

"Let's go see Andrew."

Together they crossed the hallway to Andrew's room. Elijah
sat by the door and started to stand, but with a quiet wave of
her hand, Janis motioned him to sit. Gently, they opened the
door and went in.

"Should I wake him?" Janis asked softly.

"No, he'll just cry to go. I have a hard enough time refusing
him as it is. I'll only be gone for a few days, anyhow."

The boy's blankets were twisted into a contorted pile, his
tiny body sticking half out of it. Michael rearranged the bed
clothes to cover the boy. Bending over, he kissed his son on
the brow.

He looked at Andrew for a moment, patted him lightly on
the shoulders, and took Janis's hand. They slipped out of the
room.

From the meeting hall below, the sound of the gathering
Companions greeted them. Happy shouts echoed through the
hallway at the sight of the master. Janis could feel him letting
go. The Ice was calling him—beckoning to him with its lure
of wind, sails, and blinding speed.

Daniel came forward, grinning happily. "Ready to sail again,
master. And not a moment too soon, I'd say."

Janis stifled a comment. Daniel's marriage was a constant source of amusement to her and Michael. Daniel towered over Epana, but one sharp word from her and he was rendered speechless, obedient to her every command. A voyage away from Mathin was his only escape into freedom.

"And how is Epana this morning? Isn't she here to see you off?" Michael asked playfully.

Daniel mumbled an excuse and, turning away, walked back to his men, roaring for them to get moving to the ship. None paid him any attention. They understood.

"So again I leave, my love." He drew her into his arms, unmindful of those around him, and kissed her softly.

"You are my life," Michael whispered as he drew away. Turning, he shouted greetings to the men, and they answered in kind, exuberant with the prospects of a sail to Bathan and the islands beyond.

She watched him as the men swept around Michael, shouldering their weapons and gear, then moved out of the citadel into the square beyond.

As his men pressed around him, driving forward to the ships in the harbor beyond, Michael tried to look back to Janis, but already she was gone from his view.

"All hands on deck. All hands on deck, prepare to make sail!"

A broad smile of joy on his face as his cry was picked up by the deck captains below, Michael lowered the speaking trumpet and handed it back to Finson.

"Ah, Michael, it will be a rare fine day for a sail, will it not?"

"Yes, a rare fine day," he said with a laugh as he looked up the towering mastheads of the *De Gaiuth*, light frigate and command ship of the Mathinian confederation.

The second day on the ice and they were starting early that morning. The southeastern horizon was ablaze with fiery light, while overhead the Arch cut a silvery band that rose out of the west, soared overhead, and finally merged with the rising brilliance of dawn.

Shouting to each other the sail crews poured from the hatchways and leaped to the riggings, scurrying aloft with surefooted ease. Michael looked across the frozen sea and watched as the dozen escort ships and heavy battle rams mimicked the action of the flagship. Unable to resist the challenge, Michael gave a curt nod to Finson, strode to the rigging of the foremast, and followed his men up into the crystalline light of early dawn.

Hand over hand, he climbed with steadfast ease, while the more experienced crew members scurried past him, calling out good-natured jests and greetings. He reached the fighting foretop, and several men leaned out to help pull him over. Michael cursed them with a boisterous laugh and pulled himself up onto the armored platform.

"Ah, master, 'tis a good moment to be alive now, is it not?" one of the men shouted to him above the high-pitched whistle of the wind.

Michael slapped him on the shoulder, then grabbed hold of the rigging and pushed onward to the top, leaving the lower foresail crews behind as they prepared to break out canvas.

Higher he climbed—the shouts of the crews dropping below him. The horizon arched back and away, revealing a thousand square miles of ice—the forms of his fleet insignificant specks that dotted the southward ice. He could feel the sweat under his tunic as he climbed, and it was a refreshing joy to be at sea again with the first sail of winter.

Just when he felt the need to stop for a moment to rest, he found himself beneath the foretop watchtower. Letting go of the rope with his left hand, he banged on the trap door, which opened to reveal a young bright-eyed face startled by the master's unexpected visit.

Michael looked down to the deck a hundred and fifty feet below and was conscious of the hundred pairs of eyes that were upon him. He could sense the watchful gaze of Daniel and the nervous comments of the Companions. On a wild impulse, Michael grabbed hold of the watch box and kicked his feet free from the rigging. For several seconds, he dangled as if he had lost his footing, and he could hear the wild shouts of panic. Having played the game out, he pulled himself into the watch box, stuck his head back out, and gave a playful wave to the deck below.

Withdrawing into the box, he slammed the door shut and turned to face the watchman, who sat in obvious nervousness, eying his visitor.

Michael looked him over for several seconds, then extended

his hand in greeting. "What's your name, lad?"

"W-W-Wilnarth of Sallin, master."

"How old are you, Wilnarth?"

"Seventeen, master."

Michael recognized the look of reverence in the boy's expression, and turning away, Michael concealed his smile at the boy's obvious confusion.

"Come on, Wilnarth, let's throw back the hatchway and get a better look outside."

So saying, Michael unclipped the hinges and threw the hatch open. Then he stood up and leaned far over, looking down to the antlike creatures on the deck below.

Out on the ice, the last of the anchor crews were running the lines from the stern hatch, where ice blocks and associated tackle were stored for the day's run. Far out across the sea, the other ships of the fleet were engaged in similar work, while several of the heavy battle rams were already free and running before the early-morning breeze.

As the last block was hauled in, Michael could hear Finson's commands ring out across the deck.

"Hoist the sails. All canvas, all canvas!"

The cry was picked up by each of the mast captains, and the milky white canvas burst from its casings to be run aloft by the straining crews below. From atop the mainmast, the white and dark green ensign of Mathin snapped out, catching the wind to flutter in the dawning light.

"Heave away there, smartly now, smartly!"

Chanteys of the ice were counterpointed by the creak of the tackles as the crew raced to complete its work. A mild shudder ran through the ship. Michael felt the ship's blades break free of the ice as the wind, which was running four points abaft the starboard beam, bellied the sails out, pushing the *De Gaiuth* forward.

"Sheet them in there! Pull, me hearties. Pull lively now!"

The sails tightened down, the booms straining under the pressure as the men maneuvered the sails into the best position for a fast run.

The acceleration was soon noticeable, and Michael could feel the apparent wind shifting forward as the *De Gaiuth* quickly jumped to four times wind speed.

The mast pitched over, swinging the watch box far out over

the ice, and Michael shouted with joy even as he pulled down his goggles and slipped his face mask into place. Astern the deck canted sharply as the men swarmed off the rigging, and twin trails of ice and snow shot heavenward, torn off the sea by the hundred-mile-per-hour passage of the light frigate.

As a fresh gust cut across the open sea, the *De Gauith* heeled over, while directly ahead the sun broke the horizon with its fiery golden light, illuminating the sails and casting exaggerated shadows far astern.

The rest of the fleet moved with her, thundering into the dawn—the escort ships swung out to guard the flanks and range far ahead, ever watchful for surprise. Far to port, Michael could make out the faint outline of a half-dozen merchantmen, and he read the signal rockets that identified them as Bathian trade ships bound for the Mathinian pass. The sun cleared the horizon as the *De Gaiuth* settled down into the morning passage, running straight and clear to Bathan. If the wind held true, they should reach their destination in three turns of the hourglass. Michael looked again at the boy who was standing beside him.

"'Tis a good day for a run, is it not?" Michael asked playfully.

"Y-yes, master."

Michael looked at him and smiled, remembering. Funny, he thought, the boy brings back such sharp images out of the past. He thought again of the Night of Supplication so many years earlier. Odd how we can forget the rituals—the dates only half remembered. He pushed the thought from his mind.

Reaching into his tunic, Michael pulled out a flask. "Join me in some Yawinder, boy. It will take the morning chill off."

Uncorking the flask, Michael offered it to him. He recognized the wide-eyed look—the lad was taking part in sacred communion. Michael knew how it would be spoken of that night. How the master had stood watch with the youngest aboard, sharing his wine, speaking of his dreams with the least of his followers. He knew that another anecdote would be born. How often in the past had he done the same, maneuvering them, inculcating them with his plans. Most all of them calculated, plans to help further his cause. But looking at the boy and the reverence in his eyes washed that away for the moment. For the moment, the desire to share was enough.

The hours passed. Around the flagship, the escort vessels

continued their endless weave, running ahead to probe for bad ice and swinging far out to the flanks in search of ships that could pose a threat to the Prophet. It was an intriguing display of motion and speed, revealing to a practiced eye a mastery of the Ice, unrivaled upon the Frozen Sea.

Michael watched and quietly judged as his young captains maneuvered their ships, striving to gain every ounce of advantage from the wind. It was practice now, the peaceful run across the Southward Ice, but down deep he knew that a time would come when the sailing of the Ice would again become a matter of deadly earnest.

The lad slowly loosened up to the near proximity of his leader and shared Michael's thoughts with rapt attention. The boy told Michael how his father had died as a section commander at the Battle of the Mathinian Pass, and now, as the family's oldest son, he had gone to sea to serve the Prophet. Michael easily adopted the familiar pattern of speech, so that the boy felt he was privy to the innermost thoughts and dreams— as if the master had taken him into strictest confidence. So the morning passed, until on the far horizon signal flares arched and then exploded in a red and green pattern.

Michael looked to the boy.

"It's the *Varnarg*, master, an armed sloop, signaling." The boy picked up the code book and quickly thumbed through the pages.

"Harbor in sight. We should be seeing it in several minutes."

The ice soared by beneath them, and suddenly, on the southeastern horizon, Michael saw a smudge of brown.

The wind increased, pushing the ship up again on its downwind runners, driving them with increasing speed to their destination.

"Bathan harbor, master," the boy said, pointing portside. "There, on the northward approach to the island."

"Aye, I see it," Michael shouted above the roar of the wind.

The escort craft started to come in from the far horizons to join their master's ship on its approach. Some of the vessels were already shortening sail—their crews shouting out the chanties. Michael felt a mild shudder run through the ship as Finson ordered the mainsails loosened.

The harbor was soon in view to all—its double walls glistening brightly in the morning sun. From the central icetower a triple flare rose and was quickly answered with the recognition pattern launched by the lead sloop of the Mathinian fleet. From Bathan's main gate, a number of small craft embarked with brightly colored sails as if they were sailing to a joyous festival. From all directions of the compass, Michael could see dozens of other ships coming into view—merchantmen, colliers, armed sloops, and even a light frigate riding convoy with a dozen smaller craft. All heading for the harbor of Bathan, capital of the freebooters' guild.

"Ever been to Bathan, boy?" Michael shouted above the wind.

The boy nodded his head in confusion. Bathan was known throughout the Frozen Sea as a harbor unsurpassed for its worldliness, houses of sin, and carefree abandon, as if the world would end tomorrow.

Reaching into his tunic, he pulled out the half-empty flask of Yarwinder, tossed it to the boy with a shout of laughter; then, kicking open the hatchway, he swung himself out onto the rigging below.

As their speed slacked off, the apparent wind shifted away from the bow and gradually came back abeam the ship, and Finson ordered the sails drawn in. Crew members swarmed up the rigging past Michael to pull in the sails and secure them to the booms. Michael stopped in his descent at the upper fighting foretop and watched as the men scampered out onto the booms with the skill of acrobats, shouting crude jests to their comrades about the pleasures they would find that evening in the flesh houses of Bathan.

The more daring, disdaining the slow descent of the ratlines, leaped from the booms to the backstays and slid down to deck. Michael watched in silent admiration, and the instinctual feeling coursed through him that with sailors like those, who could ever defeat him? Swinging out onto the ratlines, he followed his men to the deck.

The ship had slowed to less than ten leagues an hour by the time Michael reached the deck. The ship echoed with chanties from the straining crews counterpointed by the deep, resonant paeans of the Companions as they formed up amidship to pass Michael's and Daniel's review.

Daniel stood before Michael and with a hearty shout drained off the last of his flask, which he tossed overboard with a flamboyant gesture. "Ah, Michael, 'twas an excellent run and will be a rare fine night tonight, will it not?"

Michael looked at him with a smile. "And what of Epana, my friend?"

Daniel's smile died, replaced by a pensive gaze.

Finson broke into a deep, mirthful chuckle. "Aye, master, and what of Epana? What say you, Daniel?"

Daniel shot both of them an evil gaze of threat. "Speak not of her today; 'twill spoil the wind. You know a woman's name is bad luck, it is." Without waiting for their reply, Daniel turned from the forecastle and stormed off amidship, shouting curses at his men to form up.

"Aye, master," Cowan said with a knowing wink, "ask him about the lump on 'is head where she busted a bottle over him when he came home drunk."

Michael shook his head in amusement and followed Daniel. He spared a quick glance across the ice to observe his fleet, which was swinging into close-order approach. From several miles out, the pilot ship was bearing down under full sail and would be alongside shortly.

Daniel's commands thundered across the deck. "Stand to for the master."

Michael walked down the deck and looked over the ranks of the one hundred—all were clad in the distinctive white sealskin fur of his elite guard. He knew them all by name. Most were survivors of the Mathinian Pass and the subsequent campaign to consolidate their hold on the Southward Ice.

He stopped for a moment. "Ah, Ragnar, how's the frostbite?"

"'Tis fine now, Michael. 'Tis fine, thank you."

Michael patted him on the shoulder and moved on.

He looked each of them in the eye and had a brief word for most. There was Halnar of Zoarn, one-handed Trumarth, and the young twins Lisnor and Falcrin, each commanders of ten at eighteen. The lowest Companion held the same rank as a commander of ten of regular troops and could command a ram or light sloop in battle. If war came, they would form the officers of his fleet and the army, which would rally to his banner.

As he finished his inspection, the shout came from the foredeck: "Pilot ship coming alongside."

The portside outriggers of the pilot ship brushed up against the *Du Gauith*'s starboard side. From aboard the pilot ship came a jeering taunt. "If there's a real ice runner aboard that wreck, come on over for a yard of ale."

The challenge had been offered, and in front of his followers, it could not be denied, not even by Michael. "Come on, Daniel, let's go over."

Leaping over the rail, Michael slid down the ice-encrusted outrigger beam. The ship was still moving forward at a moderate speed, and the wind plucked at his clothing, as if trying to grab hold to toss him over the side. Reaching the edge of the outrigger, he prepared to leap across to the Bathian pilot-ship. Suddenly, the craft pulled sharply away. For a moment, he wavered uncertainly on the edge of tumbling off the craft. Looking up, Michael saw Eldric standing by the wheel, laughing uproariously at his discomfort. Eldric started to edge the craft back. Before it was alongside, Michael leaped out across the frozen sea and landed awkwardly on the other ship. Behind him, Daniel was mumbling a curse. Michael looked up to Eldric and made an obscene gesture, and Eldric's and Michael's men laughed at the sight of it.

Climbing up the pilot ship's outrigger, Michael at last reached the safety of the deck. "Eldric, you son of a misbegotten scum, so the ice has yet to claim your stinking carcass."

Eldric strode forward, his broad shoulders showing through the heavy black bearskins that wrapped his body from head to foot. He stood before Michael, his shaven skull exposed and naked except for the ceremonial scalp lock that was popular of late with Bathian pirates. With a dramatic gesture, he spit over the railing and shouted a string of oaths at his crew, ordering them to lead the fleet in at best possible speed. "So, Ormson, you've come to see them off, you have."

Michael nodded slowly and, without answering, fixed Eldric with a gaze. In a playful mood, Eldric took the challenge, and silently they stood looking at each other. It did not last long; the smirk faded and Eldric quickly broke away, Michael noticing the subtle sign against the evil eye that was flashed at him. The tone was slightly different now.

"Ormson, why I allow myself to follow you is beyond me. Sometimes I think you to be the messenger of Hell itself, come to take us all to damnation. Now, what say ye to that?"

"Are the ships ready to sail, Eldric?"

"They are, Michael; my finest shipwrights worked on them. Everything is as you paid for."

"Next week, then, as planned."

"If the wind is right."

"Good, let's go to your damned feast, then."

"Aye, Michael, as you wish. My people are here to greet you."

"You mean that your whores and pickpockets are ready to rob my crew."

Eldric slapped him across the back and let out a thundering roar of laughter. Together they stood by the prow of the pilot ship and led the Mathinian fleet into the fortified sanctuary of Bathan.

A riotous scene greeted them as they disembarked at the harbor gate. From all sides, Michael found himself in a wild kaleidoscope of dreamlike impressions. He could sense the mad anxiety of Daniel as the Companions tried to force a way through the crowd. Eldric's bodyguards were a wildly dressed lot of freebooters whose clothing seemed to be castoffs from every port on the Frozen Sea. Since the coming of the Prophet, Mathin had lost much of its pirate character, and Michael had half forgotten just how raucous a free port could be. From the decks of the privateers came boisterous shouts as men waved scimitars and battle-axes. Several cannons fired salutes that boomed and echoed across the harbor. It was obvious to all that the high spirits were fueled by the wine and ale that had been flowing since dawn.

They made their way up a narrow alleyway that was choked with the refuse and filth of winter. Overhead the small iced-over windows were open and crowded with young and old, who leaned out to catch a glimpse of the Prophet.

From several windows came invitations to satisfy the needs of the "monk," and Michael laughed at the curses that Daniel hurled at the brazen whores. At last they reached Eldric's well-built citadel. With a sigh of relief, Michael entered the gateway and allowed himself to be ushered in.

"So, Eldric, it seems you prosper."

Eldric threw his cape over a chair and faced Michael with

a cold smile. He beckoned to the doorway, and the guards ushered the last of the wellwishers from the room.

Eldric was quiet for a moment, fingering his beard and looking at Michael as if he were trying to convey some hidden thought.

He looked at the Prophet closely—the public show of mad bravado, suitable to the ice, was gone. The public Eldric was a well-rehearsed act for those who needed the wildness of a half-crazed pirate leader. In private, his actions could be as refined as any church master of Cornath.

"Take a seat, Michael." Eldric beckoned to several chairs that were set before an open fire where a heavy log of imported cedar crackled.

For several minutes, they talked lightly of the sailing conditions and Eldric's "business," until a knock on the door interrupted them.

"Ah, that be him now," Eldric said proudly. "I knew you would want to meet him as soon as possible."

The door opened, but the young man who stepped in was not quite what Michael had expected. He had an aura of refinement about him that spoke of a breeding unexpected in one of Eldric's offspring. He appeared to be nearly Michael's age— tall and slender, with a subdued strength and character revealed by his agile walk and bright twinkling eyes of steely gray.

"Ah, so this must be Jason," Michael said as he looked from the young man at the door to Eldric.

"Yes, I'm Eldric's son," Jason said evenly. "Though my father has often questioned how he could sire one such as me."

There was a pause, and Michael sat quietly, expecting an explosion from the volatile pirate. The eyes of the two locked for a moment, and to Michael's surprise, he could sense a deep bond between the two. Michael knew the boy's mother had died giving birth to him and that Eldric had never recovered from the loss. Standing, Eldric walked toward Jason and gave him a bone-crushing embrace, and they started to laugh.

"What he means is that he is somehow embarrassed that such a pirate as I could be his father. All my other bastards hate him, you know. But none would dare cross swords with him; that I assure you."

Jason walked toward Michael, and with a polite nod he pulled up a chair alongside. From under his arm, he produced a bundle of charts and diagrams and unrolled them before Michael.

"So, these are the plans for the voyage, then."

"That they are, master. I wanted to share them with you first, before you went back to the harbor to examine the fleet."

Michael eagerly unrolled them. The Northern Ice was revealed in some detail—however, on the chart of the Flowing Sea only the Trade Isles appeared, and nothing beyond that. Of the rest of the world there were but fanciful drawings, obviously the wild dreams of ancient cartographers.

"Is there nothing at all to guide you, then?" Michael asked.

"Nothing," Jason responded. "We searched everywhere for some clue of what was beyond. Rumor has it that both Cornath and Ezra have charts of the Before Time, revealing the lay of the world. But to search there would be useless."

Michael looked at Jason. A man younger even than himself would lead half a dozen ships and nearly six hundred men in the first attempt to sail around the world since the Before Time. His craft were unique in the history of the Ice. They were sailing vessels of the Flowing Sea, but each of them carried outriggers and blades that would be attached to the ship when ice was encountered. Elaborate block and tackle systems would help to pull each ship up onto the ice.

The plan was to sail the Ice southward to the Flowing Sea. Once on the sea, they would remove the ice sailing equipment, then sail south across the Flowing Sea. Rumor had it that another ice shelf existed a thousand leagues southward. There the ships would drag themselves back up onto the shelf and then sail southward and west, hoping to circle the Dead Lands, and then onward to circle the World, if such a thing was possible. Michael suddenly felt a deep longing to leave the political nightmare of the ice, and he looked at Jason jealously.

"Are you nervous at the prospect of such a voyage?"

Jason shook his head. "No, Michael. Just think what we might find! And think as well of the fact that on this voyage we might even uncover the answer to what happened Before, and in so doing, find the answer to the Loss of the Garden!"

"Now see how you have infected even my family?!" Eldric roared. "If I was to lead this, booty would be my first thought. Instead, you load the ship down with chart makers, star readers, and even *scribes* to record all that is seen. I tell you, Ormson, you are taking away the freebooter in my own family!"

Michael laughed and clapped Jason on the shoulder. "Come, let us go to the harbor and look at the ships. For that is what I journeyed to see."

Jason stood and, sweeping up his charts, started to the door with Michael behind him.

To accompany such a voyage, Michael thought. To leave the madness of this struggle behind, if only for a little while. But there is Janis and Andrew and the struggle to come. No, I am a prisoner here, after all—a prisoner of the dreams I am creating. Someday, maybe someday, I will be able to do it!

CHAPTER 5

"ULRIC, WILLIAMS NEEDS YOU ON DECK."

The urgency of the messenger's tone was unsettling. Pushing aside the charts, Ulric went topside; the cold wind cut through his clothing like a knife.

Most of the deck crew was looking astern, and following their gaze, he could see a ship running on the horizon.

"Williams, what is it?"

"Master, a heavy corsair. It's closing rapidly."

"We're on a major shipping lane. He could be bound for the Mathinian Pass."

"It's not likely, Ulric," Williams replied grimly. "She ran across our tracks, bearing northwesterly, then came about and has started to work her way to windward of us. Looks like she's trying to gain attack position."

"Privateer?"

"I think so."

Ulric quickly surveyed the deck of his ship. He was outgunned. A shame. It had been a long time since he had had a good fight at sea. "How long do you estimate before she's alongside?"

70

"Ten minutes, fifteen at best, if we put on more canvas and fall off the wind into a broad reach."

"How far to the Mathinian Pass?"

"Still two hundred miles—five hours at least, if the wind doesn't shift."

Damn, and so close, he thought. It would have to be now, damn it. The passage had been without incident; they had spotted few ships, and those that they sighted gave them a wide berth. One more day and they would have made the relative safety of the Southern Shelf. Damn it all! There was no time to debate action; turning, he faced his waiting crew.

"We'll run for it. Surrender would be too suspicious. Clear the deck; all noncrew below to the concealed storage holds."

The ten battle teams that had been taking battle drill on deck grabbed up their weapons and streamed below. Beneath his feet, Ulric could hear the shouted commands as the assassins secured the ship below and crawled into their hidden chambers to wait out the crisis.

The ship heeled beneath his feet and accelerated as the pilot turned it to run due south. Overhead, the sail crews scurried about to press on every available inch of canvas. The wind shrieked through the riggings, and the deck hummed and vibrated to the rattle of the blades. The fair wind and the smooth ice gave Ulric a surge of joy as he walked down the canted deck, calling out commands and preparing for battle. For a brief moment, he wished that he had never left the sea, but the duty to Church was far too strong, and he pushed the primitive sense of elation aside.

Eadwulf and his section, masquerading as ice runners, swept across the deck and ran below to make sure that every detail was correct. Nothing was to hint that this was something more than a dilapidated collier running from North Prydain to the Southward Shelf.

Standing by the stern rail, Ulric watched quietly as the privateer drew closer, her speed nearly twice that of the old sailing hulk. Williams's estimate was correct, and within a quarter hour, the three-masted corsair was running a half mile upwind and a quarter mile astern. A puff of smoke exploded from the bow of the pursuing ship. It was a well-laid shot and smashed into the ice not fifty yards off their bow in a shower of ice. A second shot whistled overhead, neatly holing the collier's foretop sail.

"We better strike," Ulric shouted to Williams. "Next shot will be for the deck."

Williams brought the helm over, pointing into the wind, while from overhead the flag of North Prydain, the white bear of the north, fluttered down in token of surrender. The corsair matched their maneuver, closing in and positioning herself astern of the collier, ready to deliver a broadside at the first sign of resistance. Ulric felt a grim admiration for his rival captain—the maneuver was well planned. By crossing their T astern, the privateer could deliver a full broadside in response to the collier's single six-pounder if it should foolishly decide to resist. The two ships drifted to a stop—the collier into the wind, the privateer several points off. Her crew was jumping overboard to secure temporary anchor lines. From the stern hatchway, a party of twenty men disembarked.

Williams came astern and joined Ulric to watch the unfolding drama.

"Looks like a standard boarding party. Most likely one-fifth of the crew; the rest will stand by the guns and the hatchway, ready to act if we should resist."

"What do you think?" Ulric asked, curious for Williams's opinion.

"If we're lucky, they'll take what's valuable and leave us off."

"If we're not?"

"They could put a prize crew aboard, or if they're in a hurry, they might just try to slaughter us out of hand and be done with it."

"But what of the injunctions of the Prophet against such action?"

Williams spit over the rail and laughed. "His injunctions do not mean that it becomes law with such as this."

Ulric looked at him and smiled.

Eadwulf came up from below and approached Ulric. "All secure. The attack party is waiting by the concealed hatchway, Dalmath in command."

Ulric nodded, barely acknowledging Eadwulf's presence.

"Here they come," Williams said quietly.

Grappling hooks snaked up from the boarding party and

hooked on to the stern railing. The privateers swarmed up off
the ice—the first one gaining the deck swept out a heavy, two-
handed battle-ax and eyed them menacingly. Ulric could feel
the calm drift through him as he prepared inwardly.

With hands extended in the gesture of peace, he approached
the warrior and called out in the Prydain dialect, "So now,
what might ye want of me and my men?"

Other warriors swarmed up over the side and a heavy, broad-
shouldered man dressed in ragged furs stepped forward, cutlass
in hand, his face concealed by mask and goggles. "Prydain,
aye."

Ulric nodded.

"Pull aside your mask, there."

Ulric complied, noticing from the corner of his eye the line
of crossbows trained on him and the dozen odd men that were
his "crew."

"Who be ye?" the privateer demanded in a threatening voice.

"Halnar of North Prydain, twelve days out of Mathin. A
full load of black rock."

"North Prydain, ah, Cornathian scum, then." The privateer
eyed him carefully. "Come on you pox-eaten son of a slut,
let's take a look below."

"Not much below, master," Ulric said, bringing a fearful
quaver into his voice. "A full hull of black rock, no more. I've
got two hundred lomens in silver for the shipowners' trade,
and that be it."

"Go on, damn ye, lead the way."

Three men came up behind their leader, and one of them
mumbled darkly, "One move out of any of ye and you're dead
men."

"I know that," Ulric said softly as he led the way below.

The men alighted in the darkened hull, the stench of the
black rock causing some of them to cough. The men poked
around at the mountain of rock for several minutes and, satisfied, pushed Ulric into the cabin.

"Where are the lomens?"

Ulric opened up the simple chest next to his cot, pulled out
the bag, and tossed it to them.

"Is that it?"

"Yes, master."

"You lying Cornathian pig. Smuggling most likely, goods

hidden beneath the rock. But we can search you out later."

"What do you mean?" Ulric cried, wringing his hands and forcing tears to come to his eyes. "By all the Saints, I assure you there's no other treasure aboard this miserable craft."

The boarding captain laughed viciously.

"We've got a little unplanned trip for you, you gut worm, that's all."

"But what of Mathin?" Ulric whined. "I'm just a miserable rock seller, nothing more. I'm taking this rock to the Prophet's town, and what would he say of this?"

"Why, nothing," the captain responded sharply. "You see, he'll never know."

"Go on, Yarin, get it over with," one of the men said quietly.

The captain stepped aside, and Ulric saw one of the guards bring a crossbow to his shoulder.

As the captain stepped aside, Ulric followed his motion and dived forward into the captain's arms. His open hand smashed into the captain's goggles, shattering the frame and driving the splinters into the privateer's eyes. The bolt from the guard slammed past Ulric, burying itself in the opposite wall. Ulric drove his knee into the captain's groin, and he could feel the pelvic bone shattering from the impact.

A hooded form pushed through the doorway. His dagger flashed across the throat of the rearmost guard. A shower of blood spurted outward, splashing against the low ceiling and filling the room with a sticky, metallic smell. No one had cried out yet, the shock of the attack was so sudden.

"No kill," Ulric barked in a low, steady voice.

The other two guards tried to draw their swords in the narrow confines of the room.

Ulric feigned to the left, the guard following his move, then slashed out with his foot, kicking the guard's sword hand, smashing it with a single blow. With a clear, high kick, he caught the man in the solar plexus, doubling him over, while Dalmath hooked his knife up under the other man's chin, pinning him to the wall.

"A sound and you're both dead," Ulric whispered.

The men were silent, rigid with fear.

He couldn't give them time to think. Ulric tore the mask off of his prisoner, forced the man's mouth open, and crammed the leather down the man's throat until he started to choke. Dalmath copied his motions.

"Take care of him, Dalmath," Ulric whispered.

Ulric locked his man in a pin, holding his neck at the pressure point, preventing any motion. Dalmath, with a quick, even pull, doubled his prisoner over—a sudden snap echoed through the room as the privateer's back broke. The man crumpled up with a grunt. With lightning speed, Dalmath pulled out a dagger and sliced his victim's trousers open.

Ulric forced his man over so that his face was nearly pressed up against his comrade's body.

"Do it," Ulric whispered to Dalmath, and then to his victim he said softly, "If you don't do exactly what I tell you, you can expect far worse from me."

With terrifying swiftness, Dalmath sliced upward with his dagger—his victim screamed, the sound muffled into incoherent choking. Dalmath castrated his victim.

"Finish it."

Dalmath worked the dagger up, sliding it underneath the privateer's ribs. A torrent of blood gushed out; the man jerked spasmodically and was still.

Ulric whispered softly, "I'll remove your gag. If you make a sound, you can expect the same, but for you, we'll keep you alive so you'll remember what it's like to be half a man."

Ulric didn't put the dagger up to his victim for fear he would try and kill himself.

He pulled the gag out.

The man looked at him, wild-eyed.

"Listen closely. If you don't, you'll feel my blade. Do you understand?"

The man nodded.

"How many men aboard your ship?"

"Only thirty over there."

"Why so few?"

"We took two prizes yesterday."

"What's the signal that you've secured the prize?"

"There's a flag on the captain. Raise it up, lower ten feet, then raise up again."

Dalmath pulled open the captain's tunic.

"It's here."

"Good."

"Is there any password to the men above?"

"No."

Dalmath pushed his dagger into the prisoner's face, the blood still dripping from the end of the blade.

"Are you sure?"

The man looked at him, wide-eyed with terror.

"No, I swear it, no!" Ulric could sense the hysteria rising. With a quick backhanded blow, he knocked the man unconscious. "Prepare the men. Wait until we get them below, then hit them hard. Get the strike team ready."

Ulric ripped the tunic off the captain and threw it over himself. Pulling the crossbow from one of the guards, he cocked it and set an arrow in place.

"Flag."

Dalmath tossed it to him.

"Right, get ready now."

Dalmath raced down the deck, knocked on one of the bulkheads, and soon disappeared within. Ulric waited to give his men as much time as possible, but he knew he couldn't wait too long; otherwise, the men topside would get suspicious.

Ulric grabbed a flask of Yawinder and left the cabin, closing the door after gagging and binding the prisoner.

Taking a deep breath, he sprinted up the ladder to topside, the bright light above temporarily blinding him. With a thundering shout, he held a bottle of Yawinder aloft.

"'Tis no collier!" he boomed, loud enough for his voice to carry across the ice to the waiting ship beyond. "She's a smuggler, she is. Must be ten thousand flasks of Yawinder, and there's silver—ten thousand lomen at least! By the Saint's, men, we're rich!"

A cheer went up from the crossbowmen as Ulric, hunched low, face averted, ran across the deck. From the corner of his eye, he could see several of them start to the hatchway, then hesitate, looking toward him. He knew their blood would be up with so much loot, he had to keep them moving, not allowing the privateers to look too closely.

"Go below there. Go below and take what you want. It's all ours, it is."

With a mad shout, the men swarmed to the hatchways. A

lean figure held back and walked over to him questioningly. Ulric noted the hesitation.

"Vaynar?" the man said cautiously.

Ulric rushed up to him, and tossing aside the crossbow, he swept the man into his arms, as if drunk with joy. A narrow dagger slipped into the base of the man's skull. A look of shocked recognition flickered across the man's face. Ulric watched death sweep over his victim and take him into the Darkness. All the time that Ulric held him, he continued to shout like a drunkard, while the last of the crew stormed below. Then muffled shouts began to echo up from below.

"Williams."

"Yes, master."

"Don't move until I give the word."

"Of course, master."

Ulric carried the body over to the hatchway and, shielding the view with his own body, dumped his victim to the lower deck where the sound of conflict originated.

Running over to the masthead, he ran the flag aloft, lowered it, and then ran it back up. He then mounted the sternway and shouted over to the ship.

"Come aboard! There's Yawinder—cases of it!"

A shout went up from the privateer, and Ulric counted carefully. Nearly twenty were soon swarming on the ice; a couple of gun crews and the sailing master would stay behind.

Ulric turned his back to them, training his crossbow on his own men now, as if guarding them.

The first of the privateers came over the railing.

"'Tis below, it is. Start offloading; we'll take some of the loot aboard for ourselves."

The men, eager not to be left out of the looting, swarmed below—where a knife or garrote awaited them.

Ulric could hear the stern hatchway open up. He took a quick look over the railing.

Dalmath and a dozen men clad in the furs of privateers set out from the ship and ran across the ice to the waiting privateer. Ulric smiled.

For several minutes, no sound came from the other ship; then, with a startling roar, one of the guns fired.

The shot slammed into the main deck, the ball plowing down

the length of the ship and slamming into the mainmast amid
a howling tornado of splinters. All around him was confusion,
men kicking on the deck, screaming in anguish. He looked to
Williams, but the man was on the ground, his face a bloody
pulp, with a splinter the size of a man's arm driven clear through
his skull. Ulric waited for the next shot, but none came, and
even as the smoke cleared, he could make out Dalmath on deck
cutting down the privateer's flag. The tension coiled out of
him, he looked around the deck—four men down. It could
have been worse.

Eadwulf came up from below. "All taken care of, Ulric."
His grin was bloodthirsty.

"Our losses?"

"Three dead, two wounded."

Ulric looked at the deck again; Williams and three other
brothers were dead or dying. Even as he watched, one of his
monks bent over a struggling form and with a ceremonial flourish slashed the throat of his screaming comrade.

"Let's clean it up," Ulric shouted. "They might have friends
around." Throwing the crossbow down, Ulric raced below. He
pulled the door of his cabin open and recoiled in horror. The
captive hung before him, his body hanging on the wall, the
head dangling obscenely to the side. The man had broken, but
for many the fear of death is not as terrifying as the fear of
torment and pain. The pirate had smashed his head through the
cabin's single window and slashed his throat with the jagged
glass, cutting clear to the bone. His blood was still pouring
down the wall and in the morning chill gave off a curling cloud
of steam.

Horrified, Ulric stared at the anguished, accusing eyes of
the prisoner, and before he could gain control of himself, the
reflex swept through him. Turning aside, he vomited with a
sobbing, convulsive groan.

Ulric looked across the deck of his ship. The brothers were
still struggling to repair the damage from the morning's action.
Gazing aloft to the wind pennant, he relaxed for a moment.
The wind hadn't shifted. By now the evidence of the pirate's
ship would be lost in the hot waters and volcanic steam of St.
Judean's Bane. Shaking his head, he walked the length of the
deck, the image of the ghostly vessel still haunting his thoughts.

To burn the privateer would have drawn the curious from twenty leagues around, but to abandon the ship would have been even worse. Within minutes after the action, Ulric had the dead removed from his own ship and place aboard the privateer. Ulric and a crew of ten brothers then rigged the ship for sail and started off to the southwest. As it gained momentum, his men boarded the life raft that they were towing astern. However, just before Ulric climbed over the edge, his attention was seized by one of the dead.

The prisoner who had killed himself was stacked with the others by the mainmast. Ulric ran to the pile of bodies and dragged the stiffening corpse free.

Williams and the three other dead brothers rested by the bow. Picking up a length of rope, Ulric lashed the pirate's body to the wheel. Ulric tried not to look into the eyes that gazed out in blind condemnation. The body secured, he raised his hands upward, gave the blessing, then swung himself over the side. The brothers cut the raft loose and returned to their collier. Onward the privateer sailed, until it was a mere speck that finally disappeared toward the dark smudge of clouds that marked the falling of a Saint. He pushed the memory away as he had done with a hundred other actions before, but he knew that it would be waiting for him.

"Ulric, the men are ready," Dalmath said softly.

Ulric turned to face his men. They stood before him, drawn up in ordered ranks—the units of five together, rank after rank. He felt a surge of pride. These were the best, the Chosen Ones, the elite striking force of Holy Church—all sworn to die at his command. "Eadwulf, brief them."

Eadwulf stepped forward, his compact frame lost in the heavy robes of an ice runner.

"Brothers, the hour of our mission has arrived at last. Ten leagues over the horizon is the Mathinian Pass. I shall not yet reveal our destination, but the fact that it has been kept secret should be indication enough of its importance."

There were nods from many of the men.

"We shall attempt to gain the pass before the sun sets. It would be better to approach it tomorrow morning, but our encounter with the corsair has increased the possibility of detection. As to the pass, there are two guard stations, one at the northward entrance, the other at the southward end. We will not seek action. However, if we are discovered, we shall run it by force. You all know your stations and have been drilled on the proper procedure if action must be taken."

The men stood in silence.

Ulric stepped past Eadwulf and raised his arms heavenward. "Kneel!"

In perfect unison, the Brothers of the Knife fell to their knees.

"By the Power of all the Holy Saints, by the Power of the One True and Holy Faith and with the promise of the Return of the Garden, I bless each and every one of thee. By the Pledge of your Faith and of your Mission, I absolve all of thee. For you are the Chosen, and you shall be brought before the Table, Pure and Holy, where, until the Return of the Father, we shall together feast until the ice shall give up its dead."

"Amen."

The more experienced brothers looked to each other and nodded at the significance of Ulric's benediction. He had not said, "You shall together feast." He had included himself in the prayer; Ulric had publicly pledged that in this mission he would die with them if need be.

The men rose and with the plain chant "To the Blessings of the Saints," they filed below to their positions in the secret bulkheads.

"I see it, Ulric. There, two points off the starboard bow."

Ulric looked forward, directly into the setting sun.

The channel was well marked by the deep cuts of a hundred passages, and following the pointed direction of the pilot, Ulric could see a low-lying tower of ice silhouetted by the late-afternoon sun, its icy slopes reflecting the orange-red light of the evening sky.

"Dalmath, all secure?"

"Yes, master."

"Prepare to take in canvas."

"Secure all sail fore and mizzen; jib and main hold fast till ordered!" Overhead the sails snapped and boomed as the sheets were uncleated and the booms were loosened.

As they drew closer, the collier passed a low tower of ice

and wood that stood to one side of the channel—a curious
structure that appeared to incorporate the prow of a wrecked
ship. Ulric turned to Eadwulf, who had taken Williams's position, and asked for an explanation.

"The monument to their Prophet's dead," Eadwulf said softly.
"Raised in commemoration of the battle fought here. Surrounding the structure rest the honored dead, entombed in ice and
still visible for all to see."

Ulric looked at it intently. Someday the Church would destroy this, dig up the dead, and burn their remains. Any presence of the Prophet would be eradicated—no such shrines
would remain after Ormson was gone.

A flare shot up from the watchtower half a league away.

"Signal to heave to."

"Bring her about, Eadwulf."

"Bring her into the wind." The ship heeled over as Eadwulf
turned the ship at Ulric's command. The wind shifted forward
until it was running straight down the deck, the sails cracking
overhead, while from the base of the watchtower, a small pilot's
raft emerged, hiking up against the westerly breeze.

"Now we shall learn if we are expected," Eadwulf whispered.

Ulric looked to the raft and was silent.

"Damn it all, I thought we'd be done for the day."

"Curse your whining, Olafson. It can't be helped."

Slagle stood upon the open raft and eyed the collier as she
drew closer. "Recognize her?"

"Nay, can't recall her. She ain't been on the Mathinian run.
Looks like Prydain lines to me—an old one, though."

Slagle grabbed the railing and doubled over with convulsive
coughing. He was far too old for sailing on the open Ice. Pulling
aside his mask, he coughed and gulped for air, the chill searing
his tortured lungs. The spasm passed, leaving him cold and
sweaty. Slagle barely noticed the flecks of blood that stained
his gloves.

The other two looked at their old friend with eyes that
mingled pity and fear. He was dying from the lung fire, and
they avoided him whenever possible, not wishing to share his
fate.

"Stand lively there," Slagle said, gasping for breath. "This shan't take long. Then back to the fortress and a good sack of wine for our troubles."

"Looks like she had some fun," Olafson said, his lisp slurring the words together. "There, the stern railing's been shot away."

"Must have been old Ragnar," young Pennarson said with a laugh. "He's been prowling hereabouts. But how in the Arch's name did this old wreck shake them off?"

"Bring her up across the bow, and we'll soon know," Slagle commanded, his curiosity aroused.

The two crewmen maneuvered the raft with expert hands, pulling in sail while weaving across the wind to kill off speed until the raft came to a halt—its portside blade nearly touching the outrigger of the collier. From over the ship's side, a rope ladder snaked down.

Even as he reached the ladder, Slagle turned to see the ship's stern hatch open. Half a dozen men swarmed out, dragging a pilot ship, which they quickly prepared for sail.

"Damn fools, don't tell me you plan to sail the channel tonight?"

"We've got our orders," one of the ice runners responded, spitting with the wind. "Our master's scared to death—swears he'll not spend another night on the north shelf."

Damn fools, Slagle thought as he started up the ladder. Fighting for breath, he pulled his heavy bulk upward, and helping hands reached out to pull him over the rail.

Alighting on the deck, Slagle scanned it quickly. Several of the men were wrapped in blood-caked bandages. The deck of the ship was a shambles; blood stains marked the spots where the casualties had fallen. "So, you had a little action, I see!"

A muscular, compact form walked forward, extending a gloved hand, his face mask pulled aside. "Narn be my name, twelve days out of Cornath, twenty-three out of North Prydain."

"Your cargo?"

"Black rock, of course, and the usual," Narn said with a soft chuckle. "Would you care to step below?"

Slagle nodded and followed the ship's master across the deck. He watched the man's actions. There was a peculiar walk to this master—a bit too sure of himself, not the walk of an old ice runner.

"So, where did you get hit?" Slagle asked in a disinterested tone.

"Yesterday evening, just before sunset. 'Twas a near thing, it was."

"How did you escape in this old wreck? You can't make twice the wind in this, I dare say."

"We were lucky, we were. They closed within a quarter mile, hit us once, as you can see, and then, Saints be praised, they lost a runner to a double buckle in the ice. I swore a new altar to St. Donn of Wrist for our deliverance, blessed forever be his memory."

Slagle half listened to the master's account of the battle while he did a brief check belowdeck. It was most likely a smuggler craft, to be sure—most colliers had something hidden away in the rock. Stopping for a moment, he looked at Narn with a knowing glance. As if in answer, a small pouch of coins was produced, and Slagle slipped it into his tunic.

"All seems in order," he said wearily.

The stench of the black rock started another coughing spasm that nearly doubled him over as he struggled back onto the deck. From out of his tunic, Narn produced a silver flask and offered it to him.

Slagle drained it off and started to hand it back, but Narn waved it aside with a gesture that could barely conceal the fear.

"Keep it, man. I have no use for it now."

Slagle pocketed the gift.

"Where's your destination?"

"Mathin."

"From there?"

"We should be back through in the week. Most likely, take a load of lumber for home."

There was nothing else to interest him. All he could think about was the chamber carved into the ice and the bed of furs that awaited him.

"Fine, fine, but why tonight? Why not wait till morning?"

Narn shook his head. "I'll not stay another night on the northward shelf. If that devil has his blade fixed, I know he'll be after me."

"All right, then, the channel is marked. Go carefully, and ye should reach the southward fortress the hour before dawn, if the wind holds true."

Slagle crossed the deck to the ladder.

"Fine, then, and clear ice to you," he muttered hoarsely while lowering himself over the side.

Aboard the raft, Slagle watched as the collier raised sail, backed off, then started for the entrance into the channel.

"Slagle, did you notice something?" Olafson asked cautiously.

"What was that?"

"She was loaded with rock, was she not?"

"Aye."

"She started to move rather swiftly for one that should be so heavily laden. It don't look right to me."

Another wave of coughing swept over him.

"We can still stop her," Olafson suggested. "You know the orders from Mathin about close searching of any suspicious craft."

Slagle started coughing again, and a light spray of blood sprinkled the deck. "Nay, nay, just leave it be." He sobbed. "Even if they be smugglers, they've paid enough." He jingled the bag. "Send up the flare, and let them pass. I need a drink and a warm room more than another hour out here on the ice."

The collier passed on into the shadows of the Broken Tracks. Ulric looked around to his men and could see the smiles on their faces. If they had been discovered, the southward fortress would have been alerted by the signal stations that were posted down the length of the pass—the mission would have failed.

"I'm going below," he called to Dalmath. "Wake me an hour before our arrival at the southward fort."

Returning to his cabin, he could feel the tension drain— the first great danger had been negotiated. Collapsing on the cot, he tried to will himself to sleep. Chances were that it would be the last opportunity for rest.

"And then the final sleep..." he whispered to himself.

He was alone at last. Michael struggled with the sense of frustration and worry that had plagued him all day. He thought sleep would be the answer, but his exhaustion and nervous strain were so deep that even sleep would not come as a release. Finally, in frustration, he got up, lit a taper from the wood stove, and settled down into the cross-legged position of meditation.

He started with the slow, rhythmic breathing revealed to him long before by Seth back in the monastery of St. Awstin. In the distance, he could hear the rising of the wind, and reaching out, Michael could sense the dark clouds racing across a jet black sky. His thoughts drifted between the indistinct line of meditation and dreams.

There was no sense of time, of light. But a presence, an eerily familiar presence, hovered before his outstretched thoughts.

Rifton? Was it Rifton come back from beyond? He wanted to reach out to touch his dead uncle. To see what was truly on the other side, but something stopped him. He could sense a spirit gathering beside his uncle—no, two of them, hauntingly close, reaching into his heart. Other forms gathered in the night—dozens, now hundreds, and the two led the way into the night. Down a long tunnel, they drifted farther away. He started toward them, faster, ever faster—but they stayed just out of reach. He had to know! Upward, ever upward, he soared, pursuing them into the darkness, with Rifton at their side, leading them into the light beyond. He had to go with them.

"Wait," he whispered. "Please wait for me."

The two stopped.

"Go back, Michael," an echoing voice replied. "It is not yet time; go back."

A terrible sense of dread washed over him, as if cold, unseeing hands had touched him on the back of the neck. He forced himself to confront the darkness. The vision was no dream, he realized; it was a reality, a glimpse of what is or what might be. Hundreds of shadows were gathering out of the darkness before him, closing in around the two. He could almost recognize them—their names half formed on his lips. Yes, Rifton was there, and a third was coming out of the night.

"Go back," a voice whispered softly. "It is not yet time, go back."

He looked to the shadows, and the third form appeared out of the swirling darkness. "Who are you?" Michael whispered.

The third one started to turn.

"Michael," the disembodied spirit moaned, "where were you to protect them?"

"Ishmael!"

Michael struggled forward, moving slowly, as if his feet

were trapped in mud. The shadows started to draw away from him, sliding off into the darkness of night.

"Wait!"

They stopped, turned. Their faces were no longer human; dark, skull-like eyes peered out at him. He felt his sanity drifting away. The skull-like images were known to him. There were Rifton and Ishmael, Janis's father, and between them, by All Above, he knew them, and he screamed out in his fear—

"Janis! Andrew!" He screamed until a crashing blow stunned him into consciousness.

Daniel held him by the shoulders, his eyes filled with fear. Michael looked around the room. Cowan and several of the Companions stood by the door.

"A nightmare, Michael. It was only a nightmare," Cowan said cautiously, as if trying to dispel his own fear.

The image burned before him. It was no dream, no nightmare; they were in mortal danger. "No, no nightmare, a vision!" Michael shouted in near hysteria. "Prepare my ship at once; we return to Mathin immediately!"

"But what of Sol?" Cowan replied in a soothing voice. "We're supposed to go there first."

"Damn you, Cowan, there's a danger—a terrible danger. I know at last what I have feared for so long."

"What fear, Michael?"

"The one I've struggled with for so long. You've heard my command!" he shouted hysterically. "Gather the Companions; tell Eldric to meet me in the harbor. We leave at once."

Cowan ran out of the room, and within seconds, the castle was roused into action as Michael's men turned out.

"Is it Janis?" Daniel asked slowly.

"Yes, Daniel. I should have known from the beginning. It would have had to be her."

"Master, it's time." A gentle hand was shaking him lightly. "The fortress is in sight."

To his surprise, he found that he had slept, after all, in a dreamless, deep night of darkness. He sat bolt upright, embarrassed. Never sleep so soundly that someone can approach your bed. That was a primary rule, and he had let it slip. Mumbling a confused curse, he stood up, rubbing the sleep from his eyes. Arriving on deck, Ulric could just barely make out the pilot ship leading the way down the well-marked channel.

Upon reaching the bow of the ship, he looked forward—a hundred yards ahead, the pilot ship led the way through the channel, a riding light astern to guide the larger vessel. A half mile beyond, Ulric could see a line of torches shimmering on the ice, marking the walls of the southward citadel, which guarded the Mathinian Pass. He looked to Dalmath, who had spent a sleepless night on deck.

"All's ready?"

"Yes, master."

"Let's hope this one is as easy as the last."

The last sail was pulled in, and the collier drifted to a halt, still abeam the wind, since there wasn't any room to turn into the breeze. From out of the darkness came several figures propelled by one-man skatesails. Holding the sails overhead to dump the wind, they drifted to a halt next to the portside outrigger.

"Light some torches," Ulric commanded.

Half a dozen torches flared to life, casting a cold, hollow light across the windswept deck. A slender, fur-clad figure gained the railing and swung himself up onto the deck. He quickly scanned the area and without hesitation strode purposefully up to Ulric.

This one will be tougher, Ulric thought, sensing a possible conflict coming.

"Owen, of the southward fortress line," the fortress guard said in a short, clipped manner. "I am a member of the Companions of the Prophet."

Ulric bowed low.

"Narn, I am, master of the *St. Cadrina*, thirteen days out of Cornath, twenty-two from North Prydain. Black rock to Mathin in trade for lumber."

Owen was silent, surveying him closely.

"Urgent business it must be, Master Narn, if ye weather the pass at night."

"Ah, it's me master back home, it is," Narn whined while wringing his hands. "Drives me, he does. If I don't return in fifty days, he cuts my pay a tenth for every day I'm late."

"Risk a tenth pay to run the pass at night, not a practice your master would approve of, if you ask me," Owen replied sarcastically.

Damn you, Ulric silently cursed. He bowed lower.

"You're right, noble Companion, so right indeed. 'Tis fear that drove me, as well. We were set upon by corsairs. Barely escaped, we did, and all I wanted was to be off the northward shelf and safely onto the ice controlled by your beloved Prophet."

Owen snorted and walked away.

"Let's look below."

Ulric led the way down into the bunkers where Owen spent an unusually long time sounding the rock with his sword. Ulric could feel the tension coiling around him. He waited for the moment to strike. If Owen hit one of the concealed cabins, he was a dead man.

Force the thought away, Ulric said to himself. Tension can be felt—it can be smelled and communicated without words.

Finally, after what seemed an eternity, Owen appeared satisfied. "Right, let's go up," he commanded briskly, leading the way.

"Another hour will be first light," Owen said casually, his sword still in hand. "Just pull up to the watchtower a half league forward, and wait there till dawn."

"Can't I go on?" Ulric asked, trying to use the right voice of persuasion.

"Funny, you don't sound North Prydain," Owen said, stepping forward to look closer at Ulric.

Ulric was silent.

"At dawn, we'll clear you, though. And not before."

Ulric knew that to press the issue would raise too many questions.

"Owen?" There was a shout from over the side.

Owen walked across the deck and leaned over the side. Ulric followed. Several men were standing on the ice, one with a torch in his hand, while another was down on his knees examining one of the ship's blades.

Owen looked at Ulric and pointed over the railing. "Come with me," he said with a tone that conveyed an expectation of obedience.

Ulric gave a slight gesture with his right hand. It was an

order to stand fast—he could still bluff this one out. He followed the Mathinian over the side.

"Owen, look at this," the torchbearer called, and held the light down close to the ice.

Owen bent over and examined it closely. Ulric struck a posture of easy indifference and waited, watching for any sign of tension or attack.

Owen looked up.

"Master Narn, your ship casts a light track for one laden full with rock."

"Her blades are dull," Ulric responded. "They don't cut as deep as they should."

One of the men behind Owen spoke up, his voice loud enough with suppressed tension to be heard on the deck.

"She's underloaded, I say. I know a collier track when I see one, and I say you're not showing the right track."

Ulric laughed softly; he had one last hope.

"Come, now, I've got a sack of silver that will take care of our tracks and make them look right for you."

Owen looked up from the ice and eyed Ulric with a cold, steady gaze. "We are Companions; our orders are clear. Now don't make a move. I have three men armed with crossbows in the shadows."

Ulric was silent.

"Where's she out of?" the guard with the torch asked, his voice a suppressed whisper.

"We're the *St. Cadrina* out of North Prydain."

"He's a liar!" one of the other guards shouted, his Prydain dialect ringing clear. "This here craft be from the Inar shipyards. I can tell by her lines. And ain't no *St. Cadrina* ever come from that yard."

Dalmath, who was watching the drama from above, caught the distinctive hand gesture commanding him to action.

"Down, Ulric!"

He dived to the ice. From overhead came the shots of half a dozen crossbows, their bolts slamming into the Mathinian guards. Ulric rolled across the ice, trying to gain the protection of the outrigger. A bolt slammed into the ice next to him, spraying him with crystals. Another buried itself into the outrigger support over his head. Ulric looked up and saw Owen struggling on the ice, an arrow buried in his leg, another sticking clear through his shoulder.

Their eyes locked for a second.

A horn sounded in the distance—the alarm was sounded.

"Sail," Ulric shouted. "Make sail, damn you!"

Scimitar in hand, Owen was crawling toward him. For a second, Ulric was tempted to kill him. There were other, more important things to do. Owen screamed a battle challenge to him, but Ulric turned away, leaped up onto the outrigger, and ran its length to the support beam. A bolt slammed into the railing overhead; he scrambled past it and swung himself up onto the deck.

The sails snapped out with explosive booms, the collier lurching forward as the wind started to drive the ship forward, while ahead a series of rockets went up, sounding the alarm.

From belowdecks the men swarmed up through the hatchways. The collier started to pick up speed, the distance to the gate closing rapidly.

A series of flares burst forward, and in the garish, multicolored light Ulric could see the gate that led out onto the Southern Ice.

"Damn them by all the Saints," Ulric shouted, "the gates are blocked!

"Range to gate?" Ulric shouted.

"Still another minute at least."

The roar of the wind was picking up as the collier accelerated, the rigging above singing louder and louder.

"Eadwulf!"

The assassin stepped out of the shadows in answer to Ulric's call.

"Can we force the gate if it's closed?"

"Doubtful, master. They have log booms suspended across the channel designed to rip a ship apart."

"Damn!"

"A third of a mile," Dalmath shouted. "Your command, master."

"Crash the gate; prepare to abandon ship. If need be, we'll cross the ice to Mathin by skatesail."

Dalmath relayed the commands through a speaking trumpet.

"Clear the rigging; prepare to abandon ship. Clear for collision! Reserve team to the sternway; brace for collision!"

"A quarter mile!" came the shout from the bowsprit lookout.

The mast and rigging crews came sliding down to the deck, their gloves smoking.

"Brace yourselves," Dalmath shouted. "Keep a sharp eye above."

Ulric saw the gate looming up out of the shadows. Then signal flares shot up from the towers, illuminating the log booms that barred their escape.

Eadwulf shouted, his voice carrying above the thunder of the wind and the enemy guns that were opening up on them. "Ulric, beyond the gate, ship's lanterns; looks like a merchant-man."

Ulric could make them out, two lanterns not a hundred yards beyond the gate. His reaction was instantaneous. "Belay the ramming. Crash her broadside, and block the gate! Assault teams, prepare to storm the merchantman."

The ship heeled over as the sailing master and mate pulled viciously on the wheel.

"A hundred yards!"

The ship lurched up on its starboard runners—its stern whipping around in a violent skid.

"Brace yourselves."

Ulric barely had time to grab hold of the starboard railing as the portside outriggers smashed into the south tower with a vision-blurring crash.

From overhead, tons of canvas, rope, booms, and masts came tumbling down. The deck echoed with screams as men were crushed beneath the rain of death. The pine trunk of the top foremast tore through the deck, smashing several crew men through the ship and onto the ice below.

"Eadwulf, teams one through six, over and board the merchantman!" Ulric screamed.

With a deadly silence, the men leaped over the railing and swept through the ice gate to the merchantman, which was just beginning to stir.

"Seven through ten, port tower. Eleven through fifteen, starboard."

The men went over the side, grappling hooks already snaking upward.

From overhead, an occasional bolt slammed into the deck. One of the men by the bowsprit crumpled up—his life's blood gushing out in a scarlet shower.

"The rest of you bring up the equipment from below," Ulric commanded.

All along the four-hundred-yard wall, the alarm was being raised, and from the northward ice citadel, torches emerged into the darkness.

From the citadel tower three, red rockets rose heavenward.

"There go the emergency flares!" Dalmath shouted.

Ulric turned and looked to the north. After half a minute, three more rockets rose, half a dozen miles away. "It will take the northward garrison half a day to reach here. That should give us enough time to complete our mission," he said softly.

The sound of battle rose up from the merchantman.

"Eowyn, offload the equipment and take it through the gate to the merchantman."

Without waiting for a response, Ulric ran across the shattered deck and leaped to the ice below.

From either side and above came a series of shouts and battle commands. Running on the ice, he passed several bodies of his own men. He reached the side of the merchantman, and he could hear hoarse cries of rage and fear. Ulric leaped over a dead monk by the port steering blade and made his way onto the low, open deck of the merchant craft.

Some of his men were already in the rigging, preparing to sheet in the sails. "Eadwulf, report!"

"It's secured, Ulric. Two men dead."

"Whose was it?"

Eadwulf hesitated for a second. "It was one of our own, out of Cornath, I think. We killed a priest of Mor in the taking."

"Too late to change that. Make sail. Bring her in to the tower. We leave in five minutes."

He looked back to the wall. The line of torches was weaving its way down the wall. In another minute, the ice below the towers would be a killing zone that no one could pass.

Ulric leaped back to the ice to hurry his men along. From out of the darkness, his first team emerged, laden with equipment.

"Get it aboard!" Ulric shouted. "Move it, damn you, move it!" He ran back toward the gate, his lungs burning with the exertion. More men emerged from the darkness.

A bolt whisked past him, skidding off the ice in a shower of frozen crystals. He reached the side of the shattered collier.

"Dalmath, I need light!" he shouted as he reached the side of the deck. "Send up what we have."

Four battle teams still stood on the deck—the reserve units, waiting for his command. He called the commander forward. "Ivar, when the flares go up, mark any other ships on the southward side of the gate. You're to take the reserve teams. Burn the ships and capture the largest one for yourself. You are to hold the passage at all cost until the end of the day. At all cost, you must prevent any word from traveling south. At the end of the day, you're on your own. Run for one of the eastward passes, and make your way home. Do you understand?"

"Yes, master." Ivar hesitated, as if waiting for something.

"Damn it, what is it?"

"Your blessing, Ulric."

Only half paying attention, Ulric made the sign and mumbled a brief prayer.

Ivar reached out, and grabbing the sleeve of Ulric's robe, he kissed it. Turning, he called for his men to follow.

Ulric dashed below and burst into the shattered remains of his cabin. He tore open the secret compartment, scooped out the case that held the information concerning the mission, and raced back to the deck. "Dalmath!"

"Yes, master?"

"If I fall, make sure you take these records."

"Yes, master."

"Are we ready?"

"The ship is cleared. We await your command."

In the semilight of dawn, he could make out shadowy figures running across the ice. Here and there lay twisted forms with Mathinian crossbow bolts protruding from their tunics.

"Flares!"

The rockets rose upward, bursting across the harbor. Ivar stood on the far side of the gate. "Three ships, Ulric, light merchantmen."

"Go for them. Now move!" Ulric looked around, scanning the deck. He had lost too many; that was obvious—their bodies crushed beneath the shattered rigging.

"Abandon position!" he shouted.

Ulric, leading the last battle team, went over the side with Dalmath and sprinted for the gate. From overhead, his men scrambled down the sides of the two towers. Even before the last brother was off, the Mathinians had gained the tops on either side, and a hail of arrows and ice blocks showered down on the retreating forms. Several of the men collapsed around him, but he pushed on.

The merchantman was already moving, coming across the wind, her outriggers swarming with men. A shower of ice exploded in front of Ulric, and a deafening roar passed overhead. Looking back, he saw a half dozen puffs of smoke rising from the citadel wall.

Ulric doubled his pace, but the merchantman was moving faster and faster. He pushed himself to the limit. Closer, closer. He felt as if his lungs would burst. With a desperate leap, Ulric lunged and grabbed the stern end of the merchantman's outrigger. He was immediately pulled off his feet by the ship's forward momentum.

A brother assassin reached out while holding on to a stanchion and pulled him up onto the outrigger.

With a deafening howl, the rescuer's hands were snatched out of Ulric's grasp with such violence that he nearly tumbled off the outrigger. He was blinded by a curtain of blood. His rescuer was gone, torn apart and slammed into the side of the ship by the passage of a twenty-four-pound ball.

The ship came about and, with a steady, even acceleration, raced across the eye of the wind. The blade beneath Ulric's feet chattered across the uneven ice. He looked astern and saw five or six men running a losing race. He watched them coldly. Most of them realized that the path to salvation was lost, and their training took hold. They stopped, surveyed the battle, then dashed off to the eastward, where Ivar's men were storming the iceships that were attempting to make sail.

One of the ships suddenly rose off the ice in a stunning explosion, illuminating the sky with a light that surpassed the dawn glowing to the east.

"Good, very good," he said quietly. Ulric scrambled up the outrigger support arm and landed on the deck. All around him, his men were sprawled. And he surveyed the confusion.

"Stand to by group; store the explosives and equipment below."

The men jumped to his command.

"Another volley," someone cried.

Ulric looked to the citadel. Before he even marked the smoke, two shots slammed into the ship, one striking the bow, the other crashing through the belowdeck. Screams marked the passage of deadly steel and razor-sharp splinters.

As the southward pass drifted farther astern, Ulric allowed himself to relax. It appeared that Ivar had secured all the ships in the harbor. That should block any attempt to get a message to Mathin, allowing the Brothers of the Knife at least a twelve-hour lead until reinforcements arrived from the northward gate.

"Eadwulf, how many are left?"

"Only eighty-seven, master. The rest are with Ivar or lost."

"Estimated time to Mathin?"

It was the first time he mentioned the target openly, and several of the men turned to look at him.

"Seven hours, if the wind holds," Dalmath shouted, having assumed his usual place by the wheel. "In fact, master, the wind's coming up harder by the minute. I think we might be in for a blow."

Ulric looked westward. A high-banked line of clouds cut across the western horizon, obscuring nearly a quarter of the Arch.

Another volley of shot hummed past, but wide. Only one of them holed a sail.

"Secure the equipment, then assemble the men on deck. It's time I told them of Mathin," Ulric shouted.

He looked heavenward. After the bad luck of the last day, at last there was a heaven-sent wind to send them on their way.

"Clear us away, there, Finson!"

"Master, some of the crew is still not aboard, and our escorts, sire—our escorts need another hour at least to raise their crews."

"You heard me, Finson!" He strode up to his sailing master and stared at him in a threatening manner. "Clear us away!"

Finson's own anger was rising, and words of challenge came to his lips, but froze as he gazed into Michael's eyes. Turning away, he picked up his speaking trumpet. "Move there, you bastards, and clear us away!"

The lines overboard were cut away, leaving the anchor stakes behind. Out on the harbor could be heard the cries of dozens of men who were struggling to reach the ship before it sailed into the darkness.

"Ormson, this is madness," Eldric shouted above the chanteys of the crew and the rising howl of the wind. "Our own agents would have warned us of any danger. You just can't sail off like this because of some nightmare."

Michael turned on Eldric. "But by all that we hold sacred, I tell you that I know. As sure as I stand here, I know at last what is coming, and it is aimed straight at Mathin."

Eldric looked at him. A strange, mystical light flickered in Michael's eyes—something unworldly and deeply frightening. "Michael, one more day won't matter in all of this. By the time the sun crosses the Arch, we could muster twenty ships and sail to the pass in strength. Your leaving alone like this is folly."

"But I am leaving, and unless you wish to sail with me, you'd better leave my ship!"

The deck lurched beneath their feet as the foretop sail caught the wind, driving the ship backward. The rudder was hard over, and the craft cut a sharp arc that brought the vessel up abeam the wind.

"Sheet home the fore and stern; bring her forward now. Step lively, you scum. Step to it!" Finson shouted in the background.

"Eldric, you'd better get back over the side at once."

Eldric looked at Michael closely. He still could not understand why he, a privateer, had sworn allegiance to a half-crazed renegade priest. But sworn he had, and he would not desert him in this hour. "I'll follow you within six hours and shall arrive in Mathin at first light tomorrow. And for the sake of your reputation, Michael Ormson, there better be a damn good reason for this folly, or we'll all be the laughing stock of the Southward Ice."

Michael suppressed a curse, as Eldric ran to the railing and lowered himself over the side. He leaped to the ice, nearly fell, and gaining his balance, ran alongside. The ship was gaining forward momentum. The anchor crews raced alongside the craft and leaped onto the outriggers, while in the distance the crew's stragglers ran across the ice, shouting and cursing as the ship pulled away with a deep rumble. The ship started to move faster, and as Eldric slowed, the vessel drifted past with a bone-shaking rattle that echoed through the ice.

The first light was breaking the eastern horizon as they cleared the harbor gate and defensive works.

"All sails, sheet them in and cleat down, all sails now!"

Michael paced the forecastle, looking anxiously aloft to the pennants that told the angle of the wind, and he nervously examined the angle of every sail for any sign of slackness.

He was tempted to reprimand the maintop crew for a sail that was out of alignment but suppressed the urge, leaving it to Finson, as was proper. He looked around the deck. After the mad excitement of the last hour, he had time to pause at last. He couldn't help but notice the stares that greeted him. As if his actions were those of a madman or, even more fright-ening, the act of one inspired by Above. Michael breathed deeply to calm himself, then closed his eyes for a moment's rest. But as soon as he did, the image rushed in at him—the skulls looking out of the darkness; Janis and Andrew—phan-toms.

He opened his eyes and looked to his men. Cowan, Daniel, and Finson stood before him.

"Do you understand why?" Michael whispered.

They were silent.

"I tell you, I saw it. Daniel, I saw it as plainly as I did that first time when you and I sailed to Mathin."

Daniel nodded slowly.

"How long to Mathin?" Michael asked nervously.

Finson shook his head. "Look there, Michael," he said, pointing off to the west.

Michael followed Finson's gaze, and on the horizon, he could detect a dark line of clouds, while overhead, thin, wispy tentacles of white were fringed with a darker threatening gray.

"'Tis a storm coming up. Rare for this time of year, but a storm nevertheless, and I reckon we'll be sailing straight into the teeth of it."

"So how long?" Michael asked impatiently.

"Twelve, maybe fourteen hours. The wind shall pick up at least, which will help."

Michael nodded sadly.

"If what you say is true, Michael, then as we run into the eye of the wind, a ship attacking from the pass will face a beam run, straight down without tacking."

"Damn it all," Michael cursed.

His fist slammed down against the railing. "Damn this wind to Hell!" he shouted.

CHAPTER 6

"MAMA, IT'S SNOWING!"

The door crashed open, and with an exuberant shout, a white-clad form streaked into the meditation chamber. She looked up sternly.

"Young man, what room is this?"

"The thinking room, Mama."

"Very good, Andrew. I'm glad to see that at least you remembered that."

Elijah appeared in the doorway, but with a wave of her hand, Janis indicated that he was not to intervene.

Andrew was looking at the floor, sensing with good reason that a reprimand was coming.

"Andrew, is it possible to meditate when someone is shouting in your ear?"

"No, Mama."

"Andrew, you are a descendant of the lines of Ormson and of Ishmael. When you take punishment, you take it with your head up."

He lifted his eyes up to meet hers. So like Michael's, she thought—the same cast, the same mismatched color, one light blue, the other steel gray. His eyes were almost chilling, as if the five-year-old body held a deeper, older wisdom locked within. His manner warmed her with pride, which she tried to hide in her attempt to discipline him.

He looked at her, his eyes locking onto hers with a piercing, all-encompassing gaze.

Michael, she thought sadly, her body and mind missing his presence and warmth.

"So, Andrew Michaelson, you have come to inform me that it is snowing."

"Yes, Mama," he replied gravely.

"I do suppose that means we must go for a walk," she said with a laugh, extending her arms as the boy leaped onto her lap with a joyful shout.

But the logistics of even a simple walk were troublesome to the point of distraction. She first postponed a meeting with two of Zardok's nephews, who were planning a new wing to the library at the university, then set aside the plans for the evening meal. Guards and the watchers were stationed in the woods. When they finally cleared the relatively great danger of the narrow city streets, Janis could sense Elijah's relaxation. The passage through the narrow streets of Mathin had been rough on him, as the crowds pressed in on them and called out Andrew's name. The boy had borne the attention with dignity, as Elijah and Michael had trained him, and Janis felt a surge of pride. But once the open forest was reached, his hands slipped from hers, and the five-year-old body took command at last. The boy dashed ahead with exuberant shouts.

Through the woods they ran past the stately pines that towered a hundred and fifty feet into the gray morning sky. The frigid air whisked around them, moaning through the trees as the storm raced by, dumping its moisture in the form of a fine, crystalline snow that danced and floated through the bare branches overhead.

Andrew darted back and forth through the pines, racing far ahead and then dropping back for a moment to point something out to his mother. She looked at Elijah, who walked alongside of her, and softly smiled.

"You know, he thrives under your attention, Elijah."

The guard's face mask was off, and she could see the smile of affection that crinkled up the edges of his flowing gray beard.

"He's a fine one, he is, my lady. A son that his grandfather would've been proud of."

Elijah had been her bodyguard, as well, before the coming of the Ezrians and had sailed with Ishmael for almost twenty years—the most loyal of retainers to the Tornson family.

"Elijah?"

"My lady?"

"Please, Elijah, we're away from the court for a while; just let it be Janis again."

He smiled and put his hand on her shoulder. "All right, then, my lass, little Janis it still is."

"You're proud of him, aren't you?"

Elijah hesitated for a moment and then spoke with a strange softness. "Proud and at times almost fearful of him, if I might speak frankly, Janis. He is much of you, but he is of his father, as well. You know, and I have never hidden it, that I follow not the belief of Michael. The Church of Sol has my pledge till I cross over the Shadow to join my forefathers in the Light."

"I realize that, Elijah, and Michael would have it no other way. Your belief is your own; all we ask is your help and skill for my sake and for Andrew."

"I know that, Janis, and that you shall always have. But in Andrew I see the dream of his father coming to pass. Andrew shall carry it forward, and all, all that was, shall be destroyed forever. I fear that I am the last of a dying world. Andrew has the mind of his father and shall carry his plan to its conclusion."

She nodded thoughtfully and did not respond, for she knew his words were true. Their conversation was interrupted as they reached the Sacred Grove at the top of the hill. With a shout, Andrew ran into the Sacred Place and, standing in a grandiose posture, imitated his father, speaking in soft, rapid speech that held the same hypnotic quality, that even in so young a boy carried a promise of power and control.

Janis stopped at the edge of the Sacred Grove and looked about the snow-clad summit. She could pick out the spot where she and Michael had first made love. It was the same place where they had conceived Andrew, and she chuckled at the memory of Michael's embarrassed nervousness when Daniel had come upon them in the middle of their passion in a frantic search for his missing "charge."

She sat down on the ground, smiling inwardly at the memory

of a young monk, so vulnerable and sadly desperate for understanding and love. She was surprised as Andrew, as if sensing her thoughts, came quietly over and crawled shyly onto her lap, still a little boy seeking the warm caresses of his mother.

She felt content, at ease with her life. The guards, even Elijah, had discreetly drawn back—allowing her to be alone with her thoughts and memories.

The wind was picking up, and the snow swirled down more thickly, cloaking them in a soft carpet of white. The dreams, the battles and struggles to come, drifted away into another world as she sat alone with her son. In him, she could see the fruition of Michael's striving. She hugged Andrew. For the moment, the rest was forgotten, and she was content.

The wind roared past them, blowing in from the west, carrying with it a light dusting of snow. As Ulric stepped onto the ice, he had to steady himself against the outrigger of the merchantman. The passage had been rough, for most of the day he had stood upon a canted deck as the ship ran hiked dangerously on downwind runners. The original plan called for a day of preparation, a gradual infiltration, and the taking up of positions prepared within the city. But only hours would pass before Ivar's rear guard broke and the alarm spread across the Southward Ice. He had to strike tonight, or all hope of victory was lost.

"Eadwulf, Dalmath, Eowyn, offload at once! I'll be back within three hours. Dalmath, if I fail to return, you are to lead the assault at midnight. I've reviewed all details with you. Have you any questions?"

Dalmath shook his head.

Ulric climbed aboard the two-man raft that had been stored aboard the merchantman. He hoisted the single battened sail, while the crewman pushed the craft across the wind. The sail ran up the mast, and Ulric tied off the halyard, then pulled in the downhaul, cinching the sail in tight. The crewman leaped aboard and took the rudder from Ulric's hand while he sheeted in, drawing the sail down so that the wind pressed against it, driving the craft across the choppy, snow-covered ice. Within seconds, the merchantman was out of sight in the snow squall. The acceleration pushed the two men back, so that they had to hang on for balance as the raft raced downwind on a broad reach.

"We should be sighting the harbor entrance within ten minutes, given this wind!" Ulric shouted, while his fellow assassin eyed the lines of the sail and adjusted the tiller slightly.

Ulric quietly cleared his thoughts and concentrated on what was to come. He would only have an hour, at best. They would have to get into Mathin and out again before darkness fell, then tack three leagues back to where his men were offloading in preparation for a cross-country assault. If the collier had survived, they could have sailed straight into the harbor, and then, under the cover of night, launched their assault. Instead, they would have to land on the far side of the island, cross it under cover of night, and assault the city from the landward side—in one sweeping raid.

"There it is, master. The south-side ice tower."

Through the swirling snow, Ulric made out the single tower, perched against a rock-lined coast. Its foundation set into the frozen sea.

"We better swing wide here!" Ulric shouted. "This close in, we might hit the trap zone."

The crewmen pulled the tiller over, and as they ran downwind, their speed decreased.

"Some fresh tracks," Ulric shouted, "there to port."

They guided the raft into the tracks of a light merchantman and followed them as they came abreast of the harbor entrance a half mile away. Coming into the wind on a close-hauled run, they followed the tracks straight into the harbor entrance.

"Reef her in!" the crewman shouted above the roar of the wind.

Ulric loosened the halyard and quickly drew in the sail, tying the reefing points off. The raft slowed to walking speed.

Several guards stood alongside the two harbor towers, stamping their feet in the cold, and hailed them as the raft approached.

"A rough day for a sail in that! What brings you out?" one of the guards shouted, coming forward to greet them.

"It's our father," Ulric shouted. "He's dying, and we came from Bathan to fetch our brother back to be with him."

"Aye, Bathan, you say. Did you see the master, then?"

"No, no, we missed him. We were up in the woods, didn't even know he was there. Was he and the lady in Bathan, then?"

"No, just the master. The lady stayed here."

He breathed a sigh of relief. If she were not in Mathin, the plan would fail.

The guards laughed, and Ulric heard a comment about ignorant woodcutters.

"Pass, then," the guard shouted. "And blessings to your old one!"

Ulric nodded his thanks, and leaping over the side, the two of them pushed the raft through the gate. Turning a bit off the wind, they shot across the inner harbor.

So, Ormson's at Bathan, he thought with grim satisfaction. So much the easier. Despite the falling snow, he spied a mass of shipping tied up alongside the rows of warehouses. Pulling in their sail, they let the craft drift to a halt.

"Stay here," Ulric whispered. "If I fail to return within one hour, you are to leave without me."

The assassin nodded and pulled down a section of sail to form a crude shelter against the wind.

Ulric alighted from the ship and quickly surveyed the harbor. The maps he had studied matched up quite well. Zimri's men knew their trade. Without a moment's hesitation, he ran across the harbor, zigzagging among the outriggers, anchor lines, and dozens of ships of every size and description. On all sides, the harbor was aswarm with activity—rafts towing sleds laden with supplies, groups of men holding small one-man sails whisking past on skates. Children darted in and out of the confusion—some on small, homemade rafts, while others raced on boards that mounted three skates and a single sail.

Ulric gained the wharf and, without slowing, ran across the main square, then up a narrow alleyway that was marked by a sign indicating that it was the street of the fur traders. He counted off the houses on the left-hand side as he ascended the refuse-choked alleyway. Coming to the twelfth, he stopped. Over the door hung a sign with a white bear whose forepaws extended outward in a threatening display of oversized talons. He stopped for a moment, catching his breath, calming himself in preparation for any trap that might be waiting.

He opened the finely carved door and entered the musty semidarkness.

"Can I help you, good sire?" a voice called from the gloom.

Ulric stood quietly and gazed at the thin, graying wisp of a man who stepped forward to greet him. With a swift, assured gesture, Ulric pulled back his face mask and removed the hood of his parka.

"Aye, good sire, you come to find the white fur of the great bjorn," the merchant said with a fawning voice. "I can tell by your appearance that you are a man who knows what he wants."

Ulric nodded wordlessly.

The man pointed to a doorway at the back of the room. "What is out here is trash, good sire. What I have hidden in the back is more to one of your discriminating taste."

The man turned and walked to the door, then opened it, beckoning for Ulric to follow. Closing the door behind them, the merchant took a single sooty lamp down from the wall. Approaching Ulric, he held it close to his face.

"So it is time, at last, Ulric, my master."

Ulric nodded with approval—it had been ten years since Nathan had left the cloister to enter the secular life—and wait for the Call of the Knife.

"Will it be the master, then?"

Ulric shook his head in reproach—he only revealed what was necessary, and no more.

Nathan nodded his head thoughtfully and, turning, replaced the lamp on its hook. "Ah, I know who you want. I have waited, Ulric, oh, how I have waited. Watching the danger grow, I thought at times that you in the north had forgotten how to act."

Ulric stiffened at the tone of reproach in one of his lieutenants, but then was not the time . . . "Where is the other?" Ulric demanded. "The one that you have recruited?"

"I can summon him."

"Listen closely, for we haven't much time. We had to fight our way through the barrier. Before dawn, the alarm of our passage will be raised. Our ship is sheltered in a cove on the north side of the island. We are to strike overland and enter the city tonight."

"How many do you have?"

"Only eighty-seven."

"It could be done with far less, you know."

"I know that, but I want to do it this way. I need you to

guide us from the ship to the wall, but you are not to join us. You will be needed afterward."

Disappointment flickered across the aging man's face. "I understand and shall obey," Nathan whispered sadly.

"In the citadel, there is an inner room?"

"Yes."

"I want the proper arrangements made from within. All exits are to be blocked."

"Yes, of course."

"Good, I shall step outside. Call your man, then meet me at the end of the alleyway in five minutes. My name is Narn. You are my brother, returning with me to Bathan where our father is dying."

Nathan fell to his knees.

"Your blessing, oh, master."

Ulric raised his hands in the Sign of the Arch, touched the man on the shoulder, and walked from the shop.

At the end of the alleyway, he leaned casually against a sagging wooden wall and watched the crowds of laborers, merchants, and townspeople bustling about the great square. To the north stood the citadel, where the white-clad forms of the Companions marked the corners and the main gate. It was an old fortress, built of massive logs dark with age. He looked at it and felt that he was, in fact, looking at his tomb. There was a sudden knot of fur-clad forms coming around one corner, and an electric surge seemed to run through the crowd in the square, many of them stopping and some advancing toward the group. In the center of the group was a cluster of white-clad forms, spear tips held high.

It was she! He strode across the square and pushed his way forward with a quick, sinewy ease. It is not the plan, he thought; this is not the plan. Remember your training; never on impulse.

He slowed his pace and stopped in the center of the crowd. He could distinguish a flash of burgundy, a flowing robe, and next to it a small form clad in white. The gate opened, and they were gone.

A voice whispered behind him. "See how easy it could have been."

Ulric whirled around. Nathan stood before him.

"It's late," Ulric whispered harshly. And turning, he started to run across the square and out to the harbor beyond.

* * *

"Michael, you should go belowdecks."

The voice came to him above the shrieking of the wind. He turned, and Cowan was there, holding a roll of bread and a heavy packet of aged cheese.

"Come, Michael, let's go below and have something to eat. Standing here will do nothing, and Mathin is still hours away."

"It's there, Cowan. It's very close; I know it's there."

"Michael?"

"Leave me alone," Michael said sadly. "It should be me. I am the one that caused it; I'm the one to blame. It should be me." Michael looked westward across ice that was obscured by the storm-driven squalls.

Cowan stepped back and looked to Daniel, who kept watch by the foremast, his face mask covered in ice.

Daniel nodded his head and then absently looked down, returning to the sharpening of his ax.

"We're ready, Ulric."

"Good, my brothers, gather 'round."

He gazed around the rude woodcutter's shack. The blood stains on the floor were slowly congealing into frozen pools. The bodies of the cutter and his family still rested in the corner, but he paid them scant attention.

On the table where dinner had been set only minutes before, he unrolled the map.

"All team leaders around the table; the rest of you may listen."

The men shifted positions and moved in closer.

"Our target is the citadel of Mathin—our mission, as set by Holy Church, is the elimination of the wife and child of the prophet."

From the pouch, he pulled the sketches of the intended victims. "Pass the portraits around; memorize their features."

Handing the sketches to the man to his right, he continued. "We have a three-league march ahead of us. Nathan shall lead the way. A cleared zone extends two hundred paces out from the wall. We can't infiltrate in the standard way; there isn't time. Half an hour after the changing of the middle night watch, we shall scale the wall. Teams one through three shall lead the way."

The three captains nodded as he pointed out the position to be taken.

"After gaining the wall, we shall approach the north postern gate. Team four will stay with me. I shall attempt to take the door by ruse. If that fails, a fifty-pound charge will be set to blow it. Teams five and six will lead the assault in."

"Once inside"—and he unrolled another map, showing the floor plan of the citadel—"we shall gain control of the main floor. Teams seven and eight are to take the southward corridor and hold the main gate against possible reinforcements. Teams nine through twelve are to secure the main hallway. The remaining sections are to take the living quarters on the second floor. If they follow the defense that they are drilled in, their final stand will be here." And so saying, he pointed at the meditation chamber.

"Let me state this clearly. *I* am to carry out the mission; no one else is to do it. If any one else should capture the lady or child, they are to be brought before me. If I am dead, then the targets are to be brought to Dalmath, Eadwulf, or Eowyn, who have already been briefed on what must be done. If any one fails in this, I shall condemn your soul, both in this world and in the next."

The room was silent.

"We understand each other, then. If you are the only one left, and all others have failed, only then may you complete the mission. When you slay them, you must be sure that a message has been left."

He looked at his men. "The message is this: in the name of the Lord Zimri has this act been done."

There was a stir in the room as the men looked to each other.

"Do we understand?"

He was greeted with silence.

"After the completion, you are to withdraw in the standard way. Fight through to the ship. As soon as the black thread can be distinguished from the white, the ship will sail. A dozen skatesails are concealed in the wood pile behind this house. If you miss the ship, take them and use them.

"Questions?"

"What of the master, Michael Ormson?" came a voice from the back.

"He is in Bathan and will not return for at least the next week. If our information is wrong, under no circumstances must he be injured. And that order places your immortal soul in jeopardy if you should 'accidentally' harm him."

The men stirred, many of them whispering softly to each other at this strangest of orders.

"Silence!" Ulric shouted savagely. "It is not yours to question. It is your duty only to obey."

The men looked away from the fury in his eyes.

"It is understood, then?"

The men nodded.

From within the pouch, he extracted a glass vial. Uncorking it, he poured the liquid contents onto the maps, portraits, and documents. Even as the liquid poured out, it started to smoke and within seconds burst into flames.

"Kneel!"

The monks went down as one.

"And tonight we shall be watched," Ulric entoned. "Tonight our fathers shall speak our names at the Gathering Before the Table. And they shall call out our names with pride, for we are the Chosen, we are the Select—destined to Paradise.

"For tonight a place shall be prepared at the Feast Everlasting, and our names shall be called with pride."

"For our fathers shall be watching," the monks responded.

"By the Promise of the Arch," Ulric shouted, holding his hands aloft in the Sign of Blessing, "for the Return of the Garden, and to the Glory of All the Holy Saints, I bless you—knowing that tonight we shall sup in Paradise."

"Amen." The monks rose, casting aside the garments of ice runners to reveal the black robes and hoods of the order of assassins. Reaching into their packs, they pulled out white camouflage parkas and overpants and donned them.

Ulric looked at his men with a swelling pride. Tonight they will serve the Church, he thought. Tonight the brotherhood will go to its death in a battle the likes of which has not been seen since the assault on Barandith, nearly four hundred years before.

He looked to his men, who stood before him, a light of eagerness in his eyes. "Let us move," Ulric shouted. "We stop 'neath the walls of Mathin!"

CHAPTER 7

HE ROSE FROM THE DARKNESS AND SURVEYED THE WOODS. They were ready. With a sweeping gesture, Ulric pointed to the wall, and the first wave stood up and moved past him, their camouflaged forms drifting across the snow-covered fields that surrounded the city. It would take them at least two minutes to reach the wall. Dalmath stepped out of the darkness and started to count off the seconds. Ulric could feel the ordered ranks drawing up behind him and the electric tension that hung in the air. Overhead, the aurora flared in scarlet and green as the last clouds of the snow squall drifted to the east.

"Two minutes," Dalmath whispered, "they should be there."

As if in answer, a flicker of light shone on the wall, disappeared, and flashed again.

Ulric started forward, sprinting across the field, his men behind him in units of five. From out of the darkness, the first huts appeared. He weaved past them, drifting from shadow to shadow like a breeze in the night. The hard-packed snow of an alleyway opened up before him, and he sprinted down it to the base of the wall. A door swung open on creaking hinges, and a curious, sleepy face peeked out. A dagger flickered across the alleyway, burying itself in the man's throat, while several figures leaped over the body and darted into the cabin to quietly dispatch the inhabitants within before they could raise the alarm.

The wall loomed before him, and as he reached it, a rope

ladder tumbled down. Without slowing, Ulric leaped, grabbed
the ladder, and pulled himself up, his feet barely touching the
rungs. Two hands reached down and pulled him over. He
surveyed the position.

Two bodies lay against the battlement, the white fur of their
tunics stained crimson from arteries severed by the garrote.
With quick gestures, the commanders of five reported that they
held the wall for fifty yards on either side and no alarm had
yet been raised. Every few seconds, half a dozen men vaulted,
appeared over the wall, and formed up into their attack squads.
He waited for Dalmath to appear, signaling that the last man
was in the city. The small, lithe figure appeared at last. They
were ready.

Leading the way, Ulric sprinted down the wall to the guard
tower that looked out over the western gate. His brothers had
already slipped into the tower and dispatched the lone guard
and his four sleeping Companions. The five bodies were already
stripped. Ulric quickly pulled on the tunic of a Companion,
picked up his spear, and sprinted down the stairs to the street
below.

He stepped out into the narrow alleyway and slowly walked
toward the citadel of the Prophet, a hundred yards away. Five
men fell in from behind. The rest of the assassins spread out,
their white camouflage removed, the ceremonial tunics and
trousers of black their only protection from the icy cold. Ulric
felt a shudder of excitement course through him as he reached
the edge of the open square. With four guards in tow carrying
a limp form between them, he started across the courtyard and
reached the north sally port door. Ulric gave a short, hard knock
and waited.

The peephole slid open. "Who is it?"

"Mather—Eowyn slipped on a patch of ice and fell off the
battlement."

The voice on the other side sounded tired and a bit angry
at being disturbed. "You know the rules; admittance only through
the main gate during the night."

"Damn it, man, I know that, but 'e's bleeding to death, 'e
is. Let us in before 'e dies of it."

The man on the other side hesitated for a moment. "All
right, stand back while I open up."

The sky exploded with a thundering report that echoed across the city. In the glare of the rocket, Ulric saw his men poised along the opposite end of the square.

"That be the alarm," came a voice from behind the door. "Ay now, who are you, anyhow? I don't remember your voice."

Another rocket rose, and in the distance, Ulric could hear the echo of a horn. The moment was lost; in seconds, the fortress would come alive.

Ulric thrust his spear through the peep hole into the face of the Mathinian guard. The men behind him dropped Eowyn to the ground, and from under his billowing tunic pulled out the fifty-weight charge of powder.

"Quickly," Ulric whispered, "damn it, move!"

Eowyn placed the charge against the door, while Dalmath pulled a smoldering taper out from the folds of his robe. He whirled it over his head till it glowed bright red and then touched it against the fuse projecting from the powder-laden barrel.

The men dived to either side. There was silence for a moment while overhead the third rocket exploded with a crimson flash, and the alarm horns sounded in the citadel. A howling blast of fire and splintered wood roared out, shattering every window in the great square. Deafened by the explosion, Ulric leaped to his feet, bracing himself against the wall, trying to regain his balance. From atop the battlement, a lantern shone briefly, to be extinguished with a scream of pain as a poisoned bolt slammed into the guard, knocking him off the wall to land at Ulric's feet. With a shout, the assassins stood up and charged out of the alleyways, leaping into the dense smoke, past the shattered door, and on into the citadel of the Prophet.

Ulric urged his men forward, pointing the way with outstretched dagger. They had lost the surprise. Another rocket soared overhead. He traced the direction that it came from and wondered how the guards in the harbor could have known of his coming. Word must have come from the pass, after all, he thought with a curse. He pulled out a handful of poisoned discs and followed his men into the smoke and carnage.

"Damn it, clear us through the harbor," Michael screamed as the smoke of the signal rocket whipped past him and disappeared astern.

"I don't dare do it yet, Michael," Finson shouted. "The barrier chain might not be cleared."

Michael peered into the darkness; the silhouette of the towers became clear as the snow squall passed out to sea. The first rocket rose from the guard towers and stretched across the city in response to his alarm. But it would take at least five minutes to clear the chain barriers away and pass the frigate through. Michael turned to Finson. "Run us up the channel."

Finson raised his voice to carry against the wind. "Prepare to heave to. All hands prepare to take in sail."

In the agony of frustration, Michael stood at the bow railing and felt the ship slow down. Something flashed in the city and lit up the early-morning sky; then a dull, rumbling explosion echoed across the harbor.

"By heavens, Michael," Daniel whispered, "you were right."

The towers loomed closer, and he could see the guards frantically working to clear the chains. "Call the Companions," Michael spat.

But Daniel had already placed them on alert. The hundred men were drawn up amidship, awaiting Michael's command.

Seconds passed as Finson called out the coded commands to the guard tower, confirming that it was the Prophet's ship. Filled with anxiety, Michael stood on the bow railing as the last chain was drawn aside. Overhead, the sails boomed out, filled with the wind, and the *De Gaiuth* jumped forward, clearing the towers, and skated into the harbor.

They skimmed across the harbor accompanied by the strident call of the alarm horns. Torches flared along the dockside as the ships of Michael's fleet stood ready for action, not yet knowing the form or direction of the attack.

"Finson, run her alongside the dock. I don't care what damage she takes; just get us in there!"

The inner fortress of the harbor shot past, and the docks came into view.

"Brace yourselves," Daniel shouted.

Holding on to the railing, Michael watched as Finson maneuvered the ship toward the mooring, whisking past the dozens of small cutters and the parked fleets of rams.

"Cut away the sails," he shouted. "Prepare for collision."

The speed started to drop away, and Finson pulled hard over on the wheel. The *De Gaiuth* turned into the wind, aiming for one of the long wharfs used by the ships of the Flowing Sea. At a speed that was frightening in such a close-packed harbor, the *De Gaiuth* cut into the anchorage—her starboard outrigger slamming into the dock, collapsing the bow blade and shattering the forward arm of the outrigger. From overhead came the cracking of stays; then the foretop fell.

Even before the ship had come to a stop, Michael leaped out onto the portside support beam—scimitar in hand.

"To the citadel!" he screamed, and with an answering roar, Daniel and his Companions stormed out behind him.

As the last assault team leaped through the shattered doorway, Ulric charged in behind them. The first barracks room had already been taken. Twenty or so Companions lay dead, most garroted in their bunks, so swift was the attack. Ulric recognized two of his own among the dead.

As he scanned the long room, he saw Sigurd leading two teams down the southern corridor to take the main gate, but the barracks room was too crowded—the assault on the eastern corridor must have stalled.

"Dalmath!"

"They've blocked the east door," one of the men shouted. "We're setting the charge now."

A shout suddenly echoed down the hallway. "Down!"

Ulric barely had time to hit the ground before the concussion from the blast swept over him, choking the room with smoke. From overhead, there was a brief shower of rubble. Before it ended, Ulric cast aside his dagger, drew his short scimitar, and leaped forward. Jumping across the shattered beams of the hallway, he silently charged.

The assassin before him collapsed, vomiting blood; then another stumbled, a heavy crossbow bolt sticking out the back of his head. Ulric reached the rubble-strewn doorway and, twisting, leaped through it. A bolt tore the back of his tunic, cutting a deep furrow across his shoulderblade.

Ulric rolled into the corner, hiding in the shadows cast by the single flickering torch that lit a room packed with Mathinian guards. Obviously the warning had given them time to prepare a defense. The shattered doorway vomited a silent wall of black-clad men who fell beneath the volleys of the crossbowmen, but the assassins pushed in, swarming over their fallen comrades. As Ulric regained his footing and leaped into the close-packed ranks of the Companions, an ax swept in front of him. He dodged the blow and closed in, lashing out with his feet, smashing the kneecap of the warrior. A shield struck the side of his head, knocking him over, but Ulric rolled away, avoiding the downswing of a scimitar. From his pouch, he pulled a poisoned spike and whipped it into the forehead of his opponent. Another sword slashed out, nicking him on the thigh. He thrust with his scimitar, missed, and then the scimitar was gone—smashed against the stone floor by an ax blade. A body fell over him, and he used it as a shield.

Ulric pulled the wire garrote out of his headband, pushed the body aside, and leaped at the nearest Companion, who was dressed in an ermine-lined cape. The garrote wrapped with deadly ease around the young man's throat, and Ulric drew it tight. Suddenly, a shower of blood sprayed out, blinding Ulric with its hot stickiness. He rolled backward and away and let the battle sweep past.

The defenders gave ground, but not easily, and the room was choked with the dead and dying. Dalmath maneuvered his men forward, finally pushing a way through to the far door. He reached for the bolt, pushed it, and threw his weight against the wooden barrier. "Ulric, it's locked from the other side!"

"Damn!" Ulric turned and shouted down the corridor to the secured guard room.

"Powder, twenty-pound charge!"

A black-clad form rushed from the darkness and tossed a barrel to Dalmath. Dalmath whirled the glowing taper around his head, touched it to the fuse, then threw himself into the corner where the battle still raged.

Ulric covered his head, and the blast tore through the room, sweeping both friend and foe off their feet.

"Eadwulf, lead them in. Dalmath, to me."

The room was choked with smoke and echoed with terrified screams. He could hear Eadwulf's men push out, and the sound of battle greeted them.

From out of the shadows, Dalmath appeared, his face scorched, his left arm gushing blood.

"Time?"

"Over fifteen minutes so far."

Ulric looked at him closely. He didn't have long before the blood loss would kill him.

"Dalmath, we can expect attack from the rear at any moment. Abandon the plan for escape. Set up a rear guard here to hold back the reinforcements. I'll push ahead to finish the job."

Dalmath smiled. "The blessings of the Saints upon you, and I shall meet you tonight at the Long Table of Our Fathers."

Ulric nodded. "Tonight at the Table of Our Fathers." Rising, he charged forward behind Eadwulf's men without another thought for his closest friend. The sound of battle on the staircase greeted him.

She heard the explosion as if it was the distant edge of a dream. No, it wasn't a dream. An attack.

Janis sprung out of bed, pulling on a white robe.

The door slammed open. A guard stood before her, wild-eyed with excitement.

"My lady, the citadel is under attack."

"I know, damn it," Janis shouted as she swept past him and ran into the corridor. A second explosion rocked the floor beneath her; screams of panic and battle echoed in the distance. She was nearly knocked over as five guards with drawn scimitars swept past her. They charged down the stairs toward the sounds of battle. Two men ran past her, crossbows raised, and positioned themselves by the staircase.

She ran across the hall and pushed open the door to Andrew's room. Elijah stood next to Andrew—sword drawn. A flicker of admiration ran through Janis as she looked at her small son standing next to his closest friend. Andrew stood in exact imitation of Elijah's fighting pose, dagger in hand, waiting.

"Andrew, come with me," she shouted with arms extended. The fear in the little boy suddenly burst forth as he ran across the room and was swept into his mother's arms. She started for the door.

"No, my lady." Elijah pushed her aside and stepped into the corridor first.

"Quick!" He pointed down the corridor in the direction of the meditation chambers.

A handful of guards came out from a side corridor and fell in behind Janis, covering their retreat.

"Faster," Elijah yelled. "Dominick, Zebrian, stay!"

The two Companions stopped in their tracks, wheeling with swords drawn to buy precious seconds of time.

They reached the end of the corridor and turned right; the chapel was in front of them. Two guards stood at the chapel door, spears poised.

"Open it," Elijah shouted.

The men hurried to his command.

"The escape hatch, have you cleared it?"

The guards were silent.

"Damn you, have you cleared it?" Elijah shouted.

"No, sir."

Elijah cursed as the two guards pulled open the door. Behind them the sound of battle swelled. Elijah leaped into the dimly lit chamber, dragging Janis and Andrew with him. Four guards filed in, while the others set up a defensive position outside the door.

"Quick, the escape door, there's not much time." Elijah ran over to the panel, pushed on the concealed plate, and threw his weight against the last barrier to safety.

It didn't move.

He tried again.

"Duith clom helath!" he shouted in Bathanian dialect.

Again, he threw his weight against the door. "It's stuck! Jammed from inside."

Andrew whimpered. He could sense the doom in Elijah's voice.

The floor rumbled beneath their feet as another shock tore through the citadel. Elijah looked at Janis closely. "They've blown the door into the guard room."

Janis looked into Elijah's eyes. "There's no other way out, is there?"

Elijah looked at Andrew out of the corner of his eye. He gave a curt shake of his head, then looked at the other Companions.

Janis looked around the room. "Should we put out the lights?"

"No, my lady, they're assassins. They're trained to fight in darkness; the light will help us a little."

"Jerin, Ryman, try to cut through the panel. Eberiah, take my lady and Andrew; build a barrier out of the tables at the far end of the room. We only have a minute or two."

The room echoed with the blows of axes as the two guards desperately slashed at the heavy oak panels that separated the group from safety. Another explosion, louder and almost directly underfoot, rocked the room, and the guards hacked with increased frenzy.

"Damn it all," Elijah cursed, "we built it thick to slow down pursuit. Who is the traitor?" he suddenly screamed.

Someone shouted from the other side of the door.

Elijah cautiously pulled open the peephole and looked out.

"They're in the hallway, Elijah, I think—" A confused shout echoed into the room, then the clash of arms sounded in the corridor. Elijah watched as the first assassin turned the corner and was pinned by a crossbow bolt; then a wave of black turned the corner. Poisoned discs and throwing daggers whisked down the corridor, pinning the defenders or slamming them into the heavy door.

"Down," Elijah shouted, diving to the floor. A bolt slammed through the peephole, shot across the room, and buried itself in the opposite wall.

"Bayard, your shield," Elijah shouted.

Bayard unslung his shield and slammed it against the peephole, then tilted it back at an angle. Elijah leaned against the door and looked into the mirrorlike surface of the shield, which reflected the view down the corridor.

A horn sounded in the distance, to be picked up by others.

Andrew perked up expectantly, looking at his mother.

The horn sounded again.

"Michael!" Janis shouted. "It's Michael." But it sounded so distant, so far away.

Eberiah pulled at her sleeve, and Janis stepped behind the long table he had overturned. Reaching out, she swept Andrew into her arms.

"Andrew, it's all right, Dada's coming to help us."

Andrew looked into his mother's eyes and saw the fear. He felt something cold and sharp in her left hand as her right hand pressed his head to her breast. He knew what his mother would do if Dada did not arrive in time.

Elijah's voice rang out. "Down! Down! They're blasting the—"

A thunderclap ripped through the chanber, blinding the defenders with fire and then darkness.

Michael outstripped his guards in the race up the ice paths to the citadel. The Companions were strung out behind him, the pounding of their iron-shod boots echoing in the narrow alleyways, awakening the city with shouts of alarm. He turned into the great square, the main gates of the citadel before him. With a burst of speed, he sprinted toward it, shouting, "Open, damn it; open the gates!"

An instinct reached out to him, and he dived to the ground; several bolts shot over his head, missing him by inches. He heard the cries of the men behind him as several of the bolts found their mark.

"Michael!" came the cry from behind, and two Companions swept past him, only to fall, clutching at barbs that quivered in their throats.

More men charged across the square, shouting his name, "Michael! Michael!"

Daniel drew alongside Michael, then sprawled in the snow in front of him, holding his shield aloft. An arrow slammed off it, ricocheting into the darkness.

"Michael," Daniel screamed above the roar of battle, "'tis murder here. They hold the gate."

He had to get control of himself; his men were dying by the dozen. He swept the citadel with his gaze. In the torchlight, he could make out the flash of bolts whistling from the gate and bastions to either side. But the gate wasn't blown. They must have come in from the rear postern gate nearest the wall.

"The north wall," Michael shouted, and Daniel nodded.

Together they rose up and sprinted across the square. Daniel's great voice thundered across the square, "Halnar, hold here; the rest to Michael!"

Michael reached the west corner of the citadel and was suddenly knocked flat atop his shield. Daniel's massive arms were wrapped around his waist, his heavy bulk bearing down on top of him.

"Damn you, Ormson, you'll be dead if you go first. Let the others go."

Michael felt himself losing control. Janis and Andrew—he had to reach them. He struggled futilely with Daniel, finally collapsing in frustrated rage as Daniel tightened his grip. The Companions gathered around them.

"Lisnor, Macharson, lead," Daniel commanded. "Ragnorson, your men to Michael. Ready?" They were.

"Go!"

The first men turned the corner and started at a dead run. One of them collapsed after a dozen feet, his blood showering through a severed jugular, spraying all around him. But the others chanted Michael's name with a roar as they swept up the alleyway, sacrificing their lives but taking some, at last, in return.

Daniel stepped around the corner of the citadel and watched the progress of the fight as it swept up the alleyway. A bolt from above slammed into the Companion next to Michael. The man collapsed with a scream, staining the snow with a pool of steaming blood.

"Above!"

Michael looked up and saw the form withdraw from the window. "They're in the living quarters. Janis!" Michael pulled free of Daniel's grasp and charged up the alleyway behind his men. "Elijah, hold them," he screamed. Throwing all caution aside, he charged up the alleyway—the berserker way taking hold.

Michael leaped over the bloodied bodies sprawled in the alleyway, pushing his way through the fighting mob that choked the narrow street. Michael turned the north corner, and several men fell around him from the assassins' bolts that were fired from the blown gate.

"In, in after them," Daniel screamed as he shouldered his way to the front alongside Michael. As they charged the gate with the fury of despair, an assassin slashed Daniel's parka open, but with a vicious swing, Daniel slammed the black form against the wall, then smashed the man's head with a back-handed sweep of his battle-ax.

The assassins retreated up the corridor, and the howling, raging attack pushed in, climbing over the kicking bodies of the fallen. As Michael charged into the darkness through a confused mass of struggling forms, a bolt grazed his helmet, tearing into the face of the man behind him. Then an assassin leaped out of the darkness. Michael blocked a dagger thrust with his shield and, with a vicious upward thrust, drove his scimitar into the man's groin—the bloodied blade tearing out the man's back.

A wave of men pressed over him and poured into the north barracks chamber. All lighting was extinguished, and the battle was a horrid confusion, a desperate attack of dagger and scimitar at close range. Overwhelming Ulric's rear guard, the Mathinians pushed down the east corridor to the main staircase. Michael and Daniel stood shoulder to shoulder in the fore of the attack, while the Companions attempted to push ahead to shield their leaders from the hail of bolts and poisoned disks that rained about them.

When they reached the main staircase, Lomarchson threw himself in front of Michael. A dozen assassins on the stairs waited to deliver a rain of death to the attackers. Lomarchson went down as Daniel threw himself on Michael and the shower of bolts shot over them.

"Now," Daniel screamed, "now for them!" With upraised ax, he stood and led the charge against the stairs, hacking his way forward. A Companion charged past him with spear lowered, only to be pinned against the wall by a crossbow bolt to the stomach. But Daniel cut down the archer. Immediately, a bleeding assassin leaped past him. The assassin grabbed the fallen Companion's spear and slammed it into Daniel, pinning him by the shoulder to the stairs, but even as Daniel fell, he swung, taking the man's left leg off at the knee.

Michael leaped past Daniel and started up the stairs.

"Throw the explosive," Ulric shouted as the sound of battle rose up on the staircase behind him.

The assassin lifted the thirty-pound charge, lit it with a smoldering torch, and raced to the door, placing it firmly against the barrier. Ulric braced himself.

There was a blinding flash of light and a bone-jarring explosion that slapped the men to the ground.

Michael regained his footing as the corridor filled with smoke. "Janis! Janis!"

He pushed to the top of the landing and forced his way down the corridor to the chapel, but the last few assassins gave ground only in death.

"Janis!"

With daggers in each hand, Ulric rose, leaped over the fallen bodies, and raced down the corridor through the flaming wreckage. He leaped into the room—a bolt hit him in the shoulder, spinning him around, but he recovered his footing as the three surviving assassins pushed in. From out of the shadows, a Mathinian leaped, his battle-ax splitting open one of Ulric's men. Ulric dodged but felt as if he were in a dream. He was going to die the only proper death of the master. He felt that terrible sense of calm that he had prayed a lifetime for—to guide him when death would finally reach out to greet him. That day he would sup at the Long Table of the Fathers.

His men were down; he was alone. The Mathinians were good, better than he had thought they would be. A shadow loomed before him, and he feinted to the left. Again, a feint to the left and then to where he knew the opening would be. Swinging in low, he felt his blade sink home. There was a deep guttural grunt, and the body fell away. The mother and the boy. Where are they? he thought. A high-pitched scream sounded behind him.

Pain, blinding pain coursed through his back, and he knew the wound was fatal. He started the downward thrust.

"No!" A body pushed in front of him. With a grim smile of satisfaction, Ulric drove the blade home. The woman's eyes opened wide, staring into his with a startled look of surprise. The astonishment was always the same, Ulric thought as he looked at her—the quiver of her body pulsing through the blade that he still held in his hand. She pulled away from him, and he let go of the dagger. She stood before him, her hands fumbling with the blade that stuck out of her stomach—a red stain spread obscenely across her snowy white robe.

The sound of battle swelled behind him.

"Janis!" he screamed as he pushed the last of the assassins aside in the smoke-filled corridor.

He turned the corner and charged the final steps to the shattered remnants of the chapel door. Michael stormed into the room, terrified with panic at what he would find.

She was alive! And then he froze. She stood at the far end of the room, her expression a deadly mix of bewilderment and pain.

"Janis!" he screamed.

"Don't move, heretic." From a corner stepped a blood-soaked assassin.

Struggling in his iron grip was Andrew, who kicked furiously and screamed for his mother.

Michael stopped.

Janis slipped to the floor; Michael turned from the assassin and started toward her.

"Don't move, Ormson. I have your son."

Michael looked at him and could read his intent.

All control broke. "Don't," Michael begged, hysteria crowding out any attempt at control. "Don't, I beg you, please. Take my life for his."

Behind him, he could hear his men pouring into the room.

"Don't touch him!" Michael screamed. "Don't touch him!"

The men came to a stop, terrified by what was before them.

"Why?" Michael sobbed. "Why? Janis, she was nothing to you."

The man before him smiled an enigmatic, mysterious grin.

"Michael Ormson, the Heretic, I bring to you a present from my lord Zimri."

Ulric thrust Andrew forward, holding him by his hair. His right arm swung out in a deadly arc—the scimitar cutting through the air.

"Dada!—"

The scream was cut short as the decapitated body fell to the floor.

"No!—"

Michael screamed with wild animal rage as his blade slashed into Ulric's body again and again, but the mysterious grin still held him. Daniel staggered up behind Michael and pushed him aside, and still he screamed.

He returned to his senses briefly when a voice called to him. "Michael."

Michael dropped the sword from his trembling hand and ran over to her. "Are you there?" she whispered.

"Michael . . . Andrew?"

Michael sobbed and held her, cradling her head in his lap, begging for the nightmare to end—to make it all as it once was.

She looked up at him and smiled, a trickle of blood staining her jaw.

"Oh, my love, I'll always love you. And I'll wait for you—Andrew and I together."

"Janis, don't die, please don't die!"

She smiled sadly. "I'm cold, Michael. Michael, don't hate

them. Don't let this destroy all that we've dreamed..." Her voice slurred for a moment as she coughed, her features straining with the effort and pain. "Michael, don't make others die because of me. Please, Mich—"

"Janis? Janis!" He continued to scream as all he had ever been disappeared—to be replaced by a terrifying abyss of darkness that covered him with its cold embrace.

CHAPTER 8

HE LEFT THE SHIP'S DECK WITH FULL CEREMONY, THE FORTY monks going before him, in two columns, carrying the Sacred Icons, incense, and flaming torches that marked the passage of an archbishop. The deep, dissonant chant of the bass started the hymn "To St. Mor, Protector of the Sea," and the refrain was picked up by the tenors.

Zimri descended the stern plank and stepped onto the mirror-smooth ice. The bitter wind of winter whipped past him, billowing his robes, causing him to slide for several feet until he gained his balance and fell into a slow, dignified shuffle, keeping pace with the column that preceded him.

The bells of the monastery rang out in salute, their sound rising against the wind, so that the tone had a tinny distance to it. At times, it was nearly blocked out by the high-pitched whistle of the wind.

From the monastery, whose six towers stood atop a high granite outcrop, came a procession of greeting—nearly two hundred monks carrying or following the famed Icon of Caediff, one of the most sacred relics of the Brotherhood of Mor. Behind the icon marched twenty monks on whose shoulders was balanced a great square platform nearly ten feet on a side.

Atop the platform was the great war drum of St. Gardrath. Two monks in full battle dress faced each other across the drum, each holding a large wooden mallet, which he used to strike the drum, so that its deep, rolling boom set the pace of the procession.

Zimri approached the head of the column, his own monks flanking the monastery's procession. The monks bearing the icon finally stopped directly before their archbishop, while the brothers at the rear of the line came up in orderly lines, forming a vast semicircle before their leader.

The drum beat quickened. The chanting swelled, with all voices joining together for the final stanza.

> Out of the darkness He shall deliver us,
> Into the Light He shall lead us;
> We die so that
> Paradise shall be ours.

With a dramatic flourish, Zimri stepped forward, threw aside his face mask, then prostrated himself before the icon. He kissed the ice three times, and rising to one knee, he kissed the feet of St. Gardrath. He stayed in the position of worship until the chant ended and the drum beat's final, low cadence drifted into the wind.

Zimri stood and surveyed the monks drawn up before him. The abbot approached from the ranks, and Zimri offered him his hand, which the abbot took and kissed.

"My lord Zimri, we rejoice at your safe arrival."

"My blessing upon you, Brian, and upon your brotherhood." Zimri looked past the abbot as another hooded form approached from the center of the column. Zimri looked at Brian.

"He arrived yesterday," Brian said softly.

The figure approached and knelt before Zimri, waiting for his command.

Zimri let the moment play out—Let him sweat a little bit, Zimri thought. The wind whipped around them, swirling their robes, and Zimri stood unmoving, not extending his hand. The man stayed before him without looking up. Zimri sensed Brian's tension. The abbot feared that a rebuff was coming in front of the other monks. Zimri waited for several minutes; then, with a flourish, he grabbed hold of the man and forced him to rise.

Zimri embraced the hooded form and stepped back.

"My dear Peter, I have missed you and your counsel."

The man before him removed his face mask, his cold blue eyes looking into Zimri's. "My lord, as always, I have served you and await your command."

The tone was one of humility and warmth. Zimri looked at him, seeking, trying to sense what was within. He reached forward again, embraced Peter, and whispered so that none would hear. "Forgive me, Peter. It had to be done."

Peter was silent.

Zimri released him and beckoned for him to rejoin Brian.

He gestured for the monks bearing the icon to step aside and for the bearers of the drum to place their burden on the ice. The monks edged forward, sensing that something of importance was to be spoken there. Some even broke the rule of silence to exchange quick comments about the meaning of this act.

"My dear brothers," Zimri started in a full, even voice, "my blessings upon you and this the good monastery of St. Gardrath of the Morian Brotherhood."

He raised his hands in the Sign of Blessing, and they bowed low in response.

"My dear brothers, I come to you today with a message. A message which I shall share with you first, since we are all one together in a Sacred Cause." His manner made it seem that he was taking even the lowest deacon into his personal counsel. It was a simple act, but it always generated intensified loyalty, as if he were their closest friend whose word was worth dying for.

"My brothers, Mor has been silent for too long. Our brotherhood, chosen by Ancient Decree to be the Protector of the Faithful, has been silent. Our sword has been sheathed, the cannon empty. But that time has passed!" He ended his statement with a deep, passionate shout, as if the words had been ripped from his soul.

The monks stirred.

"My brothers of Mor, prepare yourselves. Look to your cannon, sharpen your sword; the time of our brotherhood has come again!" With arms outstretched to the heavens, Zimri fell to his knees.

"So be it!" the monks shouted with one, triumphant voice.

* * *

"So, dear Peter, you look well enough," Zimri said as he pulled off his parka and outer vestments and tossed them into the hands of a waiting deacon.

Peter was silent, his face a mirror of indifference.

"Will there be anything else, your Excellency?" the deacon asked meekly.

"Yes, there will!" Zimri replied sharply. "I've been aboard ship on and off for the last month, and what I want is some heat, and I want it now, damn it. This room is so cold my breath freezes in my lungs."

The deacon bowed low and hurried from the room, closing the door softly behind him.

Zimri turned to examine Peter. The years had not set well on him. Peter had lost weight, his face was drawn, his eyes deeper set. Good, Zimri thought, very good. He's toughened.

Peter returned Zimri's gaze without emotion. He held a look of deference, but Zimri could detect a coldness that had not been present before.

"You've thought about killing me, haven't you?" Zimri asked offhandedly, as if he were casually inquiring about the weather or the state of Peter's health.

"Do you want me to lie?" Peter replied.

"Have a seat by the stove. Pour some Yawinder; we need to talk this out."

A knock sounded from the door.

"Enter."

The deacon peeked in.

"Ah, the rock! Bring it here, brother," Zimri said with an expansive gesture.

The monk scurried forward, and Zimri walked up, taking the scoop from the monk's trembling hand.

"Your Excellency, let me attend to it."

"Don't be foolish," Zimri replied. "It will be a sad day indeed if I can't attend to such a simple task by myself. Thank you for your help, brother."

He blessed the monk, who withdrew, bowing low, grateful to be out of such an august presence.

Walking to the stove, Zimri pulled open the door, shook down the ashes, and shoveled the rock in—its sulfurous stench quickly filled the room as a gust of wind forced the smoke back down the chimney and into the small study that the abbot had vacated for Zimri's use.

"You do remarkably well at that, Zimri."

"You mean building the fire up?"

"Don't be foolish. I mean making the humblest of our brothers feel as if he is important, even though you and I know that he is not."

Zimri looked up and smiled. "It makes it easier for them to die for us, Peter. I hope that you've at least learned that by now."

"Ah. In much the same way you destroyed me to cover yourself. By your logic, I am supposed to remain eternally grateful for your attention, is that it?"

Zimri looked up. He has changed more than I thought. The old Peter would never have dared to say such a thing.

"Someone had to take the blame, my dear Peter. If I had, it would have destroyed our brotherhood."

"And your ambitions."

"Yes, my ambitions for the good of Mor and Holy Church."

"I see," Peter replied sarcastically.

"Enough of this, Peter. If I had no concern for you, a dagger would have found your back years ago to protect myself against your possible revenge."

"But, such a death would have been traced to you, and what would the rest of our dear brotherhood say of an archbishop's dispatching his loyal secretary in such a way? Besides, Zimri, I've stayed loyal, though Heaven knows why. And what is more, you need me. Otherwise, you would have been content to leave me in exile in the Ezrian Court."

Zimri looked away for a moment. It was almost true. At times, he wished he had quietly dispatched Peter, a possible rival, but a bond existed between them that he could not fathom. And it was true as well that he needed Peter, now that the crisis was drawing near.

Peter sensed the conflicting emotions running through Zimri. He half expected an emotional outburst but was shocked instead when Zimri stepped forward and touched him lightly on the shoulder. Almost instinctively, Peter reached up and placed his hand atop Zimri's.

Zimri stood rigid, as if wrestling an unseen demon. Then, with a short, nervous laugh, he moved away from Peter and pulled up a chair to sit down by the open stove.

"Ah, that's better. It's so damn cold out there. Heat, any kind of heat, became an obsession, an all-consuming thought."

"I know," Peter replied lamely, confused by Zimri's curious actions.

"So tell me, Peter, how stands the mood of the Ezrian church concerning this Prophet."

"Can I not ask first," Peter responded, "why you have summoned me back after five years of silence?"

He knew the question was coming and was ready with the response. "Peter, I exiled you as ambassador to the Ezrian church for two reasons. To save your life by getting you out of the sight of our own Church after the debacle before Mathin and to prepare a way for what I knew would be the next step in the campaign. I need to know your personal observations of Ezra. After you tell me, then I will share with you what I know."

Peter took another sip of his Yawinder and looked dreamily at the ruby-colored glass. For years, he had wasted away at Cadez, unable even to speak the barbaric tongue of the Ezrians. For five years, he had plotted a hundred different ways to kill Zimri. But the light embrace had confused his thoughts of vengeance for the moment. Peter suspected it was a simple maneuver, of the sort Zimri had used to maneuver the deacon. But a deep well of loneliness was also apparent in Zimri, and he wondered if the touch was an effort to atone for the past.

Peter sipped again, watching Zimri closely.

"Damn it all, Peter," Zimri whispered. "I need you, now more than ever. A crisis is coming, one that I have precipitated, and I must confess that there are moments when I am afraid. I need someone I can trust. That is why I have sent for you, and that is why I need you."

Embarrassed, Zimri stood up and started to pace around the room. "There, I said it. And I won't say it again."

He turned away for a moment, and when he faced Peter again, his expression was one of cold indifference. "Now, as I asked before, what are Ezra's attitudes toward the Prophet?"

"It's difficult to say."

"How so?"

There were so many different ways he could interpret the information to Zimri. Ezra was waiting for Cornath's reaction in the forthcoming crisis, suspecting that somehow it was a situation created by the Cornathians to undermine Ezra's inherent advantage in the South. It was Ezra's feeling that Zimri created the problem, and Zimri would have to live with it. The Church of Ezra would, however, honor First Choice. Peter had other contacts, as well, the implied positions available inside the Ezrian structure. But, of course, nothing would be said about that.

"A strong feeling exists against the Prophet, to be sure," Peter began cautiously, "but there is just as strong a distrust of you and your intentions, concerning both him and Ezra."

"How so?"

"They believe that you set Ormson up to negate their successes against us in the Southward Isles. It will take a lot to eliminate that impression."

"I see," Zimri replied noncommittally. He wondered how much of it was Peter's and how much a true image of the Ezrian rulers.

"What of our counterpart, the warrior brotherhood of Ezra?"

"Ah, now that *is* interesting. They've been calling for a Holy War against Ormson—at least the lower ranks have—but their leader, Holiness Palao, has remained silent on the matter. Not I, nor anyone else for that matter, knows if he holds any other position on the issue besides 'wait and see.'"

"Could we get Ezra to move against the Prophet? Especially if, say, we were to offer them something for their support."

Peter hesitated. He had heard rumors about contacts from another source—contacts from Inys Gloi to Ezra. How much should he state? And after a quick calculation, he chose the path of caution.

"Look at it from our perspective," Peter ventured. "Would we ally with them if they called upon us?"

"It would depend upon the threat to the First Choice. Ormson has violated the First Choice, or have you forgotten that?"

Peter tried to feign confusion over the comment, but Zimri waved his playacting aside.

"Yes, Peter, I know you try to conceal it, but I know that you are fully aware of the First Choice. Balor told me. You are one of the few outside the archbishops and Balor's brotherhood who know about the full meaning of the Choice and have lived to contemplate its meaning."

Peter nodded slowly in response. So Zimri knew and would not have him killed as a result. One less fear to contend with. He leaned across the table and picked up the blue master's piece from a Flyswin set that rested on the abbot's desk. He examined the piece carefully while responding to Zimri's questioning.

"If Ormson has any sense to him, which we all know he has, all he needs to do is to sit back and let us come to him. Fight us in the traditional way on his home ice, while offering trade concessions to Ezra. If he does that, we will never win against him. And all of Ezra knows that."

"But, my dear Peter, you assume that Ormson is calculating enough to view it that way."

"Tell me, Zimri, are you planning a war against Ormson?" Zimri was silent.

"Zimri, I must assume that you already knew all the answers to the questions you posed concerning Ezra. Therefore, why did you summon me across five hundred leagues of ice? Surely not to rehash information you already know."

"Ah, my dear Peter," Zimri replied with a chuckle, "you *have* improved. You *are* asking for the real reasons behind our little visit?"

"Precisely."

"Then I will not hold back." Zimri sipped at the Yawinder and looked over the rim of the goblet at Peter. One decision, of which Peter was not even aware, had already been made. The armed guards would not be needed, after all. Peter could be trusted not to betray him outright, and his services could be of genuine value in dealing with Ezra.

"Peter, might I ask a favor first?"

"Anything."

"Take that damn dagger out of your tunic. You won't need it here."

Peter smiled, suppressing an inward curse. What traitor among his servants had tipped Zimri off?

Reaching into his robes, he pulled out the long, thin Ezrian stiletto and, with a casual flick, tossed it to the floor at Zimri's feet.

"That's better."

"Of course, I assume that you won't have me poisoned, then," Peter said with a cold laugh.

Zimri let out a full, deep laugh. "We are two from the same mold, Peter. No, I think we would be fools to argue at this point."

"Why this point?"

"Pour me some more of that." Zimri held out his goblet.

Peter emptied the decanter into Zimri's cup.

"It will become obvious to most within the month. I've forced the hand of Holy Church."

"How so?"

"I can't tell you everything yet, but if my plans work, Ormson will venture forth with fire and sword in a war of vengeance against us."

"You would have to hit something very close to his heart to have him drop his doctrine of nonbelligerence."

"I have."

Peter weighted the possible options. "His family?"

Zimri smiled.

"I see. So you need me to bring Ezra to our side."

Zimri leaned forward, his excitement showing. "Next spring, the Council will elect the new Holy See. At the same time, Ormson will be poised for his assault against us. Half the archbishops are in on this already. Madoc is my main concern—he stands a better chance than I to gain the chair. I need two things from you. First, you shall offer yourself to Madoc's service. It would seem logical to him. After all, it was I who destroyed your career and sent you into exile. Tell me what you can of his plans against me. Second, I want you to assure Ezra that if they will aid me in my drive for the See and guarantee their neutrality in our war with Ormson, I shall cede to them all territory owned by Sol."

"And the rewards for this service?"

"An ambassadorship from the Holy See to the Primate of Ezra, and I shall select you to be my political heir."

"I was rather hoping to be archbishop of Mor," Peter replied cautiously.

"In due time, Peter, in due time. I must control Mor for the time being."

"Highly irregular, though. Tradition demands that the Holy See turn over his archbishopric to someone else."

"I want direct control of Mor for the crisis to come, and that is settled," Zimri replied caustically. "After the crisis, there will be more than enough time to arrange for your rise in power."

Peter stood up, the Flyswin piece still in his hand, and he walked over to the window that looked out over the Frozen Sea. Five days earlier, when the summons came, he half expected death, assuming that Zimri had learned of the leaks to the hierarchy of the Ezrian church. And now this. He turned to face Zimri, a look of confusion on his face.

"Why?"

"Because I need someone, my dear Peter. I think of what I've just done to bring about the crisis. It had to be done, of course." Zimri stopped for a moment, as if confused. "Perhaps I am just afraid that this time I need someone, a friend, to stand behind me—I might have pushed the gamble right to the very edge."

Peter looked to him and nodded. "If I understand Ormson at all, I would think you most likely have."

CHAPTER 9

"Michael, it's time." A gentle hand touched his shoulder.

"Janis?"

"Michael." The voice was soft but deep, far too deep.

"Janis!" He came out of the darkness thrashing. Hands grabbed him, strong and supportive, holding his arms to his side. Cowan was holding him.

"Janis?" Michael asked in a soft, pleading voice.

"It's all right," Cowan said. "Do you know where you are?"

Michael nodded.

"Do you remember?"

"How long has it been since . . ."

"Three days, Michael."

He could remember. "What do you mean, it's time?" Michael asked cautiously, looking around the room. The chamber still wore the scars of battle, the tapestries were torn and scorched, the doorway charred. Though the carpets had been removed, the exposed floor was dark with blood.

Daniel stood beside Cowan, his arm in a sling, his face pinched and drawn by exhaustion and fever. Behind Daniel stood Seth and Eldric. They were dressed in ceremonial robes.

Polished weapons hung at their sides, and mourning bands of black cloth hung from their helmets.

"I don't remember going to sleep," Michael said wearily as he stood.

Cowan beckoned to the door, and two Companions entered, bearing a black cape, tunic, and parka.

"Seth prepared a potion for you, Michael. We didn't tell you, but you hadn't slept in two days. You needed to regain your strength."

"Yes, I suppose I did."

He looked to Seth. "Thank you."

Michael walked over to the window. "When did you get back from your voyage?" he asked absently.

"The morning after," Seth replied. "Don't you remember?"

"No . . . I guess I don't."

He looked out the window and was silent for several minutes. "It's time for the funeral, is it not?"

"Yes, master."

He remembered it all now. Yes, it was time. It was definitely time to begin. "I want the robes that I had on before," Michael said coldly.

They were silent.

"Damn it, did you hear me? I will not wear the mourning robes. I want the robes of a Companion."

"Michael, it's bloodstained and torn," Daniel responded cautiously.

Michael looked at him savagely. "I know, and you heard what I said. Now do it!"

Cowan nodded to the two guards, who left the room. Several minutes passed in silence as Michael stared through the window. The great square was packed, the multitudes spilling onto the harbor. He could see them by the tens of thousands, covering the ice as far as the horizon. And beyond the wall, a single ship waited, its sleek, handsome lines silhouetted by the morning sun.

The guards approached, bearing the battle garments that he had worn only three days before. He had forgotten how bad they looked. His shield was dented, and dark stains covered the embossed tree of Mathin. The parka—he looked away for a moment.

I must not cry, he thought grimly. I must show strength.

He felt himself shaking, the image floating up before him.

"Dada!..."

"Michael, maybe you better not?" Cowan asked softly.

"Damn it, Cowan!" he shouted. "I said I would wear them. Let the world see—let it see what happened." Michael reached out and grabbed the parka from the guard. Flecks of dry blood shook off into his hands. The front of the jacket and his breeches, as well, were stained from the shoulders to the knees.

Let them see. Unflinchingly, he eyed the men before him, and they stood silent as he pulled on the garments, washed in the blood of Janis and Andrew.

When he finished dressing, Michael looked up at the men. "It's time," he said grimly.

Michael realized that they were not looking at him so much as at the garments that he wore. But he offered no response to their concerned looks as he crossed the room and stepped out into the hallway.

Turning into the corridor, he found both sides of the wall lined with his men, many of them bearing the scars of battle. The ranks were thin; many familiar faces were missing, but he paid that no heed as he strode the length of the corridor and down the stairs.

His men stood to the side—grim, silent. As if floating in a dream, Michael walked past them into the audience chamber. Two high-back chairs still rested against the far wall. He hesitated for a moment, gazing at them. He could feel the abyss opening up, but he forced it down with a supreme effort.

No, not there.

Michael felt for a moment as if he were drowning. He gasped for breath. A hand came to rest on his shoulder, but he shrugged it off and walked to the funeral bier.

Michael walked to the bier. Struggling for control, he gazed down. She was still—cold and frozen. Her left arm was drapped protectively around the shoulder of the smaller body beside her. He felt his control slip away. With a convulsive sob, he tore himself away and strode from the citadel into the early-morning light.

The sea of faces turned, and as if a command had been shouted, they fell silent and went to their knees. He sensed the shock that the bloodstained garments caused, but the emotion of the crowd was beyond him. He walked past them, unseeing and untouched. Michael could hear his men marching, carrying the bier. A quiet murmur ran through the crowd, punctuated here and there by wild cries of mourning, but he heeded them not.

Guards, some still carrying battle-stained equipment, ranged out ahead and to either side, searching for yet another blow. But he knew that such a blow would not come, even as he wished it would.

Onward Michael walked, not noticing or caring if the rest kept pace behind him. All were silent as he passed, but behind him, the wails of lamentation swelled as his wife, child, and the hundred and fifty others who had died were carried across the great square of Mathin and on out into the harbor.

He realized suddenly that he was walking on ice. Instinctively, he changed his gait to a slow, sliding shuffle. The two towers passed behind, and before him at last loomed the *Bayeuth*, pride of Eldric's fleet of light frigates. A rigging crew was standing along the railings; the stern hatch was thrown wide open, its interior a tunnel of darkness. Michael walked to the side of the ship, where a tower of ice had been built. The stairs, carved into the side of the tower, were lined with guards, who came to attention at his approach. Walking up the stairs until he was even with the deck of the ship, Michael turned back and looked out over the sea of humanity that was following him.

In the center of the swarming crowd rose the bier of Janis and Andrew, carried by twenty men, Daniel in front. Behind them followed a hundred and fifty open coffins, each one containing a member of his guard killed in the struggle. The first of the coffins were brought up alongside the ship and carried up the stern hatchway where places had been prepared for the final voyage. Lines were lowered from the main deck, and the bier containing Janis and Andrew was hoisted up into position to rest on the open deck.

After supervising the loading of the other coffins, Daniel climbed to Michael's side.

"Where's Elijah?" Michael whispered.

"Below."

"No, I want him on deck. They would have liked that, I think."

Daniel nodded and went below. Several minutes passed; then a hatchway was thrown open. Four men struggled up from below with their burden. Michael crossed over the gangplank and joined the men, helping them bring the battered body topside. With loving care, he guided the body over to rest alongside the silent forms of Andrew and Janis. He could feel his control slipping away.

"Clear this ship," he cried hoarsely.

"Master, are you all right?" a guard replied.

"You heard me; please clear this ship. Quickly, now."

Daniel looked searchingly at Michael, fearful of some drastic action.

Michael looked into Daniel's tear-streaked eyes.

"For Heaven's sake, Daniel, I just want to be alone with them for one last minute. Please leave us alone."

Daniel nodded. "Clear the ship," he growled, waving his hand in a sweeping gesture.

Michael barely noticed them as he turned back and stood over the bier. The grief, the tears of agony, spilled out. "Why, why, Zimri?"

He threw his arms around their cold, rigid bodies and collapsed into hysterical weeping. "Damn you, Zimri, damn you forever! Why them instead of me?"

He remembered all that had been, all the life that he had lived and had dreamed of. He tried to conjure up Janis's smiling presence, wishing to see her again, praying that her ghost would appear to give him comfort and to prove the separation was not final. But nothing came of it, just the bitter, penetrating cold that had frozen her image, turning it into ice. Time slipped away into darkness.

"Michael." The voice was like a whisper, a distant shout. He started to awake.

"Janis!" he screamed, struggling to stand.

She was cold, dead, and he heard the shouts again—shouts of anguish.

"Michael, Michael, Michael..."

They were calling, calling by the thousands. He looked at her and the small form next to her, and his heart was frozen forever.

"Good-bye, my loves, my life." He bent over, kissing their

forms and then turned away to remount the ice platform.

The ship's crew, seeing him leave, looked to Eldric, who nodded.

The men swarmed onto the ship. Grimly silent, they scurried aloft, each to his assigned position. Eldric, Cowan, and Seth had come to stand on the platform along with Daniel and Michael. Eldric raised his arm and let it fall. As if guided by his single hand, all the sails shot out of their casings at the same time, the crews below pulling in the halyards and then cleating the sheets down tight. From overside, there was the clear high ringing of axes as the anchor crews cut away the ship's lines. Finson stood on the deck, tying down the wheel, locking the rudders into position. The ship groaned—a shudder ran through her, and with a start, she broke free of the icy bonds and accelerated forward. The men swarmed out of the riggings, dropping hurriedly to the ice.

The ship began to gain speed. Michael felt himself moving forward, drawn by the passing of the ship. A wild impulse seized him, and with a desperate shout, he rushed to leap onto the deck of the ship. Michael barely noticed the heavy arms that coiled around him.

"Michael, you can't; please stop."

He swayed. The strength of Eldric held him while she drifted by, and the small form resting by her side, the old warrior resting by their feet.

A sigh went up from the crowd as the ship pulled away, picking up speed as it ran abeam the wind on a southerly course. From over her stern, Finson appeared. He hesitated for a moment, looked back, then grabbing hold of a rope, he swung over the side to the ice below.

Within minutes, the ship's hull disappeared over the horizon. Soon only its highest mast was visible—a slender line of dark on the far-distant ice. Sometime during the night, the ship would reach the Flowing Sea and be lost forever.

Michael watched as it receded farther and farther. He turned away for a moment, looked back, and it was gone.

Turning, he faced his people. They were silent except for a low, distant sound of mourning. Michael watched them, drained of all feeling, and he realized that all were facing him, wondering, waiting. He gave himself over at last.

He reached to his scimitar and, with a deep guttural yell,

pulled it free from its scabbard. The sword arched overhead, catching the morning light, its blade still stained with dark blood. He held the sword up, raising his arms heavenward in a gesture of rage and despair.

As he screamed, a high, dark voice answered from the multitude that had waited for this moment.

It had begun at last, as he always knew it would. Daniel was beside him, waving his battle-ax, calling for revenge and death. Seth, Eldric, and even Cowan followed, all of them alight with a strange, fanatical frenzy.

Michael Ormson looked across the Ice. And from ten thousand men, the answer to his desire came. As if guided by one hand, ten thousand swords rose from their scabbards in answer to the master's call. An ocean of razor-sharp steel was held aloft, ready to do his bidding.

Michael embraced the calling. From the beginning, he had known that this would one day come to pass. And he gave himself over to it, purging all other thought—all other desire—from his soul.

The Holy War, the Crusade, had come at last.

BOOK IV

Frigate

BOOK IV

CHAPTER 10

"GREGORSON, LOOK, THERE TO THE SOUTHWEST. DON'T you see it?"

The Cornathian guard leaned out over the wall and looked where his comrade was pointing. "Ragarth, I see nothing."

The guard continued to point into the darkness. Overhead, the Arch still cut a shimmering band of light; however, in the east, its silvery band disappeared into the scarlet of dawn.

"There, can't you see it? By the Saints, I'm calling the priest."

Ragarth fled from the ice wall that surrounded the Cornathian trading post of Ivar and raced to the long barrack shed below, which housed the two hundred guards of Cornath's most southerly outpost.

Gregorson stood alone atop the fifty-foot-high watchtower, carved from the winter's ice. Suddenly, he heard a muffled shout from the building below. Looking down into the courtyard, Gregorson saw a dark blue robe appear in the doorway— a Morian priest. The cleric raced across the open space and ascended the ladder. Breathless, the heavy monk reached the top of the platform.

145

"By all the Saints," the monk shouted, "sound the alarm. You damned fool. It's the Mathinians."

Gregorson raced along the wall, grabbed hold of the long wooden horn, and gave breath to it while the monk called from the tower that they were under attack.

A host of men poured out of the barracks, their breath freezing in the bitter wind. Turning away from the rapidly approaching fleet Gregorson looked across the narrow harbor of Ivar and watched as the frantic crews of fifty or sixty Cornathian trade ships screamed and raged at the fate that awaited them.

"There, a rocket, three of them to the northwest," Ragarth shouted as he returned to his post atop the watcher's tower. Gregorson faced into the wind and watched the red light of the flares plummeting back to the ice. To the south, a formation of ships veered off and started to run parallel to the fortress wall at a range of several miles.

Four men rushed up the ladder, crowding the small space atop the watchtower. Two of them were carrying heavy wall-mounted crossbows; their comrades each carried a bundle of quarrels. The men lifted the weapons up onto the wall and mounted them on wooden swivels, which were permanently embedded in the ice.

"Rofeson, can we hold them?" Ragarth shouted, his voice cracking with fear.

The commander of the crossbow section was quiet, his steel gray eyes locked onto his weapons, ignoring all else around him. Rofeson worked the pulleys on his weapon, while the second bow captain imitated his actions on the other weapon. They laboriously cranked back the bows and locked the strings into position.

The ships drew closer and closer. After the initial excitement of the alarm, the Cornathians had fallen into a nervous silence from which even the priests could not rouse them with their calls for battle and prayers.

"Must be two hundred ships at least," Rofeson's assistant mumbled pensively.

"'Tis the Saint-cursed Prophet, to be sure," the monk whispered, blessing himself, then mumbling a prayer against possession.

The men looked at him with fearful expressions.

The tower rocked as the harbor-gate battlement fired a warning shot. The fleet sailed on in silence, closing with every second.

"Range is one mile," Rofeson shouted.

One of the heavy frigates of the Mathinian fleet opened up with its four bow chasers, and as it fired, it turned to windward, exposing a full broadside. All down the line, the armed merchantmen, sloops, and frigates fired their bow chasers, then turned across the wind to let fly with their full weight of metal. The monk counted off the seconds.

"There, I see one! It's . . ." Gregorson shouted. Even as he pointed, the ball screamed past, missing the tower by half a dozen yards. The harbor wall exploded in plumes of ice as dozens of shots found their mark. Overhead, the air was torn by the demented scream of passing cannon shot that arched over the wall to bound into the harbor enclosure, wreaking havoc among the parked shipping, which was now cut off from escape.

The two dozen guns of the Cornathians responded, but every minute they were answered by twenty times their number.

The attacking fleet again came across the wind, closing the range to less than half a mile. The Cornathian guns gave ragged answer. Here and there, the Cornathian crews cheered as they found their target. A sloop folded up like a smashed toy as a shot tore away its foreskates, sending it into a death roll—but still the Prophet's fleet pressed the attack. Behind the attacking screen, Gregorson could make out a series of heavy, open rafts coming into the wind at a thousand yards. The ice was aswarm with thousands of figures that formed into open columns and waited for the action to unfold.

The gunships fired their volleys, came into the wind, and closed the range to four hundred yards. As they turned to port, their broadsides fired again. One of the bow assistants screamed in anguish as the north side of the ice tower was torn away by a forty-eight pound ball. The young Cornathian crumpled up, kicked spasmodically for several seconds, then was still. The monk ran up and turned the body over. The entire front of the head was gone, torn away by a block of splintered ice. To everyone's horror, the heart was still pumping, showering blood with every pulse from the torn remains of the bow loader's face. The monk pushed the dying body off the side of the tower.

The men in the tower started to rage and scream at the Mathinian ships as they drew closer and closer. As the fleet smashed down the heavy defenses of the harbor, one by one, the Cornathian guns fell silent. Miraculously, the tower only received the one hit; a narrow target, it was difficult to hit from a moving ship.

Three green rockets rose above the heavy frigate.

"Here they come!" Gregorson shouted.

From eight hundred yards out, the host started to advance, their battle chant carrying on the wind. *"Marwth du Cornath, Marwth du Cornath, Prathe ba Ormson."*

Scimitars and axes sparkled coldly as the orderly lines swept forward, the men propelling themselves on skates. Dozens of small rafts advanced with the men, each raft carrying a tower and a defensive crew armed with heavy crossbows. A number of open-deck sloops advanced with them, and on the forecastle of each, a light carronade was mounted, loaded with grape and designed to clear the walls of defenders.

At four hundred yards, the attack force hit the antiship barrier line. Here and there, a man fell to the impalement traps, but the host pressed on. The sloops and rafts were held back until the first wave marked the channels, at which point the craft were pushed through by hand.

Several of the Cornathian guns were still firing, and their crews switched from solid shot to grape, plowing occasional bloody furrows through the advancing lines. The fleet still maintained its bombardment, aiming high in order to sweep the battlements and sow confusion in the harbor enclosure beyond.

Rofeson, his two surviving men, and the monk brought the crossbows to bear. With his first shot, Rofeson hit an advancing siege tower, the bolt pinning a man to the deck. But Mathinian crossbow bolts spat back in reply. In a matter of seconds, another one of Rofeson's men was down, an arrow driven clean through his forehead.

"Gregorson, help me!" Rofeson screamed.

Gregorson grabbed hold of the winch and worked the firing arms back into position.

The attack came closer. The chanting of the host became a thundering roar that drowned out all other noise.

The first wave of skaters hit the antipersonnel ditches. Dozens of men fell through the ice, their screams rising above the chants as they hit the sharpened stakes concealed beneath the ice. The siege towers maneuvered past them.

Rofeson fired again, sweeping the deck of a sloop and killing the pilot. The ship skidded as the tiller swung free.

The crew atop the tower shouted with insane glee as the sloop slid into an antipersonnel trap. It hovered in precarious balance for several seconds, then toppled over.

The range was less than a hundred yards, and the chanting host swarmed forward. The Mathinians reached the base of the wall, and hundreds of grappling hooks arched upward. All along the defense line, the Cornathians rained down a shower of death. Even before the siege towers were maneuvered into position, the white-clad forms of Mathin appeared along the top of the battlements. A swarm of arrows swept the tower, killing the crew of the second crossbow. In the wild insanity of battle, Gregorson watched silently as the defenses gave way under the flood of attack. Cornathians broke and ran, leaping to the ice of the inner harbor. As the siege towers were maneuvered into place, a flood of men poured out, sweeping the walls clear of defenders. The monk shouted with rage as Cornathians fell on their knees begging for mercy, only to be cut down by the enraged attackers.

"There!" the monk screamed. "Don't you see him?"

Gregorson looked to where the monk was pointing. One of the heavy frigates was maneuvering toward the wall, led by half a dozen men on skatesails who were marking the channel that led to the harbor gate. Standing on the foredeck was an armored column of men.

Gregorson looked around the watchtower. Rofeson was half dead, a bolt through his chest, but still he fought on. The battle had swept past them into the harbor. Gregorson looked over the edge of the tower. A swarm of Mathinians was scaling its side.

"The Prophet!" the monk screamed. "The Prophet is in the middle of that group. Rofeson, in the name of the Saints, shoot him!"

Rofeson swung the bow around and drew a steady aim. The

priest came alongside of him to help with the weapon.

"Shoot, damn it," the priest shouted, "before it's too late!"

Rofeson placed his hand on the trigger.

"I think I . . ." He fell backward, screaming in anguish and surprise.

The priest swung around. Gregorson stood before the body of Rofeson, scimitar raised, its blade steaming with Rofeson's blood.

"You, damn you! Saint-cursed traitor."

Gregorson smiled as he raised his sword and swung it in a hissing arc that swept off the priest's head.

There was a sound behind him. Turning, he faced a Companion who was swinging himself up onto the tower. Gregorson ripped his tunic aside and held out a silver medallion that was concealed beneath his furs.

"Marwth du Cornath!" he shouted.

The Mathinian guard looked at him closely and nodded.

"The protection of the Prophet," he replied warmly.

Gregorson bowed low, and turning, he buried his sword in the dark blue robes of the priest.

"The revenge of Ormson!" he shouted while he slashed, and slashed again.

CHAPTER 11

"SO, YOU HAVE ARRIVED SAFELY."

"Yes, my lord."

The Grand Master gazed out the window that overlooked the windswept courtyard, five hundred feet below. A dozen brothers were passing through the gate, their merchant robes billowing in the fresh northwesterly breeze. In the harbor beyond rested a dilapidated schooner. Its lines marked the vessel as an aging blockade runner out of Lismar. The traffic had been heavy of late, usually arriving in the first light of dawn and departing again at sunset.

"Did you encounter any difficulty slipping away?" he inquired, still looking out the window.

"The usual, my lord. I believe Michael knew where I was going this time, but he asked no questions."

The master turned from the window and looked at the man who knelt before him. "Rise, Seth Facinn, the Far-seeing."

Seth rose up and stared intently at the leader of Inys Gloi.

"Relax, my friend, be seated," the master said softly, leading Seth to the high-back chair next to his desk.

"Now, let us talk frankly," the master said quietly as he eased into his ivory chair.

Seth nodded, looking at the black-robed form, his face concealed by a light opaque veil. He could remember the time, so long ago, when they had been equals. But that friendship was gone forever; it died the moment his friend had reached the Sacred Throne.

"Tell me why you believe Ormson knew of your journey here."

"It cannot be defined clearly, my lord. I have often said it before—Ormson has some strange, indefinable power. It is absolutely amazing to witness. He can bend anyone to his will by a simple word and that terrible compelling gaze. And in that look, he can read your soul. When I told him that I was leaving for a while, he didn't ask any questions. All he did was look at me with that strange, terrifying gaze. And I knew he had stripped me bare."

"Describe this look."

"You've heard it before, master. It's a look that pierces your heart, as if you had been shot through the soul. As he gazes upon you with that soft, distant, dreamy look, you feel as if the lies, the deceits, and even the dreams are being torn from you and held up for his personal scrutiny. And...and it is hard to say what else."

"Try."

Agitated, Seth stood up and started to pace around the room. He swung around suddenly and faced the master. "I've seen him; you haven't. Ever since Janis, it's been worse—far worse. It's as if he has decided to let go of his power, to let go of it so that it could possess him. All he needs to do is walk into a room and everyone, everything, is riveted by his presence. He can look at a man, order him to certain death, and the man will leave his presence with a strange elation, as if it is a privilege to die for the Prophet. By all that is Holy, it is terrifying to watch. And there are times, master, when I look at him and he seems to sense my gaze, and he returns it. And when he does, I swear that he knows, that he somehow knows it all. He sees the game within the game—and that we are the ones who are the pawns."

"Do you believe that now?" the master asked quietly.

"Now?...Here?" Seth fell silent for a moment and turned away. A nervous chuckle escaped and was quickly stilled.

"When I am here, safely within the walls of Inys Gloi, I

think differently. I think then of what our collective meditation has shown us. I think of how this meditation has guided our brotherhood for two thousand years, leading us inexorably to this moment when the One True Church, carrying out the secret plan of four millennia, will finally reach its victory. Oh, no, here I never doubt. When I am away from him, it is different."

"You're afraid of him, aren't you?"

Seth was silent, his back turned to the leader of Inys Gloi.

The master examined him closely. Here was the key link between the plans of Inys Gloi and the Prophet. Here was the one who, more than any other, had created the Prophet.

The master waited for an answer, and when none came, he ventured another question.

"Do you feel as if you are a traitor to him?"

Seth knew what the wrong answer would bring. Loyalty to Inys Gloi was the sworn obligation of every brother.

"No, I am still orthodox. In his presence, I am fearful, but ultimately it is Inys Gloi that must always come first."

"Of course, I never doubted you," the master replied warmly. "I just wanted you to voice what I knew you always felt. Now let us return to Ormson and his plans. Tell me what is happening with him. I have the reports, but I want to hear it from you, as well."

"The old dream of his youth lies shattered forever, as we knew it would be," Seth replied grimly.

The master nodded. "Continue."

"The evening after the funeral, he declared that a Holy War would decide the mastery of the Ice. All except Cowan agreed with his demand. In fact, his followers would have launched one with or without his approval. Ormson's power was always compelling, but now it is terrifying. For days on end, he disappears into the scarred, foul-smelling meditation chamber. Daniel places trays of food by the door, but they remain untouched. He spends four or five *days* in there at a time."

Seth shook his head sadly at the memory of Michael's gaunt form and feverish eyes.

"Go on."

"Some of his followers whisper that he is insane, but if anything, that only makes them more fanatical in their support of him—as if his agony was theirs as well. It seems as if the collective madness of our entire race has found expression in that one man and that through him society is ready to seek revenge for all that has transpired for the last two thousand years."

"And his current battle plans?"

"Michael's fleet has gone into summer quarters. They've driven the last of the Cornathian outposts off the Southern Shelf. At the earliest possible date, the Prophet's fleet will sail north with the intent of taking Caediff by Supplication Night. He'll take over forty thousand men and five hundred ships. They'll strip the Southward Shelf of everything they have. Master, it will be the largest invasion fleet to be seen since the campaign of Sol, over five hundred years ago."

"And what of his men."

"Ah, his men," Seth replied with a strange glint in his eyes. "To lead such men into battle. The fury of the common people who live upon the Southward Shelf has at last been unleashed. Even the freebooters have given themselves over to this madness. I was with them at Ivar, not two weeks ago. It was terrifying to behold. His men went into battle chanting his name and calling for death—the death of Cornath. They swarmed over the walls, frantic to be at the front. When the Companions were unleashed, there was no stopping them. The garrison was slaughtered to a man. And Michael did not lift a finger to stop them."

"Not even at the Mathinian Pass did I see such a thing."

"What was the difference?"

Seth looked past the master as if he were gathering in thoughts from a far distant dream. A faint, flickering smile crossed his face.

"At the Mathinian Pass, they died, to be sure," he stated softly, "but it was for something different—a dream, a hope, a belief in some better future, free from Church domination. But at Ivar, they went with a darkness in their soul—to destroy and finish forever a hated foe who deserved no mercy."

"And to replace it with what?" the master asked as if musing aloud.

"With us, of course," Seth replied coldly, and again there was the faint, nervous chuckle.

The master stood up and walked across the room to join Seth by the window. The Lismar schooner was already under sail, making its way slowly out to sea—its patchwork sails pulled taut to run abeam the wind on its first tack out past the harbor gate. From astern, light plumes of slush and water were kicked up by the passing of the blades.

"Have you met Varinna?" the master asked quietly, while resting his hand on Seth's shoulder.

"No."

He could sense the chill in Seth's voice.

"You will find her interesting, to be sure."

"She will have to be if this plan is to work."

"It is her duty to make it work. You merely have to place her in Caediff before you return to Mathin. When the time comes, you will know how to make the final arrangements."

The master turned away from Seth and returned to his desk. "You opened your heart to Janis, didn't you."

Seth was silent.

"She was the one factor that you lost control of. And that is why we planted the suggestion and allowed it to be carried out and, in so doing, created our present advantage. We nearly lost complete control of Michael because of her—the one unexpected twist that softened him and turned him away from his destiny. With Varinna, we shall bring him back into complete control for as long as we still need him."

Seth nodded sadly.

"Tonight we meet with the agents for Caediff and Cornath. Tomorrow you sail."

Seth nodded.

"Are there any questions?"

From the tone of the comment, Seth knew that he was dismissed.

He started for the door and then hesitated.

"Master, you've never met him or even seen him, have you?"

"No, you know that's so. Why do you ask?"

"There might come a day..."

"A day?"

"If there ever comes a day when Ormson discovers that we were the movers behind her death, there shall be no stopping him."

"He hasn't the power to challenge us. So the thought is ridiculous. Remember the power that our meditation gives us.

It is pointless to even waste our time pondering such things."

"I've watched him grow. It was I that the brotherhood chose to send into his presence. It was felt by all of us that I, Seth Facinn, the Far-seeing, the supreme master of meditation, should be the mentor of the Prophet. I have been with him nearly every step of the way for the last ten years, and I must speak what has come more and more often to my heart of late."

The master was silent.

"You see, my lord, at times, I fear that he is the puppet master, even though he might not yet be aware of it. But if he ever does become aware, then may the Saints protect us from what would come to pass."

Seth bowed low, and with a somber flourish wrapped his swirling robes around his body and disappeared through the low arched door.

After several minutes of silence, there was a discreet cough behind a paneled doorway.

"Yes," the master said wearily.

The door slipped open. A slender, hooded form entered the room. The robes were cut tight to reveal a full graceful form. "He seemed remorseful, fearful."

"'Tis to be expected. After all, it's been ten years for him. Of course, he can't help but fall under the influence."

"It could be our undoing."

The master nodded.

"We still need him. Remember, he is the key link to the Prophet."

"But not for long."

"You can still trust him. Without him, you'll never reach Michael."

"I am concerned about him nevertheless, my lord."

The master looked at the trained assassin of Inys Gloi. "Seth is sworn to us. He will not fail. Now leave me. I must prepare for a meeting with one of our good archbishops."

She laughed darkly. "Ah, one of our sisters told me of him— how easy that seduction was—a filthy pig, from what I've heard of his preferences."

"Enough, Varinna."

"As you wish, my lord," she whispered. Her voice was rich and seductive.

He turned from the door without watching her graceful feline movement.

He gazed out the window. The Lismar schooner was gone except for the faint outline of the mainmast on the far horizon.

"The puppet master," he whispered softly. "Who is the puppet master?"

CHAPTER 12

But what was the real intent? Zimri wondered, staring at Peter in the shimmering torchlight. "Are you sure?"

"Damn it, Zimri, what would be my motivation for lying?"

Zimri turned away. He looked down the long, narrow corridor. The two hundred monks who were to escort him in honor to the Holy Cathedral waited patiently for their master to lead them in the sacred procession.

"But why didn't you tell me earlier? By all the Saints, man, we are late enough already."

"Listen to me, Zimri. I will repeat it one more time. In fifteen minutes, Madoc plans to have you assassinated as you cross the courtyard to the Cathedral. Balor is in on the plot, as well. As you ordered, I've worked my way into his trust, betraying some of your minor secrets in order to gain his confidence. Less than an hour ago, he offered me the chair of archbishop, to be confirmed immediately after your death—so I could support his bid for the Holy See."

Zimri was silent for a moment. There had to be a trap in this. What true motivation would Peter have to support him? Surely personal loyalty was not the key.

"Madoc ordered me to stand beside you in the procession. When the signal for the attack is given, I am to trip the guard in front of you, thereby providing an opening for the attack."

"And then?"

"Step out of the way, and Madoc's men will do the rest. In the ensuing panic, I am to pick up your staff and hold it aloft, calling on the Morian brothers to rally to me. It is then my duty to blame the attack on the Prophet."

"So why are you betraying Madoc?"

"I have my reasons."

"Tell me."

"You can believe my words or forget them. But if you forget them, I guarantee your death before the hour is over."

"But he wouldn't dare. It's pure madness. Madoc holds half the votes already!"

"He knows you are a master, and of late he has grown fearful that you might have some hidden plan to bring him down at the last minute. Remember our information concerning that girl and the child that she carries—Madoc might be nervous that you will use that to embarrass him."

Zimri gave a disgusted grunt and looked away from Peter. Why any man would allow himself to be compromised in such a shoddy manner was beyond him, but that was not the issue. "What do you propose, then?"

"Take Valker; you've used him several times before as your double. Let him wear the miter and a face mask. No one will recognize the subterfuge."

"Impossible. If what you say is wrong, it will be impossible to work a switch at the end of the procession. In front of all of Dulyn, I will be humiliated as a coward when it is shown that I used a double in a sacred procession. And remember, at the end of the procession, the archbishop of Mor traditionally kisses the Sacred Icon. In the eyes of our brotherhood, only an archbishop can do that; for anyone else to attempt it is blasphemy. By all the Saints, I will lose face and the support of many if I did what you say."

"If you don't, you lose your life."

Zimri turned away from Peter and strode down the corridor into the darkness. Peter followed after him.

"Zimri! For heaven's sake, you must decide now."

Is this the trap? he wondered. I could lose it all right here by a clever plan to embarrass me in front of the people. He had to decide. "Send for Valker, but by all the Saints, Peter of Mor, you are a dead man if Valker does not fall in the square."

He saw them coming out of the darkness, the softly voiced chant announcing their arrival long before the head of the column came into view. The Great Icon of St. Mor passed by in the shadows, and he bowed low, as did the fifty other brothers in the column. Next came the ring of body guards, and in the center were Peter and the mitered archbishop. They passed into the dark, and the rest of the column came into view. Peter had nodded to him, but the archbishop had not. He knew what had to be done. Rank after rank, the monks of Mor passed, illuminated but for a moment by the torchlight. Two hundred, he counted as the last rank came into view. Balor could see him now. Peter had betrayed Madoc, after all. Perhaps it was for the best, but it was time for him to act. Balor stepped forward quickly, falling in directly behind the last rank, where a tall, slender form brought up the rear of the column. He stepped up to the form.

"Peter did first what I would have done, and it is for the best."

The form half turned, nodded, and then pressed on into the darkness.

They emerged out of the corridor into the smoke-filled interior of the Cathedral of Mor. As the Great Icon appeared at the head of the procession, the organ droned out the first stanza of the plain chant "To Mor, Bringer of Victory." And the monks lifted their voices in song. *"Do Mor Thorth dun Galathin."*

At the end of each line the cathedral bell tolled in deep, rhythmic countertime. Coming from behind the altar, the column split, passing the Sacred Shrine that bore the relics of St. Mor. As each line passed the Holy of Holies, the monks bowed low, turning their faces away from the most venerated of shrines. The altar was surrounded by twenty monks, who carried incense censers that emitted rolling clouds of dark green smoke. The procession continued down the broad, open nave of the cathedral past six cannon, which had been set on display at measured intervals. Around each gun, more brothers waved censers of holy incense, so that the cathedral was wreathed in dark, rolling clouds.

"Mor Glarn Ulsach Miser Holth."

As if guided by unseen hands, the doors of the cathedral swung open, flooding the semidarkness with the brilliant light of dawn. A great shout went up from the square, then fell away into silence as the image of Mor appeared before the multitude.

They could hear other chants echoing in the plaza beyond.

The procession stepped through the ornately carved portals, led by the dozen monks carrying the portrait of St. Mor. In front of the cathedral, the pilgrims fell to their knees, covering their eyes at the presence of the Great Icon.

The monks picked up the chant "To Saint Mor, in our hour of victory."

Zimri looked across the great square of Dulyn, crowded to overflowing with tens of thousands of the faithful. As the procession of Mor cleared the doorway of the cathedral, the front of the procession of the Mord Rinn came into view in the northwestern corner of the square. Madoc was at the fore, the gold and silver trim of his vestments shimmering in the cool summer wind. Behind the Mord Rinn marched the order of St. Awstin, with Archbishop Isaac at the lead. Their numbers, however, were a mere shadow of what had once been the most powerful of all the orders. The origin of the Prophet and the sin of Rifton had dealt a near-fatal blow to the order. The people turned to Mor and Mord Rinn for guidance in these dark times.

Heavily armed monks of Mor cleared a path for the procession, driving the people back as they clamored for Zimri's blessing. There were scattered calls in support of Zimri as Holy See. Arguments and fights erupted as the procession passed, and the mob, calling for its various heroes, broke into passionate brawls. Tension rose as the supporters of the various brotherhoods called out in anger and support. A horn sounded, unexpectedly, high and clear in the distance.

Is this it? Zimri thought instinctively, recognizing that the horn was some sort of signal.

A commotion began ahead, and Zimri pushed forward through the brothers, some of whom cursed, not knowing who he was. As he reached the head of the column, he was greeted by wild shouts of confusion. Valker had stopped. A shout had gone up from the guards on either side. Zimri was deafened by the shouting of the crowd, which washed over him.

Valker turned, looking back toward him, his mouth hanging open. He appeared to be screaming, but the sound was swallowed up by the roaring of the crowd. A throwing disk protruded from his forehead, and a trickle of blood ran from the wound into the eye sockets—so that he had the appearance of a red-eyed demon. Next to him several Morian priests were down, thrashing and convulsing horribly in their agony. The mob swayed around him, so that he was knocked off his feet in the swirling confusion.

Madness reigned, and over it all came a high, clear shout.

"Zimri is dead! Zimri is dead!"

He had to keep his senses, but panic welled as the bodies crushed down on him, and he kicked out wildly searching for escape. As quickly as he had fallen, however, he found himself being dragged to his feet. Peter's arms were around his shoulder.

"All right?"

"I think so."

"Quick, my lord, we have to act fast." Peter held the miter and stained ceremonial robes. "Put them on!" he shouted above the wild uproar.

Zimri sensed the plan and followed Peter's orders. Even as he donned the miter, he pushed forward through the confusion.

"I live!" he shouted. "The assassin missed, and I live!"

Those of his men who had been close by immediately saw that a double had been used, but they kept silent. However, those who were a little farther back saw Zimri's form, as if risen from the dead, and in wild relief they called his name.

A chant started echoing across the square.

"Zimri, Zimri . . ."

He turned to Peter and grabbed hold of him by the shoulders. "I owe you my life, Peter. How can I repay you?"

"There will be a way," Peter replied with a smile.

A wave of nausea swept through Zimri—the dead man could have been him. He pushed the thought away. "Bring Valker's body."

A captain of fifty stepped forward.

"Any prisoners?" Zimri shouted above the yelling.

"None, my lord. We slew three; two at least escaped." He sensed the rage of his men, and their shock when they recognized Zimri, his hood pulled back. The guard fell to his knees.

"My lord, I thought that—"

"Never mind that now; let us continue with the procession."

Two of the monks bearing the Holy Icon had been struck down, as well, and Zimri quickly blessed them. Before any could stop him, he picked up Valker's body and made his way forward to the steps of the cathedral—his monks forming a protective shield around him.

Gaining the steps, Zimri approached the great door. The processions from the other brotherhoods broke their ranks in the confusion and clustered around him. In the press, he saw a knot of archbishops standing by the door. He ignored them.

Reaching the door, he turned and faced the multitude who pressed forward, shouting. Voices echoed and re-echoed across the square, calling his name. As he stood silent, the shouts of the mob gradually died away.

"Behold, people of Dulyn and all people of the Cornathian Brotherhoods. This is what our Church has sunk to. I came today as Protector of our Faith, and here, within the very shadow of our Blessed Cathedral, I was greeted with death.

"This, my good people, was not the work of the Prophet. This was not the work of an enemy from without. This came from within!"

Zimri turned and pointed to the open doors of the church. "This deed came from within these sacred halls. The masters of it stand even now within sight of us all. People of Dulyn, when I arrived here yesterday, I came as the Sword of Our Church, to protect us in the days to come. But I stand before you now as the Scourge of Our Church, who shall purge it of those who would betray us to our enemies. It is time now to choose, oh, people of the Cornathian Brotherhood. Shall we, in our cowardice, fall into the darkness, betraying the Faith of our forefathers who sit at the Long Table in judgment? Or shall we triumph? And in so doing, preserve the Promise of the Garden and the Return of Our Blessed Father!"

Zimri turned from the multitude. He was greeted with stunned silence. Then from the back of the mob came a cry.

"Zimri as Holy See! Save us, lord Zimri!"

Even before the words had drifted away, it was picked up, echoed and re-echoed by tens of thousands, their voices crashing against the cathedral like storm-driven waves.

As he reached the door, he looked toward Madoc and Isaac and smiled grimly.

The holy services lasted the remainder of the morning. The followers of the fourteen brotherhoods filled the cavernous nave of the Blessed Cathedral. Balor, as archbishop of the First Choice, led them in prayer and ritual. Upon entering the church, Zimri refused to sit before the altar with the other archbishops and stood instead with the monks of his order. The great mosaic of the Father dominated the front of the cathedral—the image was cloaked in a white flowing robe, its back turned, conveying a deep, all-consuming contempt, which seemed to mirror Zimri's action.

At noon, when the light of the sun arched through the green stained-glass windows that represented the lost Garden of Paradise, the services came to an end.

The thirteen archbishops before the altar formed into twin ranks and exited through the door concealed at the back of the altar table. The door was used for only one occasion—the passing of the archbishops into the Chamber of Decision, where the voting for the new Holy See would take place.

Zimri stepped forward from the orderly ranks of his brothers and strode to the front of the church. The cathedral was silent as he joined the rear of the procession and followed the ornately robed leaders into the darkened corridor.

They passed under the nave of the church, then ascended a narrow flight of stairs to the spire dedicated to St. Bonardson, first Holy See of the Cornathian Brotherhood.

An unearthly plain chant echoed up through the corridor as the Cathedral's choir sang the minor-chorded hymn "O Angry Father, Whose Rage Is Just."

Reaching the pinnacle chamber of the New Holy See, the fourteen archbishops entered the room and gathered silently around the single oaken table. Each of the fourteen chairs bore the symbol of a brotherhood. At the head of the table was a high-back chair on a dais, and each of them bowed to it before sitting. Before they were allowed to leave the room, one of them would be seated on that chair.

As head of the most sacred order, Balor sat to the left of the chair, while Isaac of St. Awstin, the oldest surviving order, sat to the right.

As was custom, all sat in silence, and none was to speak until inspired by one of the Saints. But even before the last archbishop had settled into comfortable meditation, Isaac opened the debate.

"Just what was the meaning of your words out there, Zimri, that the alleged attempt on your life came from within the Church?"

Madoc looked to his ally. Good, very good, we must attack before Zimri has solid ground to build his case.

"Precisely that, my dear Isaac," Zimri replied. "If this attack was from the Prophet, then he is more fool than I give him credit for. If he had struck me down before the Holy Cathedral, it merely would have furthered the unified effort against him."

"But is it not vengeance that he seeks?" Xavierson of St. Remardin asked in his soft, feminine voice. "After all, Zimri, it was you who killed his only child and wife."

"You are wrong there," retorted Ivan of St. Haraldson. "It was the Church that did such an action. And as our law demanded, Balor, Madoc, and Zimri had the right to exercise it."

"But Zimri never offered us the courtesy of asking our opinions," Isaac replied scathingly. "You've done that before, Zimri. Or have we all forgotten your base betrayal before the Mathinian Pass?"

"Might I ask, my brothers," Zimri interrupted, "have they forgotten the betrayal of St. Awstin, as well, my dear Isaac? Your Rifton harbored the Prophet despite Balor's warnings and then set him loose among us."

Zimri looked around the room and could see the nods of agreement.

Balor watched the game as it was played out. He would bide his time and wait for the proper moment before making his move.

"I demand that you explain your statement on the steps of the Cathedral," Madoc called.

"Isn't it clear enough already, Madoc?" Zimri retorted.

"Someone in this room planned to kill me."

They were all too experienced in such matters to register shock or indignation at his words. They were archbishops and as such had survived scores of infights. Rifton had perhaps been the last of an older breed—a breed with whom the game could be carried only so far before certain inbred rules forced restraint.

"A rather nice move that, having one of your other men take your place today. It certainly fooled the mob, who think you have some sort of immortality charm. I do hope you will tell them someday that you were hiding behind a double," Xavierson declared with a note of sarcasm.

"I received my warning," Zimri said coldly, staring at Madoc. "To shout accusations would have been useless before the attack. My double knew beforehand what might be in store for him, but he went to his death serving Good and Holy Mor." Zimri silently cursed Xavierson for the veiled accusation of cowardice. He would remember, but now was not the time or place.

Balor interrupted the argument. "My brothers, we can argue this point till the Day of the Return. Someone attempted to take Zimri's life. Fortunately, it failed. Let us select the Holy See, which is our charge and duty, and afterward we can debate who is guilty."

He looked around the room and saw nods. None of them wanted to run the risk of a schism, which would happen if the meeting broke into opposing parties over Zimri's accusation.

Balor waited for several minutes, hoping that someone would venture the first nomination. No one offered the first move.

Balor finally stood up and faced the archbishops. "If none will place a nomination, then the task falls upon me."

Madoc fixed his eyes upon the far wall. The bribes had been placed; all was ready.

"Xavierson."

Madoc looked up with a start and caught the look of veiled contempt that Balor turned to him.

Quiet murmurs circulated in the room. Xavierson was silent, his head bowed in humility. His was the order of silent monks, viewed by many as the eccentric extreme of the Church— inconsequential in politics and dedicated to a life of quiet contemplation.

"I do so," Balor started, "for many reasons. Perhaps Xavierson, more than any other, can reach a new understanding with the Prophet and avert the war that comes to us."

Zimri smiled quietly. Masterful, he thought. Very well done, Balor. Xavierson's nomination would help split the peace party.

"But we are beyond that," Harald of Narn Rin Duth replied forcefully. "Right or wrong, Balor, you, Madoc, and Zimri have forced the call of war. Perhaps it is time for Holy Church to stand for its honor and for the preservation of the First Choice."

"I merely guard the First Choice," Balor replied. "I do not set policy concerning it."

"Well, I must nominate Zimri," Harald retorted. "It will be war, like it or not, and we need the leadership of one who is trained for such a moment. For this is a struggle to the death."

"Yes, to the death, but not with the pawn of the real master," Ivan interrupted. "The Councils of Inys Gloi perhaps even reach to this chamber. We are sure of the orthodoxy of only one— the head of the Order of Inquisition, the spiritual defender of orthodoxy. For that reason, I demand that Madoc be our Holy See."

Zimri looked around the table. He would not fight it now; otherwise, all the votes might turn against both of them, and Xavierson would be the compromise. As it was, Xavierson would draw several away from Madoc, thereby preventing a majority on the first vote.

"Are there any other names to be submitted?" Balor asked quietly. No one responded.

"Then a vote shall be taken. The two who gain the most confidence shall be voted on again unless a majority is taken in the first vote."

The brothers were silent.

"Then we shall decide."

The archbishops picked up the pieces of parchment before them on the table, and marked down the symbol of the brotherhood they were voting for.

They handed the pieces to Balor, who examined and tallied each document. After several minutes, he spread them out on the table for all to see. "Madoc had six, Zimri five, Xavierson three."

There was an audible sigh around the room. It was obvious

who would be the next Holy See; it was only a formality to vote out the conclusion.

Zimri looked to the archbishops and could see the quiet challenge in their eyes. With Xavierson out of contention, he knew that he would carry only six of them. If only he could swing Balor and one other—that was the challenge.

The brothers were returning his gaze, and in many of their eyes he saw his own death. They were prepared to avoid the confrontation that even now was surrounding them. Madoc had assured many of them in private that Zimri had engineered the plot against Ormson and that, if he was elected, they could all wash themselves of the war to come and dispose of Michael at some more convenient time and in a far easier way.

"Is there anything more to be said before we cast our second vote?" Balor intoned in a mechanical voice.

"Tell me, Madoc, why did you agree to the killing of the Prophet's family?" Zimri asked casually.

"As I have stated before, Zimri of Mor, I agreed to it as an action against *heretics*. I did not know that you planned a full-scale assault that would entail the loss of hundreds of lives. You wanted a war to bring power to yourself, so you decided to launch that attack to stir up his fanatical followers. It was my wish that they be dispatched quietly and judiciously as a warning to him—not as a means of antagonizing him."

"And what do you propose to stop this war?" Balor asked evenly.

"To end this thing before it starts. To offer over to the Prophet those assassins that escaped—for his judgment."

"Tell me, Madoc," Zimri said quietly, as if asking an innocent question, "when the time comes, will you offer over the assassins that you hired to kill me, as well?"

The archbishops were shocked at the unexpectedly direct question, and a number of them stood, shouting their protests.

"Yes, damn you to Hell, it was you, Madoc, who tried to kill me on the steps of the church," Zimri shouted, pointing an accusing finger at his former ally.

Madoc tried to stay calm. "You're mad, Zimri. Everyone knows that I had the election won. Why would I risk all by trying to kill you?"

Zimri rose from his chair and walked to the door that led

out of the audience chamber. He threw it open.

"Sacrilege!" Isaac shouted. "Sacrilege to leave this room before the See has been selected."

"To hell with your sanctimonious cries of sacrilege. You and your pious mouthings of prayers while you plot your murders. Come, my brothers, let us confront what we really are. Bring him up!" Zimri shouted.

The room fell silent as the trampling of heavy boots echoed up the stairs.

Half a dozen heavily armed Morian priests entered the room. Between them were Peter and the secretary of Mord Rinn. Madoc stood up with a muffled gasp.

The secretary looked from one to the other and then fell to his knees, clinging to Peter's robes. "You promised never to reveal who I was," he wailed.

"Too late for that," Peter replied. "The good of Holy Church rests in the balance."

"What is the meaning of this outrage?" Xavierson demanded.

"It is simple," Peter replied. "This young brother will identify who attempted to assassinate my lord Zimri."

"It's a lie," Madoc shouted. "This is another of Zimri's ploys."

"Go on," Zimri shouted, drawing the group's attention away from Madoc, "who tried to murder me today?"

"Madoc," the man groaned.

"It's a bloody lie!" Madoc shouted. "Can't you see Zimri's hand in this?"

The archbishops were silent.

Zimri looked to Balor. It's now or never, he thought.

Balor gazed from one to the other—the game was to the death. If he threw in on the wrong side, the winner would kill him for sure. Buying time, he walked to the window that looked out over the courtyard. The square was strangely quiet, and he opened the stained-glass window to look out. Instead of a mob, rank after orderly rank of blue-robed monks lined the square. Before the Cathedral of Mor five heavy guns were drawn up, pointing across the square.

Balor looked back to Zimri.

"You wouldn't dare."

Zimri smiled.

The other archbishops rose up and went to the window and looked back at Zimri with shocked gazes.

"We have come to a crisis, my good brothers," Zimri said softly. "The quarreling between us, this fratricidal bickering which for a thousand years has served the First Choice by keeping our powers in check, has wound down to its bloody conclusion. The Prophet was born out of that. I dare say that some of your orders secretly take delight in his rising, especially those that serve another master—the one who waits in the wings for our decline. It is over with. It is finished."

Zimri stood up to face them while walking toward the Chair of the Holy See.

"Madoc tried to murder me, and I dare say that even after you have been presented with that fact, you would still prefer to look the other way. But I will not allow you to, my brothers. We come to the climax—the death struggle for our survival. Either we shall be united as one, under one rule and one law, or we shall perish forever from the Earth. The First Choice of our forefathers will be shattered, and with it the power of our Sacred Trust.

"Madoc would have made a good Holy See, to be sure," Zimri continued. "At least I thought so until this attempt on my life. But he would have been too weak to see us through the crisis. My good brothers, you should ask him about his personal affairs, for in such events you can see the true mark of the man. If so, you would understand why he could never be the Holy See that could lead us out of this crisis."

"But your accusations against me are a lie!" Madoc shouted.

"Your own secretary stands before us, accusing you. What better proof do we have?" Balor replied slowly.

Zimri looked to the archbishop of the First Choice.

So you have committed to me at last, Zimri thought; then the issue is decided. He nodded gravely to Balor, and in his action, all could see that the issue of power had been decided. Balor had gone over to Zimri, and the others would follow.

"Come, my brothers, let us vote," Balor called, drowning out the voices of protest and fear. "The guards and secretaries must leave at once."

Balor looked again to the square. He knew what would happen if Zimri was refused.

"Zimri, what do we receive in return if we agree to elect you as Holy See?" Isaac asked contemptuously.

"Complete autonomy over your brotherhoods. Even division of all prizes when the conflict ends, an end to turmoil, a return to the plan of our forefathers, and above all else, a continuation of your power."

"Your power, you mean," Madoc taunted in reply. "Listen, my brothers, if we surrender to his lies, then all of us will be his pawns."

"My dear Madoc, I dare say we would have been your pawns, as well, if your plans to murder me had been successful."

"I did not try to murder you!" Madoc shouted. "And might I add, I have not placed an armed threat in front of this Cathedral!"

"Enough of this!" Balor cried out. "Your arguments are useless, so let us decide and be done with it."

The brothers looked from one to the other, none daring to make the first move. Several of them hesitated and looked out the window, then glanced back again at Zimri.

Finally, it was Harald who broke the silence. "I, for one, shall answer you clearly. What has been said against Madoc is most likely true. We all know of his machinations to gain support for his bid as Holy See. I can believe that murder would not be beyond him. But on the other hand, never has an armed threat been placed in the Holy Square before the cathedral. So I believe my vote is now made simple. I shall abstain. If all of us abstain, and since the two of you are forbidden to vote for yourselves, then the issue will be deadlocked. Deadlocked we can then reopen ourselves to new nominations for the position. And I suggest that all the rest of you side with me on this issue."

One after another, the other archbishops voiced agreement with Harald and walked across the room to stand next to him. Finally, only Balor was left.

"And so it has come to me," Balor said sadly. "None of you has the courage to face this—our gravest crisis. How tragic that these two are both right and wrong. Zimri right in what he has said of our future—doomed to fall to the Prophet if we do not act and doomed to fall to Inys Gloi, as well—that order which we fear to speak of even in this the most sacred of chambers. But how wrong you were, Zimri, to try to force us by strength of arms when you knew that you could not get your votes in any other way. And Madoc, you are right in the fear of what Zimri will become, not a leader but a warrior, sword in hand, whose one concern will be his final triumph!"

Balor looked around the room. "We all know the ultimate paradox of our Church as stated in the First Choice. All is legend, created to rule the multitude. Yet such is the shock to us when we reach the Inner Circle of our Orders and the secret is revealed, that we still mouth the prayers nevertheless. Half of us probably still believe, or at least wish to believe. But the ultimate purpose is being lost. The ultimate purpose is to keep man in ignorance and, in so doing, wait for his evolution to reach and control the destructive ability of his mind. The Prophet will destroy that. He will unleash the legendary Pandora's Box of knowledge upon us.

"Even though I am master of the First Choice, I must confess that I still foolishly believe some of what we secretly call legend. Some claim that the Prophet has come to redeem us of our folly, but I believe differently—that he is the messenger of the Dark One, sent to destroy us. He is our threat, and unless united, we will fall."

Balor walked across the room and passed Madoc. He stepped up before Zimri and, taking him by the shoulders, led him to the Holy Chair.

"I cast my vote, and it is for Zimri to be Holy See. I did support Madoc, and Zimri's threat of armed force would have made that decision even clearer. But in trying to assassinate Zimri, Madoc overstepped himself. Since all the rest of you have abstained, then my vote is the majority. I kneel before you, your Holiness Zimri, and await your blessing. Lead us to victory."

The doors of the cathedral opened to the orderly ranks of Morian warriors, who stood guard around the building. One by one, the thirteen archbishops marched out in order of rank and prestige. They could sense the heavy tension in the chilled summer air as the warrior monks waited. Harald was the tenth archbishop to walk through the door, and a shout went up from the assembled warriors. Mor was the tenth brotherhood of the Church, and it should have been Zimri. The sign was obvious to all. Finally the thirteenth archbishop emerged. All were silent. The bells of the cathedral started a wild pealing, and twelve Morian deacons stepped into the sunlight bearing a platform. Atop it stood his Holiness Zimri, Holy See of the Cornathian Brotherhood. A thundering cheer went up from the warriors. From the side alleyways, the guards parted, and the mob, shouting with religious frenzy, poured into the square, chanting Zimri's name. Onward they came, and Zimri beckoned for them to be allowed forward. The square was soon packed, as the thousands pressed closer in hope of receiving the first public blessing of the new See.

He raised up his hands to the Saints above, and silence swept the square as the multitude fell to its knees.

"In the name of all the Saints, with the Promise of the Long Table, and with the hope of the Return of our Blessed Father, I bless you all and pray that the day shall come when together we shall sup in the Sacred Garden of the Father."

"So let it be."

The twelve monks bearing Zimri turned and carried their burden back into the darkness of the cathedral.

As they lowered the platform, Peter came forward and kneeled.

Zimri gave him a hurried blessing and, taking him by the shoulder, walked with him alone toward the high altar while outside the cheering of the multitude rose up.

"Has it been taken care of?" Zimri asked.

"Yes, Madoc is being arrested even now."

"Good, show him at once to my chambers."

With a purposeful stride, Zimri set off, the twelve guards falling in beside him. Exiting through the north door, reserved for him alone, Zimri strode down the ornately carved corridor and entered the office suite of the Holy See.

The guards fell to their knees at his approach. When last he had entered the chamber, Ioan was still alive, and Zimri had been summoned there with Rifton to account to the other archbishops for the action before the Mathinian Pass. Now, at last, the triumph was his.

He surveyed the room for a moment with reverent awe, then walked to the inlaid ivory desk at the far end of the room. Without hesitation, he sat before the desk and, reaching back, pulled the cord that would summon his aides.

Six armed Morian deacons entered the room.

"Do you have the lists of those arrested?"

"Yes, my lord."

"Good, give the documents to me and send in Madoc."

A shout of protest was heard in the corridor; then the door opened. Madoc staggered into the room and was pushed to his knees by two Morian priests. "Damn you to the Ice of Hell," Madoc shouted. "I will not kneel to such as you."

A guard slapped him across the back with his spear butt, knocking Madoc to the floor.

Zimri looked up at the two guards. With a quick gesture of his hand, he ordered the men out.

"Just kill me and get it over with."

"Oh, I will, my dear Madoc, but first I wish to tell you something."

Madoc got to his feet. "You wish to gloat first and listen to me beg for life. But that I will not do."

"But you will listen, anyhow. Your attempt on my life was a feeble tragedy, Madoc, without any sign of professional judgment. You could have gotten me in half a dozen other ways. Peter for one. With the right bribes, he would have betrayed me, right up till this very morning. But he was purchased by my ascension to the See."

"But I did not do it!" Madoc shouted.

"Come, come, my dear Madoc, let us stop this game."

Madoc stood defiant, his eyes brimming with hatred. "It was well designed by you, Zimri, that is all."

"I grow bored of you, my old friend. Your death awaits you in your private chambers. You have the choice of poison or the knife. I shall leave that up to you."

Reaching back, Zimri pulled the bell, which instantly brought the guards into the room.

Madoc stared hatefully at him. Then spat on the floor.

There was no gloating, no joy in what had occurred. Zimri settled down into the chair, having finally reached the goal of his life. Strangely, he felt a sad, distant sense of loss.

Peter stepped from the shadows and had the guards stand back. Bowing low, they obeyed the command of the Secretary of the Holy See.

"I did not do it," Madoc said angrily. "You know that, so

why did you betray me? I would have given you Mor if you had supported me as you said you would."

Peter laughed quietly. "I've desired much in my life, Madoc, but your petty offers were meaningless."

"But why did you accuse me?"

"You see, Madoc, it was I who engineered the assassination attempt. And it was I who arranged your betrayal."

Madoc's eyes grew wide with astonishment.

"You?"

"Precisely, my friend. Let us just say that there are some who saw that you would win and that Zimri's plan for an armed takeover would have torn the Church apart. Therefore, we organized this small diversion."

"But who?"

"Let us just say that it was I," Peter said with a soft laugh. "Now, if you will follow my suggestion, I would recommend the poison. I picked it out myself. I guarantee that it will be painless, and it's so much cleaner than the knife. May you sup tonight at the Long Table, Madoc of Mord Rinn."

The archbishop looked at him in shocked amazement.

Peter turned to the guards and called them. "Lead him away. And do make sure that his passing has some dignity to it. After all, the death of an archbishop should be a solemn event."

CHAPTER 13

"THERE IT IS, MICHAEL—THE WALLS OF CAEDIFF."

The lights of the outer fortress line flickered on the eastern horizon, standing out sharply against the darkness of early evening.

Michael turned and faced his advisors. "Cowan, are you sure that all is prepared?"

"As I have already indicated, the city of Caediff, as home citadel of the Silent Ones, has prepared to offer itself up as a free port in order to spare itself a siege. All they ask in return is nonintervention in their own monastery."

Michael turned away from his advisors and walked down the deck of the heavy frigate, *Night of Fire*. From horizon to horizon shone the running lights of half a thousand ships. The heavy transports made up the center of the flotilla. They, in turn, were surrounded by the frigates, heavy merchantmen, and the four battle cruisers. Farther out, darting smartly on the flanks of the fleet, sailed the sloops, corsairs, reconnaissance rafts, and the four hundred battle rams that made up the shock forces of the Prophet. The fleet was a moving city that housed close to fifty thousand men. Driven by a cold northwesterly, they had made an excellent passage from Lismar—losing but

176

three schooners to ice buckles and half a dozen light merchantmen and corsairs in scattered encounters with Zimri's advance
forces. They had expected Zimri to meet them in force in a
desperate bid for victory, but as of yet there had been no sign
of what he was planning.

Michael surveyed his fleet with grim satisfaction. It was
serving him well. His men asked only to be led into battle for
the glory of the Prophet and, of course, for the booty that could
be taken. There was, in fact, a sense of disappointment in
Caediff's surrendering without a fight, since this denied them
the right of pillage. Michael realized as well that he had wished
for a fight, but the bloodless taking of the small town would
cut off Conwy to the south and would provide them with a
secure Northward Shelf base of operations from which the
winter's campaign could be launched.

Michael heard footsteps behind him and looked over his
shoulder. Seth was approaching. "Ah, Seth, what do you want?"

"Does there have to be a reason for me to approach you?"

Michael nodded sadly, and grabbing hold of the ship's carved
railing, he looked out across the frozen sea. "Isn't there always
a reason for someone to come to me?"

"Let's talk, Michael. I feel a need for it."

Michael was silent.

"Remember how I first met you on the Ice after you went
out alone into the night?"

"And I didn't know that all along you were watching me."

"It was a night like this," Seth said softly, pointing overhead
to the Arch. Above them the thin band of light shimmered in
the evening sky, while to the north the aurora snapped its red-
green light across the constellations of the bears and the chalice.

"Yes, a night like this." Michael took hold of the railing,
and swinging himself over the side, he dropped down onto the
ice. Seth followed him. Together they climbed over the outrigger and walked out past where the guards were supposed to
be setting up patrol as the ship anchored down for the passage
of night. "Funny, where are the guards?"

Michael looked over his shoulder and was surprised to see
that his personal bodyguards were not following. He looked to
Seth with an inquiring gaze.

Seth smiled beneath his wind mask. "I managed to convince

Daniel that you would be safe with me. Anyhow, we'll still be inside the outer picket line."

Michael walked onward, wrapped in silent thought. "Again, I'll ask you," Michael said sadly after several minutes of quiet. "What is it that you want tonight?"

"Your peace of mind, Michael."

Michael laughed bitterly.

"Seth Facinn, you destroyed that forever the day you walked into my life."

"Do you hate me for that?"

"It resulted in Janis's death, did it not? You and the Holy Cause."

"She loved you, and when she died, she believed in what you were and what was to come."

Michael looked at him. "She believed in a peaceful answer. But Zimri destroyed that forever, Zimri and whatever was behind him."

Michael fell into silence again, and Seth did not push the direction the conversation was taking.

"Are you afraid?" Seth finally asked, breaking into Michael's quiet contemplation.

"No, Seth, not now. I know what has to be done. I have to smash the order of things once and for all—all the churches, all that stands for the suppression of thought and fights the acceptance of the one preordained."

Seth sensed something in Michael's last words and looked at him closely.

"Yes, Seth. I am the Prophet. That, I firmly believe. I dare say that is part of the equation you never expected, that I would believe what you and all the others have so conveniently arranged. It shall come at last, and it will appear with fire and sword as was intended, in a final purging—so that the new world can be shaped. And I shall not stop till all have been swept away."

Seth was quiet, not daring to probe deeper into the threat. Just how much did Michael really know about Inys Gloi? He was too afraid to ask.

"You realize, Seth, there was one question we were never able to answer concerning that night. We still do not know who was responsible for blocking the escape hatch."

Seth looked straight ahead.

"I believe someday we will."

Michael turned and started back toward the ship. "We best return. I trust all has been set for tomorrow."

"Yes, Michael, at dawn, the gates of the city will be opened. All shipping has been surrendered to you. One-tenth of all the men will serve as levies aboard our ships. The monastery of Mor, five leagues up the coast, will not surrender, of course, and shall be taken by storm at dawn. According to our agreement, Xavierson's followers are not to be violated."

"That suits my purposes for the moment," Michael said harshly.

As they reached the side of the ship, Michael stopped Seth and looked at him closely. "Tell me, Seth, what else did you and your agents arrange here this summer?"

"Only that which can help you, master," Seth said evenly.

"As I assumed you would," Michael replied.

There was no chanting, no ecstatic cheers of exaltation as Michael's flagship cleared the harbor entrance and passed into the city of Caediff. In the distance, the cannon thundered as Finson's five thousand stormed the walls of the Morian monastery. The city was strangely quiet, so different from the receptions that Michael's followers were accustomed to in the cities of the South. There his forces were greeted as the armies of liberation. As the fleet spread out into the fortified harbor, it soon became obvious that the vast majority of the population had fled during the night rather than chance a broken treaty and dawn pillage. Michael's advisors conferred in hushed tones. The strength of their revolution was based on the recruitment of new volunteers in every city that they visited. Most had expected the populace of the Cornathian Brotherhood to rise up in support of the Prophet. If Caediff was an early indication of what was to come, then they had cause for serious anxiety.

The dockside was empty except for twenty monks dressed in plain robes of white wool. One of them walked forward bearing a heavy staff in his hand and stopped before the prow of Michael's ship as it drifted to a halt.

"Michael Ormson of Mathin," the monk called out.

Michael stepped onto the catwalk and looked down to the solitary form below.

The monk held the staff up over his head. "I, Xavierson of

St. Remerdin, give unto thee the city of Caediff. My order now declares that from this day hence its holy bond to the Cornathian Brotherhood is broken. All that was has ended. All that we prayed for is naught. The dream of the Garden is dead, and the darkness manifest in your form has descended across the land. I vow from this moment hence never again to speak. And to live out the rest of my days in silence, praying for the forgiveness of our forefathers, whose folly has placed us here and whose folly we are doomed forever to repeat."

Xavierson lifted the staff up and, grabbing it at one end, swung it down onto the ice—shattering the ancient wood into splinters. A sigh went up from the monks on the dock. The archbishop bowed low to Ormson and then silently rejoined his brothers, who quietly disappeared up the alleyway.

"A hell of a welcome," Daniel growled.

Michael watched his men and did not comment as they cheered his name and swarmed over the sides of their ships. Forming into ranks, they marched up the empty alleyways and took possession of their first Cornathian city. The first invaders successfully to do so in nearly five hundred years.

He walked alone on the battlement. The shouting and laughter echoed darkly in the alleyways below. The sound of cannon fire had died in the second hour after darkness, and just before midnight, a breathless courier arrived to tell him that Finson had taken the citadel of Mor. There were no prisoners, the last of the defenders having thrown themselves off the high tower. Casualties had been heavy, nearly two hundred dead and twice as many injured—one of them Finson, who had taken an arrow in the arm.

Michael's men had quickly ferreted out those people who had stayed in the city. Many of them were women whose high-pitched shrieks and laughter indicated to Michael that not all were unwilling to welcome the new conquerors.

The palace of the shipping guild was modest but well appointed, and Michael had taken it as his headquarters while he planned their campaign. The Inner Council had already decided that the next step was to move against Cornath, to draw the Cornathian battle fleet to a final confrontation.

Michael sipped at the wine that Seth had given him. Cowan and Daniel on several occasions had made polite comments about his drinking, but he ordered them away when the subject was brought up. More often, of late, he found that he needed the wine to sleep and to make it through the night without the terrifying visions. The wine that tonight provoked a strange, pleasant warmth, and he found that he was actually relaxing under its spell.

"My lord," a voice whispered behind him.

He turned quickly and looked into the darkness. Whoever it was, he couldn't see. There was a human form—a vague outline of light surrounded by a shimmering, pulsing red, unlike anything he had ever seen.

"My lord, I was ordered to bring you more wine." She stepped out of the darkness. Blond, nearly white hair, cascaded down her back in full, heavy curls. Michael eyed the woman silently. She drew closer. Her full figure and long, tapering legs moved in a sinuous feline fashion beneath the lightly woven black dress. She drew closer, and Michael saw a strange fire in her dark blue eyes and dusky, oval face.

"Who ordered you?"

"I do not know, lord. I was a servant here before you arrived, and one of the guards approached me and said that your cup needed to be filled and that I should do it."

Michael knew it was a lie. On Daniel's strictest orders, only the Companions were allowed to present food to Michael. She was lying, but the curious thing was that her light was the same. There wasn't the slightest flicker, the slightest sign that what she said was untrue.

"You look to see if I am lying to you," she said softly.

How strange he suddenly felt.

"Who are you?"

"Varinna du Hardrin." She stepped closer to him, offering the goblet of wine.

Such a strange illusion, he suddenly thought. She holds the goblet in the same manner that Janis would. Janis, where are you now?

He sipped the wine and looked into the eyes of the woman who stood before him. The scent of her breath washed over him.

In the distance, he could hear a chanted battle paean—one that had become popular of late with his men. "Give us a prize and the endless windswept sea."

He turned away from the woman to watch the northward

sky where a flickering light rose higher by the minute—Finson was burning the monastery to the ground. He could imagine the crackle of the flames, the calls of the dying, the dark stains on the windswept ice. He suddenly longed to be there, sword in hand, to watch silently as the fire consumed the hated fortress of Zimri's power.

"My hatred is yours," she whispered behind him.

He looked at her again, while overhead the aurora matched the glow of the burning citadel.

She reached out and touched his brow, her fingers running a light tracing touch down his cheek.

"Janis," Michael whispered dreamily with half-closed eyes.

"Yes, it's been a year, Michael, a year since you've known a woman."

What was happening? He could feel himself slipping into a strange, dreamlike consciousness, unable to control or to resist the desire that welled up inside.

"Janis—then let it be Janis for tonight," Varinna whispered softly, taking Michael by the hand, leading him off the battlement to the single room atop the guild hall citadel.

"Yes, Michael," she whispered, "let it be Janis for tonight."

The door closed quietly behind them.

Seth turned away from the end of the corridor and returned to the meeting room where Cowan, Eldric, and Daniel quietly worked, examining lists of supplies taken with the fall of Caediff.

Cowan looked up with a curious gaze.

"The master?"

Seth smiled sadly. "The master is taking a much-needed rest."

Cowan nodded and returned to his papers.

Seth walked from the room. He felt a sense of loss and betrayal in what had just been so easily accomplished. Placing his own men as guards in order for Varinna to pass was simple enough. Drugging the wine, as well, was a simple accomplishment—he had been doing that and doctoring Michael's food on and off for ten years. But he feared for the morning, when the drug would no longer be there. What, then, for Michael Ormson, the master?

* * *

"My lord Zimri!"

Zimri looked up from the burden of documents that were spread across the table. A courier stood before him. His face mask still covered in ice. "We have a report from Caediff."

Zimri nodded and beckoned for the Morian deacon to enter the room.

Suddenly remembering his protocol, the priest removed his face mask and bowed low, entering the room with his eyes averted to the ground.

"You may rise, brother Ulman. I forgive your lack of manners. Make your report."

"I've just arrived from Caediff."

"You've already said that."

Flustered, the monk stammered for words.

"How long was your passage, for a start."

"One and a half days, we sailed through the night."

"Go on."

"The Prophet's fleet was last reported to be passing Lismar, and should even now be off the city walls."

"Did the Ezrians close their harbors?"

"My lord, they've betrayed us. They allowed the master's agents to purchase supplies in the city and to overhaul a light frigate that lost a runner in an ice crevice."

"By the wounds of St. Mor," Zimri shouted, rising up from his desk. Peter had given him full assurance that the Primate of Ezra had agreed in principle to deny access to the Prophet's fleet. Who had lied, then?

"It's been confirmed by one of our agents who made it into Caediff just before we sailed," the monk said slowly. "It's been reported that the Ezrians will allow the Prophet to resupply in Lismar and Gormath in exchange for a peace settlement on the Southward Shelf."

Zimri struggled to regain his composure. Peter was still in Midran. What was the game? After Madoc's assassination attempt, he was sure that Peter was solidly behind him. What had gone wrong? Now was not the time. The siege of Caediff must have started already. The time for action had come. He must get the report on the Prophet's fleet.

"It's of no consequence; with the Prophet off Caediff, we can meet him in battle at last. His supplies will be low before long. Continue with your report."

The courier hesitated.

"Go on with it. What's wrong with you, man?"

"Xavierson will surrender Caediff to the Prophet without a fight."

"By the merciful Saints!"

"Xavierson will announce that he is pulling out," the courier blurted, his fear clear. "He has decreed that his order shall be to abandon the Cornathian Confederation for the duration of the conflict."

Zimri fell back into his chair. The defections had started. If the Silent Ones left the order, then it was only a matter of time before half a dozen others would follow suit. All the battle plans of the last four months were for naught. His counterattack was based on cutting Michael's lines to the south after several weeks of siege, when supplies would become a critical problem. With Caediff in the Prophet's hands, he had a firm base to operate from. With Ezra in support as well, the situation was grim. The victory of Cornath would all rest on one desperate gamble.

The courier stood in the middle of the room, a pool of slush widening on the floor around him.

"Get out," Zimri shouted.

Ulman bowed low, waiting for absolution.

Zimri, remembering, stood, walked to the courier, and ceremonially touched him lightly on the back of the neck.

Having received the traditional and now bloodless punishment for bearing disastrous news to a Holy See, the courier rose.

"Find yourself something to eat and stay the night. I will want to talk with you at length in the morning about what you saw in Caediff."

"Yes, my lord."

"And as you leave, send in Parishson."

The courier, bowing low, left the room.

He had to draw blood, if enough was drawn, it would arouse the people against the Prophet. Even if there was no clear result in the battle to come, it would help to keep the other brotherhoods in line.

A knock sounded at the door.

To Zimri's command, the door swung open, and the lord

admiral of the fleet strode into the room. His massive bulk was wrapped in a shimmering cloak of dark blue, nearly the same color as the robes of Mor. Though his beard and hair were prematurely white, Parishson's handsome face was almost youthful in appearance.

"All has changed," Zimri said quietly, beckoning for Parishson to be seated. "Tomorrow we leave for Cornath, and from there to battle with the forces of Mathin."

Even before Michael awoke, he knew what had occurred. Startled, he sat up and looked to the other side of the bed. It was empty. She was gone. Cursing, he got up naked in the frigid air. Shivering, he strode across the room to look through the narrow window slit. The northern horizon was still dark except for the shimmering blood-red glow cast by the flaming citadel.

His thoughts were clear. So unlike last night, when a dream of Janis had appeared to him, had led him to bed and made love to him. It was in the middle of the dream, however, that he knew that it was not a hallucination, that what was being experienced was real. The movements of the woman had been full of naked animal passion and lacked a warm, sensitive touch. It was then that he remembered a bleeding corpse in a smoke-filled room. Janis was dead. Of course she was dead; it had been a year now, and her body was lost somewhere beyond the Flowing Sea.

He had called Janis's name when the realization came, but that only served to heighten the passion of the woman whose arms were locked around him. In that moment of insane confusion, Michael had given himself over to her designs.

Looking out the window, he wept for the first time since Janis and Andrew had died. Anguish overwhelmed him, seeking release. He thought of the apparition in the night and knew with self-loathing that he would welcome its return—since it was warm, and alive, in a world otherwise dark. But in his rage he screamed out his hatred for himself and what had become of his dreams, and while he screamed, he took delight in the fire that still washed the northern horizon.

The guards in the corridor heard Michael's cries and looked from one to the other, none daring to enter his quarters. And their eyes were full of fear—fear for their master, who with every passing day seemed to drift further and further into some strange, dark insanity.

As the sun passed its low zenith in the southern sky, Michael finally came down from the high chamber. Already the rumor had swept through the palace like the spreading of a plague. As soon as Daniel heard what had happened, he issued a short and direct threat to the personal guards of the Prophet. There was an unwritten agreement among those of the inner circle, and the rumor was contained only to those who came in direct contact with Michael.

He appeared in his tattered monk's robe, something that he had not been seen in since the days before the battle at the Mathinian Pass. Michael stopped at the base of the stairs and surveyed them coldly, his eyes afire with a look that was near to madness.

"I wish to inspect the fleet. As soon as our position here has been consolidated, we are to sail for Cornath. I trust that all is ready."

"Master, another week will pass before we are ready," Cowan replied evenly, looking straight into Michael's eyes.

"As soon as possible. I will tolerate no delay. I believe that Zimri will strike the moment he hears of Xavierson's betrayal, and I want to meet him as close to Cornath as possible. Do you understand?"

Cowan nodded and withdrew into the group.

Daniel stepped forward and suddenly spoke up. "Michael, during the night, we took some prisoners as they tried to sneak out over the wall—ten monks of Mord Rinn and half a dozen priests from St. Awstin. What should we do with them?"

"Stake them out on the ice. Announce to the men that any who wish to make sport of them shall have his chance."

There was a low murmur from the crowd, some nodding their approval. Cowan turned away from Michael's gaze.

Michael started to leave the room. "Eldric, come with me."

The guards fell in around him and Eldric. Uninvited, Cowan followed in their wake.

The reflected glare of the mirror-smooth ice was nearly blinding in its white intensity as they emerged out onto the harbor plain. A small cutter awaited them near the harbor gate.

Reaching its stern hatch, Michael and his followers scrambled aboard, while the crew quickly made sail to Eldric's shouted commands. Standing on the jib boom, Michael beckoned for Cowan to join him. The ship passed out of the habor gate and set a course for the vast park of ships that was drawn up in orderly rows.

"What is it, Michael?"

"You don't approve of all that has happened, do you?" Michael asked coldly.

"Why do you ask for my opinion, Michael? Your word is my command. I made that pledge to my Uncle Zardok and I've made it to you."

"Then I command you to speak what is in your heart."

Far astern, Cowan could see a small cluster of men pushing a quivering, kicking form down onto the ice, while a pack of men gathered upwind ready to launch their skate spears.

"Why the executions, Michael? To kill men in battle when they have sword in hand is honorable and just by the laws of our fathers, but to do that—"

"No more than what Cornath has done to me."

"And what was that? What did they do to you?" Cowan asked coldly.

Michael turned and fixed him with a look of barely suppressed fury.

"Destroyed my life! They destroyed everything that we worked for and wanted to believe in."

"No, Michael, you are the one who is destroying everything. When I first became your follower, you preached an end to the cycle of war, the cycle of hatred. But it seems now that you expected that to happen on the strength of your word alone. What a naive delusion. Michael, that could only happen on the strength of your actions. Take a good look at your followers, oh Prophet of the New Age. The old guard is with you yet because of the strength of your dream. Your dream, Michael— the one that first captured us and bent us to your will. But the new ones—the tens of thousands that have come to you in the last year—serve you solely on the strength of your vengeance."

"Yes, for my vengeance!" Michael shouted, so that many on the ship's deck turned to watch what was occurring forward. "My vengeance is the crucible in which will be forged the new state. A state that is free of religious tyranny."

Cowan turned away, not daring to speak.

"Go on, Cowan, say what is in your heart. Or are you afraid?"

He looked back and felt the old bond, the old dream. And he could feel the pleading in Michael's voice, as if he were asking to be led from the path that he had embarked on.

"Michael, you're not destroying a religion; you're replacing it with another one, the worship of Michael Ormson, the vengeful Prophet, a Messiah, who, sword in hand, will be the new object of worship. And by all that is sacred, that is precisely what this mob wants. It's what Seth and all the others want— a new god who can give them the power in a new age. And as for Eldric and the rabble of freebooters, they are here to serve themselves in the greatest pillaging since the Ice formed."

In the distance, the chanting started to grow as the men stationed aboard the battle-ram fleet recognized the figure standing atop the prow of the approaching cutter.

"Listen to them, Michael. Listen, but in the name of heaven, turn away before it is too late. Already their worship has led you to the brink of insanity. They no longer call for you. In their blindness, they're calling for a new god to follow. Your crusade has gone beyond all control, on your part, or anyone else's for that matter; the deaths of Janis and Andrew have become an excuse for releasing the rage of a race stranded on a hellhole of its own creation. A rage that has to be vented on something, anything, and it will culminate in an orgy of death that will ultimately destroy what is left of you."

The chanting grew louder. In spite of himself, Cowan's pulse quickened to the thrilling sound of power that the voices of the thousands conveyed.

"Michael, Michael, Michael . . ."

"And what do you propose instead," Michael asked in a bleak, distant voice. "Shall Zimri and all that stand by him go free?"

"Yes—damn it all, yes. We have Caediff. Let us keep it. Declare that to be enough. Call for a total blockade against the Cornathian Brotherhood as long as the murderer Zimri is in power. On the defensive, Zimri will not be able to defeat us. The other thirteen brotherhoods are disgruntled enough and resent the manner of his taking power—remember all of them abstained on the vote except for Balor. Zimri needs us to attack and to keep on attacking if he wishes to hold power. If we give Zimri a war, he will unite them. If we give him peace or force him to take the offensive, the other brotherhoods will drag him down from his bloody throne. By all that is Holy, Michael, don't you realize? Can't you remember that Zimri murdered Janis and Andrew for one reason only? He wanted to have you bring the war to him. You are falling right into his snare."

"But the Cornathian Brotherhoods that bred him will survive."

"So instead you offer a new brotherhood, the Brotherhood of Ormson?"

Michael turned on Cowan and fixed him with a malevolent gaze. "Cowan, I must remind myself that you are of Zardok's family. You forget who you are speaking to. And what is more, you forget the memory of Janis and Andrew. You saw their bodies and those of our friends." He turned away, covering his face with his hands, swaying as if he was about to fall. "Every moment of my life I carry their images in my heart and hear my son's plea in my brain. I cannot forget it. I can't wipe them from my mind except with his blood and that of all who follow him."

Michael looked at Cowan, and a dark, melancholy fever glowed in his eyes. He's mad; he's truly mad, Cowan thought. He wanted to step forward and embrace Michael, but he was unable to move. What can I do to stop Michael's madness from infecting the entire world?

"Please, Michael, listen to me. I've always spoken the truth to you. I have never been afraid to do so, and I will continue to speak the truth; that you can be assured of, even when you do not want to hear it."

"Leave me," Michael said coldly. "If you do not wish to follow me, you may return to Mathin."

"No, Michael, I will stay. Just remember someday that it was I who had the courage and love to tell you what was in my heart. You are mad with hate and rage, and the only one who could convince you of your folly is dead."

"Yes, she's dead!" Michael shouted, not noticing the stares of the others on the deck of the ship. "And her death crystalized it for me. We've been killing in the name of religion since time began. I am now the embodiment of religion—the Saviour, so conveniently arranged by Seth's hidden monastery.

"Well, I shall use my elevation," Michael said, his voice lowering to a whisper. "I shall use it to end the old orders. And then, from the ashes, a new order will arise—*that* shall be Janis's memorial."

"One she never would have wanted."

"And who are you to dare tell me what my wife's memorial shall be?" His words echoed across the deck, twisted by near hysteria.

It was useless; he bowed low to Michael and started to withdraw.

"Is there any other thing you wish to say?" Michael shouted, his tone giving fair warning that anything more would be dangerous.

"Look into your heart, Michael. Someday it will again show you the way and how you have departed from it."

"Leave me before I forget that you were once my friend."

Cowan turned. And, as he walked away, many looked away from him as if he were carrying a plague. It was not wise to be friendy with those who had fallen from a master's grace.

The ship glided to a halt, upwind from the orderly rows of battle rams. Disembarking, Michael walked past his ships—the four man crews standing to meet the hard gaze of the master.

Here and there, he stopped to exchange a word with the men. Scattered among the crews were the silver helms of the survivors of the ram fleet at the Mathinian Pass. After that victory, Michael had presented to each of them a silver-embossed helmet that marked them as the first, the original followers of the master. The men wore them with pride and now called out greetings to their leader, and he responded in good humor, basking in the warmth of his most loyal followers.

Cowan could feel the old enthusiasm stir as the men cheered the Prophet. Banners whipped in the afternoon wind. The battle horns were sounded in anticipation of triumph. And looking down the long line of ships, Cowan, could not suppress his pride. The calls of the thousands quickened even Cowan's pulse. The primordial summons to battle enticed him—and his reluctant soul was swept along.

While they returned to the citadel to forge their final plans, Michael barely noticed the long lines of men—the tens of thousands, formed up in battle lines, calling his name. Ahead, atop the highest tower, Michael saw Seth Facinn, the Far-seeing, dressed in white robes, staring down. Varinna was standing beside him. Michael had realized that she was Seth's doing; that his wine had been drugged; that Seth had tried to give him relief if but for a single night. Nevertheless, his soul was torn with guilt, and he tried to force the nightmare images away and imagine that another reality awaited him up there. But the images merged, and Michael knew he would have no need for drugged wine that night.

CHAPTER 14

"A<small>H</small>, P<small>ETER OF</small> M<small>OR</small>, I <small>HAVE BEEN AWAITING YOU</small>. D<small>O BE</small> seated."

Rising from bent knee, Peter stood to face the scarlet-cloaked form before him. The clamor of the streets reached even into the sanctuary of the Primate of Ezra. It was his first audience with the Primate in the new cathedral of Midran. Peter was amazed at the finely wrought tapestries that covered the wall behind the throne. They portrayed a fleet of iceships in battle formation, the lead ship carrying the blood-red banner of Ezra upon its prow. Such work was rare in the courts and abbeys of the north, where carved wood was the accepted art-form of the Church.

Peter strode to the offered chair and lowered his aching body into the satin cushions. A smile lighting up his hawklike visage, the Primate leaned across the table and poured a goblet of the rich cinnamon-scented wine favored by the high Church officials of Ezra.

"I must confess again," the Primate said with a smile, "that your counsel in months past has been beyond all ability for us to repay."

Peter nodded without expression.

"You've just arrived, from Conwy?"

"Yes, your Excellency."

"Did you encounter the fleet of the Prophet in your passage?"

He had seen it, to be sure. Peter remembered the power of Michael before the Mathinian Pass, but what he had witnessed the week before had left him speechless.

Under full sail, the Ezrian courier craft had taken four hours to pass the assembled flotilla of Ormson as it passed in the opposite direction, bound for the Cornathian coast. He knew what forces Zimri had to oppose Ormson. Zimri's fleet was heavier, to be sure, but his antiquated ships would disappear under the swarm of rams in just the same way they had before the Mathinian Pass. Peter had seen the Prophet's rams in action; Zimri had not, and the Cornathian Brotherhood had yet to accept the new way of battle.

"Yes, most impressive," Peter replied. "And I have to confess my pleasure in the fact that I was aboard an Ezrian ship when I sighted them."

"Did you convey to his Holiness, Zimri of Mor, that we would be unable directly to support him at this time due to our problems with the worshipers of the three gods, who press us on our eastern border."

Peter smiled quietly. Worshipers of the three gods indeed. It was the convenient excuse. Besides, his game depended on driving the right wedge between the two churches, which must not recognize the common foe. "My lord, I regret I was unable to do as you wished."

A slight frown crossed the Primate's face. Dog of an infidel, he thought with contempt. He knew this traitor's game. Discredit his old master, let Zimri fall, and then he, Peter, would emerge as the new power who would bring Ezra's vast reserves into play to reestablish the balance of power. The Primate would play the game for him, of course. Peter would be useful in bringing the hated northlanders to heel after the mutual destruction of Cornath and the Prophet. They would burn each other out; then Ezra would stand supreme, with the lackey Peter his faithful servant.

"I would have preferred that Zimri knew of our action before we opened our port to Michael. It would have made our action appear less—how shall I say—perfidious? So why did you fail in seeing him?"

"Remember, my lord, that it was I who first informed Zimri of your possible help, more than a year ago. *That* was partly the motivation for his subsequent actions. If I had delivered your latest message to Zimri, I truly doubt that you would ever have had the opportunity to deal with me again. If you can see what I mean.

"There was another consideration, as well, which I had to voice to you directly. If Zimri had known of your decision, it might have provoked him into attacking Ormson while the heretic was still on your ice, in an attempt to deny him a port. That would have dragged you into a war you would have preferred to wait on. But now Ormson's fleet is between your cities and Zimri's. Ormson is your shield. After the action, when both fleets are wrecked, the Southward Isles will be open to you."

The Holy See of Ezra nodded slowly as if the advice were sound words from an able advisor. Cursed fool, he thought, does he take me for a bungling idiot? Zimri would never have dared to attack me, thereby provoking two wars.

"Wise advice, Peter. With help such as yours, we can be assured of saving your beloved homeland. I forgive you for not carrying my message directly. You are indeed too valuable to lose."

Peter sipped the wine and smiled. Pig of an infidel, he thought; after they are both destroyed, and I am Holy See, then we shall deal with the question of Ezra.

"Men of Cornath, you sail in defense of Holy Church. Tonight, I call upon the Saints of Battle to bear witness to this— our moment of gravest peril. For countless generations past, we have sailed forth to battle and have returned victorious. Let each of you bear in your heart the promise of the Saints as you go face the powers of darkness."

The slow chanting of the thousands of monks rose heavenward. The ice of the harbor was obscured by incense. The cries of the thousands rose into the sterile midnight sky, flickering with a pale aurora. The deep throb of kettledrums echoed against the towering walls of Cornath, in the age old call to battle.

"Rise up, ye men of Cornath, rise up and go forth. For this is the climax of an age. We face the false prophecies, proclaiming the cult of darkness. Oh, ye warriors, upon your strength rests the future of Cornath."

His arms outstretched, Zimri suddenly stood as his platform was hoisted onto the shoulders of fifty hooded monks.

A dark-clad host swung censers that spilled forth the bitter incense of Mor. Together the monks and sailors of the fleet intoned the long chant. "Holy Church calls out in its hour of need."

The hundred-odd ships of the battle fleet stood upon the ice in orderly lines, their crews drawn up on the ice by rank and house. Every available craft had been pressed into action. But there were far too few. In the weeks before the battle, hundreds of light and heavy merchantmen had quietly slipped out of Cornath's ports, the harbor patrols unable to stop them. Nearly five hundred Morian monks had been murdered, killed by the crews of the deserting ships and dumped overboard. Many of the Cornathians were using their cannon without the necessary priests in open defiance of Holy Law. It was but one more sign that the old order was starting to break.

Zimri knew that the merchant ships had gathered several hundred miles off the coast, where they would wait out the action. If the victory was to Cornath, they would return in the spring with their rigging changed, their papers forged, and pious claims to having been stranded upon the Southward Ice or waylaid by pirates. If the Prophet won, then the owners would make their individual peace and live under the new rule.

Only one hundred ships of battle would sail—most of those the prize battle fleet of Mor, the missionary ships of Mord Rinn, and the hired frigates of the sailing guilds. The men who had stayed were the loyal followers of the Church, and they knelt as he made the Sign of the Arch above them.

Nearly twenty thousand men remained under his command, but in his heart Zimri knew they were not enough. In guns, he had a distinct advantage—nearly three times the Prophet's. But he feared the battle rams. Zimri had only a hundred against Ormson's four hundred.

He pondered such things while the procession wound through the ranks of men and ships. Along the walls of Cornath, the work crews paused while Zimri passed and then resumed building the triple line of ice walls that would defend against the Prophet's final onslaught.

The fifty monks, swaying under their burden, finally reached the stern of the flagship *St. Mor du Cornath*—a fifty-two-gun heavy cruiser—where an ornate iceladder had been prepared.

Stepping off the platform, Zimri ascended the stairs to the torch-lit deck, where the five hundred monks and priests of his crew awaited him. "All rise!" Zimri shouted. "Let us make sail," he called out in a high, clear voice that carried to the other ships drawn up alongside. "Set a course for Inys Gloi."

"I would like to sail with you to Cornath," she whispered in the dark.

He was silent, ignoring her light touch as she gently stroked his chest.

"Why?"

"To be with you, my love."

"You don't love me, and to say so is a lie."

"But Michael, my love, you have the power to look into one's soul. Look at me now and see for yourself that what I say is true."

He laughed coldly. "Don't try to fool me, Varinna. You've been trained to control your feelings."

"Then why do you allow me to sleep with you?"

"Don't ever ask that question again!"

He turned away from her. The old nightmare image flashed into mind. He pressed his hands to his forehead as if trying to drive the torment away. But it stayed, calling, driving him. Even when he was awake, walking in the world of flesh and substance, the images would hover before him. And the cries—he heard them, too, the voices and whispers, even as he lay in bed beside the beautiful woman, who only moments before had drained him of his passion.

And the voice drove him into the arms of the fanatical host that surrounded him. Their calling of the Messiah separated him more and more from the calm island of reality that he had once been. For two weeks, they had transformed Caediff into an armed camp, stockpiled with the thousands of tons of supplies necessary for a protracted winter campaign. He had watched the people, and wherever he went, they called to him—their voices full of religious fanaticism and the desire for plunder. And he took life and meaning from their cries.

Why was he betraying the memory of Janis? He tried to draw the thoughts forward into his consciousness, but he was above all human feelings, all human concern—or so he now thought.

"Shall we make love again?" she whispered, her hands softly embracing him, seeking his pleasure.

Roughly, he pushed her away and rose from the bed. "Leave me," he said hoarsely as he walked to the window. He scraped the ice away to gain a view of the harbor.

"As you wish, Michael. But you've yet to answer my question. May I sail with the fleet to Cornath?"

"Yes, damn you. Do what you want. See Seth about it." Turning, he looked at her. She stood naked by the side of the bed, her long blonde hair covering her heavy breasts in a soft, seductive manner.

"You know Seth, of course?"

She was silent.

"Of course you know Seth!" Michael shouted accusingly. "Of course he has already arranged passage for you. Now get out of my sight."

As if in a distant dream, he walked the length of the harbor— the thousands of Companions and the heavy shock troops standing to the front before their three-hundred-foot transport ships. On command, their scimitars were unsheathed to reflect brightly in the morning sun. Their calls for blood thundered around him as he gave curt nods of acknowledgment and walked on. Already the rams were making sail, and as they swept out in search formation, the picket ships were but smudges of white on the northern horizon.

The eastern sun cast long shadows across the Frozen Sea as Michael ascended to the bow of his command ship. Eldric, Finson, Cowan, and Daniel stood over the plotting board while the dozens of spotters overhead called out the positions of the battle fleet as it advanced northward.

His fleet drawn up to windward, less than a mile away, Zimri crossed the ice alone. He laughed quietly at the super-stitious dread shown by his followers when commanded to approach to within cannon shot of the towering wall of rock. Shouting down any protest, he ordered all guards to stand to and await his return. Before departing over the side in the full ceremonial robes of his office, Zimri had handed his new secretary an envelope sealed with the symbol of the silver hand pointing heavenward. Bathar was to open it if Zimri failed to return by nightfall.

A shudder of fear swept through him as he approached the west gate and disappeared into the shadows cast by the five-hundred-foot tower. There was no sign of human habitation. He knew they were watching, but what would happen if they refused to let him in or even acknowledge his presence? What a fool he would seem, standing before the gate like a rejected suitor.

As if in answer to his quiet fear, the heavy gates swung open on noiseless hinges to reveal a single form hooded in black, a large ebony staff in hand.

His head high, Zimri of the Cornathian Brotherhood advanced to meet the Grand Master of Inys Gloi. The master, his robes billowing in the icy wind, did not move.

Zimri stopped beneath the high arching gate, cast of precious steel in a distant, nearly forgotten age.

Zimri pulled aside his face mask and left it hanging to one side. The Master stood before him but left his face concealed beneath the deep folds of his heavy wool robes.

"Zimri, Holy See of Cornath, what seek ye beneath these forbidden gates?"

"The Grand Master of Inys Gloi."

"You stand before him whom you seek."

"I come to you with a simple message."

"You come to cast a seed of doubt into our plans."

"So you acknowledge that there is a plan."

"Of course, *my dear* Zimri, as you are so fond of saying. You would be a fool not to realize that we of Inys Gloi have a plan. I have been impressed by your climb to power, though we assumed such many years ago, when you were still the youngest archbishop in the history of Holy Church."

"I am glad to hear of your confidence in my success."

"You would not be so pleased to hear what we think of your chances in the days to come."

"That I know and assume, as well."

"Then why do you come here? You are wasting my time."

"Suppose I tell you that I plan to surrender everything I

have to Ormson. What would come of your plans?"

The master was silent.

Zimri laughed softly. "Not expected, is it?"

"Nor will it be done. We know you better. You will fight to the death to preserve the First Choice and, by so doing, preserve the power of the Church."

Zimri nodded. "But what if I die in the days to come?"

"There will be others."

"Such as Peter, whom, I dare say, you have managed to subvert. I must confess that when I first embarked on my campaign against Ormson, I felt I had a better than even chance of success. But betrayal of Caediff and Peter's failure to bring in Ezra have definitely weakened our chances."

"You have not come here to lament the change of your fortunes. You knew the risk when you antagonized Ormson. *That* saved you from exile and gained you the Holy See. Now you must pay the price. If Ormson defeats you on the Ice and takes Cornath, you have lost. Come, Zimri, hurry it up; I grow weary of our game. More important things await me. Why are you here?"

"To look into the face of my ultimate foe. Ormson is the mask that you hide behind. When the time comes, you will cast him aside. The pious prophecies which you have spread to the mob, which you have developed into a cult that now stands before the door of our Church, are nothing but the means to your own power. You are all that remains of the Church that once so powerfully ruled the destiny of man, three thousand years ago. Your brotherhood is all that is left of that most catholic power. You wait in the wings, ready to pick up the wreckage and start anew."

"You waste my time, Zimri, reciting that which we both know. A letter from one of the spies that you have attempted to plant in my ranks would have been sufficient to inform you of that."

Zimri smiled openly.

"You might penetrate the lowest ranks—that we have assumed. I myself was of St. Awstin, many years ago. I sailed with a master named Rifton, who found me a child in the gutter after my parents died of plague. I became such a plant, but to rise to the Inner Rank—that only comes when the conversion is complete, that only comes when you are of Inys Gloi, body and soul. Your dying Church will never penetrate our secrets, but we, we shall always be of yours. You should have asked poor Madoc, whom we corrupted without his knowing it."

Zimri tried to conceal his shock.

"Ah, so you did not know. I assumed not, and now I know. Remember how close Inys Gloi stands to you. Madoc never could have served all our purposes. His order was too much feared; his personal habits, as you knew to your advantage, were too easily corruptible. That is why we chose you over him, for you have only one overriding concern, the preservation of the Church and the insurance of your own power. Men who desire power above all else are men we respect. Men we can deal with."

"And when I no longer serve your purpose?"

"Come now, Zimri—do you really expect us to reveal *that*?"

"Then be warned, master of Inys Gloi. You need me far more than you care to acknowledge. You could kill Ormson tomorrow. It would be no problem for you, but the circle that he is leading still needs his guidance—and his madness. Strike him down now and the movement will die. No, you need him for another generation at least."

"You bore me, Zimri. State what has to be stated and lecture me not."

"You cannot kill me. I alone can prosecute this war. I realize, as well, that war is what you want, for in it the two powers will cripple each other. But if the will of one collapses and your Messiah at last becomes aware of your plan, then even the power of Heaven—if it exists—will not spare you his rage and that of his followers, whom you have betrayed. I alone can stop him—though it will most likely wreck our Church. I warn you, master of Inys Gloi, make no move against me. If you do, even from beyond death I will destroy your plans. Forever."

"Who are you to threaten Inys Gloi," the master replied with disdain.

"As long as I live, we fight, and that serves your cause. I control until my last moment the Brotherhood of the First Choice. I also control the seventy-three abbeys of Mor."

"Seventy-two," the master interrupted. "You lost one at Caediff two weeks ago, or hadn't you heard."

"Then it is seventy-two. If the circumstances of my death are suspicious, the monasteries of Mor will receive my final instruction."

"And pray, what is it that? Trembling, I await your information."

"I shall reveal to my seventy-two abbots the details of the First Choice and order my men to storm the holdings wherein all secular knowledge is hidden. They will then destroy that knowledge. But first they shall reveal to the populace the details of the First Choice and describe the knowledge to be lost; then the abbots will place all blame for the destruction on your society. And then, my dear master, where will you be indeed? What will be left of you in the chaos that follows the revelation that *all* our religions are fantasies?

"An age of humanism will result—and unrelenting fury against the secret order that destroyed what could have been. If you recall the last age of humanism, you undoubtedly remember what happened. So I bid you good day, master of Inys Gloi. But not good-bye. I am sure we shall meet again before this drama is complete." He walked away.

Soon he disappeared into the open stern hatch of the heavy ice cruiser. A hundred ships braced on sail and, hiking on their downwind runners, ran across a freshening breeze to the southwest, where less than two hundred miles away the fleets of Ormson approached in battle formation. For the first time in his life, the master stood alone upon the ice, having walked out for over a league to watch the passing of the ships. The wind increased, whipping his robes in swirling billows of blackness. For the first time in his life, he knew that he was facing an adversary who was his equal.

CHAPTER 15

"SHALL WE OFFER ACTION?" FINSON INQUIRED, LOOKING UP from the plotting board.

"Rockets again, from green scout-section," came the shout from the foretop observation post. "Enemy standing to, circling, ten leagues ahead."

"How long to close?" Michael asked quietly, leaning over the board, watching as more and more ship markers, representing the first sightings of the Cornathian fleet, were placed on the northern side.

"If they stand in formation and wait for us, half an hour for the lead fleet of rams to pierce their outer lines," Eldric replied.

Michael looked to the western horizon. Less than an hour of light remained to them.

"Think they'll hold?"

"'Tis seventy leagues northward to Cornath," Eldric replied. "Zimri will have to hold. If he turns to run, we'll be before Cornath this time tomorrow, and if we arrive without a fight, then St. Awstin and the others will fold, decrying the 'protection of Mor.'"

"What say you to pressing the action now?" Finson asked eagerly.

"I counsel not," Eldric interjected. "We'll have an hour of

action at best, and we will not be able to bring our full strength
to bear. Darkness will be to his advantage, giving aid to his
inferior numbers. If defeated, he will take advantage of night
to withdraw. Let us hold till dawn, then engage with a full day
ahead of us. Then none will escape."

Michael looked around the table.

"As soon as darkness falls," Eldric continued, "send two
battle groups of rams, their escorts, and half a dozen frigates
to the northeast. Let them hug the coast and push northward
to Cornath. After tomorrow's victory, they can be the net to
sweep up any that retreat to harbor."

The men nodded agreement.

"But I fear one thing," Cowan said cautiously. "Zimri is
desperate. He needs some sort of victory at any cost if he is
to hold the church together. I venture that he has even sailed
with the fleet as a political gesture to his followers. Remember,
Michael, desperation drove us to victory six years ago. We
had to win and we had to do the unexpected to bring about
that victory. I dare say that Zimri's thinking at this moment
might be very similar to the way ours was. Above all else,
Michael, you should take that into your counsel."

Cowan knew that several of the battle leaders saw the wisdom in what he said, but his being out of favor influenced
them to say nothing in support of his words.

Seth stood on one side, looking away from the table straight
out to the open sea.

"What say you, Seth?" Michael asked in a distant voice.

"He'll fight us to the death, but remember that this is just
the opening round. If Zimri is with the fleet, he will play the
game cautiously. He is desperate, but not to the point of fool-
hardiness as we were once."

"Still, we must anticipate the unexpected," Finson replied.
"He undoubtedly knows we are here. The heavy line of picket
ships must reveal that to the enemy admiral, whoever he might
be. We should let the pickets maintain close contact and order
the rest of our fleet to stand to here. As a protection against
any night raids, we should order Cowan's division of Companions to disembark and establish a fortified zone between us
and the Cornathian fleet."

The men nodded their agreement.

"Let it be done," Michael replied, and by his tone he signaled that the conference was at an end.

Michael turned from the battle board and walked alone to the prow of the ship, while Eldric shouted orders to the signal boys. A curtain of signal rockets rose from the stern of the vessel. Light rafts were lowered, and the fleet commanders returned to their commands.

As far as the eye could see, the fleet covered the frozen sea. In response to Eldric's commands, the main body of the fleet hove to and prepared for night defense. On the distant horizon, the twilight was soon banished by the steadily growing light of burning vessels, cannon flashes, and rocket flares signaling the initial contact between the two fleets. Even from fifteen miles away the thunder washed over them, drumming against the Mathinians, warning them of the battle to come. Hoping to catch a glimpse of the action, thousands of men crowded the decks and riggings of the ships.

Michael stood alone. Occasional ragged cheers swept across the ice in response to a particularly large explosion, and Michael felt his pulse quicken at the sound of his men glorying in battle. *He* was there. Zimri was there. And with the realization, Michael's memories merged into a bloody image. He had only one purpose . . .

"But, my lord, if I might interject, to do so is an unwarranted risk. We could fight a slow withdrawing action, delaying their approach to Cornath, and still have the fleet intact for the final confrontation before the city gates."

In the distance, the Morian monks were chanting as they led the faithful in prayer. By Zimri's order, every major ship carried a Sacred Relic aboard, and the holy objects were being carried in Holy Processions to instill courage and fortitude in the followers of the Cornathian Brotherhood.

Shaking his head, Zimri stood up and walked toward the bow of the ship. To the south the horizon pulsed with distant flashes. A half-dozen steady glows marked the places where ships had gone to their doom as the two fleets probed each other in the night. Even as he watched, a brilliant flash illuminated the horizon suddenly, silhouetting in stark detail the ships of the main Cornathian battle group. They were waiting for him, he realized; he could not show weakness or doubt.

"You have heard my orders. In one hour, it shall be done. All ships are to hoist sail. Guns are to be double shotted but unprimed so that we might avoid any premature firing. We are to pierce their picket line and attempt to fight our way through to the transports. Each ship is to strike with full speed and do as much damage as possible. When it can no longer take the punishment, the ship may withdraw. I need not remind the secular captains that Morians aboard each ship will report to me after the action. I expect every man to do his duty to Cornath. After breaking free, the surviving vessels are to rendezvous off the abbey of Inys Gloi. If the rendezvous cannot be made, then proceed to North Prydain."

"Not to Cornath?" Ulfin, commander of the heavy cruiser *Therithmar*, asked in his soft lisping voice.

"No, damn it, not to Cornath. If we fail to destroy Ormson tonight, then we must accept the fact that Cornath might very well fall within the month."

Startled expressions appeared around the table but were quickly replaced by studied neutrality.

"Yes, you heard me. Unless we deliver a crushing blow, Cornath will fall. I want this fleet to survive after doing as much damage as possible. We will fight our way back one day, but we need the nucleus of a fleet to build from. Now, are there any further protests?"

From the manner of his speech, the captains knew that any further questioning was useless.

"Good. Kneel for thy blessing."

The men dutifully bowed down before their lord as he solemnly made the Sign of the Arch. In the night breeze, his dark blue robes fluttered around him. The only sign of his high office was the purple skullcap. Its golden thread shimmered brightly in the torchlight.

"We move within the hour."

The men rose, saluted the Holy See, and going over the side, he was left alone to contemplate the final moments before action was closed. He knew he should be feeling some kind of fear, instead, he was filled with a sense of peace, a calm self-assurance that the actions he was taking were right.

He knew that his chances were slim. When he had first formulated his plan while still in exile, he had known that the odds were against him. His rise to power was linked to that of Ormson. It had almost destroyed him once, and it still could put an end to his dreams. For that matter, a stray cannon shot could do it within the next hour, but when that thought surfaced, he pushed it away.

Without the war, he never would have been made Holy See. If he had not obtained that office, the Church would have drifted from the strong course of action that was necessary to face Ormson, Inys Gloi, and the threat to the First Choice. That was behind him; now came the final challenge—the actual war with Michael. He knew even before starting the war that Ormson's power had grown beyond anyone's expectations. The only way to win was to fight on Zimri's home ground, to lure Ormson onto strange territory, and to bring the horror of war to Cornath. After the betrayal of Ezra, Zimri realized that the opening actions would result in his defeat. But defeat can fertilize the seeds of victory. Let the people of Cornath see the full horror of this new religious war, and soon they would rise up to drive the invader out. The brotherhoods that fell away were weak and corrupt with age and lack of true purpose. Let the war purge them, and new, stronger brotherhoods would grow in their place.

A series of flashes punctuated the night; several dozen flares rose into the night sky, shimmering faintly against the Arch. They drifted back to the ice and disappeared. He waited for a moment, wondering if it was a signal for attack. Long minutes passed by—the battle did not swell. A rocket supply must have been hit. Good, then Ormson was still waiting, not anticipating so desperate an action as his. Never in the history of the Ice had a full night attack been launched by an entire fleet. The odds were against Zimri, but such an action was bound to place Ormson off balance, and it would give him the proper political points, as well. Not for three hundred years had a Holy See sailed to battle. Such an action, even if it resulted in defeat, would help to unite the people around his rule.

After the battle, he would sail to Cornath. It would take weeks of siege before the city was threatened, and all the time his stature as a leader would grow. To hide in the Cathedral of Dulyn after starting the war would have been political suicide. But to lead in battle would show the entire world that the Cornathian Church was still a strong, viable entity. Of course, when it appeared that the siege would succeed, he would arrange for his advisors to force him into retreat through the secret tunnels under the mountain monasteries and then emerge triumphant as the warrior See.

There was one final factor, as well. He knew what his actions had done to Ormson. He could imagine what Michael's reactions would be when the Prophet discovered that his most hated foe stood upon the opposing line. The thought fit his plans, but it also provoked a chilling thought—one that he quickly pushed away.

There was a soft whisper behind him.

"My lord."

"Yes."

"It is time that we begin."

A flicker of light flashed on the horizon. Another followed, then five or six in quick succession. A steady glow on the horizon started to climb higher. Suddenly, the cannon flashes spread wider and wider across the horizon, running from northwest to northeast. The flickering lights were punctuated by frequent, dazzling explosions—volley fires by heavy ships. The darkness to the north was driven away by the rapidly expanding hurricane of fire and light. A deep, low booming, felt more than heard, drifted in on the northwesterly breeze.

Daniel came up to stand beside him. "Probing the line?"

"I don't know, might be a raid in force," Michael replied.

"Would Cowan's Companions be in position yet?"

"I doubt it," Michael replied. "It will be another hour, at least, before their defensive works will be up."

Rockets flashed to the north, northwest.

"Can you read them?" Eldric called, coming forward to join Michael and Daniel.

"Too far," the foretop observer shouted. "The signal relay will pick it up."

Michael waited tensely, his fears starting to form. With every second, the flashing on the horizon grew in its intensity.

The relay ship two leagues forward of the command vessel finally exploded into action, lofting four red rockets, followed only seconds later by four more.

"My bloody wounds," Daniel shouted, "the filthy bugger's attacking at night!"

"I should have known," Michael said with a detached, distant voice. "I should have known—it's what I would have done if I were he."

"It could be a false alarm," Daniel shouted above the rising clamor of voices on the flagship's deck.

"Deck ho!" came the cry from the mainforetop lookout. "Our picket ships are drawing back. The action is coming toward us!"

"Sound the alarm," Michael called. "Clear for action."

"We've broken through the outer picket line, my lord."

"I realize that. Any losses reported?"

Parishson stood before him, his robes whipping in the frigid night air.

"It's hard to say," Parishson shouted above the growing roar of battle.

A quarter mile away, a Cornathian light frigate exploded into flames—her magazine detonating with a thundering roar. Tons of debris arched heavenward as the explosive noise of destruction beat against Zimri. In the flash of the explosion, Zimri saw the ragged formations of his fleet as it ran on a broad reach toward Ormson's lines. Some of the ships were veering to port and starboard, attempting to drive in on the flanks rather than to dare a straight-on approach, where barrier lines might have been erected. A hundred yards astern, a flaming bolt from a light schooner ignited one of the sails of a Mathinian corsair, bathing the ice around them in a garish red light.

"Ease off the mainsheet," Parishson called out. "Bring in the fore and main top."

The ship was losing its breathtaking speed as the sails were drawn in. It was necessary for Zimri to start off at the head of the assault, but prudence demanded that he let the others lead the way; he would follow in their wake.

For several minutes, the Cornathians pressed in, greeted only by a scattering of shot from light patrol craft that fell back, dogging their flanks.

Suddenly, a series of rockets rose across a broad front of several miles. Arcing upward, they exploded with a dazzling white glare that illuminated the frozen sea, showing the approaching Cornathian fleet in high relief. In that moment, Zimri saw several of his ships go down, victims of the trap lines that Ormson had started to build. Ahead, the ice swarmed with thousands of white-clad men who dodged this way and that to avoid the razor-sharp blades of Zimri's approaching fleet. The heavy crossbows and onagers of Zimri's fleet came into play as it sped past the Mathinian foot troops. Dozens of men were cut down by the Cornathian bolts, their shattered bodies pinned to the ice by heavy spears. From the shadows, Zimri clearly saw a panic-stricken Companion desperately running before them. The heavy cruiser bore down on him, and with a shriek of agony, the Mathinian disappeared under the blades, his body cut in half, spraying the port outrigger with blood as the two halves of the body fell to either side.

"Hard a port!" came the shout from the spotter on the flying jib bow.

The flagship heeled hard over, rising on its runners, cutting a magnificent arc of spray as the fifty-two-gun ship swerved to avoid a series of ice blocks.

"Hard, bring it hard a starboard!"

The ship slammed down on its runners and then rose up again on the opposite tack. A bone-shattering lurch knocked Zimri off his feet. Several men tumbled from the rigging, shrieking in terror as they plummeted to the deck, impacting with a sickening thud.

"We've taken a hit!" came the call from the port outrigger lookouts.

Zimri ran to the railing and looked over the side. In the dying glare of a rocket volley, he made out the twisted runner, dragging heavily, cutting their speed.

"The fleet, there's the fleet!" came the call from above. "Damn them, they're making sail!"

"Launch all rams," Parishson called.

Zimri barely noticed the age-old ritual as the horn and drum of the rams were sounded. Before going into battle, the rams had been run out, sails hoisted and pilots in place.

Refusing to turn into the wind, the ship's master ordered the rams away while running abeam the wind. Several of the rams on the upwind side became fouled in the flagship's outrigger and had to be cut away with a loss of two pilots, who

Ram

were thrown from their vessels. But the rest maneuvered clear
and pressed the attack on the enemy fleet.

"Heretic merchantman, dead ahead."

"Bring her to starboard," Parishson called. "Prime your
pieces and prepare to fire."

Even before the ship had completed its turn, the first gun
belowdecks thundered out, aiming at a half-visible shadow
that loomed up out of the night.

The catapults and ballistae slammed out their shot, while
down the three-hundred-foot length of the ship, the cannon
roared as quickly as they could be brought to bear. But they
had no visible effect as the merchantman lurched off its course
and disappeared back into the shadows of night.

Several shots bounded in from an unknown quarter, cutting
holes in the sails, parting rigging lines that cracked and whipped
as their tension was released.

Above the howl of the wind, the roar of battle echoed through
the night, as across a hundred square miles of ice the two
colliding fleets engaged each other. In the confusion, ships

fired at anything that came close, sometimes slaughtering their own comrades while hysterically cheering the glory of their cause.

Within minutes, Zimri's surprise attack had cleaved through to the center of Michael's flotilla, leaving a flaming trail of wreckage that could be spotted from twenty leagues away.

"Master, there—to the northwest—a heavy cruiser."

Michael was silent. Dozens of rockets had been launched to order the battle, but it was impossible to tell where any substantial part of his fleet was. The sending of orders had descended into a ritual, whereby Michael and Eldric hoped that somehow they could bring order out of chaos.

A clear trail of flaming hulks stretched to the north for half a dozen leagues. In the flickering shadows, a nightmarish scene of insane slaughter was visible where the enraged Companions poured out of their transport ships to fall upon the wrecks and administered aid or death, depending on who one worshiped.

"Master, we have a signal," came a cry from above. "The transport flagship reports that all of their ships, save the Companions' fleet, are under full sail and withdrawing southward out of range of the action."

From overhead, there was a continual babble of shouts as the dozens of signal callers tried to interpret the confusion of rocket signals that rose upward in a circle around them.

"Any report from the ram fleets?" Michael shouted above the roar of battle.

"Nothing."

A shot hummed in, slamming into the ship belowdecks. Within seconds, the ship was awash in terrified screams as the wounded were dragged from the wreckage.

"Several ships closing from northeast—appear to be heavy cruisers."

Michael looked into the gloom and noticed a shadow cutting before the light of a flaming Cornathian frigate.

"Rams," a hysterical young voice shouted from above. "Cornathian rams!"

Before the cruisers, a line of rams was spreading out. To the west, there was a blinding flash of light as two Mathinian armed merchantmen let fly with volleys into the attacking Cornathian vessels. The cruisers answered in kind, smashing one of the merchantmen with a single volley that swept away its rigging and portside outrigger. The ship went into a spin and flipped over.

"Cut across their bow!" Eldric shouted. "Stay out of their broadside!"

From the south, a number of Mathinian rams came up, and even above the wild cacophony of noise, Michael could hear their death chants as they swept past the flagship. In seconds, two heavy rams collided head on with the Cornathian death craft. The rest of the Mathinian battle fleet pushed its way through the confusion. Suddenly, Michael's attention was drawn by a loud, splintering crash, and he saw the half-shadow images of a heavy cruiser's sails tumbling down.

"That was one, for sure," Daniel shouted triumphantly. "Damn my soul for not riding with them tonight."

The initial attack had been brilliant, Michael thought grimly, but they should have just hit the flanks and pulled out. The heavy cruisers could wreak havoc, to be sure, but the smaller rams, which were harder to spot, would swarm over them in the night.

"Hard a port, wreckage ahead."

The flagship nearly went into a disastrous skid as the pilot pulled the helm over. The ship jarred and rattled as it ran over spars and rigging. Screams drifted past them as the wounded survivors of a heavy merchantman cried out in fear at the sudden approach of the frigate.

"Look out!" came a terrified scream from above. "We're being wedged by two cruisers."

A heavy schooner exploded to the east and briefly illuminated two cruisers running parallel to each other, separated only by a distance of several hundred yards. Within seconds, the command ship would run right between the two.

"Hard a port!" Eldric shouted.

The ship cut an arch of spray, nearly colliding with two rams that were maneuvering to strike the heavy Cornathian ships.

As they came about into the wind, the speed of the frigate dropped off. The cruisers loomed closer.

"Prepare for a broadside," the lookouts shouted from above.

Not a hundred yards off, they cut across the bow of the enemy ship. The dozen guns belowdecks fired their double-shotted metal into the approaching cruiser. Great sections of the enemy's deck were peeled away, and several fires were ignited as hot shot buckets rolled, dumping their flaming cargo. A ragged cheer went up from the Companions as they fired their heavy crossbows and four-man ballistae into the ship's rigging to hit the foretop crews and sails with flaming shot.

"Bring her parallel," Michael called. "We'll give her a broadside from our portside guns."

Daniel and Eldric, inflamed with the joy of battle, offered no protest at the suicidal orders of exchanging broadsides with an enemy ship that carried twice their metal and could throw four times their weight in shot.

The flagship arced across the bow of the enemy ship, cutting a tight circle, while the cruiser, running on the fastest angle to the wind, cut inside the arc of the frigate and drew parallel to it. Michael drew in his breath as he saw the foreboding line of enemy guns start to flash.

"Your Holiness, are you safe?"

He had not seen the moment of the broadside when the enemy frigate had crossed their bow. Several monks had fallen upon him and dragged him behind the relative safety of the foremast, covering him with their bodies. He had felt the terrifying impact of the enemy shot as it swept the deck. As he pushed the monks aside, he swore at them with the deepest oaths, yet as he surveyed the damage, Zimri gave an inner prayer of thanks for their forethought. The forecastle was a flaming shambles—half a dozen advisors and spotters were dead. The two fore ballistae were smashed to splinters, their flaming shot causing half a dozen fires, which illuminated the deck with a garish light.

"She's coming parallel to trade broadsides."

Half a dozen monks swarmed around him again, trying to bear him to shelter.

"Damn you, no," Zimri screamed. "I'll stand here."

He was amazed at his own courage, it had been twenty years since he faced fire, and the memory of it still shook him with cold fear. But not now. Now he was caught in the fury of the moment and wished to watch. He barely noticed the looks of fear and admiration that his men gave to him. Never had they heard of a Holy See standing beside them and sharing their risks. Many called his name as they bore down on the foe.

The first gun thundered its double shot, the sulfurous smoke billowing up around him as it poured out of the vents. Then the deck catapults started to fire, one after another, their flaming shot arching out to the target not fifty yards away. All along the deck, swarms of crossbowmen raised their weapons, the twanging of their bows a high-pitched counterpoint to the deep boom of the gun: as the shot poured out.

In one blinding flash, the Mathinians returned fire in a scathing volley. The cruiser lurched sickeningly from the impact. A guard in front of Zimri spun around, screaming wildly, tearing at his eyes; then a shower of blood washed over Zimri while the heart of a monk not two feet to his left pumped great gouts of crimson blood through severed arteries.

All around him were screams of rage and hate.

"Load, damn your souls, load and feed it to him!" Parishson cried, his left arm hanging limp, a foot-long splinter of wood sticking out of his shoulder.

The frigate started to ease off into the wind, but the Cornathian pilot followed her actions, bringing the ships so close to each other that an agile ice runner could have leaped from one outrigger to the other.

The deck rumbled beneath Zimri's feet as the guns belowdecks, double shotted with roundball and grape, were run back out. They were so close to the frigate that the Morian gun deacons wasted no time in aiming. As soon as the guns were clear of the hatches, the pieces were fired.

In ragged succession, the twenty-four-gun broadside smashed into the hull of the frigate. By the raging fires that were scorching both ships, Zimri could see vast sections of hull, outrigger, decking, and human bodies being swept up and disintegrating under the deadly impact of short-range cannon fire.

A volley of arrows hailed down upon the Cornathian's deck. Another Morian guard tumbled forward, a red barb sticking out the back of his head.

Suddenly, above the roar of battle, the Cornathians heard a distant scream. "Zimri! Damn your soul, Zimri!" The cry was drawn out into a long, hysterical scream.

The two ships bumped each other; their decks were only fifteen yards apart. The crews from both vessels started to swarm over the railings in their eagerness to come to blows.

A guard directly in front of Zimri went down screaming, and the surviving monks drew closer, desperately trying to form a protective ring around the Holy See.

His own men now started to shout in wild, insane rage, pointing to the forecastle of the enemy frigate.

"It's Ormson, Saints curse him; it's the heretic!"

Several priests raised up their crossbows and fired straight at a cluster of men grouped around the enemy's pilot box. Their arrows swept into the crowd with deadly effect. The Mathinian's guns started to fire again, and the deck beneath Zimri's feet shuddered under the impact. An explosion sounded near the stern, and behind the mainmast, the deck burst open, fire shooting upward.

"The auxiliary magazine's been hit," one of Zimri's aides shouted.

The heavy cruiser shuddered as another explosion tore through the ship, ripping open the deck for nearly a quarter length of the vessel. Flames licked up, catching more than one man, to ignite his furs like a torch. Wild screams rent the air as men burned to death, while a ragged, insane cheer rose up from their rival ship.

Again, a voice echoed high and clear, with such a chilling effect that Zimri felt the voice was actually calling inside his mind. "Zimri, damn you forever!"

Looking to the enemy forecastle, he saw a tall, slender figure struggle free from a circle of white-clad men.

It was Ormson!

Fascinated, Zimri stood riveted to the deck as Michael grabbed a crossbow from one of his men and brought it up to firing position. Several men around Michael collapsed from a volley of arrows, but he didn't notice, so intent was he upon his target. As if in a dream, Zimri watched Michael aim the weapon straight at him. He was fascinated by the action. Ormson had been the enemy, the embodiment of the strife, and now less than fifty feet separated them.

All around him was fire and death—rigging tumbling from above, men screaming, guns firing—but everything was lost to Zimri as he watched Michael push forward to the frigate's railing. He felt as if he could reach out and touch the face of madness that was before him. He could almost see the hand fleck on the trigger of the bow as the ship rocked beneath his feet from the stunning explosions of half a hundred guns.

The hand closed on the trigger. And then he was lost to view as a monk raised a shield up to ward off the blow. The monk staggered backward and then tottered to one side, the arrow having driven clear through the shield and embedded itself in the monk's shoulder.

The ships began to part as a cry came down from above.

"Rams, rams dead ahead!"

In the brief moment of contact between the two ships, dozens of men had swarmed over the side to engage in close combat on the outriggers. As the ships parted, men desperately struggled to regain their own vessels, but many fell in the confusion, screaming until they were crushed on the ice. From overhead came a steady shower of flaming bolts, broken spars, torn rigging, and crushed bodies that thudded on the decks of the two vessels.

Zimri saw Ormson again when the Prophet threw the bow overboard and started to climb out onto the frigate's outrigger. Half a dozen men swarmed over him and dragged him down. A Cornathian arrow caught one of them, sending him overboard, where he slammed into the outrigger support. The body was left to hang upside down while a river of blood poured from his face, to splash on the frozen sea below.

Another volley thundered from the cruiser's surviving cannon, and the frigate's mizzenmast crashed to the deck.

"Rams closing."

"Hard a starboard."

"We're going to hit!"

Zimri was swept off his feet as the first ram crashed against the portside outrigger. He clearly heard the death screams of the Mathinians crushed beneath the massive blades of the cruiser. The cruiser's rigging lines snapped under the strain, and the heavy ropes whipped across the deck, crushing any unfortunate enough to be in the way.

"Two more to starboard."

"Turn, damn you, turn!" Parishson screamed as the pilot tried to bring the wheel over.

Zimri struggled to his feet as the ship heeled hard over on its damaged portside outrigger. He could hear timbers cracking under the strain and some of the men around him wailing in fear, thinking that the ship was breaking up. The ship hiked higher, its deck slanting over at a terrifying angle. Belowdecks two guns broke free of their moorings and crashed through the length of the vessel to burst through the portside hull with bone-jarring crashes. Hanging onto the foremast, Zimri watched as two Mathinian rams shot past the port outrigger, their crews screaming defiance as they missed their targets, passing the cruiser at over a hundred miles an hour.

"Where's the frigate?" Zimri shouted. "Ormson's frigate?" He looked back over the railing; far astern he saw a ship ablaze, its sails bursting into flame, while overhead a series of rocket flares hovered in the midnight sky, mimicking the shimmering scarlet of the northern aurora.

"More rams port beam."

"We're clearing out," Parishson shouted. "We've taken too much already."

As if in answer to Parishson's call, another explosion ripped through the interior of the ship.

Zimri looked back to the flickering fire astern, then swept the sea with his gaze. From horizon to horizon, the ice was on fire, the deep red flames of a hundred wrecks punctuated by blinding white-hot flashes as ship's magazines detonated with thunderclap roars.

Not this time, Zimri thought grimly, but then it is not yet time, after all. "Get us out of here," Zimri shouted, "we've done enough for one night."

"Abandon ship!"

"No!" Michael screamed. "In, and after him; it's Zimri!"

Four men struggled with Michael, trying to hold him down and protect him from the deadly debris that showered from overhead. He was covered in blood, and Daniel pushed his way past the men, fearing the worst. A graze to Michael's forehead was bleeding profusely—nothing more. Daniel felt the wild madness of the crew, and the hatred set the hairs tingling on the back of his neck.

"Burn her, kill him, kill him!" The cry still echoed across the deck, the blood-maddened Companions having taken up Michael's cry. Only the death of the pilot and the confused struggle with Michael had allowed Daniel to gain control of the wheel and pull the crippled vessel away. An explosion ripped belowdecks, the fire having reached the stacked powder bags piled carelessly next to a cannon.

"Abandon ship; the main magazine is going to blow!"

"Signal men, summon another ship!" Eldric cried. "Everyone overboard!"

Five red rockets rose from the launch tubes.

The frigate was pointed straight into the wind, and several Mathinian rams cut by dangerously close, having picked them for a target in the confusion and breaking their attack only at the last second.

"Michael, we have to leave!" Daniel shouted.

"No, damn you, no! In after him, after him!"

Before anyone had time to react, Daniel rushed up to Michael and delivered a stunning blow with the flat side of his ax, knocking Michael to the ground. One of the Companions, his eyes wild with rage, turned on Daniel, sword raised to strike. With no hesitation, Daniel cut the guard in half. The Companions stood back in stunned confusion.

"Now, get him over," Daniel screamed, waving the bloody ax before his men.

"A ram!" the shout came up from amidship.

Daniel looked up, then threw himself to the deck, covering Michael's body with his own. The ship seemed to lurch clear of the ice; then there was a howling explosion of wood. The ram smashed through the outrigger and crashed into the side of the frigate, tearing out the mainmast step. Rigging lines parted as if made of twine. The two-hundred-foot-high tower of wood, rope, and canvas lurched back and forth, and then slowly leaned to port. Lines parted, then the mainmast fell, raining a shower of doomed men onto the rock-hard ice, their bodies bursting open from the impact. The entire frigate lifted into the air again as the butt of the mast ripped through the starboard side of the ship, severing the craft in two, spilling its contents out onto the frozen sea, while fires exploded along the deck as flaming shot buckets tumbled over.

Scrambling to his feet, Daniel hoisted Michael's body onto his shoulders. One of the Companions took a length of rope and quickly lashed Ormson's hands around Daniel's neck. Swinging himself over the side of the ship, Daniel grabbed hold of a length of line and slid down to the ice, his gloves smoking from the friction.

After reaching the frozen sea, Daniel started off at a run, men falling in around him, crossbows raised in a circle of protection. He could feel Michael struggling weakly on his back. After a hundred yards, Daniel slowed his pace and finally stopped alongside a shattered Cornathian ram, whose pilot, his body pinned below the waist by the bulk of the craft, struggled and cried out for mercy.

The frigate exploded behind them, flooding the sea with light.

"Untie me," Michael said weakly.

Several men came up to Daniel and helped him with his burden. Leaning on a blood-spattered Companion, Michael regained his feet, then doubled over with convulsive vomiting.

Around him, the survivors gathered, dozens of them streaming away from the wreckage. Most of them were still shouting wildly—their battle lust not yet sated.

In the growing light cast by the funeral pyre of the ship, Daniel could see that the ram that had finished them was one of their own—the crew went to its death in the belief that they were finishing off a Cornathian vessel.

"I'm sorry, Michael," Daniel said gruffly, kneeling down by his master's side. "If I hadn't, you would be back there, dead."

"Perhaps for the better," Michael said with a cold, enigmatic smile. Picking up a discarded scimitar from the ice, he stood alone, wordlessly watching as the battle drifted to the northeast as the Cornathian fleet withdrew.

In the distance, he heard hoarse cries and the sounds of close combat as maddened survivors swept across the ice to seek out their enemies.

"Ships! Three of them coming in from the east," one of the Companions cried, raising his scimitar in anticipation.

The shadows gained form, the men waiting to see what fate would bring to them—several of them started their death chants, preparing for the final moment of strife.

"Cowan, it's Cowan's command ship!" Eldric shouted. The lead ship, a heavy frigate, cut across them to the south and came into the wind, a shower of ice crystals sweeping up from the stern. Even before it stopped, Michael saw Cowan running along the ship's outrigger with several of his men. They leaped from their vessel and sprinted toward the knot of men who had formed a defensive position.

"The master?"

"Alive," one of the guards shouted.

Cowan came through the press and approached Michael.

"Madness," Cowan cried. "Absolute madness—you should have stayed clear!"

"Zimri was aboard that ship," Michael said faintly.

Behind them, there was a low, guttural cry. Looking over Michael's shoulder, Cowan saw a Companion bending over the wounded Cornathian pilot. The Companion stood up, his features contorted in a demonic grin. In his hand, he waved a human head—still dripping blood.

CHAPTER 16

"I'M GOING OVER TO THE OTHER SHIP. ARE THERE ANY FINAL questions?"

"No, my lord, but I must say again that your return to Cornath is dangerous. In my opinion, suicidal. Sail with us, I beg you."

Zimri shook his head.

"I must set the example. If I fail to defend Cornath, the city will go over to the enemy, and the confederation will dissolve without a fight. My enemies would say that I started the war but fled to safety, leaving them to fight."

Parishson nodded. "Your blessing, then, my lord."

Zimri raised his hands, and the crew fell to their knees. Zimri examined the grim sight in the light of early morning. The deck was torn and battle scarred. A faint wisp of smoke was still coiling up from belowdecks where the midsection of the ship had been burned out, exposing the interior of the vessel to the sixty degrees of frost. Frozen bodies were stacked on the sternway awaiting a free moment and the proper rites of burial. Zimri looked to the shattered doors leading into the ceremonial chapel. The intricately carved wood by Dubranth, the near-legendary master woodcarver, had been shattered by the blast of heavy shot and grape that had destroyed the sacred altar concealed within.

Nearly a third of the ship's guns were permanently out of action, but that was of no consequence, since all powder had been jettisoned when the fire started to lick dangerously close to the main reserve.

Zimri was weary, infinitely weary. He had been more than a day without sleep, but there was no time to think of that now—these were his men, and the final blessing was the least he could do.

"I absolve thee of thy sins and bless you in the name of Saint Mor and all the Holy Saints. May those Above watch over you in the crisis to come, and may each of you be assured of the promise of the Long Table, where you shall sup until the Return of the Father."

"Signal to southwest. Enemy in sight," a monk called from the mainmast lookout.

Trying not to appear hurried, Zimri finished the prayer while his men knelt upon the torn deck.

"Go now to battle with my blessings and my love, and rejoice in the knowledge of your salvation. Amen." He walked to the railing of the ship and started to climb onto the starboard outrigger. His men stood up and with wild cries chanted his name. A cold chill of emotion washed through him. They were dying for him, but still they called his name. He raised a clenched fist into the air, and his men roared their response. Turning, he climbed down onto the outrigger. The ice passed by beneath him at a blinding speed, but he did not look down as he leaped across to the outrigger of the light sloop that ran alongside. Helping hands pulled him aboard and guided him up onto the deck of the Morian messenger ship, *St. Jarin*.

As Zimri walked down the length of the ship, it accelerated. By the time he reached the forecastle, the cruiser was already a hundred yards astern and falling rapidly away. He looked over the rail and swept the sea with his gaze. Nearly forty ships had made the rendezvous point, and Parishson had assured him that this indeed was remarkable, estimating that perhaps three-quarters of the fleet had survived the night action. But they had no time to loiter, since Ormson's fleet was in close pursuit. They were not six leagues astern and closing in, and Cornath was still half a day's sail away. The fleet would make for

Cornath, but only Zimri's ship and four light escort schooners would run for the harbor. The rest would sail northward and await his orders.

Ordering that he not be disturbed unless the question was serious, Zimri went below, hoping to snatch a brief rest. But before he could close his eyes he heard a cry of dismay from astern. The heavy cruiser was dumping bundles from her stern. Parishson was burying his dead upon the open ice. There would be no time for ceremony that day.

"Our losses?"

"Not as bad as first thought," Cowan responded evenly. "Four frigates, thirty-nine other craft. We lost one transport with nearly a thousand dead and forty-two battle rams, as well. It sounds bad, Michael, but it could have been far worse."

Michael was silent for a moment. "And theirs?"

"Three cruisers and at least twenty other craft."

"And Zimri's ship?"

"Appears to have escaped."

"Damn him!" Michael shouted, slamming his fist on the table. "He'll be able to call this a victory. He hit us hard and got away. This will only serve to strengthen the morale on his side and help to rally the people to support him. Damn him; he looks like a bloody hero—the great Holy See sailing forth to battle."

"Our covering fleet on the Cornathian harbor should be in position by now," Eldric said quietly, trying to draw Michael's attention back to the battle plans.

"Then crush him," Michael said grimly. "Let him not escape back into the city. This is our chance to crush him once and for all."

"We shall try our best, master."

"Don't try," Michael shouted. "Do it!"

"Sire." A hand gently touched him on the shoulder.

Sitting up and pushing the furs from him, Zimri heard clearly the sound of the wind as it whistled through the grapeshot holes in the hull. "Yes, what is it?" he asked wearily.

"The coast is in sight. Enemy ships are standing off Cornath's harbor approach."

"Damn, I should have assumed that."

The high, steep hills of Cornath glowed blood red in the afternoon sun. Standing offshore, hull down over the horizon, nearly half a hundred sails cut a patchwork pattern of brightly colored canvas. To the southwest, Zimri made out a series of dark, oily smudges across the afternoon sky.

He gave a questioning look to the sloop's master.

"Your flagship, my lord, and half a dozen others, as well. Mathinian rams have been harrying us all day. The flagship couldn't keep pace and was dragged down by their attacks an hour ago."

"Why didn't you wake me?"

"Even if I had, there was nothing you could do. You needed to rest, my lord, to be ready for what is coming."

Zimri nodded and turned away.

Nearly thirty ships were still with him, most of them straggling far astern. Even against the wind he could hear the distant boom of battle. The Mathinian light sloops and merchantmen had pushed to the fore, trading shots at long range with the hindmost of his fleet.

With every moment, the enemy fleet blockading the harbor came into clearer view. Puffs of smoke drifted across the ice.

"Lookout, what say you?" the captain shouted.

"Land action, appears that Cornath has offered a sally to keep the channel approach open."

"Good, that must be Halnar's doing."

"Order our fleet to escort us in," Zimri said grimly. "We have time for only one approach. If we have to turn and beat back out to sea for another attempt, Ormson's fleet will close in from the rear and destroy us all."

Zimri's vessel slacked off its sails in order to allow the advanced frigates of the fleet to draw up alongside. Even as they came parallel to him, the bow chasers of the Mathinian frigates opened up while running close-hauled to windward in an attempt to gain the weather gauge. The fifty rams, however, pressed straight into the attack, attempting to turn the enemy fleet before it could gain the safety to be found beneath the guns of the harbor.

In silent fascination, Zimri watched the precision maneuvers of Ormson's ram attack as tiny craft attacked in units of five. His own rams were long gone, and the few light craft available that were not escorting Zimri pressed on all canvas to try and screen the heavier ships.

"Look over there," the captain shouted. "One of our cruisers is in trouble."

Zimri turned just in time to see the splintering wreck of a ram, her crew steering clear in its survival boat, spin off the side of the ship, having shattered the cruiser's outrigger amidship. Wreckage was tangled into the ship's blades, kicking up high plumes of gouged ice that reflected brightly in the long slanting rays of the ice-cold sun.

"Eight rams approaching the center of the fleet," the lookout shouted, "bearing for us."

"They must be able to tell from our formation that this ship is being protected," Zimri said evenly.

The rams attacked in echelon formation, each one ten yards to windward and ten astern of its next companion in line. One of the light merchantmen came quickly about in order to try and run them down, but Zimri knew he would be too late.

"Hard a starboard, bring her on the broad reach!" the captain shouted.

The ship heeled over and accelerated to over a hundred miles an hour as the captain eased the sloop into the best possible sailing angle, his crew frantically tightening down the sheets until the booms nearly cracked under the strain.

The rams drew closer, while the four Cornathian escort ships sailed up to windward, forming a protective position from which they could quickly maneuver to meet the threat. In quick succession, two of the Cornathian schooners disappeared in towering plumes of ice and splintered wood, their crews taking out three rams in the process.

The four light guns carried by the sloop sprayed the ice with grape and chain shot as the rams closed in. A well-placed shot knocked out the forestay of one craft, sending its mast and sails tumbling over the side.

"Hard to port!" the captain shouted.

The ship heeled up as the sloop turned abeam the wind, its sails still cinched down tight. The momentum of their last tack carried them forward at a closing speed of nearly two hundred miles an hour. The lead ram shot by to starboard, twenty yards away; the second one came in even closer.

Zimri knew they would hit. The deck lifted beneath his feet as the ship hiked up high against the pressure of the wind on sails that were held down too tightly. The ship lurched, knocking him to his knees. Shouts and cries of rage filled the air. From the corner of his vision, he could see a two-man crossbow being fired wildly, its arrow arcing out across empty sea.

The captain came over to him with a grin and, helping Zimri to his feet, led him to the rail and pointed over the side. The entire front steering blade was gone, sheered off, the outrigger arm cracked and bent at a drunken angle.

Zimri looked astern and watched as the ram skidded wildly across the ice, trailing wreckage behind. Even as he looked, one of its crew rolled off the back of the ship and disappeared.

"We had her up high enough," the captain shouted above the roar of the wind. "The filthy scum passed underneath us with just a glancing blow to the outrigger. If luck holds, we'll be under the harbor guns in another minute."

"Captain, the outrigger, it's parting!" Even as the call came across the deck, the sloop shuddered as the entire portside outrigger gave way. The blow had been harder than both of them had thought.

"Try and hold 'er up," the captain shouted to the pilot.

As he spoke, the heavy breeze slacked off, easing the pressure on the sails, allowing the sloop to drop back down onto the ice.

"It's letting go."

The ship was suddenly out of control, still traveling at over eighty miles an hour. The outrigger snapped clean of its mount, kicking out sideways in a showering spray.

"Keep those sails taut!" the captain screamed. "Keep the pressure off the portside. If we cross the eye, cut away."

Men raced across the wildly rolling deck, drawing axes. If the wind pressed in on the other side of the vessel, it would force the craft down where there was no longer an outrigger. The ship would flip over.

"I can't hold it!" the pilot screamed. Then the wheel knocked him over as it spun wildly.

Zimri dived to the deck as the ship skidded sideways violently. The blades howled with a metallic shriek against the frozen sea, and the ship crossed into the eye of the wind. Zimri heard the men cutting the sheets, the booms releasing and weathervaning across the deck.

"We're going over!" the lookout screamed, his call ending in a shriek of terror as the ship started to settle on its crippled side.

Men fell across the slanting deck, some tumbling over the railing to fall onto the ice, where the ship ground them to bloody smears.

He waited in agony for the ship to roll over, but in the end it gently settled onto its side, the tops of its two masts snapping as they struck the sea. The lookout still hung in the rigging, shrieking with fear, his eyes closed. Zimri, coming to his feet, could not help but laugh at the terror-stricken man.

Most of the men were still uninjured as they climbed out of the wreckage. They were less than half a mile away from the cordon of blue-clad monks and guns set on sleds. The safety of Cornath was only minutes away.

"Quickly," Zimri shouted. "Over the side."

His men poured from the craft and assembled a safe distance beyond. The action still swirled around them. The injured cruiser had ground to a stop a half mile to windward with another ram sticking into its bow. Several miles farther back, several ships were burning; while to the northward, the enemy frigates poured in volley after volley at long range. Zimri could see at least ten enemy rams swinging about across the wind, preparing to run back in for another attack.

"Quick, my lord, we must move," the captain cried, grabbing hold of Zimri's sleeve.

"First send the signal for the ships to break off."

A moment later, a single red rocket shot upward, bursting high in the air with a light boom and flash. The fleet had served its purpose for the moment; now it would have to flee northward and wait for his next command.

The captain pointed off to the southwest. Dozens of sails filled the horizon, some not more than two leagues away, and closing fast.

The last escorts having been lost to the attack of the rams, no ship of Cornath was nearby. At a slow trot, Zimri started across the ice.

After several minutes, a call went up from astern.

"Sire, two rams."

They came on under full sail. Zimri's men swept out in a

protective ring, crossbows up. The rams closed and rocketed past them to either side, not fifty yards away, their men shouting taunts of death. The crossbowmen fired, but with no obvious effect. However, one of the rams circled back then slowed. As it drifted astern, a burst of rockets leaped from its open deck.

"I think that's trouble," the captain shouted.

"We'd better move faster," Zimri shouted.

Picking up the pace, they started to run, and Zimri soon found himself breathless, doubling over from the exertion.

From the protective cordon of the Cornathian line, a blue host started forward with one-man skatesails and light two-man rafts.

"Sire," one of the guards called, pointing southward. Three light sloops were closing in, trailing plumes of ice crystals that swirled behind the rapidly approaching craft.

"Run!"

The party pushed on, Zimri barely noticed the two men that fell in on either side who, half picking him up, pushed forward with the crowd of fleeing men. A deep, bone-chilling roar passed by to the left. A shower of ice shot up in front of them, and a guard tumbled to the ice, his body cut in half by a shot.

From the protective perimeter, the guns mounted on sleds opened up.

Another shot hummed past.

"Scatter!" the captain screamed.

Men bolted in every direction, like insects discovered beneath a rock.

Zimri halted and looked about him. The blue-clad monks from the Cornathian garrison were still a hundred yards away. One of the sloops came thundering in, the rumble of its blades shaking the ice beneath his feet. Without slowing its pace, the Mathinian vessel plowed into the fleeing men, scattering bodies in every direction while its guns fired broadsides of grape, which swept across the sea. The ice at Zimri's feet showered up—a shot hummed past, knocking over the captain, who stood less than a dozen feet away. The captain's left foot was torn off at the ankle, driving the shattered remains across the ice like a bullet.

The second sloop turned sharply into the wind, its spray sweeping past Zimri in its passage. Looking up, he saw men swarming down the outriggers, scimitars in hand, while the ship's four light guns sprayed their loads of case shot at point-blank range.

A third Mathinian sloop pressed in behind the advanced guard coming out of the city in a desperate attempt to cut off retreat.

Zimri started to the captain.

"Leave me, I'm dead already," the man shouted while clutching the bloody stump that pulsed out his life's blood.

An arrow whistled past, but still Zimri hesitated. Then the captain rose and, dragging his bleeding stump, staggered toward the second ship, which was skimming to a halt—its battle-mad crew already leaping off the outriggers.

"Sire!" one of the guards shrieked. "We must flee."

Without a second thought, Zimri turned and sprinted across the ice, suddenly aware that his robes would attract the heretics.

Wild screams and shouts rose up from every side. The first sloop was already several hundred yards away, coming about for another pass. Leaping past crumpled bodies, Zimri nearly slipped on the steaming blood of a man who had been cut in two by the razor-sharp blades of a Mathinian ship. The first blue clad monks from the Cornathian garrison reached him and without acknowledgment raced on, trying to form a defensive perimeter.

Wild shouts rose behind, and Zimri heard the clash of metal on metal. Looking over his shoulder, he saw a Mathinian armed with a steel-spiked mace crush the helmet of an ice runner.

The guns from the Cornathian defensive perimeter fired again, trying to drive back the first sloop, which, having come about, was starting back on a broad reach and rapidly gaining speed.

Zimri's lungs were fire as he raced drunkenly across the sea. Ax raised high, a Mathinian dashed in front of him and turned to strike Zimri down, but he collapsed wordlessly in a shower of blood. A bolt protruded from his throat. More blue-clad forms came up to him on either side. Grabbing him by the shoulders, they pushed him forward toward the safety of the fortress line. Several dozen Cornathians shot past, riding on light sailboards or carrying skatesails.

"Faster, the sloop to forward is cutting us off!"

He was off his feet, the men desperately pushing him onward. They passed a heavy sled-mounted ship's gun.

"The sloop, look out!"

"Down!"

The second sloop, as if piloted by a madman, crashed into the perimeter of guns mounted in front of the Cornathian's forward position. A tremendous explosion ripped the ice as the ship's magazine went up, ignited by a torch held in a dead hand. The shadow of the ship passed over him—screams of rage and fear tore the air. Looking up, he saw the outrigger pass by, not a dozen feet away. Men collapsed around him, shot through with arrow, grape, or splinters.

The sloop skidded into the barrel of the sled-mounted gun.

"Up, up and for it," a man to his left cried.

A two-man raft drew up alongside, and rough hands pushed Zimri onto the deck.

"No, damn you!" Zimri shouted. "No, I stand with you!"

A wild-eyed monk grabbed hold of him and tried to drag him on the craft. A heavy shot screamed overhead.

Quickly, he looked around. A hundred yards ahead, a swarming melee raged around the lead sloop. Its move to cut off Zimri's retreat had been suicide. Already dozens of Morians had gained the outrigger, and some were struggling onto the deck in desperate hand-to-hand action. The rest of Ormson's fleet was closing in rapidly.

"I shall walk into Cornath," Zimri said, calculating the effect this would have. "I shall not enter it like a fugitive."

The monks stepped back from him. Another shot hummed past, killing a man at the edge of the crowd.

"Really, my brothers, standing about in a crowd like this can be quite dangerous. Might I suggest that we return to the safety of our city."

As one, the monks held weapons aloft and cheered as Zimri stepped off the raft and, with measured step, his lungs still burning from the exertion, he walked toward the gates of Cornath, half a mile away.

All along the walls, the two hundred guns of the outer defense line started to open as Michael's fleet drew into range. To the northwest, Zimri saw the remains of his fleet disappearing into the twilight, guns flashing defiance. Overhead, outgoing shots hummed and roared, and they were soon answered in kind as the Mathinian light frigates drew into range, driving off the monks that were busy looting the one sloop that they had managed to capture. But above the roaring of the guns, Zimri clearly heard the shouts of the people as he walked beneath the protection of the gates. The siege of Cornath had begun.

Even as the gates closed behind Zimri, first the Prophet's heavy merchantmen, then his frigates, swept into position, their guns firing at long range. Atop the forecastles and in the riggings, men sat with chart boards and in the gathering darkness noted the muzzle flashes of weapons firing in response. Tallying the observers' sightings, mapmakers plotted the number and location of guns on the first line of defense.

Within the hour, the sun set, and the only illumination came from the flaming hulks of half a dozen ships. In endless succession, flares shot up from the decks of the transport ships, marking their paths as they approached the siege lines. All through the night, the fleet approached, spreading out in a vast, encompassing arc.

In the hour before dawn, Michael walked across the frozen sea, and his memories were ones of sadness. Silhouetted by the first light of dawn, was the outline of the monastery he had grown up in. Atop that mountain, he had watched endless nights pass in cold, quiet darkness as he looked out across the Frozen Sea and dreamed of what was to come.

Despite the uneasy muttering of his guards, he walked toward the smoldering hulk of a light schooner, not eight hundred yards from the wall. Bodies, twisted into the impossible contortions of the dead, littered the ice. Dark pools of blood, like deeper holes of darkness, had spread out and congealed around many of the corpses. Piled together in twisted confusion were the hated blue-robes and the hundred varied dresses of the southland ice runners.

He looked again to the gate and remembered the arrogance of that final moment—when his prey, a faint glimmer of dark blue and gold, walked through the gate without a backward gaze. Somewhere in that city, Zimri was waiting, his hands still stained with the blood of Michael's loved ones. The memory of what Cornath had once been to him washed away. Zimri was all now.

CHAPTER 17

EVERY NIGHT, FOR SIX BLOODY WEEKS, MICHAEL ORMSON OF Mathin prowled the edge of the fortified line that encircled Cornath. All routes in and out of the city were blocked, and patrols of Mathinians penetrated inland almost to within sight of the Holy City of Dulyn. Each day, a fresh convoy arrived from Caediff carrying in its holds the foodstuffs purchased from Ezra, which grew richer from the war devastating its two rivals. Many was the night that Michael stood alone, silently watching. He could sense Zimri's presence on a distant wall, gazing back at him. Taunting, waiting, tantalizingly out of reach.

The approaches to the outer ice wall were carpeted with frozen bodies, the refuse of seven assaults that had crashed futilely against the frozen barrier. He had almost despaired until the fifth week of the siege brought a breeze fresh and clear from the land. Michael climbed to the high observation tower carved from ice, and leaning forward over the edge, he listened carefully. A soft, crying chant, barely audible, could be made out as if carried from a thousand dreamlike years away. The words flooded back from memories rooted in the beginning of conscious thought. The wind bore a scent as well—half noticed, elusive, and chilling—and it carried with

232

it a silent dread that made all around him quiet and uneasy. The chant rose up for a moment as the wind carried its haunting minor key and then shifted away, disappearing into the night.

"Du Santac elvana wyrath mord plag."

"O Saints, deliver from the death by plague," he whispered in refrain.

The Death had come to Cornath's gates.

Wearily, he walked into the chamber, barely noticing the occasional short-lived screams that echoed down the corridor of the monastery. Looking out the window, Zimri watched as the procession shuffled down the narrow, refuse-choked alley-way. At the end of the dark procession, the black-robed monks drew a massive four-wheeled cart with the dead piled high; bodies hung obscenely from the sides, while more were dragged from the stinking hovels and piled onto the wagon.

A cold chill of terror coursed through him. Since the first outbreak, eight days before, nearly ten percent of the city had died. And each day the number of sick rose.

In the middle of a captain's meeting, just that morning, Salderson, a commander of a thousand, suddenly stood, and as quickly fell to the ground, then started to thrash convulsively. As he tore at his cloak, the others had backed to the corners of the room, trembling at the black rash on Salderson's throat, already swollen to the size of a child's fist.

While Salderson screamed in anguish, a geyser of black vomit poured out of his mouth. The meeting fell apart in chaos as the men ran from the room, leaving the fallen captain to kick out the last moments of his life alone and in pain. Zimri trembled at the memory and tried to push aside the recollections of what had followed. To boost morale, he led a procession of relics and icons through all the streets of Cornath. More than once he was forced to step over some who were still not dead, who, in their death agony, their bodies encrusted in vomit and filth, screamed in anguish for his blessing. He passed some who, in their delirium, had ripped open the sores on their bodies, so that a foul stench cascaded out along with the black-green rivers of pus.

His stomach heaved at the memory, and he forced the specter away as he stepped behind the desk and collapsed into a simple straight-back chair. Scattered across his desk was a chaotic pile of maps, orders, command rosters, and the frightful casualty lists.

Sixty thousand had lived in Cornath before the start of the siege. Ten thousand could still bear arms. Nearly half the men were dead or wounded. With those left, he had to defend nearly five miles of outer wall.

He tried to make sense of papers that awaited his signature, but after an hour's work, he knew that the time had come again for the nightly ritual. Pushing the papers aside, Zimri wearily rose to his feet and left the temporary haven of the Morian cathedral. Guards spread out before him as he weaved through the horrid streets. He blocked out the cries of the dying and those who mourned for the dead—and for themselves.

He passed the great square, which was a charnel house where thousands of frozen dead were stacked atop each other. They could not be buried in frozen ground, they could not be burned for lack of fuel, and to dump them over the walls would reveal their weakness to the enemy. Each day the pyramids of death rose higher and higher. Day and night the square was wreathed with clouds of incense as monks and mendicant friars offered up their prayers. A nerve-piercing keening filled the air as families kneeled before the pyramids and screamed out their anguish and rage to the Saints who had turned their backs on Cornath in its hour of woe.

His guards were frequently forced to halt as bodies were dragged aside or frenzied survivors swarmed before him, calling for his blessing or, in some cases, for his death. The square was finally left behind, but the stench of the sulfurous incense and the other, more frightening, smell still clung to his garments.

The first wall was reached—the original line of the Cornathian defenses. The gates swung open, and he passed under the high twin towers of stone that guarded the final approach to the inner harbor. A cannon flashed in the distance, its report echoing against the walls of ice and stone. For a quarter mile, he walked, weaving his way through the maze of traps until the lower, second wall was reached. Without pause, he passed through the single gate, then crossed into the dead zone that led to the third and outer line. Here and there in the shadows lay the rigid forms of the dead who had been dragged back from the barrier. The ice was scarred by hundreds of gouges marking the passage of enemy shot that had cleared the outer wall. Flashes of light flickered overhead, rockets rising up to illuminate the field of strife. After another quarter mile, Zimri and his escort reached the final barrier—an ice wall twenty feet high. Repair crews worked feverishly, repairing the damage from the incessant bombardment. Sections nearly fifty yards in length were merely splintered mounds of ice, covering half-exposed bodies and the fragments of gun carriages destroyed by enemy fire.

Climbing up onto the square, high tower of ice that dominated the line, Zimri looked across the thin circle of protection that kept the avenging hordes from a dying city.

Carnin, the wall commander, stood quietly, his shoulders hunched over in exhaustion, waiting to deliver the nightly report.

"Go ahead," Zimri said wearily.

"Less than fifty guns still operational. We lost five this evening in the last bombardment. Sixty-three men as well."

"Go on."

"Sire, I advise we abandon the wall. Tomorrow night at the latest. We've committed too many of our reserves out here already."

"No!"

"But, sire—"

"The longer we hold him here, the better. He came late in the season as is. I think his morale is starting to crack. If we abandon the wall, it will only serve to hearten Ormson and drive him onward. No, damn it, we must hold. Four months more, damn it, until the season turns, and then we shall defeat him.

"Sire, it's impossible. Our supplies will be exhausted long before then."

"Not if the plague continues," Zimri said quietly.

"Sire?"

"Every plague death is one less mouth to feed." It was the wrong thing to say, and he regretted the words at once.

The captain swayed for a moment and grabbed hold of the wall for support. Zimri waited patiently for him to recover.

"Sire, we're an eggshell ready to be cracked," Carnin said softly. "Pulling back will allow us the reserve we need to contain an assault."

"No, and that is final. Now leave me."

Carnin withdrew, leaving the Holy See alone to gaze out across the Frozen Sea. Flashes of light flickered from one horizon to another, guns fired sporadically. Flares rose, illuminating the hundreds of frozen forms that carpeted the sea. Directly across from him, a half mile away, rose a tower of ice nearly as tall as his own.

Yes, he was there again, looking at him. Ormson was there. "Come, Michael, come," Zimri whispered. "You can keep on coming at me, but you know you will never defeat me. You are slipping into madness, Ormson. I can sense it. Look into your heart, Michael, and see your doom as you destroy yourself, for behind it all you know you will never defeat me. Come, Michael Ormson, and gaze upon the face that caused your anguish and in the end shall defeat you—preserving forever the reign of Holy Church."

"Is all arranged?"

"Yes, my lord, the men have been selected and assigned the task."

Isaac of St. Awstin rose up from his desk, closing the book that rested before him.

"Where are they?"

"In the hidden sanctuary below."

"The supplies?"

"It was difficult, my lord. Two hundred-weight of powder is not easily obtained without drawing attention."

"How much do we have?"

"Only a hundred and twenty weight. I am sorry if I have failed you," Yarwin said, bowing low. His light blue robes, encrusted with filth and blood, swirled around him, giving off a distinctly unpleasant scent.

"That's not enough, by all the Saints; that is still not enough. We need seventy for each gate according to that renegade gunner."

"It can't be helped. Remember, my lord, they captured Lyfordson this morning. Even now I would venture that Zimri's men have him on the rack—if he breaks, all is lost."

Isaac again wrestled with the idea of trying to intervene for Lyfordson's release. He knew that if he did, it would arouse suspicion. No, he would have to leave the young deacon to his fate. If he drew too much attention to the issue, it would set Zimri to wondering why St. Awstin's archbishop was intervening for a deacon caught stealing a one-pound powder charge.

"How good is this, what's-his-name, this Lyfordson?"

"Tough enough, my lord. It will be a while before the tortures of Mor drag the truth from him."

"We can't delay any longer, then—powder enough or not, we'll go at dawn."

"But, sire, there isn't enough for all three gates."

"Damn it, I know, but there's no helping it. We blow the second and third gate. Let the first one stand, and pray in the confusion that they can take it. Go below to the men and get them ready. I expect you to move within the hour."

Yarwin, bowing low, left the presence of the Archbishop of St. Awstin.

Returning to the desk, Isaac tried to calm the racing of his heart. He was betraying Cornath, he thought again. No, *Zimri* betrayed us. The filthy scum had turned their city into a charnel house. The fanatic would hold Cornath till not one man was left alive, and then he would flee through the secret tunnels below the St. Awstin monastery. He pondered what was coming and offered a silent prayer to Rifton, hoping that if there was a Long Table, his old mentor would be there, watching and approving.

No, this would settle it once and for all. The siege would end, Zimri would be caught in the net, and hopefully Michael would spare the order that he had once been such a faithful member of. Michael Ormson. He stared off into the darkness and then reopened the book. Page by brittle page, he wandered through the passages written centuries ago in a thin, spidery hand. Somewhere, he reasoned, there within the Book of Prophecies, he still might find the answer to his fear.

A loud, insistent knocking echoed through the cramped ship's cabin.

"Master, it's urgent. Please come at once."

Michael sat up wearily. A light hand gently caressed his shoulders.

"Damn you—I told you never to touch me when I awaken."

She was silent and, grabbing hold of the heavy furs, rolled over in the bed, covering herself.

Pulling on a loose robe cut like a monk's, Michael walked across the room and threw back the bolts. Seth stood before him.

"Quickly, master, I've already called for all commanders. We must gather at once."

"What is it, do they sally forth?"

"No, Michael, far better—the city is ours!"

The men around the table exchanged silent glances—some of hope, others of disdain.

"Send him out of here," Michael said coldly.

A Companion took Yarwin by the arm and led him from the room.

"Well, do we believe him?" Daniel grumbled.

"We would be foolish not to," Eldric replied.

They looked to Michael, awaiting his decision.

"Prepare for the assault," Michael said quickly. "No horns, no alarm. I want Cowan's shock troops in the first wave, followed by the levies. Daniel's command of the Companions will be held in reserve." Without another word, Michael walked to the door and called for Yarwin.

The St. Awstin monk was brought before him. The guard started to force him to his knees, but with a quick gesture, Michael ordered him away.

"Why?" Michael asked grimly.

"Because my master bids it so."

"Yet I can sense that you wish it not."

Yarwin was silent.

"Speak, damn you."

"Yes, by all the Holy Saints, I wish it not," Yarwin blurted out. "You are the Dark One, sent to destroy Good and Holy Church. But I am sworn to obey my lord the archbishop, Isaac of St. Awstin. As I was once sworn to obey good Rifton as well, or have you forgotten him, Michael Ormson? Have you forgotten the Holy Order that clothed you and nurtured you? Have you forgotten Niall, who I called my friend. I curse you, Michael, for destroying everything that has ever come within your touch."

The control slipped away. With shocking suddenness, Michael delivered a crashing blow to the aging monk, who fell to the floor. All around him turned in silence and watched. Trembling, Michael had his scimitar half out of its sheath. He stood over Yarwin, whose face was covered in blood. Yarwin's eyes taunted him, dared him to strike. Their gazes locked; then Michael turned away with a wild curse and started down the corridor to the stern hatch.

Yarwin's voice followed him.

"Will you honor the request of Isaac, or will you betray him, as I expect you to?"

Michael hesitated for a second, then continued on, his men falling in behind him. As he reached the gangway, he turned to one of his guards and, with a contemptuous gesture, pointed back to Yarwin.

"Hold him till it's over."

Atop the place of watching, Isaac stood alone. A thin band of light illuminated the sky behind him—the first deep violet of dawn. Overhead, the Arch still shined brightly, while a faint flicker of a blue-green aurora played out its dying pageant to the north. He could see the torchlight of the procession as it weaved its way through the first gate and proceeded to the second. Good, all was good so far. His men carried litters normally piled high with supplies for the siege line and which were used for the retrieval of the night's wounded upon their return. Closing his eyes, he fell into silent prayer.

"Oh, Rifton, for I know you sit at the Table of our Fathers, forgive me this act. It was you who gave him life, and now he brings death to our city. It was you who saw the power of Zimri, and it is he who brings death to us, as well. Forgive me, Rifton, for what I gave myself over to long ago; forgive me for believing the Prophecies that Ormson was the new light, the new way. I pray tonight for an ending of this—that our order can survive and that your shadow can rest in peace in the land beyond."

As he raised his head up, he could see that already his men approached the final destination.

"Has he talked yet?"

The master torturer, his smock smeared with blood, bowed

low before Zimri as the Holy See entered the dark chamber below the inner gate tower.

"Nothing yet, my lord, but I can guarantee that he will soon break."

Strange, Zimri thought—a deacon of St. Awstin stealing powder. We must find the answer. From the corridor behind him, he could hear shouting, and the door suddenly swung open before a Morian deacon, who entered the room without semblance of ceremony.

"My lord, I must report something curiously strange." The deacon stood before him breathless.

"Go on."

"Sire, not ten minutes ago, a procession of monks passed through the first gate, bound for the outer wall."

"Do you disturb me to tell me that?" Zimri shouted, rising up in exhausted anger.

"Sire, please, they were of St. Awstin, nearly a hundred, bearing litters laden with supplies."

"And what is so curious about that?" Several men had crowded into the door and looked anxiously toward Zimri.

"Sire, no one bothered to check the supplies, and then I recalled hearing a rumor that a priest of St. Awstin was caught stealing powder. Sire, punish me if I am wrong, but I think this procession of monks means us harm. Even now they are approaching the outer gate."

He hesitated for a moment, then pushed past the trembling deacon. "Sound the alarm!" Zimri shouted.

He came out into the frigid air of dawn and ran up the stairs that led to the top of the stone battlement that guarded the inner harbor. The alarm horn sounded and within seconds was picked up all along the inner wall, to be echoed across the harbor and to the defense line beyond. Several rockets rose above the tower. He watched as they traced a fiery line across the Arch, then dropped downward in the direction of the outer gate. Perhaps the monks could be stopped in time. Even as the thought crossed his mind, the sky before him erupted. Without any sound, a brilliant flash filled the western horizon. The outer gate disappeared in a rising column of fire and ice.

The stone tower trembled beneath his feet; then the sound of the explosion washed over him. Suddenly, the gate of the second wall flashed, even before the debris from the outer wall had settled. The second blast was closer, louder. The roar of the detonation washed over him like a thunderclap. More rockets rose up along the inner wall—their bright flashes illuminating the harbor as men poured out of the low, ice-walled barracks and formed into ranks. Looking back toward them, his gaze lifted up to the high dark walls that were carved into the side of the mountain that was the monastery of St. Awstin. By the flicker of rockets, Zimri saw a solitary form watching from atop the highest peak. He knew it was Isaac, but for a moment a cold fear came to him—he felt as if the ghost of Rifton was returning for revenge.

"Michael, I hear horns."

"It's the alarm," another Companion whispered.

"There! Along the inner wall, they're sounding the alarm!"

Michael looked down from the tower. All along the siege line, the heavily armed shock troops waited, drawn up in units of a thousand.

He looked again to the southeast. The horizon was getting brighter by the moment; soon the sun would show itself briefly in its midwinter passage. But another sun, far closer, flashed into existence only a half mile away.

Michael turned and nodded to one of the Companions.

The Companion touched a glowing taper to the base of a long brass tube. Several seconds passed, and a single rocket shot upward. Even as it burst with a scarlet light, the second gate rose heavenward, as if in response.

"Up, men, up and to them!"

Battle horns rang out in high clarion tones. By the thousands, the heavy shock troops of the Prophet stood. Battle standards whipped out in the fresh easterly breeze.

With one voice, the legion called out Michael's name, starting the now traditional chant. "Michael, Michael, Michael . . ."

In swift orderly lines, the first assault teams poured out through the sally ports, each man carrying a skatesail. As each soldier cleared the wall, he lowered the sail, held it tight in, and started to tack inward against the wind. Strapped to their backs were rope, grappling hooks, shields, and battle-axes. Standard-bearers came out holding the dark green flags of Ormson aloft and followed the skatesailors on the assault.

Michael stood for a moment atop the wall, watching the host as it flowed forward, chanting, "Michael, Michael, Michael..."

All along the siege wall, the guns opened and quickly built to a mind-numbing crescendo as their shot was poured into the gap left by the explosion. Waves of thunder washed over Michael, while overhead shot screamed past from the fleet beyond.

Nearly a thousand skatesailors advanced along a front of several hundred yards. The second wave was already starting to advance. Skaters, they carried no sails. Each carried a long wooden plank, which would be used to bridge the barrier lines.

Cowan appeared alongside Michael's tower, his signalers, flag bearers, spotters, and other staff streaming behind him. His skates kicked up showers of crystals as he sprinted forward across the ice. Behind him advanced the main body of the legion, nearly four thousand strong. They started across the ice at a slow trot, saving their strength for the final hundred yards. Several guns opened up from the Cornathian wall, the round shot bounding across the sea, plowing through the formed ranks.

"Close up, close up your lines!" the file closers screamed, pushing men forward to fill the gaps caused by the enemy shot.

The Mathinian artillery rounds screamed overhead and along the entire length of the Cornathian wall, geysers of shimmering ice erupted. Cowan looked back with approval as the ice sleds were being pulled across the ice by teams of twenty men. Each sled mounted one gun, its crew standing ready, the barrels loaded with double grape to sweep the enemy from his defenses. They advanced, through increasingly heavier fire as more and more guns opened up from the Cornathian wall. Great gaps were slashed in the lines as dozens of men were tumbled over, screaming and kicking in agony. A signaler went down, cut in half by a solid shot, but his comrades rescued the rockets from his rucksack while a torrent of blood poured from his steaming intestines.

Along the forward edge of the advancing skatesailors, men disappeared as they fell into traps or were crushed by the murderous short-range cannons, designed to fire grape and chain shot. Hundreds fell. Reaching the barrier ditch, they tossed their sails aside and skated straight in across the fifty-foot-wide ice path that stood directly before the gate. Grape swept away the first wave, and yet another went in. A maddening crush pulled up in front of the one passage to the inner wall. The first wave of skaters reached the ditch and started to position their planks to broaden the passage to the enemy wall.

"In, men, in!" Cowan screamed as he reach the press.

Looking back, he saw the orderly ranks of the shock troops advancing steadily, though every step cost another bloody hole in their lines.

The gate was only thirty yards ahead, and the ruins were still smoking. He could hear the clash of metal on metal and a rising crescendo of screams. Occasionally the attackers caught sight of the thin shield wall of monks and ice runners who held the top of the wreckage.

"Onward, onward!"

The press started to heave forward. A green standard appeared atop the rubble. A shout arose.

Cowan was knocked off his feet by a bloody torso, the concussion from the cannon shot jarring his vision. A series of rockets exploded around them as a torch still held by a lifeless hand slammed into the back of a signaler. Screaming, the signaler rolled briefly on the ice, then fell into the ditch where the rockets thundered off, ricocheting against the walls and slamming into men before exploding with deadly effect.

The shoving, screaming troops pushed forward, Cowan with them. Suddenly, he was tripping over mounds of rubble—falling, rising, being pushed inexorably onward. He looked up and realized that they were inside the wall. Calling for his staff, he scrambled up the south side of the broken gate to try for a better vantage.

The ice was aswarm with men. The leader of the skatesailors rushed up to him, his helmet missing, a river of blood pouring down his face.

"Push on," Cowan screamed. "Don't stop! Push on to the next gate, and hold it at all costs!"

The man saluted, raised up his scimitar with a shout, and charged away into the advancing horde.

Lifting his gaze to the wall that loomed above the gate, Cowan saw that some of his men had gained the top. Turning, he beckoned to his staff.

"Up," Cowan screamed, "we need to see what is happening!"

Ropes snaked upward—his staff starting to climb up the

icy walls as soon as the grappling hooks were secure. Grabbing hold of a rope, Cowan scaled the wall. Gaining the top, he crouched low as an arrow whistled past.

Looking back toward his own lines, Cowan noted the orderly ranks of the advancing shock troops. The leading edge of the column was less than two hundred yards away. Their foothold on the wall was already fifty yards wide and spreading. Several hundred of his skaters were already a hundred yards forward, advancing on the next wall.

All along the outer perimeter Cornathians were dropping over the side and running madly to the next line of defense. Explosions rippled up and down the line as gun crews detonated powder supplies, shattering the wall and destroying the guns.

The gate was carpeted with twisting and screaming bodies. Among the fallen were dozens of light blue robes. Cowan nodded his approval. The monks of St. Awstin had fulfilled their promise.

"Signal first wall secured."

Three green rockets shot upward. In a few seconds, Cowan heard the answering cheer.

The first wave of foot troops reached the gate and poured through the opening. A team of sappers broke from the line and ran along the outside of the wall, smashing holes into the barrier. In a few minutes, they had placed powder charges and shouted warnings, "Down!"

Explosions raced along the wall at fifty-yard intervals. Then hundreds of men ran forward with heavy planking, which they laid over the shattered ice, opening new avenues for the assault to continue.

Cowan's men pushed on, driving toward the next barrier. The guns of the Cornathian second line fired with deadly effect. His men fell by the hundreds, dying, disappearing in showering splinters of steel and ice, but still the assault pushed toward the second line.

"Time we pressed in!" Cowan shouted, grabbing hold of a rope and swinging back onto the ice. Pushing his way past the heavy foot troops, he skated forward. For the first several hundred yards, he encountered few bodies; then, as if a mysterious line had been crossed the corpses grew in density until at times he had to stop skating entirely in order to step over the fallen or move around traps his men had fallen through.

The guns of the second wall had the range of the attackers, but they pushed on, overtaking the fleeing survivors of the first wall and cutting them down as they fled. Here and there, Cornathian commands attempted an orderly withdrawal, but they were surrounded by enraged Mathinians who cut them down without quarter.

A knot of fighting soon developed around the remains of the second gate, and a number of rockets rose from the wall beyond.

"Quickly," Cowan shouted, "quickly, before they can abandon the wall and withdraw!"

He drove his men forward with the fury of despair as the guns of the inner line began to fall silent. No barrier ditch had been dug before the second wall, and with hard, fast pushing, Cowan reached the relative protection of the wall. Out of breath, he bent over, feeling as if he would vomit from the exertion, but he saw his men swarming through the break, throwing themselves upon the shield wall while they chanted their death songs.

Suddenly, the defense gave way. A group of men appeared out of the carnage bearing a ladder, and to the shouts of his staff, they raised it up next to him.

Kicking off his skates, Cowan scrambled upward, shield held high, expecting an enemy bolt. Reaching the top, he peered over, and to his amazement found the parapet empty except for a scattering of corpses.

Standing up, he looked across the last quarter mile to the final inner line. His advance units were still pushing forward, but the defense had stiffened; an orderly shield wall was pulling back—their faces to the Mathinians while withdrawing at a slow, steady pace. Along the inner wall, dozens of guns flashed in the early-morning light and their shot screamed overhead to bound across the frozen plain beyond. Thousands of men, Cornathians, were clamoring up the side of the defensive works using ropes and ladders, while a solid mass poured into the still-open gate.

"In that confusion, we can still break through," one of Cowan's staff shouted.

"Press the attack!" Cowan yelled. "This is our final chance!"

The command rockets went off. Across the plain behind him flowed an endless swarm of men. Cowan turned to a lieutenant.

"Find the flag squads. The channels have to be marked for the rams and siege craft."

"Lord, it will take time in this confusion."

"Damn you, find them! We haven't much time. When you do, have them mark the channel as far as they can. We'll try to take the final wall by storm, but chances are we'll need the rams to finish it."

Minutes passed and the assault pressed forward, nearly reaching the base of the wall, but the hundred cannons along the icy battlement commanded overlapping fields of fire. Cowan's men were bottlenecked by the two outer lines and were arriving at the inner line with insufficient mass to overrun the position. Demolition teams appeared on the second line and blasted several holes to aid in the advance, but it was too late— the slaughter in the plain before the third line showed the Cornathians were covering the retreat. They were too well prepared now for a frontal assault to succeed. Before his position, the first red flag of the channel-marking team appeared, the unit commander looking up to him and waving. Every fifty yards, two more flags went up as they advanced into the fray. Then the enemy gunners began to register their weapons on the red flags, and the commander went down, his leg torn off—but the squad pushed forward.

Soon the last of the retreating Cornathians were inside the protective barrier or cut off as the defenders closed the gates, severed the ropes, and pushed the ladders away. In desperation, the unfortunate men turned and traded their lives grimly. Wave after wave of assault pressed forward.

"Goes poorly," a grim voice said.

Cowan looked over his shoulder and found Eldric standing next to him, panting for breath.

"I was up there briefly," Eldric shouted above the roar of battle. "We didn't have enough men forward to gain the inner wall."

Cowan pointed to the marker unit; they were less than two hundred yards from the wall. Retreating Mathinian units poured back around them, then a shower of grapeshot swept through the flag unit, knocking down half of the men.

"Damn all the Saints to hell," Cowan cursed grimly.

The survivors pressed forward, marking the channel at a hundred and fifty yards, and then advanced to less than a hundred yards. All along the battle line, the Mathinians were falling back.

The squad reached the fifty-yard mark and hammered in its flags. The ice appeared to explode around them, their bodies rising up in the air from the impact.

"Finished," Eldric said quietly.

"Order the attack off," Cowan shouted as a shot struck into the wall next to them, killing several of his staff.

The five rockets soared upward.

"How many guns on this wall?" Eldric asked.

"Not many. Fifty at most, I would reckon. This line was built to slow a breakthrough, not necessarily to stop it."

"Signal from the master," a spotter shouted.

Cowan looked back to the west, noticing that the sails of the distant patrol craft were now highlighted by the slanting rays of the early-morning sun.

"What does it read?"

"We are ordered to press the attack."

Cowan looked back to Michael's position and muttered a quiet curse. Ormson was ordering a suicidal assault; they could never take that position without first breeching the wall.

"Signal back, 'Impossible.'"

The staff turned and looked at him.

"Do it!" Cowan shouted. "I'll not waste my men."

The rockets rose, and all looked to the west, ignoring the howl of shot and the screams of the wounded around them.

Even before the three rockets burst in reply, he knew what message they carried.

"Press attack," the spotter said quietly as the two red and single green burst over the high watchtower a mile away.

Cowan looked to Eldric.

"How long before we can clear a path and bring up the siege equipment and rams?"

"Not till nightfall."

"You could wait," Eldric said in a low voice.

Cowan shook his head sadly. "I swore to follow his command. If I refuse, what little influence I have over him would be gone forever. I must trust to his leadership."

Unsheathing his scimitar, he started over the wall, his staff following him. "Bring those rams up quickly," Cowan said grimly. "Elsewise, our leader will have no army left to assault with by the time the wall is breeched."

"Here they come!"

The monks braced the heavy, iron-shod gate, putting their shoulders to it while the spotter closed the loophole and backed away. The battering ram struck with a bone-jarring shock. Hairline cracks coursed up and down the beams. The ram struck again, and wild shouts of rage sounded from the other side.

"My lord, there is nothing to be done here," a frightened deacon shouted. "Go back where you'll be safe."

Isaac nodded, waved an absent blessing to the monks and deacons who held the door, and retreated up through the long labyrinth of corridors carved into the mountain side. He was tempted to go again to the place of watching and observe the state of the siege, but that was impossible now—Morian guns were trained on the position, ready to sweep it the moment the door was opened. He could do nothing but wait. The city was falling, but Zimri fully intended to take the monks of St. Awstin to their doom, as well.

Under a covering unit of archers and flanking shield walls of Morian priests, Zimri returned through the city to the place of final refuge. Crossing the square, he found the way clogged with frozen bodies that had to be climbed over to reach the approach to the inner citadel. Dozens of men ran past him, each one carrying a frozen corpse. He would have stopped it had he known about the order, but it was too late now. Still, the idea of using the bodies as barricades was an efficient one, so he offered no objection. A line of heavy crossbows was emplaced along the steps of the cathedral, their crews looking anxiously to him as he strode past without acknowledgment. Several sections of the city were on fire from the hot shot the enemy was lobbing with mortars placed directly behind the second wall. Shouts of panic echoed up and down the streets, confirming the reports that rioting had broken out in some quarters.

A deafening roar echoed through the city as Zimri reached

the steps of the church. Overhead, the stained-glass window-pane shattered from the blast. Stunned, he looked off to the northern quarter of the city where a fireball, wreathed in black smoke, hovered.

"One of the powder storehouses. The mob must have taken it and started a fire," an aide shouted.

"Saints preserve us," another whispered.

Stepping into the arch wall protecting the door, Zimri watched as a shower of debris rained down on the square, killing several of the work crew he had passed just moments before. A wave of nausea swept over him.

The echo of the explosion died away, leaving a boiling cloud of black smoke, and the sound of the struggle on the wall half a mile away became audible again as the shouts of tens of thousands of men echoed through the city. The thunder of guns and the wails of terror in the city all blended together into one maddening roar that washed over him, buffeting him, as the defense of Cornath, strongest city of the Confederation, dissolved.

Zimri crossed the threshold of the church, and the heavy iron-shod doors swung shut behind him, blocking out most of the noise. Several dozen monks slid heavy bars into place, the sound of which made him think of the closing of a lock on a tomb.

Reaching the altar and sanctuary, he bowed low, and as he did so, the assembled monks stopped in their chanting. Without offering a blessing he walked up to the altar and stepped behind it, opening the hidden door that led upward to the place of watching. The door slid shut, and the chanting rose again as the monks begged for the intercession of the Saints.

At the top of the tower, Zimri opened the trap door. Climbing upward, he came to rest in the small room that looked out upon the doomed city. He was trapped. There had been a way out of the city. A single tunnel carved under the mountain that emerged beyond the siege lines. But, damn Isaac to hell forever, that path had been betrayed. The way out was through the fortress monastery of St. Awstin. "Damn St. Awstin to hell forever!" Zimri shouted in frightened rage.

They had betrayed him, blown the gates, and then sealed up the monastery, blocking the one avenue of escape. Even now, his men, precious men that should be on the wall, laid siege to the position, but by the time they took it, the Mathinians would be in the city.

From atop the tower, he could watch all that would occur in the hours to come. Already the sun was low in the western sky, silhouetting the hundreds of ships that lined the approaches of the sea. Around him, the city was in flames, and hordes of panic-stricken citizens clogged the streets, blocking the movement of troops and, in some places, falling upon the Morian warriors. Looking out toward the wall, he felt a cold chill knot through his stomach. Four heavy rams were moving into position, and alongside them were a dozen fifty-foot siege towers, their ice-coated walls shining brightly in the late-afternoon sun.

He was trapped in Cornath, and the raging host of Ormson was preparing to deliver its final assault.

"My lord, your arm, it must be attended to at once."

"Leave me be," Cowan shouted at his aide. But his words could barely be heard above the roar of battle.

Daniel came up to stand before him. "Listen to your men, Cowan," Daniel said grimly. "Elsewise you'll be dead from loss of blood."

Exhausted, Cowan slumped back against the wall, fighting off the battle-mad hysteria. "Go on, then, damn you all," he whispered, his words trailing off into mumbled curses.

Two of his aides ran forward, one bearing a heavy fur robe. Unsheathing a knife, the officer sliced open Cowan's sleeve, while another man unbuckled Cowan's chain-mail armor. The attendant pulled out his knife and cut Cowan's tunic off, exposing his bare flesh to the seventy degrees of frost. The cold wind shocked him into a fit of violent shivering. The men bundled him up in the heavy fur, leaving his shield arm exposed. Sticking through his bicep was a heavy crossbow bolt that had smashed through his shield and buried itself in the upper arm. Dark red blood still pulsed from the wound, steaming as it hit the frigid air, then quickly freezing into icy slush.

Daniel extracted his flask and poured a generous helping of liquor down Cowan's throat.

"Ready?"

"Go ahead," Cowan mumbled, looking away from the arm

while Daniel leaned over and helped to brace his friend for the shock of the knife.

The blade sliced into his arm, cutting around the base of the arrow. In spite of his attempt at control, a scream of anguished pain burst from Cowan's lips as the attendant cut the barbed point free and tore it out of the arm—a hunk of muscle still hanging to the reddened point. From a protected spot by the wall, a fire had already been kindled, and another aide pulled out a red hot knife and stuck it into the wound, burning it shut in a cloud of steam and smoke.

"Dress me," Cowan called weakly, "I must go back."

"Down!"

The ice wall above them exploded from the impact of a cannon shot, showering the bloody ice around them with a rain of fragments.

Pulling the tunic off a mangled body lying nearby, a staff member gently dressed Cowan after tying his useless arm to his body.

Cowan attempted to regain his feet, but a wave of nausea drove him back down to his knees. Gasping for breath, he fought down the sour taste. He had to regain his feet or he would be out of the fight at the crucial moment. The memory of his command and the field covered with his dying men flashed before him. He slowly stood swaying, then leaned on an aide's shoulder and pointed his men back into the fight.

Huddled beneath the second wall were hundreds of wounded, suffering from every injury imaginable. Their pitiful screams rent the air—many of them called for a knife to end their anguish. Cowan had to harden himself. They were all that remained of his once-proud legion, they and the hundreds upon hundreds of bodies that choked the approaches to the final wall. Scattered among the wounded were exhausted soldiers waiting for the command to return to battle. Less than a third of Cowan's command could still do battle, and the thought brought tears to his eyes.

Daniel gently placed a supporting hand on Cowan's shoulder. "'Tis grim business, this. Never have I witnessed such madness in battle."

Cowan was silent.

Toward early afternoon, they had managed to gain a brief

foothold atop the wall, and Cowan was one of the first up. For nearly an hour, they had tried desperately to expand their position and sweep the Cornathians off, but the Morian priests fought with the fury of despair. From atop that high position, Cowan glimpsed a city in panic. A fair portion was in flames— the streets were choked with panic stricken peasants who ran aimlessly through the confusion. Cowan's men were driven off the wall at last by a suicidal attack. They might have held on, but the bolt had knocked him over, and the cry went up that he was dead, breaking the morale of his soldiers. His staff had sacrificed their own lives when they had bound him up and lowered him to the ice below. Only two escaped, the other twenty, close friends and relatives all, were lost forever. Gone and dead, and for nothing, since all knew it was insanity to attack until the towers and rams could be brought to bear.

"You grieve for what you lost," Daniel said quietly. "But you served a purpose. It kept the pressure on them and allowed the ice to be leveled and cleared for the rams."

"We could have taken it with far less loss," Cowan cried. "The city is in revolt. If only Michael had waited, he could have taken it without this insane bloodletting!"

Daniel looked at him sadly. "But he does not have the time, Cowan, or don't you understand that?"

"Michael, Michael . . ."

The chanting rose in the distance, louder with each second, swelling above the roar of combat.

He looked back to the west, and silhouetted against the setting sun came the advancing wall of heavily armed men. The command of ten thousand was advancing at last, the ten thousand Companions, the elite troops commanded by Daniel, held in reserve throughout the long bloody day for the final assault. Before them rode four heavy rams, each one nearly fifty feet abeam. The logs, taken from five standard ship rams, had been bundled together to form the striking core of the wall-smashing unit. Each ram carried four masts, set two by two alongside each other. On the riggings swarmed a host of men. For the present, only the mainsails had been set; the rest of the canvas would be sheeted on after the second wall had been cleared and there was an open path to the final target.

Behind the rams, a dozen towers advanced, each one pulled by half a thousand men. However, one tower soared higher than the rest, and it advanced slowly in the middle of the marching horde. It was the command post of the Prophet. A giant, twenty-foot-square pennant snapped in the breeze above the tower, the personal flag of the Prophet, and he stood beneath it without armor, dressed in a plain brown robe.

Cowan did not know whether to curse Michael or to cheer and shout his name as the host drew closer and closer.

The few guns still firing on the inner wall turned their weapons to bear as the host came into view. Shot hummed, bounded, and fell among the men. As quickly as a gap appeared, the orderly ranks closed up. They never ceased their chant.

Daniel grabbed Cowan on the shoulder and looked at him. Cowan could see the wild light of fanaticism in his eyes. Unsheathing his heavy two-handed battle-ax, Daniel turned and ran to the fore of the advance, leading his men on the final attack of a long and bitter day.

The rams rumbled past, heavy, ponderous, and awe-inspiring in their raw power.

From behind the column came the low rhythmic beat of the death drums, mounted on six sleds, each fifteen feet across. Half a dozen Companions surrounded each instrument and struck it in turn, signaling the cadence of the chant, sending a spine-tingling thrill through the host, and striking terror in the hearts of the defenders who braced themselves for what was to come. A signal flare arced into the sky, and a thunderous roar rose from the ten thousand as they reached the second wall and started to pour through the gaps the sappers had prepared for their passage.

As the first ram cleared the second wall, the men on deck and in the riggings unleashed thousands of square feet of canvas to catch the late-afternoon breeze. Instantly, the craft lurched forward, gaining speed. A distant cry came up from the wall as doom approached.

The hundreds of men aboard the accelerating ram frantically sheeted in the sails—already it was a hundred yards forward and gaining in speed. The first men started to leap off, rolling across the ice like insects abandoning a rotten carcass.

The second ram passed Cowan and accelerated away, following its sister ship. Behind came the third vessel, its crew wildly calling Michael's name. The first ram was roaring down on the wall, and in the gathering twilight, Cowan could see that many of its crew would not get off in time.

Several shots screamed overhead, one of them hitting the right foremast of the second ram, splintering its port topgallant mast. Spars and rigging cascaded down, but the heavy craft continued forward. The pilot crew was swept away by the wreckage, but more swarmed in to take its place on the tiller pole.

An unexpected hush fell over the field as all eyes watched the first ram closing on its target. Even as antlike figures tumbled off the rear of the ship, the heavy craft slammed into the wall twenty yards north of the gate. A silent explosion soared upward—the icewall collapsed, broke away, and disappeared beneath the impact of wood and iron. The four masts snapped off, the rigging and wood catapulting against the wall, whipping off the unfortunates who had not been able to get off.

The second ram closed in on its target, and the others followed behind as the rumbling echo of the first collision rolled across the ice. The next ram struck to the south of the gate, but the third one hit dead on between the two stone towers, smashing down the entry for the approaching horde.

"For Michael!"

Their roar filled the air, and as if with one step, the ten thousand rushed forward chanting their war cry, leaving the siege towers behind. The fourth ram never made it to its target. Missing the channel, its portside outrigger fell into a trap hole, spinning the craft around. Rigging and masts collapsed; the other blades buckled under the weight, and the craft rose up on its side, flipping over.

"For Michael!"

The host pressed forward, scimitars waving in the blood-red light of the setting sun, which was rivaled by the flames of the city that awaited them.

Wearily, Cowan watched them pass, until finally the last of the men crossed through the broken wall. The tower of Michael had stopped not twenty feet away. Looking up, Cowan could see him alone, silently watching as the column swarmed up through the wreckage and came to grips with the shield wall that offered the final defense. For a moment, he thought of approaching the tower to mount it and stand beside his friend in the moment of triumph. But he hesitated as he looked around at the hundreds of silent forms on the ice.

"My banner," Cowan called weakly.

A blood-smeared boy fetched the scorched and torn standard of the house of Zardok.

"Let us go in," he said grimly.

Picking up a scimitar from the ice, he ordered the rally call for his legion to be sounded. Wearily, the men rose to their feet and, at a slow walk, followed the chanting host into the breech.

Even before the splinters and debris from the last ram had been cleared, Zimri made out the white-clad host advancing into the wreckage. In the gathering shadows, he watched thin lines of dark blue smothered under the Companions. By the thousands, the demoralized defenders threw aside their shields and sought safety in the burning city. Around him, the flames rose higher, cutting a ring of light into the descending night.

Within minutes, the wall was aswarm with the Mathinian host, which did not pause but plunged forward, cutting down the panic-stricken defenders as they fled. As if the city had been linked by a single consciousness, the cry suddenly echoed up and down the streets, even to the farthest point of the landward wall where the guns were silent.

"The city has fallen!"

A wild, hysterical mob pushed into the square, streaming in from every direction, rushing to the cathedral, hands stretched heavenward beseechingly. Families clung together, surrounded by the pyramids of frozen dead still unburied from the plague. Screams rose up as priests, monks, ice runners, and peasants called upon the Saints to deliver them. Never had he heard such desperation and anguish. In their prayers, some fell upon their own swords; others slew their families before the steps of the cathedral as they called out to their patron Saints for deliverance. It was beyond the worst images of hell ever imagined by the church's artists.

A strange, dissonant keening filled the air as the few surviving monks of Mor started the chant "O Mor, in my hour of death." As their words echoed in the plaza above the roar of battle, the people fell to their knees, joining the chant, hoping beyond hope that the Saints would appear from the sky to deliver them from the Dark One, as the Holy Writings had described the deliverance of cities in ages past. He looked heavenward as well and found the prayers coming to his lips, even though in his heart he knew that no Saint or God would ever hear their call.

As he looked to the Arch above, which appeared surrounded in a circle of flame, a light appeared, flashing bright and quick. Silently, it crossed up over the sky, illuminating all in stark, clear white.

A wailing scream coursed through the city.

"The Saints, the Saints come to deliver us!"

The people clung to each other, crying out like children, wishing to believe a story that in their hearts they knew was not true.

The light crossed the sky, racing southward, and disappeared. A strange hush fell over Cornath as all turned to watch its passing. Both sides watched in superstitious fear. The quiet hung over all with an intensity as frightful as the din of madness had been just a moment before. All waited for a sign. But there was nothing, only the crackling of the flames. In the distance, a shout came up high and clear.

"He is the One. Ormson is the One ordained!" A wild cry of triumph thundered outside the city, and the people in the square bowed their heads in despair. The Saints had forsaken them. As he looked out across the city, Zimri saw the white-clad hosts drawing closer and closer. Soon he heard their battle cry as their swords flooded the streets with blood.

He turned his gaze away and looked to the gate of St. Awstin's monastery. The signal rocket that would have told him that the three great doors had been pierced would never rise. It was finished. Again, St. Awstin had defeated him. Whispering a silent curse, he lowered his head in prayer.

"'And the fire of the sky shall light the night of his coming,'" he whispered softly. The sound of battle reached him even here in the dark chamber, hidden within the confines of St. Awstin.

A monk appeared in the doorway, breathless, his face blistered and scorched.

"Isaac, they flee; the Morians flee from our gate. The heretic's men approach even now."

"Then it is time at last," Isaac replied, his thoughts distant, far away. Isaac looked up at the monk. "You are the commander of the gates, are you not?"

"Yes, my lord."

"Then open them."

"What!"

"You heard me, open them. Open them to greet him whom we bred and gave forth to the world."

"My lord, it is madness out there. They are the Companions, the fanatics of the Prophet. They will slaughter us."

"Don't fear," Isaac said quietly. "The Prophet knows who it was that cleared the way. We shall be spared."

The monk stood by the door, hesitating.

Isaac looked up at him. "You have received the command of the archbishop of St. Awstin, who holds the power of life and death over you."

Bowing low, the guard left Isaac to his meditation. The book was open before him. By the light of a flickering candle, he continued to read. "'And upon that night shall come an end to all things, as the passing of an age is complete. Amen, the passing shall come in the night.'

"'And upon that night shall come a lighting of two fires, from beyond the reach of the Saints above, and from the fire that brings an ending to an age.'"

He turned the heavy parchment page of the *Book of Prophecies*. Oh, Michael, he thought, I cry aloud in my fear, for the frozen darkness is still upon the land.

There was an echo of screams.

Looking down at the book, he continued to read. "'And upon that night shall come the ending of all that was and of all that was dreamed by Him, as well.'"

The screams grew louder. He heard the clash of weapons in the corridor.

He looked up from the book. A monk ran past the door and collapsed wordlessly, an arrow sticking out of his back.

He started to rise but stopped. So, as I feared, as I had feared all along. Not even Awstin will survive.

He sat down, trying to concentrate on the reading as the screams drew closer.

He looked around the bare, empty room. The room that had been the sole refuge of Michael Ormson for fifteen years.

So this is where it began. Briefly, he recalled glimpsing the bundled form of a whimpering boy who clung to Rifton's robes. It was the only time he had ever seen the Prophet.

Poor Michael, he thought, and what have you become now? Poor Zimri, as well, the voice inside him whispered—together they are linked.

He leaned forward, his weak eyes searching the illuminated text. "'And upon that night the two shall be linked, one together, life unto life, death unto death.'"

He heard the approach but never saw the ax that severed the life from his body.

Cowan climbed over the piles of dead and dying and passed the remains of the ram that pierced the gate. Even though the sun had set nearly an hour earlier, the scene was as bright as day. Cornath was being offered up to the flames. Wild cries of combat thundered around him as he staggered up the death-choked alleyways. Ahead, the Companions still chanted their cry, but it had taken on a deep fierceness as battle lust consumed all around him.

Pushing forward to the square, he suddenly came upon vast pyramids of dead. He could not believe that all of these were the results of the battle, and drawing closer, he was transfixed with horror at the realization that these were the unburied dead from the plague, frozen into rigid blocks of ice, the corpses used as a final desperate barrier to the onslaught. Wild cries of combat echoed about the square; heavy crossbow bolts and ballistae shot cut through the air above him. Pushing through the men, he saw a heavy unit of Mathinians swarm up the steps of the church, overrunning the guards. A log was brought forward as a battering ram, and the assault was mounted on the door. From atop the cathedral wall, rivers of boiling oil rained down. As quickly as men fell, others pushed forward to pick up the ram. Blow after blow was struck, the door gradually giving against its hinges. Finally, the barrier fell, with a resounding crash, and scimitars gleaming red in the firelight, the Companions swarmed forward.

Following the men in, Cowan stood in amazement as Daniel appeared at the front of the crush, cutting down Morian priests, who retreated grimly before the assault.

The Mathinians pushed into the cathedral and the vast hollow chamber echoing the shouts of battle. A line of hooded priests stood at the top of the altar, crossbows raised. As quickly as the first rank fired, they withdrew, exposing the next rank, which fired in turn. The Companions hesitated until Daniel leaped out, battle-ax high.

"No prisoners!" Daniel screamed as he rushed headlong to the altar. A thundering cry went up at his words, and the men swarmed after him. Daniel went down, knocked off his feet. Staggering, he rose up again, ax on high, crashing into the Morian line. The altar disappeared beneath a swarm of struggling forms.

Cowan retreated from the cathedral. Men passed in the flickering shadows. As if Daniel's call had been picked up by ten thousand at once, a sudden cry echoed up and down the streets.

"No prisoners, no prisoners!"

Horrified, Cowan watched as white-clad soldiers smashed down the doors of houses facing the square. Loud screams echoed from within. Companions poured into the buildings. Cowan started across the square to the nearest structure, which was already half consumed with flames. A warrior came out of the building covered in blood; in his hand, a screaming infant gave forth a high-pitched wail of terror. Raising up the child, the warrior dashed its life out against the wall, then threw the still-quivering carcass aside.

"No prisoners," the cry went up, echoing in the streets.

Cowan looked back to his command. It was slipping away, joining in the pillage and rape of the city. Not twenty of his men remained by his side, looking about themselves with shocked expressions of confusion.

Wandering up an alleyway, the battle having passed on, Cowan confronted streets choked with dead, occasional warriors, a few blue robes, but mostly old men, children, and women tangled together in death.

"Michael!" he screamed, his voice rising up in anguish. "Michael, can you see what we have become?"

Turning, he fled down the streets of the dying city, passing house after house of death. Most were already engulfed in flames.

Reaching the harbor, Cowan climbed back over the wreckage. Behind him, the city was a madhouse of screaming death. As he crossed over the wreckage of the rams, he was forced aside as another column passed him in the night. Their chant sounded grim and dark, as if the rage of two thousand years was at last to be released in a climactic orgy of darkness.

"No prisoners, no prisoners!"

At last, he came to the command tower, surrounded by the five hundred select—the elite guard of the Prophet.

Cowan passed through their ranks, reached the base of the ladder, and climbed upward, his heart racing. He reached the top of the platform where Michael stood alone.

"For God's sake, Michael, stop it. You've got to stop it!" Cowan screamed. "They're killing them all; they're killing everyone. For God's sake, stop it!"

By the light of the flaming city, he could see Michael's face and eyes as he turned and looked upon Cowan.

"Yes," Michael said with a distant, hollow voice, his eyes two mirrors of madness. "Yes, kill them all, for if there is a God, he will know his own."

CHAPTER 18

THOUGH THE SUN HAD RISEN TWO HOURS EARLIER, THE RUINS of the city were still cloaked in darkness—choked in smoke and swirling ash.

There was no cheering now; no strident calls of command sending the hosts to battle. It was the hour of triumph, but all was strangely still.

He felt himself walking in a dream in which his feet would not touch the ground. He felt no emotion as he climbed over the shattered hulk of a ram and passed into what had once been his home. The stone towers were new. He remembered them not; where they stood had once been a pinnacle of ice—and a sad, lonely man atop it, calling out a silent prayer while Michael sailed away into the darkness.

They had tried to clear a path for Michael, but still he found himself tripping over the bodies of the fallen. The guards looked one to the other, wondering if he was drunk by the way he walked forward into the clouds of smoke.

A feeble cry whispered up.

He stopped and looked down. A young Companion, his eyes already distant with the look of death, reached up to him. Michael bent over, taking the bare, frozen hand.

"Michael, we died gladly for you."

Michael bent his head down and kissed the hand lightly. Rising up, he walked on as if his spirit had departed from the body.

He followed the path of death into the burned out city. Quietly, Seth tried to guide him away from the square, but he would not listen, wanting to see, wanting to let what he had finally accomplished wash over him.

Without order or rank, wandering groups of Companions weaved in and out of the burned-out homes, bent over under the weight of their booty. Occasional drunken shouts drifted through the smoke, as if coming from disembodied spirits. A swirling cloud of smoke eddied down the alleyway, obscuring everything for a moment. Like a phantom spirit, it drifted past, revealing a cluster of bodies in the middle of the street.

He stopped for a moment, looking down at the form of a young woman lying in the street, her dark hair moving softly in the breeze. In death, her frozen eyes looked up at him, as if begging for intercession. By her side was the smashed remnants of a young boy, his hands intertwined in hers, his features contorted with a final cry of terror. Her dress had been slashed off at the waist, and the savagery of the rape accused him mutely.

He looked to Seth, who stared past him into the smoke.

Reaching up to the brooch that clasped his cape, he held it close for a moment. It had been a gift of love long before, in a world lost to shadows. Unclippping it, he let the cape fall and, bending over, placed it across the body of the woman. Swaying, he felt himself falling, falling into darkness blacker than the worst hell of imagining, and as he fell, he screamed, the pain and anguish at last ripping through his soul.

Pale and distant, like a blood-red host, the sun hovered darkly in the eastern sky. The screams had died away with the coming of dawn. He felt frozen and removed and wondered grimly if perhaps he was the last survivor of Cornath. What had once been the narrow, weaving maze of streets known as Cornath was now nothing more than charred wreckage. Here and there, flickers of light shone wanly through the choking clouds of smoke. But there was little left to burn. Already some of the men, weaving drunkenly in small groups, were starting

THE FLAME UPON THE ICE

back to the ships, appearing out of the smoke like ghosts, their backs bent with loot.

A dagger lay on the table, but he could not bring himself to that final action. During the night of madness, he had picked it up, trying to nerve himself, posing the blade at his stomach. Each time, the dagger had fallen from his shaking hands and clattered to the floor.

Let me join them, he prayed fervently, but he could not bring himself to cross the shadow. Zimri was not sure whether it was from fear or a sense of not yet being defeated. He should feel that all was lost. A brief look out the window would overwhelm him with grief, but he could not bring himself to die alone, unnoticed, within the secret chamber.

Any that know of this hidden room are long since dead, he thought. I will die alone, and in time my body will rot and turn to dust. I would not even be able to share the final tomb of ice with those who had so foolishly followed me to this disaster.

He rose from the table and looked out the window. Across the far side of the square, there was a commotion. Some of the men were scurrying away into side alleys, while others were dropping their loot and standing to attention as a small knot of helmeted warriors, battle standards hanging limp behind them, strode purposefully across the body-choked square.

Was it the master? Was it he?

If I am to die, then let it not come till I face him, Zimri thought with a flicker of a smile. He has defeated me this time. I shall die, but I shall face him for one last time. Leaving the dagger on the table, he pulled open the hatch door and started down the long, narrow, circular stairs to the remnants of the church below.

They looked one to the other as the blood-smeared entryway to the church enclosed them in a dim, smoke-filled half-light.

"Have they found Finson's body yet?" Cowan asked quietly.

"Nay, I heard tell it was consumed in the flame when the barracks hall collapsed," Eldric replied sadly.

"He and my uncle sailed together many times. I shall miss him sorely," Cowan said, struggling with his emotions.

"Cowan, you should not have come back here. There is

nothing to do now but let the fires burn out and then bury the dead."

"Burying the dead will take a long time," Cowan replied weakly. "Perhaps our entire lifetime to bury the dead of Cornath."

He looked to Daniel, who hobbled along, a fresh trickle of blood breaking through the bandage around his thigh. The arrowhead had yet to be removed. He could imagine the agony it must cause him, but Daniel was quiet, speaking not, as if lost in a dream.

From one end of the cathedral to the other, there was barely a spot where a man could touch the ground with his foot, so thick were the piles of the fallen. Before the altar, the men appeared to be lying in rows, frozen to the ground where they had fallen in the final charge to the altar.

The altar looked as if it were encased in red and deep blue from the pyramid of Morian priests who had defended it to the last. Here and there in the cavernous hall, blood-smeared Companions poked among the wreckage, looking for friends or loot. Eldric, Cowan, and Daniel walked down the smoke-filled length of the church, followed by their standard-bearers and half a dozen men armed with crossbows.

"Nothing more to see here," Cowan said wearily. "We have inspected enough of the city. Let us go to Michael and report."

Turning, they started to leave.

"Hold!" a guard shouted behind them.

Looking over his shoulder, Daniel saw the guard bringing up his crossbow to fire.

"Zimri!" Daniel screamed. His ax flashed from its scabbard, and with a backhanded sweep of his hand, he knocked the guard down.

"He is mine!" Daniel shouted, limping forward, waving his blade on high.

Stunned by the swiftness of what had happened, Cowan turned and saw Daniel lumbering forward. Standing next to the altar was a tall, slender form dressed in dark blue robes trimmed in gold. The hood was pulled up, concealing his face. It was not a ghost. It was Zimri!

"Daniel, no!" Cowan shouted, starting forward.

The ghostly image did not move or raise a hand to defend itself.

"Eldric, stop him!" Cowan screamed, unable to keep up with Daniel's lumbering advance.

The cathedral echoed with Daniel's screams of rage as he charged to the altar, battle-ax raised high.

Eldric came up behind him, and suddenly his blade flashed out as well.

"For Janis!" he shouted coldly.

Cowan stopped, knowing he was unable to prevent them from again falling to the lust of death.

Zimri made no attempt to flee but stood still, his hooded form staring out at them.

Daniel reached his side and raised the ax, the blade cutting the air with a deadly hiss.

He stood before Zimri, poised like a statue, but the blade did not fall.

Eldric came up behind him, scimitar drawn, pointed low.

Zimri looked from one to the other and waited for death.

For long seconds, Daniel stood before him, trembling; then, ever so slowly, he lowered his blade.

"No," he said sadly. "No, I've had enough of this business. Let Michael decide."

This was familiar, strangely familiar. His senses returned, registering the impressions that swarmed around him. There was a deep, hollow sound to their steps, a warm flickering glow to the torches. Yes, he remembered it now.

"Seth?" he called weakly.

A face appeared above him. Was it Seth or was it a memory of long ago?

"Where am I, Seth?"

"Do you remember?" Seth asked softly, almost tenderly.

"Yes, I think so."

He looked around and realized that he was being carried on a litter.

Slowly, he swung his feet to the cold, hard floor and stood up, shaking.

"St. Awstin the beloved," Michael said in a whisper.

"Yes, Michael, St. Awstin the beloved."

"How long?"

"Not long, Michael. You were asleep for only a little while."

He remembered the young woman and child. For a moment,

he wished to block them away, but no, he could never do that again. This was the penance, the penance to be enacted forever at the place that had given birth to the dream and the sin.

"Are any left at all?" Michael asked sadly, looking up and down the corridor that was carpeted in light blue robes.

"No."

"Why?" Michael asked with the voice of a little child.

Seth looked into his eyes, and he could read the thoughts.

"You should know why, master."

He had no need of a guide. He stepped away from the guards, and removing a flickering torch from a wall socket, he passed into the labyrinth beneath the city.

So familiar, and yet somehow now, so small. He had remembered a time when the caverns had the dimension of an entire world, yet now it seemed so small and pitiful. He wanted to look upon the faces frozen in death but dared not, fearful that he would know them and would see them again—all dead by his hand. Rifton, Niall, and the beliefs of two thousand years gone forever because of him.

He reached the end of a corridor and stopped before a low, rounded door. Hesitating, he looked back to Seth.

"Perhaps it's best not to, Michael."

He turned away and opened the door, stepping over a body soaked in blood with an arrow sticking out of its back.

A single candle still flickered upon the table. Slumped next to it was a rotund form, its skull split open, a pool of black blood puddled on the table before him. At the edge of the desk was a book, its pages spattered with blood.

"Ah, Isaac," Michael whispered sadly. "So this is where you chose to die."

He wanted to turn on the men and place the blame for this death, but the words stayed within. St. Awstin, where he had been hidden for so many years and had at last gone out, ultimately to destroy.

"Bear him out with honor," Michael said to the guards, "for he is the last of a most sacred line."

He looked to Seth.

"Did you ever think, Seth—did you ever wish that perhaps on that first fateful night your course had been stayed? What then would have transpired today? How different it would all be."

Seth was silent.

"Leave me alone," Michael said quietly.

The guards behind Seth looked to Michael and then back to Seth with a grim, expectant air.

Michael noticed the tension.

"What is it?" Michael asked. "What are you hiding?"

"There is someone you'd better see."

"Who?" Michael asked wearily. "Can it not wait? I wish to be alone for a little while."

"I'm sorry, Michael. I don't think this can wait."

They were always pressing, always asking. Couldn't they just leave him alone forever? "All right, show him in," he said quietly. "Who is it?"

"Perhaps it would be best if he introduced himself."

Seth motioned to the guards, who turned and walked back up the corridor. In the distance, Michael heard the dark, grim curses of Daniel echoing down the corridor—the harsh voice, painful in its loudness.

"Here, damn you, here it is."

Michael walked over to the blood-stained desk and sat down behind it. Curiously, he started to gaze at the pages of the book, sticky with drying blood.

A shadow crossed the doorway, he looked up. He stood up slowly, as if the weight of his anguish were nearly too much to bear.

"You! It is you?"

"Yes, Michael Ormson, deacon of St. Awstin, it is I."

Still dressed in the robes of the Holy See, Zimri of Mor stood in the doorway, Daniel and Seth behind him.

"I prayed with all my hatred for this moment, to confront you with sword in hand, and here at last it has come."

"Yes, Michael, it has come, but is it as you wished?" Zimri replied in a cold, steady voice. "Look around you, Michael Ormson. The ghosts of Cornath, the ghosts of your dead order, witness this moment that you wished for."

"The ghosts of Janis and Andrew, as well," Daniel growled.

"Leave us," Michael commanded.

"Kill him now!" one of the guards cried out in the hall. "Kill him; kill the bastard!"

Michael looked up and stared beyond Zimri to Daniel, who stood ready to deliver the death blow, and Seth, who stood quiet, wrapped in mystery.

"Leave us," Michael said quietly.

"Master?"

"You heard me," Michael replied with a low, forceful voice. "Leave us immediately."

Daniel hesitated, the hatred flashing in his eyes.

"Let me take him the way he took Andrew," Daniel shouted, raising his ax on high.

Zimri stood motionless, his eyes fixed on Michael.

"No, damn you, you heard my order. Now leave!"

They looked one to the other and, finally bowing their heads, left the room, closing the door behind them.

"And so, Michael Ormson, it appears as if you have won for the moment," Zimri said quietly as he advanced into the room, stopping at the far side of the desk and placing his hand on the blood-stained book.

"Not for the moment, Zimri. The Church is destroyed."

"As you wished."

Michael was silent.

"A bit more than you expected, my dear Michael, if I might be so bold. You unleashed war, but you never expected what war would finally bring."

The memory flashed back to him—the streets of Cornath. He started to sway.

"But I have you."

"Yes, Michael, you have me."

"Why?" Michael asked sadly. "Why did you do it?"

"They were pawns, Michael. I did not want them, but I did want you, and through them I knew that I could reach you— unbalance you and fill you with hate."

Michael looked down to the floor.

"Yes, Michael, you were too logical, too pure, and in that pure logic, you would win. Thank me, Michael Ormson, for I made you human, capable of hate, like the rest of us trapped on this frozen planet, cursed by our own hands."

"You have cursed it by the First Choice," Michael replied.

"Ah, the First Choice is it? Look at our world, and remember the Garden. It was not the First Choice that brought us to the edge of extinction in the first place, it was man and his quest for knowledge. No, Michael, we at least gave mankind a chance and a dream."

"The prophecy is the dream."

"Do you really believe that rubbish created by Inys Gloi?"

Michael was silent.

"I dare say you finally do," Zimri replied, gazing intently on Michael. "Yes, you do, the dream of the Messiah has taken hold of you at last. Oh, Inys Gloi would be proud of this moment. Their pawn has come to believe the legend they created.

"So what now, Messiah?" Zimri shouted mockingly. "Can you raise the dead that you slaughtered this day?"

"Damn you forever, Zimri. The blood is on your hands— their blood and the blood of my own."

"And what of the innocent thousands that your hatred killed this day in the streets of Cornath?"

Michael started to sway as if he were looking over the edge of a deep, dark abyss—that led back into madness. He could still see them, remembering every detail of their broken forms.

Zimri started to laugh.

"So, you have me. Kill me. But you will not be able to unmake what has happened here—what I knew would happen here. Until this morning, many believed you to be the liberator, the Bringer of the New Age, but the mask is off you now, Michael Ormson. You have at last come of age in our cold, harsh world. At last you see us all for what we are, and for what you are."

He screamed a deep, primal voicing of horror and pain. With all his strength, he swung a mighty blow that crashed into Zimri, knocking him off his feet. Coming around the far side of the table, he unsheathed his sword and held it on high, ready to deliver the death blow.

"Go on, Michael," Zimri whispered. "Become like me; strike the blow with your own hand."

He stood above him, hesitating, looking down on his enemy. He could hear her voice still calling to him her last words, crying from a distant dream. With a scream of rage, he brought the sword down on the stone floor next to Zimri. In a shower of sparks, the sword shattered, the blade skidding across the floor.

"Get up, damn you. Get to your feet!"

He could see the hesitation in Zimri's eyes. He had expected death and had prepared for it, but death had not come.

Standing up before Michael, Zimri looked into his eyes. Their gazes locked and held; never had he encountered one as strong as this and Michael actually found himself hesitating for a second. This was the murderer of his family and of all that he once was. He stepped back from Zimri still holding the hilt of his shattered sword.

"Behold all that shall be!" Michael shouted. "It has come not as I wished, but it has come nevertheless. I shall shatter the First Choice, I shall end the church's rule forever, I shall bring about the new renaissance, and the Church shall be but a memory of a dark age."

Zimri tried to maintain contact, but the power before him was too strong; he lowered his eyes.

Michael raised the hilt of the sword upward and, turning, slammed it into the book on the table behind him. Removing his hand, the blade vibrated with the violence of the impact.

"Yes, I am the Chosen One," Michael said grimly, looking back at Zimri.

"You're a common murderer like the rest of us."

"For that I shall have to one day atone," Michael said sadly.. "You and your Church destroyed the balance, and I shall finish it once and for all. Even now your orders fall away, and you, the Holy See, stand before me powerless."

Zimri laughed grimly. "If I was powerless, then you would not have granted the time to meet me. No, Michael, you and I are linked together. If you believe the Prophecies, then in those words you will see that. For it is written that the two shall be bound together as one."

The adversaries looked at each other in silence, their shadows flickering on the floor by the light of a single torch. Michael looked back to the book and then to Zimri.

"Why?" Michael asked again sadly.

Zimri could see the anguish, the pain. There was a passing moment of empathy, but he forced it away. Here was the enemy.

"As I said, Michael, Janis was nothing to me. It was you whom I wanted, and you did as I wanted."

"And now you expect me to kill you?"

"Would that not bring you satisfaction?"

Michael hesitated. For a year, he had dreamed of this moment, but now it was purged, washed away in blood.

"I do not know," he said weakly.

Zimri looked up at him, shocked. His entrapment in Cornath

had been a mistake—in Michael was the object of his own fear, and he had come before him expecting the end of existence. They had lost the battle, but in losing it, they might have won the war, so brutal had been the taking of the city. He knew that by the tens of thousands the Cornathian Brotherhood would rally in hatred and fear, just as Michael's legions had rallied—but somehow that was beyond him, until now, with this sign of hesitation.

"Will you not send my shadow into the beyond as an offering to your wife and child?"

Her voice came back to Michael calling out as she drifted away.

What was to come? he wondered sadly, remembering her cry and then the memories that rested just outside the monastery. Penance, he thought sadly, penance.

"Daniel," Michael shouted.

The door swung open, showing Daniel's heavy form.

"Take him to the prison below. Seth knows the way."

Zimri looked at Michael. "Why do you hesitate? Was this not the moment that you prayed for?"

Michael looked to Zimri. "We shall soon meet again, Zimri. Unlike you, I have indeed found too much blood on my hands. Let us say that the love of another has spared you for the moment. The love of another and the memory of all that once was in this very room. But when next we come together, we shall perish. Take him away."

Daniel laid a rough hand on Zimri and started to push him toward the door.

Zimri turned to Michael and looked at him.

"My dear Ormson, we are indeed linked together in this drama. Remember that, and also remember that which stands beyond all of us—Inys Gloi."

"We shall meet again, Zimri," Michael said coldly.

"Oh, yes, my dear Michael, of that I am certain."

CHAPTER 19

AND SO THE CITY SLEPT THE QUIET SLEEP OF EXHAUSTION. The frenzy of blood ended in stunned silence as the men looked one to the other and wondered what had become of them and all that they had dreamed. As if sensing that the slaughter had ended, dazed survivors crawled out of the rubble. Beyond mourning, they picked through the wreckage of their lives and watched as the warriors of the south marched past them back to the ships. Here and there, some of them tried to recover their dead, but most, taking what few possessions they had, made their way eastward, and crossing unmolested through the landwall gate, left the city of death behind them. And the word of what had occurred traveled with them—into the world beyond.

A shadow stood before him in the darkness, and he knew her form.

"Is all prepared, then?" she whispered.

"Yes," he replied wearily. "One other thing must be attended to."

"Ah, when I heard that Zimri was still alive after meeting him, I suspected something to that effect."

"Damn you to the Ice. You got what was required of you. Now finish it and leave him."

She laughed quietly. "Ah, my good friend, I wonder if the Grand Master would approve of your sentiment."

She saw a glint of steel.

"You would not dare," she replied with a coarse laugh.

He turned away. "The hell with you, bitch. Do what you have to do, then leave him."

There was the sound of a scuffle in the corridor. It lasted but a moment, and then all was silent. Zimri got up from his cot.

The door to his prison squealed open on rusty hinges. Four shadowy figures entered the room.

"Remove your robes, Zimri."

He hesitated, and before he could voice a protest, the men were upon him, ripping his golden cape and tunic off.

"Put this on."

They tossed him the foul-smelling robes of an ice runner.

"Who are you?" he asked quietly while donning the garments.

They were silent.

"Quickly now," one of them said.

Two went out ahead, and the other two fell in behind as they drifted through the dark corridors. On several occasions, they passed weary guards, and the man up front mumbled a few words, and the group pushed on. They came to a door at the end of a long, dark corridor, and the lead man opened it with a key. The two men at the back of the party pushed Zimri forward.

The lead man came up to Zimri and pushed a bag of provisions into his hands.

"This is the tunnel you were supposed to have escaped through at the end of the siege. Here is the door, open for you."

Zimri looked at him.

"Are you of Inys Gloi, as well?" Zimri asked.

The man was silent.

"What is at the other end of this tunnel?"

"You will find nothing; this is where our help will end. I

traveled this tunnel once myself, and at the end of it I still do not understand what I have found."

"Suppose I do not go?"

"You will, Zimri of Mor. Your destiny is for you to go. Of that we are certain."

"If I live, you know we will win," Zimri replied.

The hooded form was silent.

Turning, Zimri went through the door. For nearly half an hour, he walked in darkness, his hands pressed against the wall to guide him on his way. Finally, a dim light showed before him. At the end of the tunnel, he peered out cautiously. He was greeted with silence. He stepped out into the night. Overhead, the Arch shone brightly, the sky alight with the flickering aurora. He looked back to the west. There was still a faint glow on the horizon as the last fires of Cornath burned softly down into ashes.

Somehow there was a vague sense to it all. Zimri had looked into Ormson's eyes and for a moment had sensed a link, a bond. He felt that Michael knew he would be freed. That Michael had in the end returned him his life as a penance for what had been done in trying to take it. He thought on it for a moment and then shook the thoughts away. It was foolishness to assume so. Mathin and the Brotherhood of Cornath were locked in battle till the death. The brotherhood for the moment was shattered, but in time it would be rebuilt. Shouldering his pack, he set off into the darkness of the east.

"Michael?"

The voice came softly to him. The torch had gutted out, and now only a single light flickered before him. It showed a soft feminine form in the darkness. For a moment, he thought it was a dream. No, that was foolishness, he thought sadly. It was no dream. It was her.

"Come in, Varinna," he said sadly.

She approached out of the shadows. In the one hand, she carried a candle; in the other, a goblet of wine.

He looked at her without feeling. She had, after all, been a dream. He had slept with her, made love to her with a near-violent passion, but through it all she had been an elusive fantasy.

She drew closer, her warm, feminine scent reaching him,

calling him, taunting him. "I thought you might wish something to drink," she said, quietly holding out the cup.

Without rising, he extended his hand and took the cold silver goblet.

"Do you wish to come to bed?" she asked with a whispering voice.

"No."

"Shall I wait for you? I've seen that a room has been prepared for us."

"No, that will not be necessary. I think we should have an understanding," he said quietly.

"Yes."

"You are to leave here before the dawn. I shall see that a ship has been prepared for you. It will take you anywhere upon the Ice that you desire. Even to Inys Gloi, if that is your wish."

She was good, he thought, so well trained. Only the light change in her breathing betrayed the fear.

"Why, Michael?" she asked, playing the game to the final moment, wondering what had happened.

"Because you are a lie. You knew that when I held you, when I made love to you, it was not you, it was Janis. That is gone forever. I must live alone, without her, and your order cannot arrange who I shall love."

She nodded softly.

Taking the cup, he raised it to his lips. He looked up to her and smiled sadly. "Poison?"

She shook her head.

"No, Inys Gloi needs me yet, as it does Zimri. But know, Varinna, that both of us are aware, and whichever one of us wins, the other will be waiting. I have won for now. Know that I am aware."

He drained the cup. "Yawinder, from my uncle's private cask, I dare say."

She smiled.

No, it was not poison, but it was something else. He could feel a drowsiness coming over him. Why would she do that? he thought. He looked up to her.

"Yes, Michael, my love, but it's only a potion for you to sleep, to sleep without interfering in my voyage. I shall not take your ship. There is another, and I shall be gone within the hour."

She came closer to him; the perfume of her breath washed over him. Leaning over, she kissed him on the forehead, her heavy breasts brushing against his shoulder.

"I carry your child, Michael Ormson, and Inys Gloi shall have him."

He looked up to her through sleepy eyes.

"Good-bye, o Prophet, and know that your seed will be trained to our needs."

As if in an apparition, she was gone, but her words echoed into his sleep.

They had come to him in the middle of the night and awakened him from the stupor of a drugged sleep and told him that Zimri was gone. He knew their words even before they spoke them, and dismissing them, he lay back down on the floor of the room that had once been his entire world and passed the night in the realm that he alone could travel.

CHAPTER 20

HE STOOD ALONE ATOP THE PLACE OF WATCHING. A FAINT promise of warmth hung in the air, the temperature nearly within ten degrees of frost. In another month, the ice would be impassable. Already communication had been cut to the Southward Sea, and the last report said that the journey to sail around the world, postponed at the start of the war, had finally embarked. Under the command of Jason Eldricsson, twenty ships and a thousand men had sailed not in quest of war but for knowledge alone—to find the lands beyond and perhaps one day to come full circle, bearing with them a link, a first step toward reuniting with the dreams of old.

He looked down to the streets of Cornath. A small section of the city had been rebuilt during the night of winter, mainly to house the thousands of men who occupied the city and for the storage of supplies needed in the taking of Dulyn. Only a handful had abandoned the Cornathian cities to join him in the cause. How unlike Mathin, he thought sadly, when tens of thousands had come after the victory before the Pass. But he shook the thoughts away.

The Protectorate had been formed. Of the fourteen brotherhoods, nine had been swept away or surrendered, severing their ties with the old Confederation. Secular rule had shattered the Church once and for all. Gone was the Inquisition, and gone as well was the First Choice.

Word had come only the night before. Under the lead of Cowan, Dulyn had fallen with a minimum of bloodshed. Somehow Balor and most of his brothers had escaped with nearly all the library—but a few books, a few documents, had been found, and it was enough to shatter all that the Church had been built upon. He smiled inwardly. They had two thousand years to catch up with. Today he would go before the Council and hear the theory put forth by a young renegade priest of St. Awstin that he had found a way to prove the size of the earth by measuring the angle of light from the sun at two different places at the same time. A year before, the Black Brothers would have sought him out and killed him. Today he would have Michael's protection.

He stood alone, purged at last. From this place, he had traveled into a full realization of all that he could be. He had shared a love that was gone forever, and a hatred; each was purged in blood. Now he stood alone—the Prophet, the Bringer of the New Age.

He looked to the east. Somewhere beyond Dulyn, Zimri waited. He was still Holy See, a rallying point for those who believed. Michael felt no emotion, just a sense of infinite loss. Why he had faltered and not killed Zimri was something Michael had pondered throughout the winter. The words of *Prophecy* came back to him. If he was the Prophet, then he and Zimri were linked. And the two would fall together, as in *Prophecy*. Perhaps it was something beyond himself that had stayed his hand or the desire for penance. But of Zimri, that was no longer a concern—the Church was dying of its own weight, the weight of two thousand years coming to end at last in the New Age of Knowledge.

But to the west was something that no prophecy spoke of. He knew full well why he had awakened in the night. It had been early, nearly a month so. In the darkness of a cloistered hall, new life had started. He would never know him or touch him. They would have the boy forever. But now, at last, he knew.

The sun started to break the horizon to the east, flooding the high pinnacle with light. Much needed attending to—there would be the reports from Cowan, a review of new recruits with Daniel, a meeting with Eldric concerning the continued action against the remnants of Cornath's fleet, and, of course, a quiet conversation with Seth, who was increasingly distant of late. But he knew the reason for that.

It is begun at last, he thought with a sad smile. What we have started cannot be arrested, for too big a mark has been made upon the pages of history. Even if we lose, still, the final victory will be ours.

The wind started to pick up from the north, blowing free and clear. The signal horn, marking the start of another day, echoed throughout the city. Soon the streets would echo with the voices of thousands as they labored and prepared to carry the word of the New Age that had dawned with the coming of the Prophet. The coming of the Renaissance long foretold.

As if on impulse, he reached into his pocket and drew out the stained remnants of a light blue ribbon. It had belonged to her, given so long ago. He looked at it and smiled softly. Michael raised his hand up high, and with a gentle toss, the ribbon soared outward with the wind, blowing free and clear to the south—to Mathin and the Flowing Sea beyond.

About the Author

William R. Forstchen, who makes his home in Maine, was born in 1950. Educated by Benedictine monks, he considered the calling of the priesthood but decided instead to pursue a career in history. Completing his B.A. in education at Rider College, he went on to do graduate work in the field of counseling psychology.

In 1978, William moved to Maine where he is currently an instructor of Ancient and Medieval History at Maine Central Institute, Pittsfield, Maine. He also coordinates activities as director of the Medieval Club, Live Dungeons, and Catapult Team Competitions at the school. His student team recently set a new national distance record with a sixteen foot crossbow. Forstchen lives with his wife, Marilyn, and their dog, Ilya Murometz, in central Maine.

William's interests include iceboating, Hobie Cat racing, sailing, skiing, pinball machines, Zen philosophy, and participation in Civil War battle reenactments as a private in the 20th Maine Volunteer Infantry.